I0713557

WORKBOOK PRESS LLC
187 E Warm Springs Rd
Suite B285 Las Vegas NV 89119 USA

Website: https://workbookpress.com
Hotline: 1-888-818-4856
Email: admin@workbookpress.com

Ordering Information:
Quantity sales. Special discounts are available on quantity purchases by corporations, associations, and others.

For details, contact the publisher at the address above.

Library of Congress Control Number: 2020921581
ISBN-13: 9781960752789 (Paperback Version)
           9781960752796 (Digital Version)

REV. DATE: 07/30/2024

M HARLAND-SUDDES

Psychopython

Part 1

Dark Odyssey

"What a well-told and eye-opening, if brutal, story. You write well, and the depictions of characters' interactions and dialogue are among the book's strong points. Readers will feel deeply for the predicament of Delia Grey and her two daughters, hoping they not only survive, but also thrive after their difficult ordeal with PP."

*****

"Five stars... This is a brilliantly written story, with many triggers for Mental Health and Abuse...Written from the heart of a strong woman, who didn't realise how strong she was until the end.

The words and writing give a perfect view of what can go on behind closed doors. Not to be taken lightly, this book is full of trauma and heartache."

*****

"Brilliantly written and recommended... This is written from the depths of Delia's heart; a truly moving account of a life almost destroyed by abuse. You will understand how badly, torture, and abuse, AND words, can affect even the strongest person."

*****

"A moving testimony of life and marriage to the wrong person; and how sick and ill a person can be who tries to destroy you. Brilliantly written; and highly recommended."

*****

Dedicated

To my beloved husband and our beautiful daughters,

and in loving memory of our son.

And even in our sleep, pain which cannot be forgot falls drop by drop upon the heart, and in our own despair, against our will, comes wisdom to us, by the awful Grace of God.

—Aeschylus (525–456 BC)

Chapter 1

Ill Met By Moonlight

My dark odyssey began one Friday evening in March, five months after Alan's death.

I had been to an evening class. And to keep a promise to my teenage daughters, I had stopped off to pick up some fish and chips for their supper. It was just after nine o'clock, with only occasional glimmers of moonlight coming through the heavy clouds, and I was in a rush to get home. The rain was driving almost horizontally, straight inland from the sea, and I half wished I hadn't made the promise and had just headed straight home.

As I pulled onto the empty seafront car park, I noticed another car was close behind me. And for some reason the driver was now parking, almost nose to tail, directly behind me, just about as close as he could get. It struck me as odd that the only other arrival should do that, with dozens of empty spaces all around. But it was only a fleeting thought and of no particular significance. All I cared about was getting my fish and chips and going home.

Grabbing my soaking umbrella, I splashed my way around the corner to the chippy.

'Damn!' I muttered under my breath, seeing the darkened shop. 'Wouldn't you just know it? They're shut.'

I hurried back to the car, feeling rattled and inclined to forget the supper plan and just drive home. But I didn't want to disappoint my girls, and there was another place, nearer home, which I decided to try.

Flipping the water from my umbrella, I got in, harnessed up, and switched on the ignition. I sat for a few seconds, watching as the wiper blades cleared the blurred windscreen. It was one of those evenings when the dazzle of the headlights reflects back in the heavy, moist air and makes it difficult to see through the streaming windows. The interior glass was fogged, so I rubbed the windscreen hard and took a quick glance in my rear mirror to be sure I was clear behind. Pushing the gears into reverse, I began backing up.

Suddenly, my heart gave a sickening lurch; the car parked in the bay directly behind me had also begun reversing, and the driver seemed in a reckless hurry. I could hear his engine revving and saw he was coming directly at me with no lights showing.

Ramming on my brakes, I gritted my teeth and braced myself in anticipation of an almighty crash; I could almost feel the horrible judder and crunch of colliding metal. But, miraculously, both cars lurched to a halt before it happened.

A wave of nausea swept over me, and I sat in the darkness with my engine stalled. My eyes were transfixed by the dull glow of the ignition light and its small red bulb, which seemed, belatedly, to be warning me of danger.

It was a brief incident, a momentary thing, but it left me shaken and unnerved.

Since Alan's death, I had been living on my nerves. I was pretending to be fine and coping well, but every small incident out of the normal run of things made my heart thunder and my hands tremble and left me in a cold panic. My assumed facade was fragile and barely skin-deep.

A sudden, heavy banging on the window beside me shocked me back to reality, and I jerked my head towards the bulky silhouette of a man peering in through the glass. He was wearing a dark green oiled jacket and shouting something, but the noise of the wind and the rain were carrying his voice away.

I wound the window down a few inches, and he tilted his head to speak through the gap. I saw rain trickling down his face from his flattened hair but not much else.

'Yer orright, luv?' he shouted roughly, drawling the words and emphasising the word luv. 'Yer wuz goin' a bit sharpish wasn't yer? Giv uz quite a turn, yer did, comin' at uz in the dark like that. Yer might've 'it uz if ah 'adn't slammed on me ankers sharpish.'

His obvious coarseness and unapologetic justification for what he had just done riled me. He had been revving his engine and driving without any lights, and it seemed as though he might have been attempting to cause a collision to prevent me from leaving the car park.

Is he crazy? I thought angrily. This man's a bigoted loudmouth, a brainless idiot trying to blame me for his reckless driving.

'You must be blind if you didn't see me,' I snapped. 'My headlights and tail lights were all on, and I was barely moving, whereas you were showing no lights at all and revving your engine like a complete idiot.'

He scraped his fingers through his lank, rain-soaked hair, pushing it from his eyes. 'Well,' he slurred, 'mebbe no 'arms bin dun, an' we wuz boaf at folt.'

'We were not both at fault,' I snapped. 'That near go was all down to you. This is a car park; it's pitch-dark, and you should have switched your lights on before you started moving.'

I anticipated him swearing and saying something aggressive at that point, before storming off, but he surprised me by remaining where he was, with his hand still firmly on the top of my partially open window.

'Look luv,' he replied mildly. 'Ah kin see yer a bit shaken up, so we'll lerrit go. It doan matter oos folt is wuz, since no 'arms bin dun. Why doan ah tek yer fer a drink or summat, ter calm yer nerves? Ah'm a decent bloke, an' Ah allus duz the right fing. Ah kin see yer put abaat.'

'No thanks,' I said frostily. 'My nerves are all right. I don't know who you are, and I really don't care. So please, just remove your hand and let me go.'

For some reason he was still determined to delay me. 'Look luv,' he began again, drawling his words coarsely and smirking at me in an over-familiar fashion.

Now his attitude had begun to make my flesh creep. I always react negatively to loud-mouthed men who try making themselves familiar by calling me love or darling or any other uninvited term of endearment. I find it insulting and sleazy, and this obnoxious character was having a very negative effect on me for a whole variety of reasons.

'Naw,' he said, chewing on a mouthful of gum, 'Ah caan't let yer go in this state...yer aal over the place wiv yer nerves. If yer wone 'ave a drink ter patch fings up, then ah insist yer let uz tek yer fer a bite ter eat. Someplace very public, no funny bizzness. Ah'm not that kine uv a bloke. Ah'm a decen' ornarry fella, and Ah doan like upsettin' women. Ah've got kids meself, so Ah no 'ow angshus yer mus' be abaat 'em lef' on theer own.'

'No! No!' I said, shaking my head. 'It's, err … well it's gone nine, and I can't waste any more time.' The sound of my own hesitancy shocked me, and I could hear the slight uncertainty creeping into my voice. 'I really should go. You see, I need to get home; I promised not to be late.'

My suddenly subdued reactions were inexplicable, but something about his strange, conciliatory manner had begun to penetrate my defences. Since Alan's death, everyone I knew had been kind, but in a distant sort of way. People I thought I knew well seemed to be avoiding me, as if I had developed some seriously infectious illness and become someone they didn't want to know anymore. Maybe I was being too sensitive, but it felt as though they were all afraid my experiences were contagious, and they didn't want to get too involved.

My recent bereavement had left me feeling socially rejected and isolated. It was obvious men felt awkward being caught speaking to me alone, and I noticed how their wives clung to them as though they suspected I had ulterior designs, and had suddenly turned into a weird sexual predator. Even family invitations had suddenly dried up. Widowhood had left me feeling distinctly ostracised, very much on my own, and akin to a social outcast.

Unexpectedly, for the first time in months, in that dark, rainswept car park, a total stranger was showing some sensitivity towards how I was feeling. This strange uncouth man seemed to be offering me a kind of rough-and-ready human compassion, empathising with me beyond anything my so-called friends ever had.

My reactions were involuntary, but for some inexplicable reason I was starting to find myself disarmed by his crude attempt at cajoling. I had never seen him before in my life, yet after only a few rough, kind words, he had me lowering my defensive guard.

A fragment of my cautious common sense reminded me he had never apologised for scaring me; but even so, he seemed to be oozing concern and even a little too much familiarity. Something prodding my brain was making me wonder... Was this just an act or was he being genuine?

Then another sudden thought flashed through my mind... Was it possible he had been following me?

Something buried deep inside my head seemed to be trying to send me warnings, and it was making me feel uneasy. I had never seen this man before, yet he seemed to know more about me than any casual stranger could.

I still don't understand why I didn't end the matter there and then by simply restarting my engine and driving off. But right then, my hesitancy provided the opportunity he needed, and he seized upon it to press forward with pursuing an acquaintance.

Squeezing his huge hand through the narrow window gap, he grinned disarmingly and said, 'Ah'm PP, luv, an Ah'm very pleased ter meet yer. Naw are yer goin' ter tell uz oo yer are?'

Suddenly, two quiet voices were competing inside my head. One, the voice of common sense, was urging me to drive off, go home, and stick to my original plan. But the other voice, the more persistent of the two, was tempting me to throw caution to the wind... kick over the traces and play the rebel. What harm was there in accepting the offer this rough stranger was making? It would make a change to share a meal, and maybe even an hour of his crude company. It might even be amusing to steal a few moments of light relief. What harm would I be doing by walking a few steps down an unfamiliar road? If I wanted to, I could always leave.

Without realising it, I was confronting a significant moment of destiny; and for some inexplicable reason, the rebel in me won.

Even after the space of many years, I still have no rational explanation for my crazy decision. But on that cold wet night, I chose to travel an unknown road, and that has made all the difference to my life. Against sense and reason, I allowed a complete stranger to bend my will to his, and disarm me with his rough seductive charm.

My hesitation was brief, and seconds later I wound down the window, and tentatively shook his extended hand. 'I'm Delia Grey,' I said awkwardly.

'Well, Delia,' he grinned, 'there's a phone box on tha' corner. Why doan yer ring yer kids and tell em why yer'll be a bit late 'ome?'

I still hesitated, biting my lip in uncertainty.

'Go on,' he urged. 'Ah'll walk over wiv yer. Jus' let yer kids no yer ahrite, an tell em wot's 'appened.' He gave me another broad, disarming grin. 'Ah jus wan the chance ter mek fings ahrite wiv yer. Afta tha' yer need nivver see uz agin, if yer doan wan ter.'

A faint trace of reason was still struggling to whisper in my ear. How does he know you have children? How does he know there's not an anxious husband waiting for you at home? Don't trust him. Something's wrong. Leave while you still have the chance.

But I chose to ignore those uncertainties without a second thought, and adopted the docile complacency of a feeble-minded rabbit.

Chapter 2

The Yellow River

The Yellow River Chinese restaurant was arranged with secluded private booths. The setting was intimate, the food good, and the atmosphere tranquil. No one tried to rush you or pester you while you ate. You could talk privately without any intrusion, and it was a pleasant relaxing place to spend an evening.

For Alan and me, it had always been our favourite restaurant. Etched lanterns, in pale yellow glass, glowed on the tables like oriental moons, each cleverly designed to cast golden shadows across the faces of the diners. It was a very romantic setting, and one that held many happy memories for me.

On every visit, I would look across the lantern's glow at Alan's handsome face and see him smile as he reached across to take my hand. And I remember how the tenderness shining in his dark brown eyes glowed even more brightly in that golden lamplight. It was all so memorable because we were very much in love.

On that miserable Friday night in March, the place was quiet, but the atmosphere was as warm and inviting as ever. Suddenly a mixture of emotions came welling up inside me. As PP and I were being shown to an empty booth, I panicked. Being there with this strange man suddenly felt like a betrayal of Alan.

I became confused and awkwardly embarrassed, overwhelmed by a desperate urge to make an excuse and leave. My girls were at home, and I knew I should be there with them.

I turned, intending to go, but a firm hand gripped my arm, and my retreat was blocked by the bulky shape of my companion. He had sensed my sudden reluctance and continued gripping my elbow firmly as he steered me towards a table. My wet coat and umbrella were whisked away, and we were seated.

While we examined the menus, I surreptitiously began to study him. Up to that point, he had been nothing more than a bulky outline against the rain and darkness... just a rough-voiced, cajoling stranger.

Now that I was seeing him more clearly in the subdued lighting of the restaurant, my overall reaction came close to revulsion. I shivered involuntarily, as though someone had just walked across my grave.

This man was no Alan.

Seated in front of me, I saw a gross, brooding man, with the outline of his distended beer belly straining against the buttons of his blue shirt, where it was pressed hard against the table's edge. But that distasteful reaction was nothing, when compared with the one I had to his facial features, which persisted in focusing my attention.

A more bloated, sensuous face I had never seen. But for some inexplicable reason, it was one that bore an indefinable hypnotic quality about its ugliness. He was clean-shaven, with heavy jowls and a stubborn-looking, deeply cleft, bulbous chin. It was a coarse face... the face of a man given to self-indulgence and excess. And it exhibited an indefinable air of brutality.

To my eyes, it was akin to the faces of the medieval peasantry in paintings by Pieter Bruegel, and suddenly I realised how much its coarseness repelled me. I read it as the face of a manipulative man who always achieved his own way using unflinching willpower, and force, and I could see no signs of gentleness or refinement in it.

Dissecting the features, I noted the wide sensuous mouth and fleshy pendulous lips. When he smiled, he exposed uneven, discoloured teeth. It was a remarkable smile, not simply because of his thick lips and awful teeth, but because his pale eyes remained empty and unresponsive, as though the smile was nothing to do with them and never reached that far up his face.

More than any other physical feature, it was his eyes that focused my attention. They had a cold hypnotic energy, which disturbed me and left me feeling uncomfortable. A brief glimpse into their emotionless void sent shivers down my spine, and brought back unwelcome memories of a nightmare that had haunted my childhood dreams.

Sitting across the table from him in The Yellow River, I found myself drawn again and again to glance surreptitiously at those pale, compelling eyes, now unexpectedly calling back unhappy reminiscences I had thought were long forgotten. In my childhood, an unpleasant recurring nightmare had disturbed my sleep, when night after night I had been haunted by such emotionless eyes. There was no glimpse of a tender soul hidden behind them, no fleeting trace of compassion or empathy, only calculating deception and cruelty.

Those long-ago eyes had belonged to a cold-hearted, malevolent dream python. Now suddenly they had returned, and this time they were real. After the peaceful space of so many years, I was disturbed to be once again contemplating my terrifying dream python's eyes, suddenly resurrected in the face of the living man who was gazing at me, a man who seemed to be attempting to penetrate my mind.

His close proximity made me shudder involuntarily for a second time. My imagination... along with my guilt... was working overtime. For a fleeting moment I fancied I caught sight of Alan, quietly standing behind him in the shadows, looking at me, and shaking his head sadly.

Then PP was talking, commanding my attention, and compelling me to focus on him... effectively blocking any further negative thoughts I might have. Under the influence of his animated repartee my darker thoughts gradually subsided. He was jolly and affable, without inhibitions; a skilful and well-practised raconteur, a man brimming with self-confidence, and well used to dominating any situation and captivating his listeners' attention with his bluff bonhomie.

Gradually I became caught up by his stories, until I forgot the underlying misapprehensions I had felt. I even forgot the time, as he rambled on about his life and his sorrows. Like the rest of him, his language was rough and uneducated... a mangled mixture of travellers' slang and estuary English, mixed with another strange vernacular I couldn't place. I had to concentrate hard to follow what he was saying. That fact alone kept all my attention focused on him. And if it was one of his deliberate ploys, it worked. His talent for telling convincing stories and concentrating his listener's attention was riveting.

Grinning at me across the table, he began by informing me he was the director of a profitable building company. TBM Builders Ltd, built private housing estates; and he and his two co-directors also contracted building projects for various local councils around the county. The three partners had run their successful company in Essex for sixteen years.

He certainly knew how to tell a good tale. But for some reason, I failed to ask myself... Is this man really telling me the truth? And why is he telling me his life story? We've only just met, and we'll be unlikely to ever meet again.

A few moments of clear thinking would have had me wondering if some ulterior reason lay behind his setting out to impress me with his tales of his success and his wealth.

'Ah doan speak posh, an' Ah ain't got no oonivarsety degree, but Ah know wot's wot, an' Ah'm flush wi' the dosh. An' Ah aren't mean, nyver.'

Could it be that my earlier impressions had been unfair, and even premature?

'Ah'm a self-made man,' he went on, 'an though yer wuldn't guess it ter look at uz, Ah've dun very well fer mesel. Ah'm wot's called, a genwine ruff dymon; one uv nachur's gennelmen, that's me...but wivv a 'eart o' gold, as yer'll very well fin' out wen yer gits ter no uz better. Naaw, luv, wot yer 'avin ter eat?'

There it was again, that assumed familiarity that had made me cringe. Only now it was part of the general vulgarity of the man, and somehow it didn't seem quite so grating, and not at all personal.

For the remainder of the evening, my attention was saturated with a stream of graphic details about his early life and his struggles to achieve success. But mostly his narrative persisted in returning to accounts of his diabolical first marriage, and of the terrible blighted life he had endured at the hands of a madwoman. She was so insane there had even been a time when the police had to escort her from the local cathedral, where she had climbed into the pulpit and started preaching about her amazing husband...himself!

Our meal was eaten to the accompaniment of this non-stop life recital, which also involved tales of his drunken, good-for-nothing, abusive father and his downtrodden mother. All of this was regularly interspersed with graphic details of his disastrous marriage, at age nineteen, to the deranged Scottish woman he had finally divorced.

It seemed she had spent their twenty years of marriage having affairs with every man she had ever met... fitting her affairs in between confinements in various psychiatric institutions as a sectioned patient under the Mental Health Act.

It was a terrible life history he was relating, but one that somehow seemed a trifle too well rehearsed. The way he claimed he had borne all his grievous experiences bravely, and done his best to give her and their son a happy life struck me as just a trifle glib...more like some sort of contrived search for sympathy.

Nevertheless, he kept my attention. And by the time the meal was over, my perception of his character had undergone a significant shift. The gut-wrenching stories I had heard, had gradually won my sympathy, and my initial scepticism had slowly evaporated. After three hours of his non-stop storytelling, I had found myself beginning to empathise with him.

I was willing to admit, he did have a certain … je ne sais quoi.

By comparison, my personal troubles had begun to seem verging upon self-pity. While he had spent years struggling to escape from poverty, and a disastrous early marriage to a madwoman who deceived him at every opportunity, my life from childhood onward had been filled with security and love.

Under the influence of his convincing stories, my initial view of PP had been turned around, until I saw him through new eyes. Now I saw a man more deserving of my compassion and sympathy, than my criticism and censure.

That feeling of empathy continued while we shared the evening, and it lasted right until the moment came when he inadvertently turned my carefully elicited opinion onto its head.

At the end of the evening, as I stood quietly waiting by the till for my coat and umbrella to be brought, he unexpectedly made such a flamboyant, vulgar spectacle of paying the bill, my carefully conditioned opinion of him was annihilated in seconds. With a sudden careless flamboyant exhibition, he sent my carefully moulded impression spinning into space, and I returned to my earlier more realistic and cynical opinion of him as a vulgar ignorant oaf.

As we waited, he inexplicably engaged the Chinese cashier in a loud, bombastic, one-sided conversation, calling him John, and announcing to all who were within earshot that he had spent part of his life living in Hong Kong and was familiar with its geography. He went on to make a loud vulgar show of reeling off Chinese street names and those of backstreet traders he recalled.

The cashier nodded politely and listened patiently while he waited to be paid.

For me, it was a cringingly awful experience. I had anticipated PP would simply hand over his credit card and settle the bill; instead he began fumbling about inside his jacket. Eventually, to my further embarrassment, he produced a large bundle of banknotes, held together with a thick elastic band. There must have been at least five hundred pounds in the roll. Then after licking his thumb, he flamboyantly began peeling off bills, counting aloud as he did so. I shrank back, shocked by his vulgarity. Suddenly he resembled an itinerant scrap metal merchant doing a shady deal, and I wanted to hide.

Disgusted by this sleazy exhibition, I backed away, and began edging towards the cloakroom, wishing with all my heart I could be a million miles away from such a crass display. I kept my eyes averted as he stuffed the fat bankroll back inside his jacket, complete with its elastic band.

People were watching him, listening to his exhibitionist monologue with the cashier, and gawping at his strange vulgarity with his cash.

I already felt guilty enough about being there, and now I just wanted to escape from all association with him. He made me feel cheap, as though I was some sort of common tart he'd picked up, by flashing his money about. The balancing see-saw of my earlier empathy came crashing down again, in the light of reality, and I couldn't get away from the restaurant and him fast enough.

If there was some hidden motive behind his ridiculous behaviour, and he had been hoping to impress me with his knowledge of Hong Kong and his flamboyant wealth, he had failed completely. I couldn't have been more disgusted if he had suddenly spat on the floor. To my mind he was a vulgar loud-mouthed braggart.

I already half suspected he might attempt to inveigle me into inviting him home for coffee; but there had never been the remotest chance of that happening. This strange man was someone I had encountered by mischance, only three hours earlier, and suddenly his crass exhibition confirmed my opinion that I wanted nothing so much as to see the back of him, as quickly as I could. If I never saw him again, it would be too soon.

After thanking him for the meal, I took my leave at the door with a stiff handshake. That was as much as my offended feelings would allow. It was still raining hard, so I said goodnight and hurriedly got into my car and drove home.

When I pulled onto my drive it was almost midnight, and the house was in darkness. Samantha and Nathalie were long in bed, and I didn't want to disturb them, or my four little Yorkshire terriers asleep in the kitchen... Slipping off my shoes, I tiptoed up the dark stairs.

Before leaving the house that evening, I had half drawn the curtains of my bedroom, and now the street lamp provided enough light for my bedtime needs.

I took a brief look down into the street before I got into bed and was shocked to see the dark estate car belonging to PP parked on the road directly opposite my house. I could even make out his bulky shape, huddled behind the driving wheel, just as it had been in the seafront car park earlier that evening.

I knew I hadn't given him my address, and it was no pleasant surprise to realise he must have followed me home.

Whatever had possessed him to do that?

As I stood concealed behind the curtains, watching the street below, I saw two bright flashes of light come from the open window of his car. I felt sure it was a camera flash.

What was the man up to? I wondered. And why was he taking flash photographs of my house? There was something seriously strange about his behaviour which was now spooking me. It wasn't simply odd behaviour; it was unnerving.

Seconds later, I peeped out again, just in time to see him driving off.

I stood for a while longer, waiting to see if he would come back, before taking off my dressing gown and getting into bed. The entire evening had been weird, and I was left feeling distinctly uneasy about the behaviour of the strange man I had encountered.

That night, I was much too overwrought to sleep. I knew I had behaved badly and completely out of character. And I felt as guilty, as if I had wilfully betrayed Alan with some low life I had picked up. What on earth had possessed me to consent to go for a meal with such an awful man? For heaven's sake, he had deliberately tried to crash into my car.

Telling myself I'd had a silly little adventure was pointless. My guilt continued to distress me for hours, making my heart thump like a steam hammer and churning my brain so much there was no sleep left in me.

Alan's sudden senseless death had left me broken-hearted, with my world turned on its head. Everything that had ever given my life meaning had suddenly vanished. The aftermath of my bereavement was that I had lost my way and had become very confused and erratic. I realised I was often not thinking straight, and at times, my behaviour was irrational. My brain could no longer be relied on to assess things normally. I was doing illogical things, in a sort of desperate panic, convinced they were the right things to do.

Now this latest situation had caught me off balance, and I was desperate to sort myself out and get back to normal.

I hadn't slept properly for months, from grieving, and worrying about my family's future; and I was constantly driven by fears of dying and leaving my daughters destitute.

My irrational grief was turning my life into a living hell.

As I lay awake in the darkness, churning over my deep suspicions concerning that evening's supposed accidental encounter with PP, I was overtaken by another panic.

Now I was convinced the man I had encountered was some sort of an opportunist, a conniving chancer. He was a self-obsessed domineering low life, who had almost certainly deliberately attempted to crash into my car in order to establish an introduction to me.

But why would he do that? It seemed inexplicable. We had absolutely nothing in common. So why had he been there? Why had he followed me onto the car park? Why almost crash into me? Had he actually been stalking me?

I tossed and turned all night with a hundred questions jumbling about inside my head, and I was left sleepless, confused, and angry with myself.

Eventually just before dawn I fell into an exhausted half-waking sleep, and with it came a tragic vision of Alan to depress me even more. He was standing with his back towards me; his head was down, and his shoulders were slumped. For me, he conveyed an attitude of abject misery.

Tears poured down my cheeks as I watched him slowly walking away from me.

I cried out to him to come back, but he didn't turn to face me. And from somewhere nearby, a hollow disembodied voice began repeating over and again, 'Look behind the facade. Don't be a fool.'

The dream slowly faded, and the voice fell silent. I felt enveloped in the nothingness of silent darkness, and then suddenly my mind became fully conscious and alert. I realised I was no longer asleep, and my brain was urging me to get up and move about.

I struggled to get out of bed, but for some reason, my body was paralysed. I couldn't move a muscle; nothing was responding. Only my eyes were working. My legs and arms were useless and refusing to move, and I couldn't help myself at all.

Then, horror of horrors, I felt a thick layer of cobwebs creeping across my face; the web was heavy and made from shiny steel wire.

I knew beyond question I was conscious. I could see and feel, and I knew I wasn't dreaming. But my head was fixed rigidly to the pillow. I could move my eyes just enough to see the silhouette of an enormous spider crouched malevolently in the darkness beside me. It was touching me and tasting me, with an evil that was tangible, while I lay immobilised and helpless beneath its horrible web. I felt sick from fear and totally incapable of doing anything to help myself.

My heart thundered in my chest, as if it were about to explode. But I was trapped, motionless and terror-stricken, lying helpless and suffocating in the ominous gloom. With my eyes bulging, all I could do was look on as the spider began to change shape. Forced to watch its horrifying metamorphosis, I saw its legs being shed and its gross body lengthening. Then its pale gleaming eyes flattened, leaving the cold lidless gaze of my childhood nightmare python, once again staring at me.

The hideous creature was slithering closer, feasting on my fear. Its forked tongue flicked, and its sharp menacing teeth gleamed as it prepared to embrace and devour me. I felt the hair on my scalp bristling from terror, and I was truly convinced I was within seconds of death.

Never before had I experienced the proximity of such overwhelming evil, and such fear, as I continued to battle with all the will-power I could summon to regain control of my body.

Suddenly, my limbs broke free and responded to my panic-stricken brain. I threw back the bedding and stumbled from bed, shivering from terror and gasping for breath.

The hideous python dissipated into the light of the early dawn, and I sat, gasping and weeping, propped against my bed in a dishevelled heap on the floor.

When I had pulled myself together, I wandered into the bathroom, feeling depressed and exhausted from my waking nightmares. I washed my tear-stained face, dragged on my dressing gown, and staggered downstairs to make some tea.

I carried the mug into the study and slumped at my desk, the latent depression still hanging around me like a black impenetrable curtain. I desperately wanted something to calm my nerves and put me back in touch with reality.

Putting the scalding tea aside, I unlocked the bottom drawer of the desk and took out the metal deed box I kept there. It was filled with my precious family mementoes. During the past months the box had come to represent something resembling a security blanket for me. It held the most treasured memories of my life with Alan. It was just a collection of bits of paper really... scraps that meant nothing to anyone else. But they were beyond value to me. Every item was a link with my beloved husband. And right there and then I desperately needed to find a way to reconnect with him.

I tipped the contents out onto the desk and began a familiar ritual of sorting, handling, and placing each item into one of three piles. I forget how many times I had performed the same routine over the past five months. Perhaps it was symptomatic of my morbid mentality, but the reminiscences gave me comfort in their own way.

I made one pile of the cards and letters of condolence I had received. The next pile was for the birthday, anniversary, Christmas, and Valentine's Day cards from Alan over the years. I read for the umpteenth time the sentiments, and loving, hand-written verses in them, while my face grew wet, once again, with tears. The third pile comprised the collection of certificates, diplomas, and academic awards belonging to various family members. It was just an assorted collection of family bits and pieces, worth nothing to anyone else, but precious to me beyond measure.

Included in that sentimental pile were some papers tied with blue ribbon. They were of particular poignancy and never failed to release an emotional outpouring. Each scrap reminded me of my lost child. They were all that remained of Richard, our first child. Richard. I repeated his name aloud... my darling firstborn, our son, Alan's and mine, our tragically stillborn little boy.

A bungled pregnancy had brought him into the world dead. We had never been allowed to see him, or even touch him. And my only remembrances were his birth certificate and his burial document, along with a few condolence cards and letters.

I had been told to forget the experience... to put it behind me and move on. But no one had explained how I was ever to achieve such amnesia of my emotions.

Now all I had left of Richard was that little collection of papers tied with blue ribbon. Nine months of eager waiting and dreaming... and then only empty arms and an empty crib.

That morning, I desperately needed to make some sort of emotional contact with my dead husband and our lost child. I needed to revisit my ocean of anguish and release some of my pent-up grief. Sometimes I felt so heartbroken it seemed I would die from all my silent repressed emotions.

Lowering my head onto my folded arms on the desk, I cried silently, until the hurt eased. My entire being yearned for Alan. I longed for the comfort and security of sleeping wrapped in his arms each night, for the touch of his strong, gentle hands, and the unfailing loving tenderness with which he had filled my life. This shadow of a life I was now condemned to live, was an emotionless desert, and the burden often too heavy to carry.

Eventually I pulled myself together, dried my eyes, and carefully tidied my memories safely back into their box. Then I locked the drawer... until the next time.

It was almost eight o'clock and I could hear the girls moving about in their bedrooms. My untouched tea was stone cold.

Chapter 3

A Family Discussion

Overnight, the weather had cleared, and the early sun was doing its best to break up the heavy clouds. The grass was wet, so I pulled on my wellington boots and tucked my pyjama trousers inside to keep them dry, before wandering aimlessly around the garden with my little dogs, while my mind remained in a ferment of uncertainty.

The air smelled cool and fresh, and I hoped it would help clear my head and straighten out my chaotic thoughts. Taken together the experiences of the previous night had left me confused and depressed. I was finding my enforced coming to terms with being a widow a difficult journey to travel, and my emotions remained raw and fragile. It didn't take much to unsettle me and leave me seriously nervous and unsure of myself.

Putting on a brave professional front at my school and in public wasn't easy. Neither was pretending at home that everything was just the same as before. It was a contrived performance and hard to sustain.

I felt in control of myself only so long as my days were tranquil and nothing unpredictable happened. Like flying on autopilot, I was fine so long as I didn't have to face the unexpected realities of life's ups and downs.

The unwelcome intrusion of the strange man, PP, into my controlled schedule had thrown me out of kilter. And the discovery that he had followed me home had been enough to disturb my sleep and produce fearsome nightmares.

For some illogical reason, that morning, the memory of him was continuing to disturb me. He was something like a worm, which had gotten inside my brain, and I couldn't shake off the night terrors that persisted in hanging over me like a menacing cloud. Even at the worst of times, after Alan's death, I had never experienced such terrible dreams and premonitions.

PP was a strange man... like no one I had ever met. I tried to reason with myself that it was just possible everything about the previous evening might have a logical, completely innocent explanation.

But the more I focused on him, the more convinced I became that there was something deeply unsettling about the whole episode. The man was undeniably an ignorant, ill-mannered, uneducated, and loud-mouthed braggart; and every instinct warned me to steer clear of him. He was no kind of a diamond... and a long way from the 'genwine ruff dymon' he had insisted he was.

All I could be sure of was he could tell highly convincing plausible stories. For some reason, he still seemed obsessed with his former wife and found some kind of pleasure in dredging up lurid tales about her. From his accounts, I knew their marriage had ended years previously, though their divorce had only been finalised around three years ago. But it was obvious he still retained a strange obsession with her, and for unexplained reasons, he still could not put their relationship aside and move on. He seemed driven by hatred, judging by the way he persisted in denigrating her, and claiming she was mad. To my mind, it seemed a seriously unhealthy obsession, but one he appeared to be incapable of leaving behind.

That morning, I would have preferred to say as little as possible to my daughters about the previous evening. But with Nathalie and Samantha, there was never any chance of that. Something unexpected had happened to keep their mother out until almost midnight, and they were determined to get to the bottom of it. Plus, I had gone out at seven o'clock for a couple of hours, promising to bring home fish and chips for their suppers, and had ended up disappointing them. Quite naturally, they wanted an explanation.

Now they came galloping down the garden to drag me back to the house for questioning. Talking about PP or recounting the details of my strange evening in his company was the last thing I wanted to do. I'd had little sleep, and felt too shattered and too emotionally disturbed to want to relive any of it. But there was to be no escape; my daughters wanted details.

Heaving a big sigh, I left my boots in the conservatory and was soon followed by four excited little dogs and two excited daughters. We all stumbled our way into the kitchen. Nathalie and Samantha sat impatiently at the table while I fed the Yorkies.

The interrogation continued over breakfast.

'So, this weirdo deliberately tried to crash into you in the car park?' Nathalie was first in. 'What I don't understand is why you didn't just give him a piece of your mind and leave. He hadn't actually bashed into you, so giving him a piece of your mind is what I'd have expected you to do. I've never known you to suffer fools gladly, Mum, and he sounds a right devious dickhead.'

I was pouring milk onto my breakfast muesli, but my hand shook nervously, and it went onto the table instead. I got up to fetch a cloth.

'I know what you're saying, but it was more complicated than that,' I said feebly. I was embarrassed and groping for a satisfactory explanation for my ridiculous behaviour. 'Sometimes awkward things happen, and they sort of make you confused,' I added weakly. 'You don't understand. I was pretty shaken up by what had happened. Maybe I just went a bit crazy. I don't really know why I didn't drive off. But for some reason, I let him persuade me to … Well I let him take me for a meal… as his way of making an apology.'

Now Samantha joined in. 'Mum... you let this yob, who'd pretty well scared the living daylights out of you, and who you didn't know from Adam, take you for a meal? What on earth were you thinking? Can you imagine what you'd say if we did anything like that?'

Now I was beginning to feel like a naughty teenager being reprimanded by my parents. 'Well, I was seriously shaken up,' I volunteered apologetically. 'And as you know, he did insist I should phone the pair of you to let you know I was all right.'

'So now he's got your phone number, and he knows where you live.' Samantha was really giving me a ticking off.

There was a longish pause, before Nathalie said, 'Well what I'd like to know is how he knew you had us two at home waiting for you?'

I shrugged thoughtfully. 'That's a very good question, and I've been wondering about it myself. I've really no idea. I didn't tell him, but he seemed to know already... and about you dad not being here waiting for me. As for the phone number, I definitely didn't give it to him.'

'Well he was standing watching while you rang us, wasn't he?' Nathalie sounded exasperated. 'I'll bet the so-and-so made a note of it; he sounds a crafty piece of work to me.'

'Oh, Mum,' Samantha said, sounding in despair, 'which century are you living in?'

'Oh my God.' I gasped. 'The crafty bugger! So now he's got my phone number, and he knows where I live. He's even taken photos of the house. What on earth is the man up to?'

'I don't know.' Samantha sounded puzzled. Then after a moment's thought, she added, 'Not unless the whole thing was a set-up, and he's been stalking you without you knowing it. Maybe he's trying to find out how much the house is worth.'

'Oh, come off it,' I said. 'Why would he want to do that? He's a company director of a building firm, for goodness sake; he already has a house. This is going too far. Now you're turning the whole thing into some sort of James Bond spy story.'

'Well, mum,' Nathalie said quietly, 'what's your explanation for all the stuff he did last evening? He sounds like a real creep to me. I don't think you ought to have anything more to do with him; he might even be dangerous. There're some nasty pieces of work about. I've read about these blokes who stalk women and try to wheedle their way into their confidence. They're really cunning characters, and this PP guy could easily be one of them.'

Talking to the girls had certainly started alarm bells ringing inside my head, and fired up a heap of uncertainties about my strange new acquaintance and what his motives might be.

'What I can't work out is how he knew I had children,' I said, feeling confused. 'And it was really odd how confident he was that I didn't have a husband at home waiting for me. How could he possibly have known that? I've never taken off my wedding ring. And I certainly didn't tell him I was a widow. That only leaves one thing, and it's ridiculously outrageous. You don't think he read my mind, do you? But going so far as to follow me home and photograph the house? Well that beggars-belief.'

'No, of course he couldn't read your mind.' Samantha grinned. 'My guess is he must've gotten the information from someone who knows you. Think hard. Who do you know who might know him? Maybe a parent at school or someone in the church who might have been talking to him? He's a nasty sneaky piece of work, hitting on you like that. But to come after you, stalking you and taking photos of our house; I'm sure that counts as criminal behaviour.'

'How on earth could I possibly know anyone he knows?' I said. 'He's not from around here. But I agree with you about the criminal behaviour. No respectable man would do those things... especially to a woman he's only just encountered by accident. It's totally outrageous.'

'I think you should ring the police,' Nathalie said, 'and tell them, just in case he comes back and does something else.'

'And what would I tell them?' I said. 'He never attempted to lay a finger on me. Yes, it's true he did almost crash into me, but that was on a car-park, and I let him make up for that by taking me for as meal. I can just imagine what the police would say about it.'

'Normal people don't follow a stranger home in the middle of the night and take photos of their house. He's not a normal person, Mum. He could be a burglar or a con man with plans to rob you.' Nathalie was getting really agitated.

'Does he know you're a head teacher?' Samantha interrupted anxiously. 'For all you know, he's already worked out you're not on benefits. Nobody living in a posh five-bedroom house is poor. My guess is he already knows a lot more about you than you'd ever imagine. I'll bet he's got some secret agenda, and it's all to do with money.'

Listening to their matter-of-fact opinions was making me increasingly worried.

The three of us sat thinking for a few minutes, before Nathalie said, 'If you had to make a list of what you really know about this man, what could you put on it, except he's fat and ugly and carries loads of cash around with him like a gypsy? You don't know who he is, or even where he lives or anything much at all. But for some reason, he's made it his business to find out loads of stuff about you. Sam's right. I'll bet he knows more about you than you'd ever guess.'

'Well,' I began defensively, 'I know he's a director of the building company called TBM Builders Ltd, and I know he's divorced and has a son the same age as Samantha. He can't be all that disreputable.'

'Oh yeah!' Samantha chipped in. 'He says that's what he is. Like he says his ex-wife's a madwoman. Mum! You know what Dad always told us about taking sides without knowing the whole story. He said we should hear both sides before we make up our own minds about what to believe. You shouldn't believe bad things about anyone just because someone slangs them off. It's obvious he hates his ex-wife. But you've never met her, so you really don't know what's true and what isn't.' She gave me a reproachful look.

'I reckon he was just trying to impress you, and all his stories could be a pack of lies,' Nathalie said quietly. 'If his wife was mad, why did he marry her? She couldn't have been crazy all the time; and if she was, why did he stay with her for twenty years? Nothing about any of it sounds right to me. Maybe he did things to her that drove her mad! Whatever! I still think he's creepy for telling you all that horrible stuff about her, when she wasn't there to defend herself. Can't you see he's like a spider, spinning you a load of lies, to trap you? He's what Dad would call "a nasty piece of work and not to be trusted".'

For a second while she was speaking, the memory of the horrific dream spider flashed into my mind. There was something creepy about the man. That was a fact. It seemed even my suppressed intuition was rebelling against him, but I had no idea why.

'I agree,' Samantha joined in. 'He's shameless, disrespecting his ex-wife. A really nice man wouldn't bad-mouth her like that, not to a stranger. He would keep their differences private. I'd tell him that to his face if he was here.'

It was obvious the girls felt protective towards me and highly suspicious of the man I had encountered the previous night. I really didn't want our discussion to go any further and sensed a family row could easily blow up.

'Okay,' I said. 'Let's leave this for now. If you're right, and if by any chance he does try to contact me over the next couple of weeks, here's what we'll do. We're on holiday over Easter. So even if we're home, we'll let any calls go onto the answering machine, or one of you can take them. If the worst does happen and you can't avoid speaking to him, just tell him I'm out shopping or away for the day. Get his number, but just make sure he doesn't get to speak to me. Agreed?'

Both heads nodded vigorously, and Samantha murmured. 'Uh-huh, you bet we'll block him.' While Nathalie enthusiastically added, 'Let him try, he won't get past us mum.'

'So, what are we doing today?' I asked brightly, attempting to change the subject. 'I was wondering if you'd fancy a trip into town, sort of to make up for me letting you down last evening? I thought we might do some shopping and then go to the cinema, and finish off with a pizza and salad before we come home.'

There was a thoughtful silence, while they watched me placing some twenty-pound banknotes on the breakfast table.

'Here's your dress allowance for this month,' I said.

I looked up to see two crestfallen faces. 'Now what's wrong? What have I said out of place now?' I said. 'What have I forgotten this time?'

Neither of them hurried to reply. They just glanced awkwardly at each other.

'Oh! I see,' I said. 'You already have plans for today, and I've forgotten, haven't I? Silly me.'

'We did tell you, Mum,' Nathalie volunteered. 'We said we'd be meeting friends in town this afternoon and going to the harbour disco later on. Sorry.'

I really couldn't remember being told anything about these

plans, but I nodded as though I did. 'Of course,' I said. 'My memory's getting to be like a sieve.' I paused thoughtfully and then added, 'And if I'm not mistaken, there's something I should remember about next weekend as well, isn't there?'

They exchanged sheepish glances, and then Samantha gave a big sigh, before coming to give me a huge hug. 'Everything's changed, Mum,' she said softly, and I realised she was trying to let me down gently.

'Dad's not with us anymore. We don't do the same things we used to when he was here. We'll always be a family, but we have to arrange things ourselves now, and get used to how different life is. It's never going to be just the four of us anymore, at weekends and holidays, not like it used to be.'

She looked out of the window and pointed towards the garden where our two sailing boats lay under tarpaulins, and the touring caravan stood unused.

Nathalie joined in. 'We didn't want anything to change, Mum. It just happened. Dad didn't abandon us or leave us. He was the best dad in the world, and we'll always love him. But nothing can ever be changed back to how it was. He's never coming home. We all have to accept that. Everything we had is gone; it's all lost. We're big girls, and we have to get on with our lives … And so do you. I'm going on sixteen. And Sam's nearly fifteen. Nothing's ever going to change how we feel about our dad, but he wouldn't want to hold us back and keep us miserable, would he? We all need to accept that and get on with our lives. We both want you to be happy, Mum... maybe in time even meet some really nice new guy. Only not one like that creep you got involved with last night.'

I could see tears glistening in Samantha's eyes. 'Nat's right,' she said softly. 'We both love you, Mum, and we'll always love Dad. But we're not your babies anymore.'

'Of-course you're not,' I said quickly, swallowing a big lump of emotion, and quickly changing the subject, before my feelings got the better of me. 'So, what are these plans for next weekend? I'll need to get myself sorted and make some of my own I guess; it is going to be Easter after all.'

'It's Amelia's birthday,' Samantha said, brightening up and surreptitiously dabbing her eyes. 'It's her sixteenth. She's having a beach barbecue on Saturday afternoon and then a disco party in the, Marine Pavilion, until midnight.'

Nathalie chipped in. 'After it finishes, we're having a sleepover at Tamsin's house. Her dad's going to bring us home on Sunday afternoon.'

'We showed you the invitation weeks ago,' Samantha added.

'Like I said,'…I sighed… 'my memory is still playing me tricks at present. The party sounds a great idea. I hope you both have fun and the weather improves.' I took a deep breath. 'Anyway, I want you both to have a great time this afternoon and at the disco tonight. Any idea what time you'll be home?'

'Oh, somewhere around the same time as you got in last night,' Samantha said, grinning cheekily.

'No way!' I called after them as they rushed out of the kitchen. 'I want you home by eleven. Get a taxi and don't walk. Do you hear me? You're not grown up yet; I'm still in charge here, so don't be late.'

Two voices called back from the hall, above the noise of their feet thumping their way upstairs. 'Heard that!' 'Okay. We'll see you at bedtime.'

I sat staring out of the kitchen window into a blank nothingness. Inside, it felt like a big black hole had just opened in my heart, and my thoughts were chaotic. So, is this what the future's going to be like?

Nothing had prepared me for these feelings. It had been only five short months since Alan's death, but somehow time had galloped away from me, without my ever noticing the changes going on.

In that short time, my daughters had changed. They were becoming independent-minded young women, just as I'd once been, eager to fly the nest and taste adult life.

The changes must have happened while I had been looking the other way, or was blindly buried in my misery. Whatever had gone on, I had been insensitive to noticing the reality of what was happening under my nose.

The dark winter days had been bleak for all of us, and we had clung together from desperate sorrow and confusion. But the winter was passed now, and for my two young daughters, their lives were moving on. Now it was spring, and I was the one still stuck in my widow's weeds and clinging forlornly to the dreams of our past life.

Without recognising their feelings or even my own, I had wanted time to stop, because emotionally my mind couldn't keep up with it. Strange things had been happening inside my brain for months. And deep down I had desperately wanted to go on believing I was in the middle of a bad dream and that, in a little while I would wake up and find it was all just a big mistake. I wanted to believe my fantasy... Alan would be coming home again, somehow, someday.

The reality was I still hadn't managed to work out how I was going to survive without him.

We had been an item from our schooldays, and nothing had ever split us apart. After losing him, I had just gone on living my life in a sort of state of suspended disbelief, like a fictional romance which is bound to have a happy ending.

The girls still had me, and I didn't want anything else to change. But I really couldn't expect them to remain buried in grief just because I couldn't sort out my own emotional realities. That realisation was a disturbing shock, and it suddenly forced me to face how different life was going to be for me in the unfamiliar landscape of the future.

I hadn't allowed myself to think about it before, not seriously. Of course, I had faced the practicalities of life as a single parent, and the financial implications that come from having only one income instead of two. But I had not given any thought to how I was going to feel when my daughters flew the nest and I would be left facing a solitary future.

Their growing up, leaving home, going to university, and getting married, were all things my brain had put firmly on hold... as problems to be dealt with later but not yet. Now it felt like I had suddenly been pushed to the edge of a void, and was left staring into the dangerous empty space of an unfamiliar country, a place devoid of love or even companionship. The awful feelings of panic and vulnerability returned, and my emotions began turning cartwheels inside my head again.

My thoughts were interrupted by two sets of elephant feet coming downstairs. I went into the hall and watched as they dashed out. Samantha blew me a kiss, before they both waved and rushed off to catch the bus into town.

'Don't forget,' I yelled after them, 'eleven o'clock, and you get a taxi home.'

Once they had gone, I knew I ought to get ready and take myself off to do the weekly shop. Instead, I went back into the conservatory and slumped in a chair. Today was not a good day.

My four little Yorkies came bouncing in beside me, jumping about on my knees. They were so tiny I could cuddle them all together. They were always a lovable distraction whenever I felt the world was a jungle I couldn't cope with.

Just then, they were all fussing and wriggling, as they each vied to be the one snuggling closest in my arms. I think I belonged to them as much as they belonged to me. It was love of the devoted doggy variety; they were my perpetual substitute children and would never grow up or want to leave me.

I began thinking about the coming Easter weekend. I would go to church, listen to Reverend Norman preach his Easter sermon, take communion, and then prepare a late lunch for whatever time the girls got home.

And, of course, there was always something or another to be done for school. I had a briefcase full of paperwork I had brought home to be dealt with.

It suddenly struck me that, in future, my life would be made up of anonymous irrelevancies. I was destined to become a set of mechanical functions, not a real woman anymore. I was no one's wife, and almost not even a functioning mother. What I did could be performed by a mechanical automaton programmed to do what I did.

How far I had travelled in five months, along a road I had never even noticed. Now I was confronting a turning point, where my future life would be a very different one from everything I had ever known and loved. It took some effort of will for that to even scratch the surface of comprehension, much less acceptance.

And what of that unknown future? Where on earth was that road taking me?

From where I was sitting, I could see the upturned sailing boats, lying where Alan had left them, still covered by green tarpaulins to keep them dry until their next outing ...an outing that was never going to happen. I stared at the green blurred silhouette of the girls' tub-shaped, Mirror-dinghy, lying alongside the sleeker profile, of our sixteen-foot, Fleetwind. I had to turn my head away. Sometimes the memories of how things used to be were just too painful to revisit.

I realised I needed to get up and motivate myself... go and do something to change my gut-wrenching reminiscing about the past.

Today I had been forced to recognise the hiatus between the past and the present; it was a chasm called death, and that was something I needed to face square on and not keep hiding from.

I went upstairs, took a shower, and got ready to go shopping, resolving as I did not to think about my problems anymore... well at least not for the present.

 Chapter 4

An Easter Sunday Revelation

As the church emptied on Easter Sunday morning, I hung back, deliberately dawdling my way to the door, while everyone else was chatting and heading towards the vestry tearoom.

I didn't feel inclined to join the Sunday morning social chit-chat, and I wasn't in any hurry to get back to my empty house either. The girls wouldn't be home until later. And with time on my hands and no lunch to cook, I was feeling a bit lost... at a loose end and with time to waste, even if it was just to admire the floral displays.

My faith had taken something of a battering over recent months, and I had become a half-hearted communicant since Alan's death. Along with all my other uncertainties, I was no longer really sure what I believed in; in fact, I had been half expecting to hear from Norman Forester, our vicar, querying my unexplained absences.

On that Easter Sunday morning, I was trying to avoid him; and taking my time to admire the flower arrangements provided an excuse not to be in the noisy queue, waiting for tea and pleasantries or, at worst, a friendly inquisition.

Gradually I made my way along the nave towards the vestry, wondering what I would find to say to him if he caught up with me.

Alex and Moira Wright were standing just outside the vestry door, and it was obvious they had seen me approaching; in fact, it looked as if they might have been waiting for me. Before I reached them, I noticed Moira say something to Alex and then pat him reassuringly on the arm, before disappearing into the vestry.

Our families had been church friends for years, but I hadn't seen, or spoken to Alex or Moira more than three times since Alan's death. This lack of contact seemed to be significant. I felt I had been ditched in a sort of ecumenical brush-off. If I didn't attend church regularly, then the church didn't want to know me, and I could stay home and stew in my own juice. Maybe I was being overly sensitive, but sadly, that was how it seemed to me.

However, as I came closer, Alex held out his hand to greet me, at the same time looking rather embarrassed, as though he had something awkward on his mind and didn't know how to begin saying it.

I smiled and took his outstretched hand, surprised to find him holding on to mine and steering me away from the noisy doorway.

'Are you in a hurry?' he said quietly. 'If you can spare a moment, I'd appreciate it. I would really like a word with you.'

'Of course,' I said. 'I'm in no particular rush. There's nothing wrong at home, is there? No one ill I hope?'

He shook his head. 'Oh, no! Nothing like that. Everyone's fine.'

After an awkward pause, he cleared his throat and then continued. 'Well … I'm not really certain how to start this conversation.' He grinned briefly. 'It's just that Moira and I have agreed something needs to be said to you. It's rather awkward… none of our business really. But after the shock of Alan's death, we couldn't help wondering …'

'Whatever's the matter?' I said, starting to feel uncomfortable. His hesitant awkwardness was making me nervous. 'What needs to be said, Alex? Whatever it is, you can be up front. This isn't going to embarrass me, is it?'

'Oh! For heaven's sake, no! It's just we wanted to know … Is everything all right?' His voice sounded strained and anxious, as if he couldn't find the right words to say what he wanted. 'What I mean to say is… are you coping?'

'You've got me there,' I said uneasily. 'Are you asking me if I'm getting myself back on track after Alan's death?'

'Well, I suppose that's sort of what I mean.' He still sounded uncertain how to continue.

'I think I'm doing as well as can be expected, considering the circumstances.' I said, becoming slightly defensive. 'I can't pretend this is the happiest time of my life, or the easiest for my girls either. But we're stuck with it, aren't we? We don't have any alternative.'

Suddenly, and for no logical reason, my pent-up emotions seemed to reach bursting point. All the repressed rage I had been controlling for months flared out of control. 'Well, actually, our situation is intolerable and very difficult to come to terms with.' I heard the anger sharpening my voice. 'Particularly in view of the fact that Alan shouldn't have died. If he had received proper medical treatment from a dedicated physician that morning, he would still be alive. I still find it incomprehensible that a qualified doctor was incapable of differentiating between a hiatus hernia and a cardiac infarction. When Bormann first responded and examined Alan... he told me categorically there was nothing wrong with his heart... I might as well have been consulting a plumber.'

I looked around at the empty church. 'No one seems to know or care what we've been put through because of that incompetent man's stupidity. Is there a way back to … being all right, when you know your husband died because of the medical incompetency of your family GP?'

Hot angry tears began oozing from the corners of my eyes. I brushed them away impatiently, while Alex stared in silent embarrassment, not knowing how to respond to my angry outburst.

'If justice had been done, there would have been an official inquest,' I went on, fishing in my pocket for a handkerchief, 'a proper legal enquiry into what Alan endured that day. His dangerous, life-threatening condition should have been properly identified and dealt with. I phoned for help, and for him to be taken into intensive care immediately. Instead I got a bumbling idiot who wasted two hours doing absolutely nothing before my husband finally died. Bormann's insistence that the problem was a hiatus hernia was a farce; he did absolutely nothing to help Alan, and neglected him shamefully.'

I wiped my eyes and continued my angry outburst, without

ever giving Alex any time to respond; and I felt no tinge of embarrassment, even though I knew Dr Bormann was a friend of his. 'Bormann told me not to worry and then calmly left the house and went home for his breakfast. And as Alan rapidly deteriorated before my eyes, it was left for me to give him CPR and call an ambulance and the crash team. There should have been an inquest into the circumstances of why Alan was criminally neglected by that man. He was an incompetent idiot, masquerading as a qualified doctor. In my eyes, it was manslaughter. Bormann killed Alan because of his incompetence, and I was left to bury my husband because of his medical failure. There can never be any forgiving or forgetting. This situation is what I'm left to live with, for the remainder of my life.

'My husband is dead. He can't be brought back. That's not something for me to … get over, or ever again be all right about.' I wiped my eyes and struggled to regain my composure.

Alex's face had blanched during my outburst, and I saw him glancing nervously towards the vestry door... empathising with me but not knowing what to say next.

'I apologise for exploding like that,' I said quietly. 'Please excuse me, Alex. Unfortunately, you pressed the button, and triggered some very raw emotions. Alan was only forty-three, and it's only been five months since his death; neither my anger nor my grief have subsided.'

He shook his head. 'No. Please don't apologise, Delia. I'm sorry … It's obvious I chose an inopportune moment to speak to you.'

He turned to leave and then stopped. 'I'm really sorry to have intruded on you like this, Delia. I honestly had no idea how deeply traumatised you were. Your bereavement was clearly a terrible experience. None of us have ever heard any of the details, and now I'm left feeling really awkward.'

He was about to go and then he suddenly thought better of it. Putting a hand on my shoulder, he said, 'Look. I may have been clumsy in approaching you like I did, and nothing came out the way it was intended to. What I was meaning to speak to you about was something that happened on Thursday afternoon. We had an incident at the agency, which was worrying, and unfortunately it does concern you. It's been troubling Moira and me ever since, and that's the reason we decided you ought to know about it. My speaking to you this morning, seemed preferable to just phoning you.'

'Well you have my attention,' I said. 'What's the matter?'

After a thoughtful pause, he said hesitantly, 'Can I just ask you straight up? Are you by any chance considering putting your house on the market?'

I felt stunned, and for a moment, I must have looked as shaken as I felt.

'I'm only asking because we've known one another for a long time, and I do have a good reason for enquiring. Your decisions are nobody's business but your own. But we wanted you to understand, if there's a problem that Moira or I can help with, you only have to say...'

'Sell my house?' I gasped. 'Whatever gave you that idea?'

Taking my arm, he drew me towards a pew behind the font, where we could sit without being overheard. 'Like I was saying, something very odd happened at the agency on Thursday afternoon.' He took a quick glance around to make sure we were alone before continuing. 'That's what prompted my approaching you this morning.'

He suddenly stopped speaking and looked seriously embarrassed for a moment. 'Oh! Good grief! Please don't think I'm touting for business. Heaven forbid... No! No! We were just concerned for you, that's all!'

For a few seconds, I remained speechless. 'What could possibly have made you think I want to sell my house?' I blurted out. 'As if getting my head around the problems I'm already trying to deal with wasn't enough, moving house would be the last thing on my mind.'

'I can see that now,' he said quietly. 'There's obviously been some sort of mix-up... crossed wires ... We just got the idea you might be thinking of downsizing... maybe looking for something smaller?'

'Or cheaper?' I retaliated swiftly. 'So, were you wondering why I hadn't come to Wright's Estate Agency if I was putting my house on the market?' I was trying hard to keep the irritation out of my voice.

'No! Good gracious me, nothing like that. I assure you, my dear. Please don't imagine for a second, I'm touting for business. For God's sake, I'm not a ghoul!'

'Then I really don't see what the point of this conversation is, Alex,' I said sharply. 'Let me assure you, I have no mortgage to pay. I work for a living, and financially I'm in a reasonable position to maintain my girls and myself, without needing to downsize. The girls are in a good grammar school, and we all like where we live... I have no plans to move now, or at any time in the future.'

He listened without interrupting and then quietly said, 'Well, even so, you really do need to know that someone has designs on your property. A young woman came into our office on Thursday enquiring about your house. That's what I've been trying to get around to telling you, and making a pig's ear of it in the process.'

The news left me temporarily stunned. 'Someone has been enquiring about my house?' I eventually said, curiously, 'Who was it? Did you get a name?'

He raised his hand to stop me going on. 'Please, just hear me out, and I'll tell you what we know. I don't know who she was.

'This young person turned up at the office around closing time and said she was looking to buy a large five-bedroom detached house near the grammar school. According to her story, she had heard from a private source, one would be coming onto the market quite soon. She claimed her informant had recommended our agency as being the most likely one to handle larger properties.

'Well, of course I told her I didn't know of anything on the market answering her description. So next thing, she produces a couple of photographs of the house she says she's interested in buying. They were poor quality grainy pictures and looked like they'd been taken in semi-darkness, but I recognised them immediately as being of your house.'

'Did she leave her name?' I said sharply. 'Do you have the photos?'

He shook his head. 'Neither, I'm afraid. She was very … well … err … strange. To be frank, she looked and sounded... well not really very intelligent and certainly not affluent. In fact, quite frankly, I would describe her as being somewhat common... coarse-featured and dressed in a tight skimpy skirt, with straw-bleached hair and heels she could barely totter in... definitely not the sort to be in the market to afford the kind of place she claimed to be looking for. I couldn't get my head around what she was up to. In fact, the whole episode seemed pretty suspicious.'

'Did anyone else get a look at her or hear what she had to say?' I was becoming alarmed. The story I was hearing was an unpleasant shock, and one I hadn't been anticipating.

'Yes,' he nodded. 'Moira was sitting at one of the other desks, so she overheard everything. All the rest of the staff had gone. But if you want any confirmation, she's over there in the vestry.'

'There's no question of my not believing you,' I said. 'Of-course I do.'

'Well I tried to put her off and said I didn't recognise the house in the photos. But she persisted... began by describing exactly what she wanted. Then unexpectedly, she turned the conversation around to asking me directly to give her an estimated valuation of the house she was looking to buy.'

'And what about her personal details?' I said. 'Her name?... address? Didn't you get her to fill in one of your registration forms? I mean that's what usually happens when new clients come into your office looking to buy or sell property, isn't it?'

'Absolutely! We would never take anyone onto our books without knowing who they were. We explain to new clients how much effort we put into finding them exactly the sort of new home they're looking for. But this, err, person was far from our normal run of clients. She didn't stop talking at me, at the top of her voice, and I couldn't get a word in edgeways. All she kept harping on about was how much was the house in her photographs worth.'

'And did you eventually offer her any price guide?' I asked.

'Well, she persisted in pushing me and pushing me for an estimated valuation, until I admit, out of desperation, I finally said, "You've got to be looking at a ballpark sum of anything up to half a million for a one-off architect-designed house." Then I asked her point blank, "Are you sure you can afford that type of property?"

'Moments later, while I was reaching in my desk, to get a set of client registration papers, she jumped up, and shouted at me, "I've decided I don't want to do business with a snotty-nosed freak like you," and stormed out.

'I don't believe she ever had any serious intentions at all. Moira listened, and she agreed. There was something deeply unpleasant behind it; the whole thing seemed seriously contrived. We decided you should be told, because if something underhand is going on behind your back, you have every right to be aware of it.'

I had already guessed something of what might lie behind the situation he was describing, and I was biting back my anger. If this was a further development in the strange events surrounding PP stalking me, then what I was hearing was deeply disturbing. 'You were absolutely right to tell me,' I said. 'I'm indebted to you, Alex. I have no idea what's going on, or who the rude woman was. Perhaps something will eventually happen to clarify her ignorant behaviour. All I can say is I'm sorry you've been involved like this; it's obvious there's something here I shall need to look into.'

I glanced at my watch and stood up to leave. People were clustered in groups outside the vestry door, and I wanted to be gone before anyone else caught up with me. I turned back towards Alex briefly. 'Did those photographs happen to look as if they might have been taken with a camera flash?' I said.

'Why, yes. Now you come to mention it, they did.'

I paused a moment, recalling what I'd seen from my bedroom window. 'Is there anything else either you or Moira remember about the incident?' I asked. 'If that young woman ever turns up again, would you recognise her?'

He nodded thoughtfully. 'I'm sure I would, and Moira got a good look at her as well. We both agreed she had a terrible accent. And she certainly wasn't intelligent or well educated. There was nothing about her to suggest she could possibly be in the market for an expensive property. Maybe it sounds judgmental, but being estate agents, we have to assess potential clients who walk through our doors. Otherwise, we would be taken for a ride by con artists every week.

'We're very selective about who we show over our vendors' homes. There's a lot at stake, and security is crucial to our good name and our business credentials; you'll understand when I say we have to assess clients carefully. It was plain as a pikestaff that girl could never aspire to buy an expensive property. Nothing about her suggested she had two pennies to rub together.'

He paused and then added as an afterthought. 'Oh! There is one other thing Moira said I had to tell you. It was something that happened when she followed the woman to lock up. She saw her getting into a scruffy dark-coloured estate car... I think it was probably black but smothered in dirt... beside the male driver. She couldn't get a good look at him, but she did notice the outline of a large heavily built sort of guy, with dark untidy hair. Confidentially, in her opinion, he looked like, well … err … the travelling type of person. You know, the sort of dodgy bloke that buys and sells scrap metal and stuff that's supposed to have "fallen off the back of a lorry". If you take my meaning. Very rough-looking. I'm sure you must know the sort I mean?'

'Yes,' I said thoughtfully. 'I know exactly the sort you mean.'

Chapter 5

The Old Man of the Sea

When I arrived home from church, there were three missed calls on my answering machine.

The first and the third both simply said, 'Caller withheld their number.'

Of course, there was no proof, but I had a pretty good idea who the mystery caller had probably been.

The second message was from Samantha. She sounded her usual happy bubbly self, eager to tell me she and Nathalie had enjoyed the beach party and the disco. Their sleepover at Tamsin's had been great fun, and she was calling to say she hoped I didn't mind, but they wouldn't be coming home until six.

They had been invited to stay at Tamsin's for lunch and then take a trip to the wildlife park with the family in the afternoon.

Tamsin's dad would drop them off on his way home.

I naturally felt disappointed. But they were happy, so I quickly pushed my disappointment aside. In our present circumstances, more than anything else in the world, I wanted my girls to be happy.

In any case I had an idea taking shape in my head, which I would need time to carry out... particularly while the girls weren't around.

A quick glance at my watch showed me it was just after one, so I had plenty of time to do what I was planning, and still be back before the girls got home. I fetched the telephone directory and sat down at the kitchen table.

Following my offbeat conversation with Alex, I had decided to do some follow-up investigating. I needed some serious answers relating to what devious plans PP might be devising. Clearly something was going on behind my back, which I needed to get to the bottom of. If PP was a bone fide builder, then he would probably have a landline listed.

I flicked the directory open at 'Building Contractors' and began running my finger down the columns. There it was, in heavy type, 'TBM Building Contractors. Ltd'... along with a list of contact numbers, one of which was in the village where he had told me he lived.

I felt sure it must be the same man. I made a note of the address and the telephone number. The village location was about seventeen miles away. I had enough time to drive there and back, and do a bit of surreptitious snooping before the girls got home.

Suppressing feelings of apprehension, which were making my

stomach queasy, I picked up my sunglasses, pulled on my coat, and grabbed my handbag and car keys. Then as an afterthought, I pushed my camera into my bag. I was determined to get to the bottom of my suspicions about who this strange man was, and what he might be up to.

Less than half an hour later, I was driving slowly along a winding country road, looking for the address I had scribbled on my notepad. I was in the right place, but I couldn't have felt more guilty about being there if I had been planning a burglary.

A stream meandered through the centre of the village, with the road running alongside it. But there was no sign of the address I was looking for. I drove on until I found myself surrounded on both sides by cabbage fields, with no more houses to be seen. Essex has vast acres of similar fields, all filled with a variety of market-garden produce. This was just one of them.

Maybe I had gotten myself lost or taken a wrong turning?

Changing down into second gear, I crept along slowly for a better look, but an unkempt hedge, straggling along the road frontage blocked my view. After keeping going for another five minutes, I finally found the place I was looking for.

The house had been built in the fenced-off corner of a vegetable field. It wasn't an attractive rural site... just a piece of rough agricultural land with derelict farm buildings as its closest neighbours, and acres of cabbages.

I drove on until I found a field entrance where I could reverse, and then set off back in the direction I had come to get a better view of my target. My heart was pounding. I didn't want to be spotted, or challenged by anyone for behaving suspiciously. Now that I was on the opposite side of the road, I had a slightly more advantageous view of the house.

It was small and unremarkable... a three-bedroom detached property built close to the road frontage. It was a very ordinary kind of house, like something out of a bog-standard design book, available at any newsagents. It might typically have been built on any large housing estate, surrounded on all sides by dozens of identical ones.

No one was about, but there were three vehicles parked in the drive. One was a dark green Morris Minor; one, a dark maroon commercial van, sign-written, TBM Builders Ltd; and the last, a scruffy, mud-splattered black estate car. I had definitely seen that one before.

There was no need for photographs. I had seen enough to satisfy my immediate curiosity. As I drove home, I was preoccupied with wondering who the dark green Morris Minor could belong to. Perhaps it was the young woman Alex had spoken about. It couldn't possibly belong to PP's son; he was only fifteen, presupposing what I had been told about him had been true.

My little snooping adventure had resolved some of my curiosity. But there seemed a whole can of worms still to be opened before I got to the truth about what PP was up to, and why he wanted to know the value of my house.

For the present, I decided to keep my afternoon's activities to myself. It was possible I might never hear another word from the man, so I decided to say nothing to Nathalie or Samantha.

On Easter Monday, my Yorkies woke me at 5 a.m. It was still dark, and they were creating merry hell at the kitchen door, barking and scratching to get into the hall. From the racket they were making it seemed as though the devil himself was spooking them.

I dragged on my dressing gown, and staggered barefoot and half-asleep, downstairs to see what was going on. Feeling nervous, I grabbed the wooden rolling pin I kept handy, and switched on all the lights as I went.

As soon as I appeared at the kitchen door, the Yorkies raced past me and ran snarling and barking to the front door. I couldn't get them to calm down; something unexpected and outside their normal routine had disturbed them, and they weren't happy about it. My initial fear had been that someone might have been trying to break in. But the alarm hadn't gone off, so I decided maybe a fox had been rummaging about outside, and that had spooked them.

I went around checking windows and doors for any signs of an attempted break-in but could find nothing unusual. Then the girls appeared on the scene yawning sleepily and both wanting to know what all the noise was about.

When the dogs had calmed down, we gathered in the kitchen, drinking coffee and all still half asleep. It was almost daylight before I persuaded them to go back to bed, after convincing them we were all safe and nothing else was likely to happen.

After they had wandered back upstairs, I fed the dogs and settled them back in their beds. But my mind was still uneasy. I had a feeling that something might have been pushed through the letter box, so I went to check it out.

The box was empty, but beyond the glazed door panels, I could see something bulky had been attached to the door handles. With the aid of a torch, I could see a cardboard box hanging from the handles between the two glass doors. I fumbled to undo the lock, but the doors were held rigidly on the outside with strong twine, and wouldn't open.

Fetching a sharp knife and some scissors, I did what I could to cut the handles free. But after ten minutes I was no further forward, so I gave up and went back into the kitchen, where I slipped on my gardening shoes. Taking the knife and scissors with me, I walked around to the front of the house.

The large cardboard box hanging between the door handles advertised the contents as being an electric drill. But most of the original lettering was now covered in brown parcel tape, and the box had clearly been reused to hold something else. I cut it free, and carried it into the kitchen, surprised by how light it felt. Perhaps it was some kind of prank... a joke carried out by some teenage Romeo the girls knew?

In the lamplight, I found a handwritten label, addressed to me. I ripped off the tape and a large quantity of squiggly poly packing instantly fell all over the kitchen floor.

Concealed inside the packing was a huge chocolate Easter egg. It was the largest, most garish one I had ever seen. The light brown chocolate egg was elaborately decorated all over with florid green and yellow icing sugar, piped to look like grass, and with fluffy yellow chicks wandering over the surface, attached by their feet with green icing. The garish effect was completed by an enormous red icing sugar heart attached to a spring, which wobbled when you shook the egg. And the hideous creation was topped off with a lavish red ribbon bow and a gift card. The card had been crudely decorated in red felt-tip pen, with a roughly drawn heart and the words, 'I (heart) you, xxx PP' scrawled on it.

My heart sank, and my hands began to tremble. He was stalking me. I wasn't amused, and didn't find it at all funny. The stupid man had scared all my family half out of their wits that morning, and fastened my door up with twine manacles to deliver this hideous, unwelcome gift.

He was a virtual stranger but was behaving as if he knew me well. And to complete the insult, he was taking deeply unwelcome liberties. I was not encouraging his attentions, and I was furious.

While I was wondering what to do about the ludicrous egg, Nathalie and Samantha reappeared. They took one look at the enormous thing sitting among its deluge of plastic curlicues and then grabbed the card and began laughing their heads off.

'Whatever are you going to do about this weirdo?' Samantha said between giggles.

'I've absolutely no idea,' I replied weakly. 'It's gone beyond a joke. I barely know this man, but he's behaving as if we know one another really well... even familiarly.'

'I think you're going to have to put him right,' Nathalie suggested. 'I mean you need to find out what he's up to and put a stop to it.'

'We've been blocking his phone calls all week, Mum,' Samantha added. 'He knows you're not out all the time. I think that's why he's ended up doing this.'

Nathalie picked up the monster egg and shook it. Some of the yellow chicks fell off, and the big red heart wobbled madly on its spring.

'This thing must be as big as his ego, or his head, and just about as empty. He's not giving up easily, is he?' She said grinning.

I looked from one to the other of my girls, took a deep breath, and then said, 'There's something you don't know about. Something happened after church yesterday. It's connected to all of this. I wasn't going to say anything about it because I didn't want you to worry. But now I think I'd better clear the air... because you have a right to know.'

Spilling the beans to my daughters about my conversation with Alex and my Sunday afternoon trip, actually made me feel better. But it left both of them looking worried.

Following the unwelcome arrival of the monster egg, the phone call we had all been anticipating came later that morning.

Samantha let the phone ring six times before she picked it up. I heard her speaking politely to someone before she put her hand over the mouthpiece and waved the receiver at me. 'It's him, Mum,' she said softly. 'Do you want to take the call? Or shall I just hang up?'

I took a deep breath and nodded, before walking hesitantly across the hall. In my best professional voice, I said coolly, 'Hello. Who is this? How can I help you?'

I was answered by a throaty chuckle. 'Well, 'ello there moy deer. 'Ow meny 'ansom men woz yer expectin' ter 'ere from this mornin'?' PP's half-baked greeting echoed in my ear.

'So, 'ow cum yer've bin avoidin' uz this las' week?' he said, continuing his sleazy effort at seduction. 'Yer dorters 'ave bin sayin' yer've bin bizzy wiv yer schoolwork, an' Ah've nivver seemed ter pick the righ' time ter call. So, wot 'ave yer bin up ter? 'Ow meny men 'ave yer bin aout wiv?'

'Oh! It's you,' I said, feigning mock surprise. 'What a surprise. I thought you might have gone away for Easter with your son. He's on holiday this week, isn't he? Unfortunately, teachers have holiday obligations. We aren't so lucky; I have a stack of work to get through preparing for the new term.'

"Ave yer?' His manner sounded vague at best, and not in the least bit interested. 'Well, Ah didn't phone ter tork abaout yer work or moy lad. I rang ter tell yer... Ah want yer ter come aout wiv uz. Ah'm invitin yer on a date see, like we cud go daawn the pub somewier, an' Ah cud lern yer ter ply darts. Or if yer doan fancy tha', Warringford is playin' at 'ome.'

I grimaced towards the girls, who were standing a couple of feet away. 'You are offering to take me on a date to teach me to play darts?' I said flatly, 'Or watch a football match at Warringford?' I pulled a silly expression. 'Well, what can I say? It's very kind of you, but I'm not really into the pub scene. And I'm sorry to say, I don't have any inclinations urging me to learn how to play darts or watch football. Thanks for phoning, but I'll have to say no thank you to your invitation.'

I was about to hang up, relieved to put an end to the embarrassment, but he hung on doggedly. 'So, wot wud it tek ter gitcher ter cum out wiv uz? Wot kine uv fings does yer like doin'?'

The unexpected question threw me. I had intended to end the matter quickly, and hopefully never hear anything more from him. I paused frantically trying to think of something that would be a complete turn-off for him.

After a short pause, I said reluctantly, 'Well, err … the sort of things I would choose to do would be a visit to the theatre or the ballet. I enjoy the opera and classical music and visiting art galleries. I even like visiting stately homes and gardens and antiques fairs. They are what I'd call my sort of entertainment. But I don't suppose you and I really share any of those interests in common, do we? In any event, I don't need to remind you, we're virtually strangers. We know nothing about each other, and I doubt we really have much at all to talk about. So why on earth would we go out on a date, which one of us would find deathly boring?'

'Yer not entyerly correc' there, luv, and it doan mean uz can't git ter no eachuver. Ah really likes classic moosik, speshly country an' weste'n classic moosik. Ah wuz at ther feeater a couple uv munfs ago ter see a show. An Ah took me dorter ter see Jesus Christ Super Star in London. So mebbe Ah cud git ter loik the stuff yer duz, if Ah got arf a chance. Ah reely likes yer, luv...an' Ah've taken quite a fancy ter yer. An' Oi'm determined ter see yer agin an' git ter naw yer.'

Brain lights flashed. A daughter? He'd told me he only had a son? Was it just a tall story? Or could it be true? Did he have two children? I decided not to question him. As things stood, it really didn't matter.

However, hearing myself once again being called love did matter, and it set my teeth on edge. 'Look, PP,' I said frostily, 'if you really want to avoid irritating me, please don't call me love. I've mentioned it before. Please respect my feelings, or I really don't want to talk to you.'

'Yer! Yer! Mus respek yer feelin's.' He showed no signs of being the least bit bothered about my feelings or my sensitivities, and just ploughed on with his own agenda. "Ow abaat if Ah got sum tikits fer the feater. Then wud yer cum aaut wiv uz?'

'Oh … umm … maybe,' I replied cagily. 'It would depend if it was something I wanted to see. As I've already told you, I have a busy life. And I'm not ready for making new friends for the time being. I don't know anything about you, not even where you live. You just can't walk into someone's life and expect her to instantly want to spend time in your company. It takes time to get to know someone.'

I took a moment to psyche myself up for what I wanted to say next. 'And apart from that, something is really puzzling me.

I'm actually ex-directory, and I don't know how you can have got hold of my phone number? I have to say I find that quite disturbing.'

It was as though nothing I was saying was getting through to him. 'Yer kin axe uz enfink yer wan, luv, an' Ah'll tell yer. By the way 'ow did yer like me choklat egg? It ware a bigun, waren't it? Becher nivver 'ad won as big as tha' afore?'

His unexpected change of tactics left me speechless. He had quite deliberately avoided answering my questions, and had rudely changed the subject.,

'Well,' I began again, picking my words carefully, 'to be honest I thought it was...' I stopped, suddenly not sure how to express my real feelings. I wanted to say quite a lot about the egg and about the way it had been delivered, beginning with...It was awful. I have never seen anything so grotesque in my life. And how dare you come to my house disturbing my family in the middle of the night and fastening your stupid parcel to my door handles so that we couldn't get out of the house!

But being me, I treated him politely and let him get away with his diabolical behaviour. 'It came as quite a shock,' I said. 'I've not seen one quite like it before... nothing so ... um ... large or quite so colourful. And I found it extremely difficult to unfasten my door handles after the way you had tied them up. You must have put yourself to quite some trouble in delivering it, especially at that time of the morning. Yes, it was quite an unexpected surprise.'

He was totally unfazed. 'Ah'm well known fer givin' fowks unexpicted surprises,' he said smugly and then laughed. 'Sum of 'em aren't allus nice uns eyver, not like that'un Ah gived yer. Neebody can ivver guess wot stunt Ah'll pull nixt, cos neebody kin read me mind, see. It's cos Ah'm too sharp fer 'em. Ah'm too cliver. But fer yer, luv, Ah'd go te the ends uv the erf.'

His mangled English made me cringe. The words were totally insincere, and even patronising, and I wanted to slam the phone down on him.

Still choosing my words carefully, I said, 'You certainly gave me a surprise I wasn't expecting. It took me almost half an hour to unfasten the door.'

I heard him chuckling to himself at the other end of the phone. 'Wonce ah meks me mind up to git summat, Ah alus gits wot Ah wonts, evenchally. Ah've gorra way wiv uz see, an Ah doan giv up. Ah'll tell yer summat else, luv. Ah kin reed yer mind.'

Smiling to myself at his crude arrogance, I said, 'That would be truly amazing, as you don't know me, and you can't possibly know what I'm thinking.'

'Wanna test me then?' he said cockily.

'No,' I said slowly. 'I don't think so.' I was beginning to feel nervous again. The conversation was going on for far too long. 'That won't be necessary.'

'Well, Ah'll tell yer onyways. Wot yer finkin rite naw is, Stoopid bugga, wot's ee ramblin on abaat? Ah'm right, ain't Ah?'

I laughed aloud. 'I couldn't possibly deny or confirm that. I'd rather keep my thoughts private.'

'Ah kin see Ah'll ave ter tek yer daan a peg er too. You's a bit too cocky by arf, missis. But yer doan need ter fank uz fer th' expensive egg. Ah wuz tryin' ter pleeze yer, so doan trouble yersel te fank uz. Naw lissen, Ah'm goin te git them tikits, an as soon as ah do, Ah'll let yer no. So meentimes, yer kin git yer best bib an' tucker ready fer ower date. Bye fer naw.'

Before I could make any reply, the phone went dead. He had controlled the entire situation. Then he'd hung up before I could finally reject his plans.

I slumped onto the hall chair with the receiver still in my hand, feeling browbeaten and overwhelmed. When I looked up, the girls were standing watching me and grinning.

'Well, that certainly put him in his place, Mum.' Nathalie smirked.

And then Samantha joined in. 'You won't be hearing from him again in a hurry, will you?' She sniggered. 'Well, not for a couple of days at least, not until he's got those theatre tickets sorted out. He's really weird, Mum, and determined not to give up. I don't think he's going to be all that easy to get rid of. You'd better watch out, Mumsy. That man has his eye on you.'

'Yes,' I said thoughtfully, 'that's just what I've been thinking. I just wish I could think of a way to poke him in it. He really isn't someone I want to get to know.' I shuddered. 'Ugh! He's so vulgar, so presumptuous. What an awful man! I wish I had just driven off that night in the car park and left him standing.'

'You sounded really stuck-up, telling him about what interests you,' Nathalie said. 'If that didn't put him off, he must be really keen; it was amazing the way he ignored all your deliberate put-downs.'

'Or more likely, he's just thick-skinned and determined to get his own way, for some reason,' Samantha added thoughtfully.

'Well he reminds me more of, Sinbad and the Old Man of the Sea,' I said. 'That story was about someone determined to take advantage... an old man who wouldn't leave Sinbad alone. No matter what Sinbad did, he couldn't get him off his back, because the old boy clung to him like a leech. I have a horrible feeling PP is going to turn out to be my version of that story. That man has a hide like a rhinoceros. He's shifty and manipulative and just bulldozes his way to get what he wants.'

I sighed and shrugged my shoulders. 'I know nothing about him, and I really don't want to. But he won't go away. How am I going to get him out of my hair?'

Looking helplessly from Nathalie to Samantha, I said, 'You must have heard him? He's an ignorant yob. We're from opposite sides of the track, and I honestly don't know what is going on in his head, or why he's latched himself to me. I've not encouraged his attentions, so why does he imagine I would want to go out with him?'

I wasn't being snobbish. What I had said was true. The last things I would ever dream of doing would be going to a football match, or learning to play darts. And as for hanging around in pubs, well, that was something I had never done in my life. Enough said.

Chapter 6

Cunning Tactics

I was unwittingly travelling through murky waters and entirely unaware of the motivations of the strange character who was attempting to inveigle his way into my life.

Dislodging him, and blocking his intentions was never going to be an easy or a painless process. My mild, polite tactics had no possibility of dissuading him. His secret motivation, and the agenda driving him to pursue me, were totally resolute and inflexible.

Unfortunately, and entirely without my approval, he was determined to make whatever efforts were necessary to achieve his Machiavellian ambitions. In his view, the end always justified the means.

A few days after his previous phone call, I received another.

He was cock-a-hoop. Having obtained tickets for the London theatre production of Starlight Express, he assumed I would be overjoyed to accompany him to London the following Saturday.

Naturally I was surprised, even a little bit flattered. No matter how I might feel about the man, a London production was something I found very hard to resist. And after a minimum amount of persuasion, I accepted. I couldn't remember the last time I had been to see a top-class show in London.

It didn't take me long learn that whatever PP set out to achieve, he would brook no opposition to it. It had nothing to do with academic learning or simply being an amenable person, but everything to do with cunning animal instinct and determination. Whatever he fixed his sights on, he never took his focus off the target.

The devil does not tempt you with roast beef if you are a vegetarian, and I had made it clear I had no desire to learn to play darts or watch football. But I did love the theatre.

A couple of weeks after our trip to see Starlight Express, he produced more theatre tickets, to keep me interested. This time they were for a musical, not in London but in the nearby city. Now he knew where my recreational interests lay, he was determined to capitalise on the knowledge and use whatever leverage he could to insinuate himself into my life.

Any serious doubts that still might be lingering about him in my mind were being carefully erased, and I was being offered tempting inducements, intended to gradually win me over. He intended to break down my resistance and persuade me into believing he was a genuine, good-hearted, and honest person, who was desperately trying to please me and gain my trust. The theatre tickets were tempting carrots, dangled before me to encourage me to believe his good intentions and his benevolent personality.

I was back on the emotional see-saw again... back to the uncertainty of what to believe and what to doubt.

He was, after all, never slow to remind me what a 'genwine diamon' geezer' he was, and how he wanted 'to please yer, and git yer ter trus uz'. By hook or by crook, he seemed determined to install himself in my life, and he invented a hundred ways to convince me there weren't many good-natured, generous-hearted, fun-loving, laugh-a-minute blokes like him around.

And as he constantly reminded me...

'but for my lucky break in meeting him, I might've fallen prey to some devious old bugger who just wanted me for my money. Instead my luck was in, and here he was, an honest, self-made man... a company director with a heart of pure gold, who enjoyed my company and liked me for myself and wanted to do everything he could to make me happy.'

I think an old expression aptly describes his efforts: 'Self-praise is no recommendation.'

Following the two theatre trips, he never let a day go by without trying to move things along in other ways, using his version of 'love bombing' me. Mostly, he was working hard to gain my confidence and my sympathies, by continually filling my mind with lurid stories relating to his former unhappy marriage and divorce. His catalogue of criticisms and complaints against his ex-wife seemed endless.

I was also concerned about his inclination to be sparing with the truth, particularly about his children. This characteristic of ambivalence about trivial things seemed so unnecessary, and left serious doubts in my mind about his character. What possible reason could anyone have for lying about how many children he had? It was totally pointless, and something only someone with seriously unpleasant things to hide about himself would do.

Then something happened that added some insight into a darker and more unsavoury side to his character; and it gave me new reasons to mistrust him. The situation came about when he accidentally dropped his wallet, and a bundle of photographs of semi-naked women fell out of it.

I bent down to retrieve what at first glance I assumed were family photographs, before I recognised what they really were. Each picture had a name and address on the reverse, along with a score out of ten, and the woman's vital statistics. It shocked and disgusted me that he would carry such lewd trash around with him, and that he was into soft porn.

He tried to bluff his way through my barely concealed disgust with even more lies, and a crazy story claiming they were just pictures of women who had responded to his advert in The Lady magazine for a live-in housekeeper, more than a year earlier.

How could he imagine I would be that simple-minded or naive to believe such a cock and bull tale, and that the CVs of his applicants included semi-naked photographs? He even claimed to have forgotten, after eighteen months, that the photographs were still in his wallet... another hard to believe tale indeed.

At that point his plans to insinuate himself took a serious nosedive. Too many things about him just didn't ring true, and I decided to put an end to our association, such as it was. He tried to gloss over the incident. But my doubts were not easily removed, and all my previous misapprehensions about him were revived.

I had already caught him out with his silly pointless lies about his children, first telling me he had only one child, his son. Then it unexpectedly emerged he also had a daughter, Liz. Then eventually, the full truth emerged; he actually had two daughters and a son.

He hadn't spoken to the oldest daughter, Mandy, for over two years, as she had left home, and gone off to marry a man he considered to be a low-life character, and a no-good wastrel. The man Mandy had chosen to marry was a divorced lorry driver with three children.

I had begun to wonder if PP ever told the truth about anything, if he could get away with it. He was certainly extremely sparing with it, and only seemed to say whatever suited his purposes. At that point, I told him I didn't want to see him again.

However, he ignored my decision and refused to give up his efforts in pursuing me. Even after I'd told him categorically that I didn't see any prospect of our friendship continuing, he persisted and would not accept defeat. He just kept on pestering me.

Following up on the two theatre visits, he began insisting he wanted me meet his parents, and the two children who were still living at home with him. Suddenly, he was at pains to fill in their background history. And for some reason, he seemed to feel I needed to know everything about them. But why this should be still remained a mystery.

Liz was his younger daughter. She was nineteen and had always been in a remedial stream at school because she was not very bright. She had been slow to learn to read and write or understand maths. After leaving school, she had taken a cookery course, and currently had a job working in the kitchens of a local hospital. At some point during the previous year, she had told her father she wanted to leave home and join the air force. Very recently, she had been accepted as a recruit by the WRAF, and now she was waiting for her registration papers to arrive so she could leave home and become an air force cook.

Judging from the way he spoke about the girl I got the impression he found her difficult and disobedient. He described her as 'bolshie and loud-mouthed', and gave me to understand that he was rather relieved she was leaving home, and would no longer be his responsibility. He said he didn't approve of her behaviour, and thought she was too fond of drinking and discos, and would probably end up in some kind of trouble and most likely pregnant.

From what he had said about both his daughters, there seemed to be something strange about his relationships with each of them. I felt I was hearing conflicting mixed messages, which left me feeling uneasy.

It was obvious that beneath all the bluster and pretence, he was massively aggrieved about both of them deciding to leave home so soon after the divorce. Whatever their personal reasons were, neither of them had wanted to stay with him. And it was a bone of contention with him that each of them had eventually re-established a close link with their mother. He certainly wasn't pleased about their loyalty to her. I got the impression that, although he seemed to have wanted the family split up, he believed their loyalty should have remained focused only on himself.

However, I was left with the strong impression that the underlying situation, for both his daughters, went much deeper than that. Mandy, the elder one, had been his favourite. But following some serious unpleasantness, she had left him and gone off to get married. Now Liz was increasing his annoyance by her determination to leave home to join the WRAF. He made it very clear that he believed one of them should have stayed at home to look after their brother and himself; he was furious that he was probably going to have to pay someone to cook and clean for them.

His authoritarian attitude to both his daughters struck me as very controlling and domineering. To my mind, such a disturbing chauvinistic mindset implied he regarded women as inferior to men, and that daughters were under an obligation to renounce their personal freedom, and attend to the needs of the men in their families.

I was already aware that he considered cooking, cleaning, washing, shopping, and general housekeeping, even gardening, not activities that were part of his remit. These were not domestic activities men should be expected to do... not even single men who could very well look after themselves. In his opinion, Liz was committing an unforgivable offence by leaving home.

But I was still left wondering why she had made up her mind to leave, now her sister and their mother had both already gone?

However, as the consequence of what he considered to be her perverse waywardness, he had decided he would punish her by putting their house up for sale. It ensured there would be no home for her to return to, if she didn't find life in the WRAF to her liking. Her boats would have been burned, so to speak, and she would be stuck with the problem of having nowhere else to go.

The significance of such senseless vindictiveness, along with several other aspects of his behaviour, struck me as strange. Viewed retrospectively, they should have been a timely warning to me of his vengeful disposition. I should have had the common sense to flag up potential dangers ahead. But I paid little heed to any of it. I was an independent woman and felt it was nothing to do with me how he and his dysfunctional family organised their lives.

His son, Steve, was the same age as my daughter, Samantha. According to PP, the boy attended the local Comprehensive school, closest to where they lived. He claimed his son was bright, but had an antipathy towards formal education. He didn't like teachers, and resented anyone who attempted to make him do as he was told. As a consequence, the boy absconded frequently and was habitually truanting.

Hearing the facts about his various offspring left me feeling distinctly uneasy about meeting them. And I began to wonder just what reason he had for wanting me to get to know them.

I had been unaware his house was up for sale, or that he would soon have to find a new home for himself and his son. But from what I did know, I found their entire family relationships strange and contentious.

I hadn't known him more than a few weeks, and consequently I was in no position to understand anything of the reality of what was going on. For reasons only known to himself, PP was deliberately keeping me in the dark about a great many things. Consequently, I had no idea of what he was actually planning, or how important I was to those plans.

However, before taking me to meet his children, he had a visit to his parents planned. The old couple lived in a three-bedroom council house in the village where he had grown up.

He had once casually mentioned that he had an older sister, Mavis, but they didn't get on, and rarely met. I had been told that Mavis had two young adult daughters. She had been widowed for several years and had only recently remarried. Her new husband was a German man, who PP scathingly referred to as 'Adolph Arsehole'. Mavis now lived in Hamburg, but occasionally she visited England to see her girls, and visit her parents.

PP's family dynamics sounded perplexing, to say the least, and nothing I had heard attracted me to be in any hurry to become involved with them. But to keep the peace, I agreed to go with him to visit his parents.

I found them a pleasant enough old country couple. His father, Arthur, referred to by one and all for some reason as, Old Charlie, was a sturdy old chap. He had spent his life employed as a farm labourer, and for most of his married life, he had worked as a woodsman on a local estate. He wasn't much of a communicator. A lifetime of woodland maintenance work involving chainsaws and heavy machinery had left him stone deaf, and had reduced his conversational skills to little more than monosyllabic grunting. He sat in his chair smoking incessantly, and spent a great deal of time watching horse racing on television when he wasn't in his garden. I had been told that his greatest claim to fame was being the oldest of fifteen children, thirteen of whom were still living; although to his credit he was a very productive vegetable gardener and tended a flourishing greenhouse.

His mother, Gladys, on the other hand, never stopped blathering. She rambled from one subject to another, until the thread of what she was talking about became obscure. PP clearly found her endless chatter monotonous and boring, and after our arrival that Saturday afternoon, he and his father quickly went outside to look at the old man's garden and greenhouse.

When they had gone, Gladys turned her rambling conversation

onto the subject of PP's ex-wife, Beryl, whom she still regarded as her daughter-in-law. The old woman needed no input from me, but rambled along with a series of confusing stories about Beryl, mixed with stories about some other woman called Val Evans, someone her son had brought to visit them after his divorce.

She talked on and on, while I half-listened, as she ranged from subject to subject, relating incidents from her son's childhood, along with stories about her older daughter, Mavis, and her youngest child, Joan. The little girl had died tragically and mysteriously, just before her third birthday at the time when PP was seven.

At that point, I pricked up my ears and began to pay attention. I was curious to know more. I hadn't heard PP ever mention his little sister Joan.

'He was always jealous of her,' Gladys said with a sob, wiping tears from her eyes. 'Then when he came home from the woods that day alone, and hid in the coal shed, I found him and said, "Where's Joanie?"'

'He claimed he didn't know. But me and Charlie knew he often took her up to the woods, and we knew he sometimes used to try to leave her there. Well, we went up looking for her. And we did eventually find her... poor little mite. When we did, she was dead... left where he'd put her, hidden under some bushes. The poor little thing had been shot in the chest. He wouldn't tell us anything, just kept on saying it weren't his fault; they'd just been playing, and something had happened. But he never would say what. He was always a strange lad. Never did tell us what had happened to little Joanie... not even after her funeral. He just wiped her out of his mind and never mentioned her name again.'

The memories clearly still pained her. She had a quiet little weep, and then she wandered back to talking about the new woman in her son's life. He had brought Val Evans to meet them two years earlier, and told them she was the woman he was now intending to marry. A while later, she'd heard they'd been away on holiday together to the Balearic Islands and had a lovely time. But it was a while since he had been to see them, and she wasn't sure if the wedding was still going ahead.

From her loquacious ramblings, I learned quite a lot about PP and his ex-wife Beryl. What I was now hearing were things PP had never troubled to tell me. What did become clear was that he was inclined to focus only on stories about Beryl that denigrated her. I had never heard him say anything nice about her. And he consistently made a point of focussing on his former matrimonial woes, which he claimed were all caused by her sexual excesses, and her mental derangement.

So far as the divorce was concerned, Gladys confided that Beryl had behaved sensibly. She hadn't enraged PP by disputing the divorce terms he had offered her. In fact, she had agreed quite willingly to everything, once he had instigated the divorce.

His decision to get divorced had only come about because of his plans to marry Val Evans. He had told Beryl that, if she went quietly, he would settle the house he owned in Leicestershire on her. But he would be keeping the matrimonial home and the children, along with his business interests and everything else.

I discovered, by way of Gladys' chatter, that he had originally bought the small house in Leicestershire as an investment property, and had put it in his daughter Mandy's name for tax-avoidance purposes. But a couple of years later, when his plans to marry Val Evans began, he told Mandy she would have to sign the house back over to him, as he now intended to give it to her mother in their divorce settlement.

'The foolish girl kicked up no end about having to surrender the house,' Gladys confided. 'She actually tried to claim it was legally hers. She argued her dad had given it to her as a permanent gift. How ridiculous was that? No one gives a seventeen-year-old girl a house. Well she put up quite a fight with him, and argued long and hard that the house belonged to her. She led him quite a dance, I can tell you. Refused to accept the fact that putting it into her name was just the trick he'd used to conceal it from the taxman. Having to give it back made her so furious she hasn't spoken to him for over two years... well that and a few other things they disagreed about. Mandy's very stubborn, just like her dad.'

Gladys paused in her diatribe and took a look out of the window to ensure both the men were still sitting in the greenhouse. Then she leaned closer to where I was sitting and said, quietly and confidingly, 'But that wasn't the end of their falling out. Mandy made things a hundred times worse by leaving home and going to live with Joe Jackson and his three kids. Then, would you believe it, she really drove her dad even more wild by marrying the man?

'I think her mother egged her on. But together the two of them made my son furious. He had always expected Mandy to stay at home and live with him and the boy, but she wouldn't. There must have been more to their falling out than I ever knew, because she called him some terrible names. Said he was a deviant and a lecher, and she wouldn't live under his roof again... not after all the things he'd done to her.

'Anyway, Beryl made a wedding party for them, but they didn't invite PP. Well, you can't imagine what a fury that put my son in. He doesn't take insults lightly. But he soon got his revenge on Mandy. One night, when her and Joe were in bed, he drove over to the council house where they were living, and smashed her car to smithereens... left her with just a heap of scrap metal to teach her a lesson she'll never forget. Well, as he said, he'd bought the car... so if he smashed it up, he was within his rights. It was in his name, after all, and not hers. That just made things a lot worse I can tell you. They're still not speaking.'

'So, what about Beryl?' I said. 'Where is she living now? Did she go up to Leicestershire and live there?'

'Oh no, dear. She sold the Leicestershire house as soon as she could. She has a brother living there, but she wanted to be over here in Essex, near her sister, Marjory. That was what really decided her to sell... that and her own girls of course. Leicestershire was too far away from Marjory.'

After a brief pause, Gladys continued, 'Yes, she bought herself a nice little bungalow on the edge of the city, close to where Marjory lives, and near the local hospital where she works.'

I listened while Gladys rambled on, going into details about how often Beryl still drove over to visit them, whenever her shift work at the hospital allowed, and how she was a lovely woman and a very good mother, as well as being a good nurse. In fact, she had recently been promoted to sister in charge of a ward.

When I casually enquired how Beryl's health was, the old woman looked at me curiously and asked why I thought anything was wrong with her. I shrugged and said I'd been given to understand she'd had some serious mental issues, and had been ill in various specialist clinics for a long time.

'Oh no, dear,' she said. 'I don't know who gave you that idea. She's a good strong Scottish girl; there's not much ails her.

She had a miscarriage fourteen years back, not long after her son Steve was born; and then she had a couple of breakdowns afterwards...maybe it was three...I forget...but they were all caused by stress I believe. But whatever it was everything was all sorted out, and she's been fine for years. Beryl's a quiet sort of girl, a devout Catholic, you know. She doesn't really believe in divorce or in loose moral behaviour.'

She paused briefly, and I noticed a puzzled look on her face, as though she was mulling something over. I waited quietly, wondering if something could be troubling her. Then pushing whatever it was aside, she gathered her thoughts together and went on. 'In fact, I never did understand why she so readily agreed to being divorced herself... But she made no objections to it at all. She's a woman who takes her faith seriously, you see... church every Sunday without fail. And she's never looked at another man since she's been divorced from my son. They've been apart now for going on three years, but she's got no inclinations in that direction, if you take my meaning. She says she wants no more men in her life.

'She's been getting along fine on her own and hasn't lost a day's work through ill health. Well, I mean to say, she wouldn't be working in a psychiatric hospital if there was any sort of mental illness wrong with her, would she?'

She suddenly broke off speaking, and gave me a sort of puzzled look, then suddenly said, 'Who did you say you were, dear? You do remind me very much of my little Joanie. She had blonde hair and blue eyes just like you.'

Our strange conversation came to a sudden end, as PP and 'Old Charlie' returned from the garden. PP was instantly suspicious. 'Wot yer two bin gobbin abaat?' he challenged.

'Oh, just this and that,' I said. 'Just two women getting to know one another over a cup of tea, while you men gossiped in the greenhouse.'

I made no reference to his mother's conversation, but it certainly left me with plenty to think about.

Later that evening, when I began to turn Gladys' enlightening stories over in my mind, they set me wondering about the collection of lurid tales PP had been eager to fill my mind with about Beryl... and her purported lecherous philandering and her serious mental issues.

Clearly somebody had been lying to me, big time.

Chapter 7

The House in the Cabbage Fields

Following my visit to PP's parents' home, I was left seriously troubled by the stories I had heard from his mother. Everything she had related had left me with unanswered questions about PP's motives regarding myself... about his general honesty...and about his ambivalent attitude towards women in general. It had come as a complete surprise to learn of his inconclusive plans to marry a woman by the name of Val Evans. This was something else he hadn't bothered to mention to me.

What this woman meant to him was really none of my business, but I wondered why he had never mentioned her, or his plans to remarry. If their relationship was a serious one, what on earth was he doing pursuing his weird acquaintance with me?

He and I had no meeting of minds whatsoever. Nor did we even have any shared interests... or anything else, for that matter. In fact, we didn't even seem to speak the same language. And prior to the contrived introduction he had initiated several weeks earlier, in the seafront car park, I had never even known he existed.

There were so many discrepancies between the conflicting strands of the stories he had told me, and the more authentic-sounding ones I had heard from his mother. I felt seriously uneasy about the direction in which our developing relationship might be heading. None of it made any sense. I was most definitely not enamoured of him, and far from ready to consider any man as a replacement for Alan... and certainly not one with whom I had so little in common.

But PP was persisting in going out of his way to pursue me for some reason, and I found it disturbing, as I could not figure out what his genuine motives were.

The endless recital of unpleasant stories he had told me about his ex-wife now appeared to have been deliberately twisted, and a long way from the truth as his mother told it. In fact, his version of events seemed nothing short of vindictive and deliberately malicious, and constantly repeated only to blacken Beryl's character for some unknown reason.

Why would someone do that? I wondered. They were divorced, and it sounded as though, in the end, it had been quite amicable... not forgetting she was, after all, still the mother of his children.

To my way of thinking, there could be no foundation for any sort of friendship with someone who bears grudges, is vindictive, and is a habitual liar. In my reasoning, a man who tells distorted lies about one woman and enjoys blackening her character, would be highly likely to make a habit of behaving in a similar way towards any other woman he became involved with. That thought made me even more suspicious about the honesty, and sincerity of his motives. All these collective feelings of unease made PP seem an even more dubious, and less likeable or trustworthy character.

Now he was insisting I must meet his children, and I really didn't understand why. With my head already full of uneasy thoughts about him, I was reluctant to be hawked around his family like a fairground sideshow. I told him I didn't think it was a good idea, and I would rather put the visit off for a while, until I knew him better.

However, he remained adamant it was time I met his kids, and saw the fantastic house he had built for Beryl... the one she had walked out of when she had callously abandoned their family.

It had become obvious there was no dissuading him from anything once his mind was made up. Therefore, come what may, the introductions to his children would happen the following Saturday. I would meet his son Steve first. Then after we'd had tea, we would drive to the hospital and meet Liz, when she finished work.

He was, of course, unaware that I already knew where he lived and had already seen his much-lauded house from the outside. But he put me under so much pressure to agree to the proposed visit, I was finally left with no alternative but to consent.

I admit to some lingering, guilty apprehensions as we approached the village. But I felt sure no one could possibly recognise me from the Easter Sunday visit I had paid there. I had never gotten out of my car. Nor had I been seen by anyone. But pangs of guilt still troubled me, as we drove to the house in the cabbage fields.

It was just before three o'clock when we arrived that dull

Saturday afternoon. The red sports bicycle propped up beside the front door obviously belonged to his son.

PP unlocked the door, and I followed him inside. A first glance around told me more than he could ever have imagined. I recognised the property from my previous clandestine visit, but I had only seen it from the road. Now I was being invited to take a closer look at its 'luxurious' accommodation as a visitor.

Before I even got inside the door, I knew something about it was not quite right. It was immediately apparent that PP did not share his father's gardening interests. The 'luxury house built for Beryl' had a wilderness for a garden, with nothing remotely cultivated growing in it. On the contrary, the jungle of weeds, and untended grass enveloping it, might very well have concealed a herd of illegal elephants.

But it was only after I stepped inside, that the real story began to unfold. It has always been my belief that any house becomes a home because of the intimate atmosphere generated there. It has nothing to do with the central heating or the value of its contents, but everything to do with family warmth. I think of it as an indefinable feeling that welcomes the visitor... an integral quality of contentment almost breathing in the air; a peacefulness that radiates love and generates a sense of belonging. I believe whatever it is, grows from loving security. It fills the spaces between the walls and comes from the people who call it their home. The place doesn't have to be scrupulously clean or neat and tidy, or full of expensive gizmos, just lived in and enjoyed... a relaxed comfortable space that reaches out to enfold its occupants, and welcome them home each time they return.

This place was none of those things. It was just a house... an anonymous waiting area, used by people who came and went from it. It was a weatherproof, functional shelter, with no soul, and no love in it, and not a lot of comfort either.

The overall interior design was haphazard, and almost illogical, as though the designer had started with a square box and slotted walls in here and there to create spaces and call them rooms. It wasn't badly built, just badly designed, and with windows so small the place seemed to be in permanent gloom. It was immediately obvious that very little money, or even effort, had been spent on household comfort, and the resulting interior was Spartan, cheap, and shabby. Whatever else it was, it bore no comparison whatsoever to my own home.

The grubby rooms were all painted in bog-standard Magnolia emulsion paint; while the floor coverings, such as they were, were the cheapest possible corded nylon. They appeared to have a dark brown pattern on them but were so ingrained with dirt it was impossible to make out what the design had ever been.

Upstairs were three cramped bedrooms, plus a small bathroom, while downstairs, all the living areas led from an enormous room-sized hall, with a minute cloakroom squashed into one corner of it.

A large dismal living area opened from the hall. It overlooked the road, and doubled as the dining space. It was the only place where anyone could sit down to relax. An annex leading off from one corner and measuring about ten feet square was grandly referred to by PP as, 'maa persnal offiss'. It was crammed with a seven-foot long chipboard sideboard, a pretentious six-foot long chipboard desk, and a chair.

The last door from the living space led into an incredibly narrow kitchen, which had been tacked on along the entire length of the rear wall as an afterthought. It more resembled a wide corridor than a kitchen, but led to the outside area and the garage. It was a single-storey construction and projected about seven feet from the house.

The original tiny kitchen, also accessed from the front hallway, was now crammed with a scruffy washing machine and tumble dryer, along with a small sink. It was just another walk-through from the hall, back into the living area, and was now referred to as 'the laundry'.

As I was shown around by its proud owner, I could think of nothing complementary to say about the place. Nothing in it impressed me with any warmth or taste, and I saw little more than rudimentary comfort. This then was the 'luxurious house' PP claimed to have designed and built for Beryl. The council house his mother and father occupied was better designed, and contained much more comfortable furnishings; and it certainly had more of a cosy homely feel to it, than the cabbage field house ever would.

I could barely restrain my surprise and dismay as he walked me back into the living area. The rear of the room was in shadow, but I saw a veneered chipboard china cabinet, positioned alongside the wall. In front of it was a deeply scratched refectory table, with five cafe-style bentwood chairs parked around it. Not half a dozen, as I would have expected, just five... the minimum to seat two parents and three children.

The centre of the room was filled with an ugly brown, imitation leather three-piece suite, so dilapidated it appeared to have been attacked by animals... its entire surface had been clawed, or peeled, off in large patches, leaving only the underlying dirty cream-coloured canvas fabric visible. In front of it was a chipboard, sapele-veneered coffee table with metal legs. This arrangement had been placed so as to face the outer side-wall, where a chimney breast might have been; only no chimney existed, not even a simulated fireplace, as a focal point. Instead, all along this blank wall stretched another chipboard monstrosity... a sort of general-purpose unit, twenty feet long and stretching almost the length of the room. It was stacked, untidily, from end to end with a large television set, some hi-fi equipment, videocassettes, and a video recorder, along with piles of twelve-inch country and western records.

There were empty cups and dirty dishes scattered everywhere. And significantly, the thing that struck me most... there wasn't a single book anywhere in sight.

In the middle of the wall, above the long general utility unit, hung the only concession to culture in the entire building... a three-foot wide unglazed print of a mountain scene by Van Gogh. It was heavily coated with brown nicotine, which largely obscured everything except the top of the mountain, and was quite clearly of no particular artistic interest to anybody.

Taken as a whole, the place left the impression of being a depressing dump. Luxurious it most certainly was not. It was scruffy, cheap and tacky; and above all, it was unloved.

As my eyes grew accustomed to the subdued light, I glanced towards the damaged display cabinet and noticed its only contents were bottles of alcohol. There was nothing in the house worth a handful of beans... not a prized piece of china or a book, or any other object of value or culture. There was nothing of any significance anywhere, but I did notice most of the glass panels in the display cabinet had been smashed.

This was not a place a happy woman had ever been proud to call her home. And very clearly, Beryl had never felt motivated to stamp her personal touch on it. There was nothing significant about it at all, except for the feeling of cold detachment. I found myself staring blankly at the hazy mountain view of the Van Gogh. It seemed almost as old as the original, and much less discernible. Its vivid colours were a blur behind the veneer of brown nicotine-stained scum, and it was all deeply depressing.

After pointing me in the direction of the threadbare sofa, and telling me to make myself comfortable, PP went into the hall and called to his son, who was upstairs in his bedroom. He then joined me on the sofa while we waited for the boy to appear. Several minutes went by, but no one came downstairs.

PP called up to the boy again, still without response. By now, clearly enraged, he stormed up the stairs, thumping his feet on the bare treads as he went.

For the next ten minutes, I sat cringing, on the edge of my seat, listening to what sounded like a battle going on overhead. There was a barrage of aggressive shouting and yelling, followed by the sound of objects being hurled about and smashed. This was immediately followed by doors being slammed and more aggressive terrifying yelling. Then I heard battering and crashing sounds, which seemed, for all the world, like a door was being battered down.

Finally, heavy feet came thundering down the stairs. The front door slammed, and I caught sight of a tall youth haring out of the house, and heading into the cabbage fields that lay beyond.

So much for my anticipated introduction to his son. It was nothing more than a deeply embarrassing fiasco.

The boy was clearly pretty nimble on his feet. And when his father came thundering downstairs in close pursuit, I watched from the window as a shocking episode unfolded. The youth raced off like a hare, deep into the distance of the green cabbages, with his father chasing behind him, waving his fists and shouting things I couldn't hear.

Eventually after an hour of this pursuit, the youth disappeared from sight into some hiding place, obviously determined not to return to the house while I was there. Eventually his father gave up and came back alone, livid, and out of breath.

For another hour we sat, waiting for the miscreant to return, while PP entertained me with his favourite 'classic' record, which he insisted upon replaying six times for my amusement. I doubt if I will ever again want to hear the maudlin sounds of Kenny Rogers singing 'Lucille'.

After wasting all afternoon, and still with no sign of the boy reappearing, PP eventually admitted defeat and said he would deal with him later. Time was getting on, and we needed to drive to the city hospital to meet Liz, when she finished her shift at six o'clock.

That plan produced results equally as baffling as the earlier one, and was an even more distressing experience from my point of view. However, it proved to be unexpectedly informative, and taught me a lot of things I had never guessed, or been told by PP, concerning his former life.

Liz was alone in the hospital kitchen when we arrived, and just getting ready to leave. It was apparent she knew her father was coming to see her and bringing me with him. But quite deliberately she went out of her way to blank me, and ignore the fact that I was there at all. Her behaviour was incredible, totally out of order, and ignorant beyond belief. She had never seen me before, but she made no effort to disguise the fact that she wanted absolutely nothing to do with me. I had reluctantly agreed to meet her, because her father had insisted I should, but my feelings of incipient friendship were no warmer than hers.

Even so, I recognised her very quickly from the description Alex had given me of the uncouth, coarse-featured bleached blonde, who had visited his estate agency some weeks earlier. She was, without doubt, the woman who had been making enquiries about the value of my house, and the owner of the dark green Morris Minor.

Now here she was in the flesh, being just as objectionable and rude as Alex had found her. Setting aside the platinum straw, with its black roots, she was recognisably her father's daughter, and bore many of his clumsy physical and coarse facial characteristics, including the thick flabby-lipped mouth.

Turning her back on me and totally blanking my presence, she spoke only to her father. "Oo's she?' she demanded in a loud aggressive voice.

'Ah've told yer,' he retorted. 'This 'ere is Delia. We're gettin' married. Like Ah teld yer on the phone. Ah sed ah wuz bringin' 'er 'ere terday ter meet yer.'

My heart lurched violently inside my chest. Married! I had made no such commitment to him. He was supposed to be getting married to someone called Val Evans. Where on earth had this idea come from? I was appalled to hear him telling his daughter we intended to marry. Up to that point, I had known very little about him. And the more I learned, the less I liked him.

Suddenly it dawned on me that, from our first encounter, this had been the idea he had been formulating inside his crazy brain. I glared at him, furious from shock. But he didn't even turn to look in my direction. It appeared that my presence, along with my consent and even my emotions, were equally irrelevant to the situation.

'Well Ah want nuffink ter do wiv 'er,' the girl snarled. Then amplifying her voice to the point of screaming, she shrieked, 'We've bin 'ere afor a fowsan times, Dad, wiv yer an all yer diffren wimin. Ivery week, yer've gorra diffren one paradin' abaat the 'ouse in 'er knickers. 'Ow many ov them wuz yer planning ter marry?

'We've 'ad wimin livin' in the 'ouse, sharing yer bed an s'pposed ter be yer 'ousekeepers, an' wimin cumin an goin at all hours ov the day an night. There's bin black wimin an' yeller uns, as well as white uns. Duz she no that?

'An wot abaat the wimin standin' ou'side the 'ouse screamin' 'ow yer'd got em pregnan' an' wantin' money off yer fer aborshuns. Ah fort yer wuz marryin' Val Evans? Yer teld us yer wuz. Me an ower Steve like 'er. We've even been on 'oliday wiv er. Yer sent er money ter come aout ter the Balearic Islands ter join us, even arter yer said it wuz only goin ter be the free ov uz on 'oliday. Yer 'ad ter git 'er out ter sleep wiv yer, didn' yer? Yer even teld me nan yer wuz goin ter marry 'er. Me an' Steve won' forgit yer carryin-ons in an 'urry. Yer bed's nivver bin cold wiv all the diffren' wimin in an' aout uv it. Wierivver yer dug this un up from, Ah doan wan' ter know, an Ah doan care eyver. Ah nivver wan nuffink ter do wiv anovver of the dirty whores yer carry on wiv.

'Yer did the dirty on ower muvver fer years, wiv yer leching, an then got rid o 'er, and called 'er a whore an sed she wuz mad... called 'er a crazy womin. Yer the whore in this fambly, Dad. Yer the crazy un. Yer got rid uv all the uvvers, so git rid ov this un an all.'

She suddenly paused for breath. Then she lowered her tone to end on an almost pathetic, pleading note. 'If yer do wot Ah'm sayin, Dad, Ah'll stay at 'ome wiv yer, an not go inter the WRAF.'

Her hysterical revelations had both shocked and sickened me. If what she had been screaming really was true, then it was a terrible indictment of her father.

On a personal level, I had never been so insulted and degraded by anyone in my life... nor so humiliated. She had obviously pre-planned and rehearsed the entire production, aided and abetted, no doubt, by her brother. Their two antisocial performances were clearly not individually accidental. And what I was now left to think about was terrible beyond belief.

But I suspected something else might lie behind this pair of orchestrated performances I had witnessed that afternoon. The picture Liz had painted for my benefit was of a disgusting filthy lecher... a low life, scum of the earth who had deceived his first wife, and paraded an endless procession of loose women in and out of their family home in front of his children, for years.

It sounded as though I was merely the latest deluded female he was setting up, with his empty promises and his vile treatment, while ahead of me stretched a long line of women with whom he had previously been sexually involved. Such a loathsome mentality was beyond sordid. And if what she was claiming was true, then he was nothing more than a grotesque, evil, lecherous monster. But for all that, I suspected a vital clue might lie in her last pronouncement... the pleading suggestion that, if he got rid of me, she would stay at home and not leave him to go into the WRAF. Perhaps her motivation for the outburst was not quite what I had initially suspected. Maybe jealousy lay at its roots... or something much sadder... an aching desire for him to want her, and beg her not to leave home.

My mind was in a ferment, and I was immediately reminded

of the things PP's mother had said the previous weekend about Beryl. Now Liz had been screaming things that brought all those stories back to make me wonder where the truth about his ex-wife, and their marriage, really lay. And why did he feel it was necessary to make up such terrible lies about her?

Someone was clearly lying, but who was it? Was it one or all of them? They each seemed to have some sort of individual agenda, with every one wanting to achieve whatever ending suited them best. The truth was hidden somewhere under a heap of muddled obfuscation and duplicity, and I felt overwhelmed by it all.

What had I got myself mixed up in concerning this weird dysfunctional family? And why had PP suddenly announced we were going to get married? I scarcely knew the man. My head was swimming in confusion.

The girl had screamed herself hoarse during her abusive verbal attack on her father and me. Then suddenly, she stopped screaming, burst into floods of tears, and fled out of the kitchen exit. I saw her wrench open the door of the Morris Minor parked nearby. She fumbled with the ignition and then drove off like a mad thing, grinding and crashing the gears in her panic, without ever looking back.

After the debacle, and the stinging insulting experiences I had endured that afternoon from his two awful children, I needed some space to myself. I just wanted to go back to normality, and the sanity of my own peaceful home, and put PP and his family behind me. Whatever marriage plans he had made concerning the woman called Val Evans were no concern of mine.

I asked him to take me home, and I did not invite him in. I simply said goodbye in the street and went indoors. So far as I was concerned, the sordid history I had just heard, and the relationship, such as it was, were at an end. If he was playing some sort of strategic emotional game with different women, or trying to inveigle himself into my life, for some unknown reason, I wanted nothing to do with it.

My personal emotions were fragile enough. I wasn't looking for anyone to replace Alan, and I doubted if I ever would. I had my own children to concern myself with, along with an essential and demanding job. The last thing I needed was some weirdo like PP complicating my life even further...especially someone with seriously deranged sexual issues, a failed marriage, and two aggressive, and emotionally disturbed teenage children.

Chapter 8

Cheating, Lying, and Manipulation

Between the pair of them, Liz and Steve almost wrecked their father's carefully laid plans to hook me into his ultimate power-game. For a week after my encounter with the pair of them, I did everything I could to avoid all contact with him.

Had I stuck to my guns all might have been well. Perhaps eventually, PP would have given up his pursuit and set his sights elsewhere. And I would certainly have had a lucky escape. But I was being cunningly manoeuvred into a spider's web of deceit, by a man with a relentless agenda.

Although I was being kept in the dark, and knew nothing about his convoluted plans and intentions, time was against PP. His house was already on the market, and it was barely six weeks until Liz was due to leave home. He had known she was going for almost a year. Now with only six weeks left, he needed to press forward with his diabolical schemes, if he was going to succeed in manoeuvring me into the situation he had in mind.

There could be no doubt; I was not the first woman he had targeted as a replacement wife. His ultimate objective was ruthless, and dedicated entirely to self-interest. He was aware that, once his house was sold, he and his son would need somewhere to live. For two years, he had already been touting around to find a suitable woman to manipulate into becoming the replacement he was seeking ... a woman he could deceive into becoming his unpaid servant and future financial provider.

But the choice had been limited, and time was running out. Finding his ideal had been difficult. Physically, he had little to recommend him to any discerning woman. There had been some women who would have taken him on, but they had been far from his ideal, and certainly not rich enough to satisfy his greed.

PP had a clearly defined idea of what he was looking for. His overriding plans were to significantly improve his financial situation by hooking himself a wealthy wife. He had every intention of ensuring that the next woman he married would keep him in the style to which he intended to become accustomed.

He was a hunter out to make a kill.

Some years later (when it was much too late to be of any benefit to me), I learned that he had openly boasted to the workmen on his building site that, in meeting me, he had finally found the most suitable candidate to fill his matrimonial vacancy. I was the woman he intended to pin down and marry. I was rich, and a good-looking blonde; a widow with no family to speak of, just a couple of young daughters, who wouldn't have the wit or the strength to give him any trouble. He was absolutely certain he would soon have me manipulated into providing him and his kids, with everything they could desire in life... new cars, luxury holidays, and eventually even a house apiece. Everyone working at TBM Builders had heard these crass boasts. Even his two partners knew all about his plans to enrich himself at my expense.

These plans had been no secret from anyone who knew him... except of course, me. And it had been his open boast that once he had got me married, he would take possession of everything I had. His ultimate plans were finally on course, and coming to fruition. Finding himself a millionaire was the luckiest break he had ever had.

According to his distorted view of the law, all the assets a woman owned, legally became her husband's property upon marriage. He was so gleeful at the prospect of fulfilling his plans he could barely contain himself. According to his imaginative, but seriously self-deluding legal knowledge, the law would guarantee he became a very wealthy man once he had tied me down in marriage.

His self-confidence had been so over-inflated, he had boasted to his son and daughter about his plans. They had been instructed that they were to make themselves agreeable, at least until it was too late for me to back out. After that, it wouldn't matter what they said or did. But until he had got things sorted, and his hands securely on my assets, he wanted no more scenes like the ones they had created that disastrous Saturday, or he might lose the golden opportunity to get his hands on my house and my money.

What a pity some kind soul hadn't telephoned me anonymously

and put me in the picture. Unfortunately, none of his business acquaintances knew me. And they already considered him something of a loud-mouthed, aggressive weirdo with an inflated ego.

With hind-sight I believe there was a perceptive part of my muddled brain still trying in vain to wake me up to what was going on in my life. But the reality was, I remained oblivious to PP's devious plans, and never suspected I was already partially caught up in his sinister web of intrigue.

Before Alan died, I had always considered myself to be a strong-minded, discerning woman, with a clear sense of right and wrong... someone with ethical values and a forthright personality. I was no wimp; and in my normal state of mind, I certainly did not suffer fools gladly. Under normal, less stressful circumstances, PP was a man with whom I would never have passed the time of day, much less given a second glance, or ever remotely considered as a marriage partner. But for some reason, my shattered emotions had turned me into a gullible fool... I had lost my way, and inadvertently ended up being manipulated by a devil in disguise.

Like a hunting snake, PP had his mind fixed upon one covert objective, and I had been selected as his prey.

Bad things do happen to good people. You do not need to go looking for evil; it can unexpectedly come hunting for you. It's easy now to castigate myself for lacking the moral fibre to stand up to PP's emotional manipulation. But there are times in life when we are at our lowest ebb, and PP slithered into my life at just such a time.

He had begun his affair with Val Evans a year before he decided to divorce Beryl, and she had been the catalyst that had precipitated it. She was younger, sexier, and more fun than Beryl, and he had quickly lined her up to be his next wife, before instigating the legal proceedings.

As his wife of twenty years, Beryl had put up with his brutality, his callous indifference, and his sordid affairs for many of those years. But their relationship had long been in tatters. Things between them had deteriorated to the point where she had taken a hospital job working permanent night duties, to get away from him.

The shameful circumstances surrounding the birth of Steve had been quickly followed by a suspicious, and very bloody miscarriage, which had resulted in their marriage being over for a very long time. He'd made no secret of the fact, that each evening as he arrived home, Beryl was on her way out to work. Their paths had rarely crossed in years, and certainly never in the bedroom department. They had shared a bed, but never occupied it at the same time. He spent his weekends at the house in Leicestershire with Mandy, and sometimes Steve, while Beryl had stayed at home with Liz.

However, even before his decree absolute was granted, PP had already begun to develop cold feet regarding his contemplated remarriage to Val. He'd had time to weigh up the financial aspects of the commitment he was about to make, and was no longer sure he wanted to saddle himself with another woman who would not bring him any significant financial benefit. His motivations were entirely avaricious, and upon reflection, he had begun to realise Val was not really a woman he wanted to commit himself to. She obviously expected her prospective husband to provide for her; and it wasn't long before he completely changed his mind about the marriage.

Love was an emotion that meant nothing to him; it never had. He could find sex anywhere, whenever he felt the need. But the long-term reality of what he really wanted was a woman who would keep him, as well as fulfil all his avaricious and sexual fantasies, without costing him a bean.

At that point, he had come to the conclusion it would be best if he kept looking. If he could find the right woman, he would go all out to marry her. But money would be the prime objective, and there would have to be no interfering relatives to get in his way and cause trouble.

Val was not entirely without assets. She owned her own small terraced house. But she had a supportive family, and they were not overly keen on the domineering vulgar boyfriend under whose influence she had fallen, and who was taking advantage of her good nature.

After their parents' divorce, Mandy, Liz, and Steve had welcomed Val to their home, because when she came, she helped out with the cooking and cleaning and caused no trouble. Since Mandy's departure, these household responsibilities had largely fallen upon Liz's reluctant shoulders, and Val had remained a very welcome all-round help, and eager to ingratiate herself. The situation had suited PP, as it had cost him nothing. He saw no need to spend money paying any woman to do the necessary housework if Val was there to help, free of charge. For a while that arrangement had suited them all.

Once the decree nisi had been granted, PP had suggested that he, Steve, and Liz should have a two-week holiday in the Balearic Islands. That had really pleased the pair of them. They had never been abroad before, and were excited to be going away together to a Mediterranean island.

Their excitement quickly faded when they discovered, as soon as they arrived, that PP was phoning Val to invite her out to join them. Just as Liz had revealed, (in her screaming match at the hospital), her father had even gone so far as to arrange for the cost of her flight and accommodation to be paid by the company offices at home.

The terminal disillusionment eventually set in after the holiday was over. Val had regarded it as a sort of partial payment for all she had been doing to help the family. And she was fully anticipating the promise of further commitment from PP as soon as he obtained his decree absolute. She had been sleeping with him for months, but there had been no formal arrangements between them... no engagement ring or planned wedding date.

When, out of the blue, PP had suggested she should move into his house and sell hers, she'd been more than happy to agree, as the proposal had come with the added promise of marriage.

All seemed to be going along fine, until she made her fatal mistake of confiding in him that her brothers had advised her not to sell her house. They felt she should hold on to it. Renting it out would provide her with a regular income; and it was sound financial sense for her to keep the house as her security blanket, just in case anything went wrong.

PP's reaction to that proposition was fury; he had no intention of agreeing to her retaining possession of her house, and he objected vehemently. He gave her an ultimatum. If she expected a wedding ring, then he expected her to sell her property, and hand over the money she received as an indication of good faith, and as a financial contribution towards moving into his luxurious family home as his new wife. There was no way he intended to share ownership of his house without Val contributing her own assets to compensate for his generous offer.

A stand-off had ensued. But being a sensible, practical woman, with sound advisers guiding her...Val had refused his ultimatum and stuck to her guns... insisting upon keeping her own property as security. A short while later she flew to Canada to visit relatives, and to think through where their relationship might be heading.

He was waiting to collect her at Heathrow on her return, to show her his decree absolute, and also to inform her of his final stance... no money, no marriage; either she handed over her assets, or their romantic plans were over.

Val Evans faded from his thoughts as quickly as old news. PP never indulged in regrets, and he was not an emotional man who ever felt lasting attachments were necessary. He didn't do heartbreak. He just moved on to his next potential victim.

Men like him have no capacity for grief, or meaningful emotions of any kind, and he rapidly found himself a new potential marriage interest, in the form of the divorced wife of a local doctor. Bettina Gowan owned a large detached house on an exclusive golf-club development. She was quite amenable to having a brief fling, with the bit-of-rough-builder she had just met. But there was no way she intended to lower her social standing, or sacrifice her lavish alimony, or her comfortable home, to actually marry a domineering uncouth man like PP. That affair also quickly fizzled out.

These unpleasant truths about PP were a long time in emerging. I had almost stumbled on the truth when he had dropped his wallet, and the salacious collection of photographs had fallen out of it. But it was a long while before I eventually discovered the truth behind the motley collection of women, spread all over the country, with whom he had been involved, in one way or another.

Finding himself the right replacement for Beryl's vacancy had seen him travelling from one end of the United Kingdom to the other for two years. Unfortunately for me, the discovery of this collection of sordid information came too late to save me. The truth only came to light after I was well and truly trapped in his malevolent coils.

He had made up his mind that any second marriage was going to benefit him financially. And his plans were already in place. Once he had married the right woman, he would make very sure he quickly got his hands on all she had, before engineering some way of getting rid of her. He had found the lecherous lifestyle something he had come to enjoy. For an unemotional man like himself, women were an easily dispensable commodity. They were like buses; let one go by, and there'll always be another one coming along pretty soon.

Unfortunately, at the time of which I am speaking, I knew nothing of any of these activities. Nor did I ever guess how many other disgusting secrets he was hiding, or that he considered me the most well-heeled and vulnerable female he had managed to line up, in order to bring his cunning scheme to its final and satisfactory conclusion.

My girls had guessed right when they'd suspected he already knew who I was, long before we ever met. Truth sometimes emerges slowly. And in my own case, it came too late to save me.

I had first come to PP's attention several years before I met him. This had come about through a business contact he had in the building industry, and he had been taking a perverse interest in me ever since... during the period when his marriage to Beryl was on the rocks, and I was happily married to Alan.

It seemed a crazy and unlikely story, but it was completely true. During the months while the construction of my school had been underway, it had been necessary for me to make several visits to the site to meet with Chris Mayling, the council's clerk of works. (Chris was the person in charge of overseeing the building project.) By way of the network of builders, who carried out contract work for Essex County Council, Chris Mayling was already acquainted with PP and TBM Builders Ltd.

At some point, after a business meeting, PP and Chris Mayling had met in a bar, and their discussion had involved their shared interests in a variety of current council building projects. Somehow my school and my name, as the newly appointed head teacher, had come up. And after the fashion of how some men talk and discuss women, Chris Mayling had waxed quite lyrical about the attractive, youthful, blonde headmistress he'd met. I have no idea what was said, but whatever it was, PP's strange sexual appetite had been whetted, and he had later telephoned Chris, and persuaded him to let him visit the school site to look it over. The pretext for the visit was PP's interest in the innovative architectural design; but covertly, and for a man of his sinister personality, he had wanted to get a good look at me.

One thing had led to another, and without me ever knowing anything of what was going on, PP had been 'keeping an eye on me' ever since that time. For some crazy reason, he had developed a perverse interest me. I was being kept under observation from a distance, and was entirely unaware of anything unusual going on. However, for reasons best known to himself, the strange man had made up his mind that I was a millionaire, and consequently someone he was very interested in.

Four years later, when the news of Alan's death had reached his ears, his interest became reignited. At that time, he was already playing the marriage-market game, and he made it his business to check me out, and learned that my only living relatives were my two young daughters. That had settled the matter for him. And recently he had decided the time was ripe to make a move on me. All of these activities had been going on, entirely without my awareness, and he had been surreptitiously stalking me for quite a while, waiting for the right opportunity to present itself.

Having already convinced himself I was a millionaire, and exactly what he was looking for, he had made me his target. My imaginary assets were adequate to satisfy all his avaricious ambitions; and suddenly he had found his ultimate quarry.

Once he had found his way to engineer an introduction, he was sticking to me like a leech, and love bombing me to ensure I didn't escape.

After having made such a relentless effort, my getting rid of him was never going to be easy.

Following the fiasco of the meeting with his two awful children, my own intention had been to bring the strange, and highly undesirable, relationship to a rapid end. I found him completely unattractive; he was rough and ignorant, and his behaviour was beyond my comprehension. I also found his personality and manners distasteful and inconsistent; and generally speaking, I considered him a very dodgy sort of person, about whom I knew very little, and had no wish to know more.

What I had recently learned about his character, and his strange behaviour, I definitely did not like. I simply found him disgustingly uncouth, and I had the gut feeling he was both untrustworthy and ambivalent with the truth... clearly a man with an enormous ego, who talked endlessly about himself, while denigrating everyone else. I had already made up my mind. He was not a nice person at all.

I still could not get my head around the fact that, although we had known one another for less than eight weeks, his warped mind had become fixated with the idea of a marriage taking place that summer. To me, it was crazy...unreal. Yet suddenly there he was, swearing that he had fallen passionately in love with me, and couldn't wait to make me his wife.

Looking back upon the entire ridiculous situation, I think my brains must have fallen out, for me ever to have allowed myself to be flattered and persuaded into believing a single word of the absolute garbage that poured out his mouth.

But at that time, I knew nothing about the wedding dance he had been performing all over the country during the previous two years, or anything about his motives in stalking me. When he insisted that I was the best thing that had ever happened to him, I failed to appreciate what he actually meant. He was speaking financially, and certainly not referring to my personality.

Silly stupid me! To allow myself to be taken for a complete fool by PP, the snake oil salesman.

In life, we all eventually do what we want, I suppose. And deep down, I think I wanted to believe in something again. I was a bereaved, lost soul, in need of some sort of an anchor...Maybe I subconsciously wanted to regain my basic security for myself and my children?

But the love and trust I had always known with Alan was not something I could ever hope to rediscover with PP.

In everything which had been happening since PP had manipulated his way into a devious acquaintance with me, the quiet perceptive part of my mind had been constantly urging me to hold back from any commitment, and wait until all my uncertainties were resolved, and my reasoning processes had returned to their normal state of rationality.

A more honest man, one who had any genuine feelings would have wanted to slow the situation down, and allow me space to come to terms with my bereavement. I'm sure anyone with a modicum of decency would not have been manipulating me, and rushing me headlong into an ill-considered commitment, merely to suit his own selfish agenda.

Unfortunately, as usual, wisdom too often only comes with hindsight. The devious character I had met in a deserted car-park, was a completely unknown factor...and as it was eventually proved, PP was a thoroughly dishonest individual... masquerading as an honest man.

I recall feeling something was seriously wrong with his emotional compass, and especially his concept of grief, when he vehemently argued that his divorce, almost three years previously, (from the woman with whom he had shared no kind of married life for many years,) was a much more devastating and traumatic experience than anything I was suffering because of Alan's death.

Alan, my devoted husband... the man I had loved, and shared my life with from our schooldays until the moment of his death only months previously, was being dismissed as irrelevant, by a man whose marriage had been non-existent for years.

It was beyond my comprehension how PP could possibly create an argument of comparatives, or even attempt to draw parallels between our lives. They were polar opposites. From his own accounts, his marriage had been over for ten years before their divorce; yet he was taking every opportunity to make me feel ashamed of the emotional devastation I was struggling to come to terms with. Alan and I had never fallen out of love; our marriage was enduring and strong... I had suddenly been bereaved of the man I still loved with all my heart.

Quite simply, PP had begun doing his utmost to poison my mind... demanding that I must forget Alan, and put him behind me, as though he were of no consequence or had never really existed. PP even had the audacity to set about arguing that Alan had only been a temporary, meaningless nobody in my life.

This heartless man was actively trying to shame me for my grief, and seriously imply my heart-rending sorrow was nothing but pathetic self-indulgence.

In his opinion, my grief could never come anywhere near to his own maudlin feelings, regarding his divorce. He even went so far as to lecture me that I was wallowing in self-pity, and needed to pull myself together and get over it.

Time and again he berated me, denigrating Alan, and attempting to downgrade his importance in my life; returning always to reminding me of his own generous nature, and how our wedding and the honeymoon would cost me nothing, because he was fully prepared to finance the entire affair. I found his comparisons and concepts, incomprehensible, and confusing... He was working to undermine my emotions, as though I had reason to hate Alan for dying... because it demonstrated how easily, and callously he had deserted me.

What does money have to do with grief? I asked myself. No one can buy his or her way out of the devastating death of a loved one.

In every way he could devise, PP was cunningly and relentlessly overshadowing my life with his towering negativity. He took pleasure in constantly manipulating my guilt and my sorrow... carping and criticising, and attempting to distort and negate my feelings for Alan, and manipulate me into accepting the cruel reality of my situation. At every opportunity, I found him reminding me that Alan was dead... He was not coming back... And apart from my daughters I was alone in the world, without a relative, friend, or companion. There was no one I could turn to for advice or help. Nobody cared if I was dead or alive... I was occupying an emotionless void... But he was there, full of love and support, ready and willing to fill that void for me.

It was a cunning, maliciously orchestrated scheme, deliberately intended to distort my emotions, and wear down my resistance, in order to insinuate himself further into my life. He was brainwashing me, and attempting to mould my mind to his way of thinking. In actuality, PP was actively working to deepen my insecurity and my depression.

Somehow, deep down, I intuitively knew, there was something seriously not right about him. Perhaps if I'd had some close male relative to talk to and trust, PP might have been persuaded to back off, and not persist in inveigling his way into my grief. I like to think another man would have more readily seen through his facade than I did at that time.

I was alone, of that I needed no reminding. But he had made me his target not out of compassion or sympathy... but because I was vulnerable, and because he had decided I was rich.

Financially I was self-sufficient, nothing more. I had my career, my children, and a substantial and valuable, mortgage-free home. These were the sum total of all the positives I had left in my life.

What I lacked was a calm state of mind, and the stability and comfort of a supportive, loving family. I wasn't ready to grow old alone. And the prospect of changing my solitary state was one that PP continually played upon; reminding me an opportunity such as that which he was offering might not come again. He played a convincing game of being hurt by my lack of enthusiasm, and claimed I was toying with his emotions, and causing him unnecessary personal grief. Did his generosity and affection not demonstrate how much he genuinely cared about me, and how seriously his mind was set upon marrying me?

I listened while he talked... I could have anything I wanted, if only I would agree to marry him. He was persistently at pains to paint a rosy picture of how we would each overcome our individual grief, and make a happy life together with our combined children.

In the constant onslaught of his complex propaganda, I began to feel insidiously torn between my life-long loyalty to Alan, and my desperate need for tangible emotional support. My love for Alan was enduring. He would always remain the one and only abiding love of my life. Even the notion that I might be considering the idea of remarriage seemed a betrayal of that love.

But over and again, PP kept up his arguments and appeals. If only I would just say the word, he would take me anywhere in the world I wanted to spend our honeymoon. Anything I wanted could be mine.

But set against all this flim-flam of generosity and passion, there was a constant drip-feeding undercurrent of negative propaganda intended to undermine my self-confidence, and my personal sense of worth. I was continually being reminded that, at forty-one I would not find anyone else remotely interested in me. I was old, and my looks were a thing of the past. I was ugly, and too fat; and if I didn't accept him there was no likelihood anyone else would ever want me... But in-spite of all my negative attributes, he wanted me, and if I would say yes, I would make him the happiest man in the world

By some foolish oversight I never thought to ask... if I was so old and ugly, and so physically undesirable, why was he so keen on marrying me? And did his future plans for happiness, include endeavouring to make me the happiest woman in the world?

Could it possibly be nearer the truth that the anticipated arrangement was intended to be just one-sided, and for his benefit alone?

His persistence, and his strangely ambivalent declarations of affection, were beginning to have an effect on me. And as the love-bombing increased, and my self-esteem was increasingly undermined, I became increasingly vulnerable to his attentions.

I have no explanation for how I eventually lost sight of his strange manipulative behaviour; or why I failed to take account of the dreadful things he was telling me about his past activities. In reality, we had absolutely no background, or life-history in common; and everything about this man was alien to the world I had always inhabited. Yet by some quirk of his glib, mesmerising tongue, and my own self-delusions, I was blinded to what was really staring me in the face.

In some strange way he was able to tap into my current emotional confusion, and deepest insecurities. And by dint of his driving resolve, and his plausible tongue, he was successfully getting inside my head and making me question...might I possibly find some sort of companionship and security, even happiness again? Would Alan have expected me to mourn forever, and spend my remaining years alone?

I had already looked into that abyss, and there was nothing but emptiness and loneliness waiting there. If I did remarry, then the girls would have someone to look after them, should the worst-case scenario happen, and I were to die.

My mind, my self-esteem, and my emotions, were in a terrible state of demoralisation and confusion. But I never seemed to have a moment's peace from PP's cajoling and persuasive voice, alternating with his harping criticism.

When I did finally fall blindfold, off the edge of my dilemma, and said a hesitant, 'Yes...but....' he was elated, and unbelievably over the top in triumph. He instantly began making wedding plans, and galloped at break-neck speed, to get everything settled as soon as possible. I wanted to take my time, but for some reason, my wishes were disregarded, and all the arrangement must all be completed that summer.

It was, indeed, a very satisfactory outcome for PP. The marriage-trap had been sprung before I was even aware a trap existed...and he was determined I was not going to have any time to re-think the situation, or make my escape.

Before I had time to change my mind, everything was sorted. The church was booked, and a honeymoon in Sorrento, paid for.

Having to continue pretending to be someone he was not, for five long months must have been wearing; but in the guise of Dr Jekyll he clung on to completing his secret agenda. Now there was to be no stopping until the service was over, and the wedding ring firmly on my finger.

But I was still not entirely convinced I was making the right decision for my daughters and myself, and I made it very clear that there remained a number of important considerations I felt it was necessary to raise with him. For me these were very significant issues; and I insisted until we had an agreement on them, I was not prepared to let any arrangements go forward.

My terms were not negotiable. There had to be a clear agreement... under no circumstances would I ever move out of my home. I was adamant I would never relinquish it, or consider living in his house. My second and third conditions were that I would never consider moving my daughters from the excellent school they attended, nor ever give up my own career. My final condition was he must be in full agreement that there could be no thought, whatsoever to our ever, having children. For me the prospect was much too dangerous and life-threatening. Without his acceptance of these conditions, I simply could not agree to marry him.

He listened to what I had to say, and made no argument about anything, just fell over himself to agree to each condition I had insisted upon.

It was only a few days after the wedding arrangements were settled that the first inklings of his dubious interests in my finances began to surface. Quite casually one Saturday afternoon, he suggested we might take a look in a local automobile showroom to see what new models they currently had in stock. New cars did not particularly interest me. Alan had always dealt with everything to do with our motor vehicles. I had only ever been interested in driving whichever car I owned, for work and shopping, or transporting the girls to their various clubs and out-of-school activities.

However, during our visit to the showrooms, he was very keen to draw my attention to a three litre, golden-metallic automatic Mercedes. I said it seemed very luxurious. Then, as an afterthought, I asked if he was thinking of buying it. He said he was, just as soon as his house was sold.

We went for lunch afterwards, and as were eating, he casually returned to the subject of the car we had just seen. He said he had spoken to the salesman and agreed to a good deal on it, for cash.

Naturally I enquired if he intended to settle the deal.

'Well,' he said. 'Tha' all depends.'

'Oh, I suppose you mean upon when you sell your house?' I said.

'Well, it's more ter do wiv if yer'll lend uz the muney till Ah do sell thee 'ouse.' He was grinning broadly and disarmingly, and waiting for my agreement.

'Yer wouldn't deny uz a few quid tempraly, till Ah do, wud yer? It's jus fer a month or two, an yer know yer'll git it back. By the time weer married, yer'll 'ave it back in yer bank account aal safe an sound, an yer'll be ridin' around like the queen herself, in a fancy golden coach. Payin' up front fer the weddin' an aal 'as sort o run uz short at presen'.'

Like a total idiot, I eventually allowed him to persuade me to agree to the loan, and I withdrew the thousands he required, in cash, and handed it to him. That was financial pay-out number one to PP.

A couple of weeks later, he craftily set about manipulating me into financial coup number two... by prevailing upon me to open a joint bank account with him. He said it was an act of good faith that we should share one account, and contribute all our individual assets into it, on a fifty-fifty arrangement.

Initially I did not view the proposal as unusual. Alan and I had always shared a joint account, into which both of our salaries were paid. At a personal level Alan was not the least bit interested in money. So long as there was enough in our account to cover our living expenses, he had always left me to get on with running things. I never recall him ever questioning me about our finances. Ours had always been a marriage based upon total trust. Whatever we owned belonged to us as a family; nothing had ever been specified as being yours or mine.

After thinking through PP's joint banking proposal, I was not so sure the idea was a good one, and I dragged my feet for as long as I could. I had begun to experience certain misapprehensions about his attitude towards money. Also, my uneasy intuition had begun bothering me again; it was demanding to know why he was insisting upon rushing things along so quickly.

Was I being overly suspicious? I wondered.

Whatever was whipping it into activity, I couldn't seem to close my subconscious down. It persisted in nagging at me, until I finally admitted to myself there were things in the proposed arrangements that were making me uneasy. Could there be any possibility PP was manoeuvring me into a position of total financial commitment, to benefit himself?

Now my suspicions really were worrying me. Everything was going much too fast, and too many bridges were being burned. I had my daughters' welfare to concern myself with, and I had begun to realise I ought to retain my financial independence. I hadn't known PP long, and I didn't know much at all about his personality or his background, except for what he had told me, and the bits and pieces I had gleaned. And that, I was beginning to realise, was something short of a clear picture, or the whole truth.

I didn't even know anyone one who knew him, who could fill in the gaps for me.

My uneasy thoughts had begun to make me feel increasingly unsettled about his motivations regarding our marriage...

particularly taking into account the various conflicting things I had recently heard, and what he had told me about his former wife. Taken together, there were quite a number of unresolved issues troubling me.

Now, with the planned wedding date set, he was pressing me to agree to a joint bank account, which involved handing over access to my entire salary. Then I discovered he intended to pull a devious trick on me. It emerged he had never had any intention of following through with the plan for the fifty-fifty split he had originally suggested. Suddenly, and autonomously, the plan had been changed, and merging all our assets was definitely not his intention after all.

His revised arrangement now involved my salary being paid into the new account, while he would arrange for an amount, which he would decide upon, to be paid in each month, from his business account. In future, the new bank account would cover all our expenditure, including holidays, household outgoings, clothing, housekeeping, and everything else. But I could see that this revised suggestion was completely one-sided, and suspiciously wide-open to abuse.

While he intended to continue retaining his personal account with an unspecified amount going into it each month, he expected me to have my entire income paid into the new account, to be held in our joint names and with either party entitled to draw on it.

When I attempted to voice my disquiet feelings about this unexpected change in arrangements, and suggested, as an alternative, we should come to an agreement upon a monthly figure we could each agree to contribute to cover our outgoings, he instantly turned the tables on me. I found myself being angrily accused of dishonesty and distrust, and of attempting to rob him and ruin him.

Within moments, his fury exploded, and I was left seriously intimidated. He was accusing me of trying to manipulate the situation for my own purposes in order to deceive him, and make a fool of him... I was attempting to take advantage of his good nature in order to squirrel away secret assets for myself, in order to rob him.

I found myself being accused of greed, and all kinds of dishonesty... by a manipulative rogue, who was no better than a devious money-grabbing low life.

My genuine concerns over the obviously skewed proposed arrangements were rubbished and totally dismissed, and I was given to understand I was a conniving bitch who was intent upon ruining him. This sudden display of fury, over my alternative suggestions upon how we should arrange our finances more equitably, shocked me. It was a side to him I had not seen before.

In money matters, as in everything else, PP was as cunning as a snake. He had craftily turned the tables on me, and turned my genuine concerns into ridicule. I was being accused of devising a devious plot to get my hands on his money; when the cynical reality was, it was the very scam he himself had in mind to perpetrate on me.

It was a defining moment in the relationship.

In my own best interests that was the moment I should have pulled out of the entire commitment. Common sense would have prevailed. I should have sent him on his way, and thereafter remained financially secure, happy, and free from his devious schemes, and his bullying.

But at that time, I could not entirely trust my own judgment. I recognised there were times when my emotions were still not as logical as they should be. Maybe his accusations that I was being irrational were true? And eventually, in the face of his display of righteous and incandescent indignation, I reluctantly withdrew my objections and conceded to his plan

He had won; and I had allowed myself to be intimidated into surrender. He had browbeaten me into handing him the financial whip-hand over my personal finances.

It was a major psychological defeat for me; and one that held more significance for my future financial security and happiness, than I could ever have imagined.

Chapter 9

The Takeover Begins

After being manipulated into agreeing to open a joint bank account with PP, on his terms, my quiet voice of reason continued its constantly niggling. Looking back, I now see what a convoluted mess I was cunningly, and unwittingly, being manoeuvred into. I was walking into disaster with a blindfold over my eyes.

But at that time, I was struggling from day to day just to keep going. I knew things weren't right; but my only excuse for my weak out-of-character behaviour was my confused state of mind, which PP was capitalising on. Retrospectively, I believe I should have found some way to pull myself together, and regain control of my life. But at that time, I was way out of my depth, and emotionally in a very bad place. I was wallowing in a state of misery, clinging to the belief that my vacillating mental state was only temporary and that, before very long, things would all correct themselves.

I recognised that my bereavement had sent me whirling into a dizzy vortex, where my life had become like a boat without oars... And I was left drifting helplessly in a fog of confusion.

The unwarranted advent of PP into my life was piling layer upon layer of confusion on top of my problems, and I was trying to cope with too much pressure too soon, and suffering from stress overload as a result.

But I soldiered on, because I had no idea what else I could do; there was no-one I could consult, nor anyone except myself to rely upon. Perhaps I was going through some form of an emotional breakdown? All I can remember is that, while it was all happening, I refused to accept there was anything wrong with me. I needed to be in control of my life, and do all the things I felt were right for my daughters. I had to go to work... I had to keep things going. It was the only way we would survive.

A jumbled mixture of insurmountable stresses and anxieties were at the heart of my problems, but as I tossed and turned each night, reviewing my situation, the same recurring torment haunted me. If I die, who will care for my children?

I was already halfway persuaded to trust PP, and I clung to the blind hope he would prove to be the answer to my problems.

But the truth, if only I could have recognised it, was that he was the last thing I needed in my life; he was exacerbating my situation and becoming my major problem. This man was actively working to undermine and wreck what was left of my life and my sanity.

Because of everything I was attempting to deal with, a constant state of confused turmoil was continually buzzing in the back of my mind. I desperately wanted security for my daughters. But was PP the answer to my worries? Was he as reliable and trustworthy as he vehemently claimed to be?

He had set about convincing me, right from our first encounter, that he was a genuine, caring person...someone honest and savvy who would be a genuine support, and someone I could trust and lean on. But there was no getting passed the fact he was nothing remotely like Alan.

Without really knowing anything about him, or suspecting his hidden motives, I was being subversively and successfully groomed by him.

In spite of all his plausible mind-bending brainwashing, somehow my suppressed, 'perceptive and wiser mind' was still attempting to communicate with me. My 'inner guide' was still struggling to draw my attention to glaring inconsistencies about him. There were ambiguous unpleasant characteristics about his manipulative behaviour, which had all been there from the start, and which my wise inner counsel had persisted in attempting to try to communicate to me.

I kept on asking myself... Was he the honest character he would have me believe? Or was he just a devious, skilful liar out to con me? I had never met anyone like him before, and he was undeniably an expert at self-promotion.

I asked the questions... But I never listened to the answers.

What I felt for him was certainly never love. But breaking free from his influence was a massive dilemma. He had successfully inveigled his way into my life, and capitalised on my vulnerability using his strange animal magnetism and intuitive psychology to deceive me. The more he worked on me, the more difficult it became to differentiate his true underlying identity, from the one he was portraying as genuine.

This man was possessed of a personality that was resolute and forceful, and he was like no one I had ever met before. And for some unknown reason, he had me mesmerised, much like a snake fascinates a timid rabbit. I was confused by his mixed messages, and his persistent controlling and conflicting behaviour. But at the same time, I was effectively blotting out what my gut instincts were persistently trying to draw to my attention about him.

Inexplicably, I ended up colluding with what he was doing to me, and allowing him to draw his web of influence ever more tightly around me... My confused mind wanted to believe in him and rely upon him. And I was inadvertently allowing him to take control of my life.

I had already registered that money seemed of utmost importance to him, because everything always invariably led back to that subject. He claimed to be financially sound; and he had made a huge issue about it, emphasising his personal generosity, when pressing the marriage idea on me, by telling me how he would happily pay for everything.

It gradually occurred to me that his way of constantly reciting the facts regarding his personal generosity, seemed almost as though he was making an investment, or paying upfront in a business deal. My mind continued performing somersaults in its efforts to rationalise things; and the constant confusing dichotomy going on inside my head was tearing me apart, like an illness that gave me no peace.

Did he believe he was buying me? I was not a commodity, and I had never been for sale. The fact that I was an intelligent, independent woman, responsible for my own decisions, seemed to have temporarily been obliterated from my mind.

He and I had absolutely nothing in common, and the truth was we still barely knew each other. But it seemed as though he'd had the whole marriage scenario already planned in his head, from the moment we had met... almost like a script he had been following. I was troubled that there had been no gradual emergence of his declared emotional attachment, no gradual strengthening of our companionship, and no cautious hesitancy about making a serious commitment.

Instead the entire relationship had been instant and full on... from start to finish in six months. These were some of the thoughts which bubbled to the surface of my thoughts in my disquiet moments. It seemed PP had been determined to rush me into a commitment before I had any opportunity to regain my equilibrium, or find peace for my troubled mind after losing Alan. I hadn't even had time to get to know WHO he really was.

There was certainly nothing refined or educated about him. At face value, he was totally unattractive, and exactly what he appeared to be... a rough-and-ready, badly spoken, badly educated, and coarse-mannered builder. But in spite of all the things I didn't like about him, he exuded a deceptively crude kind of hypnotic charm... a charisma, I suppose... which he had used to very good effect.

In reality, if I had been able to push aside the blinkers, I would have seen there were a great many carefully obfuscated dimensions to his character. And it was only when it was too late to pull back, that I recognised I should have paid careful heed to my accurate, and perceptive, intuitive feelings.

I had allowed myself to be too easily overwhelmed, when I

should have been more critical and a good deal more cautious, and discriminatory. I should have slowed the hectic pace, and been much more reluctant to believe, and less willing to overlook his controlling ways, and his strange preoccupation with money.

My subconscious judgment had always been opposed to him. But for some illogical reason, my conscious mind had influenced me to trust him.

The entire situation proved to be the triumph of blind hope over wiser instinct. My better judgment had always seen what I hadn't wanted to recognise, and it had persisted in nagging at me, telling me very clearly that my uncertainties about his character were well founded, and I should insist upon making haste... slowly.

But nothing was telling me WHY. What was the piece of the puzzle I was missing? And why was my mind going in circles, and unable to come to a resolution concerning PP's real character?

I had no family of my own to turn to for support, and no one to entrust, or name as guardians for my children. During all the months following Alan's death, there had been only silence in response to the letters I had sent his father and mother, and his married sister and brother, telling them the heart-breaking, tragic news of Alan's sudden death. Incredibly, they had never acknowledged his passing with so much as a condolence card or a flower. Not one of them had even telephoned to express their sorrow. The three of us had been abruptly and cruelly excluded from their lives, as though our entire family had been wiped out.

This detached callousness had shocked me, and made my sense of isolation and rejection even worse. I had been forced to face the fact that we were simply of no further concern to anybody, and what became of us was irrelevant. Alan was dead, and we were no longer anything to do with his family.

My children's only remaining grandparents cared nothing about them, and we had all been effectively and permanently deleted from their lives.

Soon new doubts from my troubled inner voice began niggling inside my mind, over my decision to marry PP. This anxiety persisted like an unpleasant worm inside an apple; but I could not work out what was constantly eating at my conscience... that is until one night, when in my anxiety-ridden tossing and turning, I finally recognised what was wrong. The new problem bugging me was not a hidden worm; it was a significant legal flaw.

This realisation came as a shock, but it was an undeniable fact. Once I was married to him, PP would become my legal next-of-kin. As such, he would take precedence over my children. If my deep instincts eventually proved correct, and my worst fears materialised, my death would entitle him to claim everything I possessed. He would legally be entitled to disinherit my daughters from everything their father and I had worked for. And should he really be maliciously inclined, he could sell their home, pocket the profit, and disclaim all responsibility for them. Unless I took rapid action, both he and his own children would stand to benefit from Alan's and my estate, and leave our own daughters destitute.

Without me, my children had no one to defend them. Not even their paternal grandparents cared what happened to them.

Maybe I was overreacting, but I felt so confused I really couldn't be sure of anything. All I could think was, whatever else I did I had to protect my girls from all eventualities, real or imaginary.

The following Monday, I made an appointment with a solicitor. Then I called on my way home from school and drew up my will, in anticipation of the marriage. Everything I owned was to be divided equally between my children, with no other beneficiaries or claimants.

I felt satisfied I had done the right thing. I had protected them. If and when I died, I was now certain Samantha and Nathalie would be safe from any risk of being left destitute or homeless.

There was one more thing I still needed to do, to finally put my mind at ease before it was too late, and that was arrange with a monumental mason for the erection of a memorial on Alan's grave. No one in the world would ever mean more to me than my beloved Alan. He was not only my cherished husband; he had always been my devoted, loyal lover, my companion, and my best and most trusted friend. We were two bodies with one soul, and I was not ashamed for the world to know that was how I would always hold him in my heart.

The irrational, persistent premonition about my own death had been bugging me ever since I had lost Alan. But now I was finally satisfied that, whatever came of my decision to remarry, at least I had safeguarded our children's future, and respected their father's memory. I believed I had successfully tied up the loose ends of my life, and if I was about to embark on a dark journey into unknown murky waters, there was little more I could do now, except go with the flow.

Foolishly I had overlooked the fact that most rivers are full of hidden hazards. Some are infested with crocodiles… man-eaters lurking silently in the darkness, waiting to tear the unwary traveller into shreds.

It was early in May when the sale of PP's house was completed. Liz had already departed for the WRAF, and we were still a few months away from the date set for the wedding. The school term still had two more months to run before the summer holidays began, and in the meantime, PP had arranged for his son to temporarily board with a family in their village. I was told the boy would continue to travel daily on the school bus until the term ended. Then, once the holidays began, he intended to bring him to live with us.

None of this had been discussed with me. I was merely informed of his decisions, although I did have serious misgivings about the prospective situation. My own view was that, given all the circumstances, I would have found it preferable for Steve to spend at least part of each week at his mother's house. He clearly resented me, and had serious issues to deal with concerning me. We didn't even know each other, and I could foresee potential problems arising from the instant full-on residential arrangements being planned by his father. But I was never consulted about it. PP merely informed me what was going to happen... no ifs, no buts.

I felt concerned that I was being bulldozed into something highly contentious, with serious implications involving my home, my daughters, and myself, all without being allowed any say over anything. Things were moving far too quickly; events were being taken out of my hands, and huge assumptions made that could adversely affect all of our lives. No one had asked my daughters how they felt about any of these plans. Their feelings were being disregarded as irrelevant. It was all about PP and his son, and what he wanted.

The house was, after all, first and foremost, mine and my children's home. It was my property. But the ownership of it, and who would live there, were facts being bandied about without any discussions with me. I deeply resented not being consulted, or asked for my consent over any of PP's decisions. He had not even requested my opinion.

In addition, nothing had been said about where PP would live once his house was sold, and during the months before we were due to be married. I assumed he would find himself a temporary flat or a bedsit. But once again, I was never consulted on the subject.

Being a dominating, self-obsessed character, PP saw things very differently from me. But just how divergent our views were, was not immediately obvious.

From PP's angle, he needed somewhere to live, and he expected … someone to feed him, cook for him, and generally look after him. He was not prepared to do any of these things for himself. Nor did he plan to pay for such arrangements, or spend his money on renting a flat. So, without any prior discussions with me, he decided to force my hand.

Quite unexpectedly, and without any by your leave, or even the courtesy of a telephone call, the Sunday following the completion of his house sale, PP turned up at my house with a wagonload of his household furniture, and announced he was moving in. He didn't even trouble to ring the doorbell to inform me of his arrival. The first I knew of it was when the men he had brought with him had already begun unloading his household junk onto my driveway.

His unexpected arrival caught me completely off balance and left me at a dumbfounded loss to know how to deal with him. Admittedly I had never come across anyone so forceful or so determinedly autocratic before.

From the state of my drive, it looked like a rag-and-bone man had just invaded the neighbourhood. I watched in silent dismay as his possessions were carried into my hall, completely cluttering it with his collection of tasteless chipboard rubbish.

I had been manoeuvred into a fait accompli to house him. Suddenly there he was, sweeping into my home to take advantage of my vulnerable situation, without any request for permission, or even a word of apology for the assumption he was making. His behaviour was nothing short of an invasion; it was unforgivably ignorant, and presumptuous beyond belief. He was making a fool out of me, and taking my good nature to the extremes of credibility.

I had nowhere to house his tacky rubbish; my house was already fully furnished with antiques. Every last thing I owned was made to totally different standards from the scruffy junk he was in the process of dumping on me. It came as little consolation to hear that his bedroom furniture, and many of his other 'choice household pieces', such as his glassless china cabinet and threadbare three-piece suite, had been distributed to his parents, and to the family of farm labourers currently housing his son.

When I viewed the collection of rubbish cluttering my hall, I could have wept. The place was chock-a-block with his huge table and its five bentwood chairs; a yellow plastic-laminated kitchen table, along with two plastic covered benches; a scruffy sideboard; a dresser; his grotesque twenty-foot-long chipboard unit... split into several sections... and his oversized chipboard desk and accompanying chair.

Elsewhere among the array of clutter, I could see his television set and all his second-rate hi-fi equipment, plus endless boxes of records and tapes. And for some unknown reason, he had also brought his scruffy old fridge-freezer; his battered washing machine with its accompanying tumble dryer; and several packing cases filled with an assortment of aluminium kitchenware, nylon bedding, and heaven only knew what other tacky household goods. It was impossible to walk across the hall because of all the obstacles it now contained.

The only place I could think of putting this motley collection of useless rubbish was outside in the garage.

However, true to form, PP did not wait for any instructions from me as to where his clutter might be housed. Once the wagon was emptied, he began shuffling the furniture around in my dining room, and instructed the men with him to stack his possessions in there.

I was devastated, when I saw the disgusting chaos they had created, in my dining room; it was suddenly crammed full, and stacked beyond belief with the jumble he had dumped in it. Now I couldn't even get inside the door.

His planned takeover of my house and my life, had begun in earnest and I didn't know what to do, or how to stop him. It seemed as though I had been paralysed, and left with no resistance against him.

The following day while I was at school, he ripped out my expensive, dual-action, washing machine / tumble dryer. When I arrived home, I found my shiny kitchen appliance had vanished, and his two scruffy machines had been installed where my neat one had previously been. There had been no permission sought, and certainly no apologies or explanations offered for what he had done.

Now he lived in my house. This demonstration was the first in a series of similar events, performed as fait accompli to illustrate he could do whatever he wanted with my property. He had moved in on me, and taken over my home and my life, without my being able to put up any fight, and without even asking for my agreement for anything he intended to do.

Having invaded my home, he now gave himself the rights to make all the decisions. Whatever he decided was final and non-negotiable. My ownership rights to decide anything in my home had been cancelled, and my property was being stolen from under my nose.

How would anyone feel other than outraged and incensed? I immediately demanded that he return my expensive missing machine; but he just laughed at me and ridiculed my anger, and claimed what he had removed was 'a load of old rubbish', and the two scruffy items he had installed in its place were superior in every way.

He claimed I had no idea about anything mechanical and, in effect, didn't know my arse from my elbow. In fact, I should get down on my knees and thank him for being so thoughtful and considerate, and for spending all day working his guts out to please me, while I was at school...playing stupid games and wasting my time shuffling bits of paper about. I was nothing more than a jumped-up clerk, who knew nothing about anything.

It was the first time anyone had ever disrespected me in such an offensive way, or rubbished my academic credentials and years of professional success. Within moments, he had annihilated my whole life, as though it was nothing but a collection of worthless trivialities. And all this was happening in my home.

In his eyes, I was...'a waste of space... an overpaid idiot, doing a pointless job. My opinions counted for nothing, and I was just... a stupid ugly twat, full of bullshit, who knew diddly-squat about anything...'

His vile disrespect left me humiliated and angry beyond words. I suddenly got the impression he enjoyed belittling me with his vile contemptuous opinions, and was doing it quite deliberately to denigrate my intelligence.

If this was what he really thought of me, then I didn't want either him or his rubbishy old equipment in my kitchen. I demanded that he return my own expensive property, and remove his junk from my dining room. In fact, I went the whole hog and ordered him out of my home, and told him everything between us was finished.

The reaction I got was incredible. He totally blanked me, and just continued ridiculing, and making a fool of me... imitating a petulant child crying for a lost toy. 'Waa, waa, waa, ah wan me dolly back. Waa, waa, gimme back me dolly. Yer a nasty 'orrible man, and ah wan me dolly back.'

It was a savage, disrespectful way to behave, and it left me devastated. I was being intimidated, and effectively emasculated by him, with no idea what I could do to get him and his rubbish out of my house. He was there, imposing himself on me like a determined, aggressive squatter. I boiled with fury, but I hadn't the least idea what I could do about the situation.

Ruthless ridicule and aggression were invariably his ways of doing business. This was how he dealt with anyone or anything that opposed him. Like an enraged bull, he charged straight for any impediment in his path to control and annihilate it.

He only ever lived by one rule... 'I can and will do whatever I want. I will blitz anyone who attempts to stand in my way or tries to stop me because I am bigger and tougher, and I listen to no one. I dare you to attempt to oppose me or challenge me...

because I'll grind you into the ground if you try.'

His moving into my home without my agreement had tested my parameters. He had taken a major step into my territory, and had quite brazenly disposed of a valuable item of my property without any consultation. And he had no intention of returning it. What I said, or how I felt mattered not one jot.

Adding insult to injury, I had also been confronted by another kind of challenge... his seriously offensive and derogatory denigration of my intelligence, my academic work, and my qualifications. I felt helpless, angry, and totally defeated, with no idea what I could to do to get him out of my home. This demonstration of uncivilised behaviour was totally outside of anything I had ever met, and I was immobilised by it.

Common sense and lack of knowledge concerning my legal entitlement to exert my ownership rights failed me, and I was already halfway to becoming an emotional prisoner of this awful man.

Alan, my gallant, loyal knight, was dead. And I was now left facing the devilish fiery dragon of PP, alone and defenceless.

The more he pushed his implacable intentions forward, the more intimidated I became by him... until I ended up being conditioned into silently giving way to appease him, and keep him from further harming me.

I can now recognise with certainty, what I was blind to identifying at the time; right from the beginning of the relationship, he had been working to dominate and control me, as well as undermine my self-esteem and decimate my sense of self-worth. His manipulative scheme began at a time when I was emotionally already at a low ebb.

I have never been able to reconcile my reasons for failing to listen to the persistent warnings of my intuitive instincts. Right from the first moments I had encountered this man, something inside my brain had constantly been attempting to alert me to his dangerous, untrustworthy nature, while there was still time and opportunity to rid myself of him. Perversely, I chose to render myself deaf to all those warnings.

For such persistent, personal, crass stupidity and ignorance, I have castigated myself a million times over the years. Why did I fail to dig my heels in, and demand the return of my property; or pursue legal action to get him out of my house, that very first time he used his control tactics on me? Why did I not take out an injunction and have him ousted from my home? Why did I not put a stop to his takeover of my life while I still had the chance to escape? Why? Why? Why?

The only answer I have found lies in his cunningly reprehensible reptilian psychology. Somehow, from the moment when he first insinuated himself into my life, PP had been intuitively working out my psychology. It was easy for him to see how fragile my emotions were. Then with amazing rapidity, he began to play on my vulnerabilities, in order to dominate and control me.

Moving himself in on me was a test, which I unfortunately failed, and he passed. My confused mentality at that time, along with my weak responses to his confrontational behaviour, eventually resulted in my powerless, downtrodden submission to him.

As time passed, I became so increasingly overwhelmed by fear of his multidimensional brutality, I failed to recognise how invidiously and effectively I was being coerced and manipulated by him.

The sinister Nazi Gestapo had the system worked out to perfection; and PP was a great admirer of the whole Nazi philosophy of the Hitler regime. It was based upon rapidly gaining control over the mind and body of the victim. The tools used were both physical and psychological. And from the outset, fear and intimidation were instilled by means of shouting, swearing, vicious physical abuse, and mental torture; along-side endless programmes of persecution and denigration; add in contradictory behaviour; and sleep deprivation inducing mental breakdown and psychological disorientation. PP's version of the Nazi master plan worked, because he remorselessly ensured every weapon of abuse and intimidation was systematically brought to bear upon me...as his victim... without pause or respite.

Brutality, domination, fear, sleep deprivation, and the like... was, in essence, was how PP intended to gain complete control over me. And he had made a start by claiming the first advantage, when he moved in on me.

Under the rigorous, and relentless intimidation designed by the Nazi regime, the victim was rapidly reduced to a state of subservience, paralysed by fear, and in a condition of total mental terror and subordination...

History can teach us many important lessons, if we are willing to learn.

My state of mind, during the early months of our relationship, was fragile, and entirely naïve. Without my normal perceptive understanding of the threats from PP's warped personality, I was at a very serious disadvantage. Right from the start of the relationship, and before we ever married, PP began applying his cunning manipulation to my mind... conditioning me by introducing his coercive tactics to weaken my self-confidence ever further, and drive forward his ability to dominate and control me.

His early success in moving into my home, was the beginning of exerting his will to dominate me; it defined exactly how he intended our relationship would develop, and had been the opening salvo of the sinister mind games he intended playing with me... games where he was always in control, and seriously working to strengthen his cold and calculating Jekyll and Hyde reptilian power.

From the outset of the relationship, my confused, and out-of-character weakness found his dominating behaviour totally demoralising. It was impossible for me to understand exactly what he was doing to me, or why.

The devious motives that drove him remained an enigma for a long time, right up to the time when I eventually regained my emotional strength, along with the capacity to think rationally again. Only then was I able to work out what was going on inside his head, and what he had been scheming to do to mine.

Until I reached the point where I felt re-empowered to start to reclaim control over my life, an awful lot of tears were destined to be shed.

Chapter 10

The Golden Lion Incident

As the date for the wedding slowly edged its way closer, I found myself beset by increasing doubts over the integrity of PP, and the honesty of his intentions. My perceptive, but still suppressed, deep cerebral source was constantly attempting to warn me that I should not trust him. The message, 'deeds not words' was persistently coming into my head, as my inner awareness kept on repeating... Start judging him by how he's behaving towards you. Wake up. Open your eyes and see the truth. Ask yourself... Why do you need this man in your life?

This strangely conflicting mental dichotomy was constantly stirring up a whole raft of confusions for me, and battling to draw my attention to things my conscious mind was choosing to ignore. The logical reasoning part, realised I should delay all major decisions, and certainly all thoughts of remarriage, until I knew PP a great deal better that I did.

Nevertheless, at the every-day level of reality, I was emotionally floundering, and so devoid of confidence in myself that I had already been brainwashed into believing that I needed him to be my prop, and bolster my lack of self-worth. I had been persuaded that he was my only hope of surviving my deep-seated fears of being on my own. The overpowered, conscious part of me wanted to believe in him and trust him.

I remained in this crazy emotionally anaesthetised state, regularly doing battle with my perceptive subconscious, and actively silencing it, throughout two deeply distressing, damaging, and confusing years.

PP was a great deal more streetwise than I was. He was a cynical, savvy, cunning con artist, with years of practise, and he was in a hurry to press forward with his plans and consolidate them, sooner rather than later.

He knew if he was to succeed, the longer things were delayed, the more likely I would be to wake up to what he was doing to me, and call the whole thing off. It was a case of 'strike while the iron is hot'. For him, nothing was certain until the wedding ring was on my finger.

During those first six months of knowing him, he wasted no time in bulldozing his way into my confidence; testing the measure of his success by deliberately conniving to defraud me of substantial sums of money, with the convincing, and sincere-sounding, promises of paying everything back, as soon as his own property was sold.

Weeks had now passed since his house sale had been completed, and he had still made no effort to repay me. Subsequently, he had inveigled me into agreeing to open a joint bank account, with more plausible promises... this time to pay money into the account every month equal to my salary. This had also failed to materialise.

Added to these deceptions, if the writing on the wall wasn't already clear enough, he had then wasted no time at all, following the sale of his house, in moving himself and his remaining possessions, lock-stock-and-barrel into my house, without so much as a by your leave. Currently, he was living free of all expenses in my home, and already beginning to take it over. He showed no compunction whatsoever, over sponging off me, and seemed to believe he was entitled to take my good nature, and my property entirely for granted.

He was relentlessly working his way towards taking over my life and my home, and establishing his domination and control over me. The evidence of what he was up to was clear for anyone with half a brain to see. But at that time, and for very significant reasons, I was that foolish woman with less than half a brain.

However, the working half, my subconscious, was still attempting to save me from a serious life-changing disaster.

The only significant financial gesture PP had made, since contriving his weird introduction to me, had been to impress upon me his willingness to pay for everything involved in the wedding costs. With expansive largesse, he had insisted I could have free rein over all the arrangements, and organise everything in whatever way I wanted… the venue, the honeymoon, whatever I wanted, no expenses would be spared, and he would happily foot the bill.

It was a calculated gesture of generosity, from a seriously avaricious, vindictive and conniving man. From the outset, this pseudo generosity had been intended as nothing other than 'a sprat to catch a mackerel'… as my wise grandmother would have said.

Unfortunately, his one flamboyant gesture had been enough to blind me to all his other glaring financial manipulations, and

I had allowed myself to be convinced his intentions towards me were honest. I had accepted that one impressive gesture, as outweighing everything else he had subsequently done. That was how things were rolling along, until something happened that forced open a chink in my obfuscated conscious mind, and let some light shine upon the hidden reality of his deeply manipulative, and disgusting character.

It was a seriously unwelcome and unpleasant shock when I discovered there was a much darker personality lurking out of sight behind his carefully constructed Dr Jekyll facade. In reality, there was a serious sadistic nastiness to him, which up to that point, he had worked hard to control and keep hidden from me. This darkness of his soul, surfaced one Friday evening after he announced he was taking me to meet his aunt, who lived about twenty-five miles away in the village of Fenbrook.

He had never spoken about any of his father's relatives before, and it puzzled me why he suddenly wanted me to meet his aunt. Yvonne was the widow of his father's youngest brother Fred. She and her two adult daughters owned a modern bungalow in the village where PP's paternal grandparents had originally lived.

I already knew 'Old Charlie', PP's father, was the eldest of a large family of fifteen children, of which his brother Fred had been the youngest. Having such a wide age range between the two siblings had resulted in Uncle Fred and his nephew being of a similar age. In fact, PP's aunt Yvonne was only a couple of years older than I was.

But I was at a loss to understand why he suddenly wanted me to meet her ahead of the wedding, having never previously mentioned her name before.

As I dressed that evening, I naively anticipated we would be taking Yvonne out for dinner. It seemed the natural, family thing to do, as he hadn't seen her since his uncle's funeral five years earlier.

We arrived at her house at around seven o'clock. After chatting for an hour, PP suggested we should drive to the local pub, where, I assumed, he was planning for us to eat.

When we arrived at, The Golden Lion, I was shocked to find the place was nothing better than a small rural pub, of the spit-and-sawdust type, and somewhere that did not serve food. It was the scruffiest, dirtiest establishment I had ever been inside, and his subsequent behaviour there was nothing short of disgraceful.

No sooner had we arrived than he immediately abandoned Yvonne and myself in a small side room, and disappeared out of sight into the bar. I couldn't believe he wasn't coming back and spent the first half an hour anxiously watching the door.

During the course of the evening I became increasingly disgusted by his loathsome and degrading behaviour. His aunt and I were complete strangers, with absolutely nothing to talk about. Nevertheless, he callously chose to ignore the pair of us and left us dumped in a filthy side room while, for the next three hours, he continued drinking himself stupid in the bar, consuming round after round of Bacardi and Coke. The entire evening was a pointless fiasco, which he appeared to have organised simply as a way of embarrassing both myself and his aunt, while he remained in the bar indulging in a drunken binge.

Why he had ever suggested our meeting that Friday night remained a mystery for some long time... until I discovered, by chance, there actually had been a devious convoluted motive behind it. It was just one more example of PP's perverse way of carrying out one of his sick acts of revenge. He had arranged the evening for one reason only... to relay a spiteful message to his ex-wife, and make her aware of the new woman he was now intending to marry.

Beryl and Yvonne had remained close friends, following both the divorce and Yvonne's bereavement. And it also happened that the two women regularly attended the same Catholic church. That Friday meeting had been arranged for the purely malicious reason of ensuring Beryl received a first-hand account of the new woman in her ex-husband's life. He knew she would hear the story from Yvonne the following Sunday in church, and he had fully intended it to cause her distress.

It was the first time I had experienced a practical demonstration of the crazy vengeful side to his personality. And when I did finally learn the truth, I was disgusted. Apart from his malicious never-ending thirst for revenge, the meeting was otherwise completely pointless.

I found Yvonne to be a gentle, pleasant lady. But we were both left embarrassed and at a loss to understand why we had been brought together and then dumped for three hours in the filthy backroom of a scruffy pub, with nothing at all to say to each other. In all the years that followed, Yvonne and I never encountered each other again. And PP never once felt motivated to arrange another meeting with her.

However, that Friday evening, by the time we came to leave the Golden Lion, he was staggering about, belligerently drunk, and in a highly offensive condition. His abominable drunken behaviour left me absolutely repelled and nauseated by him. To make matters even worse, when we had left my house that evening, he had insisted upon driving my car. At eleven, he was drunk, foul-mouthed, and aggressive, and refusing to hand over my keys. Nothing I said could dissuade him from taking charge of my car, which was not insured for him to drive.

The state of his inebriated erratic driving, may be imagined. But having dropped Yvonne back at her home, he set off to drive the twenty-five miles back to my house. I sat in fearful silence, gripping the side of my seat and praying for a police car to appear and stop him. But none did.

Not only was he very drunk, he was also vilely threatening, and scaring me out of my wits. The drunken PP was even more offensive and vile than the sober version, and I was terrified of him. It was a side to his character I had neither seen nor suspected before; he had kept his heavy drinking habit a complete secret from me.

The entire evening had been a disgraceful charade, and seeing him in such a disgusting state did nothing to endear him to me. I sat silently petrified, as the car swerved and lurched about the road, while he cursed and swore at me like someone deranged, and unpredictably dangerous.

The entire evening was a significant moment of enlightenment for me, and I realised this was not someone I ever wanted to marry. PP had frequently and obsessively talked about Beryl as the mad woman he had married. Now I began to understand there probably had been a mad person in their marriage, but it was unlikely to have been her.

After driving in his drunken state, for ten miles along the motor road, he suddenly veered off into a narrow side road and slammed on the brakes. I didn't know what to do. We had come to a halt on a narrow unlit road in the middle of nowhere, surrounded in every direction by woodlands. It was almost midnight, and now he was shouting and raving at me, threatening me in a maniacal way, and accusing me of having stolen his wallet. His behaviour was terrifyingly intimidating, and suddenly I found myself threatened that if I didn't hand over his money what he planned to do to me would result in my body being dumped in the woods.

This display of aggressive, gut-churning bellowing rage, together with his threats of violence, seemed to go on for what seemed ages, and I was reduced to cowering away from him in a state of terror and tears. Then suddenly, he snatched my handbag from me and began rifling through it. His search ended when he tipped the contents all over the floor of the car, and kicked everything about. Finding nothing he was looking for, he followed up by suddenly flinging open the door and storming off into the woodland shouting he needed 'a slash'.

I was left shaking from fear and blinded by tears, as I tried to pick up my things and stuff them back into my bag. Such crazy, unbalanced, drunken behaviour was something I had never experienced before in my life, and all I wanted to do was get away from him. Had he left my keys in the ignition, I would have happily driven off and left him to his own devices... most probably permanently. But drunk or not, he had seen fit to remove the keys, and I was trapped in the middle of nowhere.

When he staggered back, he seemed to have calmed down slightly, and muttered grudgingly that he had found his wallet. But significantly, he offered me no apology for his outrageous behaviour, or his vile accusations. He just climbed into the car, slammed it into gear, and continued the harrowing journey.

I had never been more relieved to see my own front door. All I wanted to do was get as far away from this awful man as quickly as I could, and crawl into bed. However, that was not going to be permitted. He grabbed hold of me and demanded I make him a meal before he would allow me to go to bed.

Having sat in petrified silence for almost an hour, listening to his vile, abusive language and threats, while we drove home, I had no idea what new violence he might be planning to unleash on me, and I was too afraid to refuse. But I cooked the greasiest meal I could think of, and hoped it would give him chronic indigestion for the remainder of the night.

His outrageous behaviour that evening had opened my eyes to the reality of his unbridled, insane, and vindictive real temperament. I had been confronted with a deeply unwelcome reality, and left with serious doubts about the wisdom of any continued relationship with him.

For several days afterward, I ensured I kept a very cool distance, while I considered what my options were for getting out of our arrangement.

I finally made up my mind I would begin detaching myself from the ill-advised wedding arrangements by attempting to recover the money I had loaned him. Then I would reorganise the joint bank account. I realised I was already in serious trouble, and into the situation well over my head. He had cunningly installed himself in my home, and complicated my life and finances with his manipulative arrangements. Now I finally began to realise what a potentially ominous situation I was facing. Somehow, I needed to work out how I could rid myself of him.

I was already aware that the proceeds from his house sale were sitting in his bank account, so I decided to begin by telling him I wanted the immediate return of the money he owed me. In approaching him about the debt, I made no attempt to disguise my belief that he was quite coolly and deliberately intending to defraud me.

Being the canny-operator he certainly was, I am sure he recognised what was going on in my mind, and was already working on some new scheme to prevent me from getting away from him. His first reaction, as usual, was to try ridiculing me, attempting to make me feel stupid and childish about asking for the return of my money. 'Oh wot's the matta wif diddum's? 'As the nasty man takin 'er sweeties? Poor diddum's, won't 'e give 'em back?'

Then he progressed to blatant lying, claiming he didn't have a chequebook at present... that the money for the sale hadn't cleared the banking process... all a pack of deliberate lies, and I knew it.

This calculated prevarication went on for another week, while he put me off with one manufactured excuse after another. Then when his new plan was ready, he arrogantly informed me that he had decided to invest the entire proceeds from his house sale, including the money he owed me, into the purchase of another house, because it was the safest investment we could make.

I was speechless and couldn't think what to say to this outrageous scheme. I certainly hadn't been consulted about this decision, and it came entirely unexpectedly. Without my being given any choice in the matter I was merely told what was going to happen to my money. For sure, I was not going to get it back.

I had handed thousands of pounds over to him, in good faith, as a loan, and now he was blatantly showing me that he regarded the money as his. He had no intention of returning a single penny of it. Now he alone would decide what he did with it, and I could take a running jump if I thought he was returning any of it.

He was pretty clearly, or more or less telling me, 'If you break off our arrangements, you'll get nothing.'

His latest crazy excuse for not returning my money was, as a builder, he was much more knowledgeable about financial matters than I would ever be. No investment was safer than land ownership, along with the bricks and mortar built on it. It was his right to make any financial decisions concerning the money, and he had decided the amount involved, which I kept insisting was mine, was going to be absorbed into a new investment, about which he would tolerate no further argument. He had my best interests at heart, and there was a very good reason for what he was doing.

As a very special pre-marriage 'treat' for me, he had decided to purchase a weekend cottage for us, miles away in rural Wiltshire. A small estate of three-bedroom detached houses, was being built in a lovely village outside of Salisbury, and we would be travelling there to see the development plans the following weekend. Together, we would decide on which one of the available sites we would like to own.

He ended in turning the tables on me and telling me what an ungrateful suspicious woman I was, demanding the return of a trivial amount of money, when my generous husband-to-be was proposing to buy me a country cottage as a wedding gift.

There was nothing I could think of to say to that. It was another victory to PP.

Chapter 11

A Succession of Very Bad Decisions

Without ever bothering to discuss the idea of investing in a country cottage or seeking any agreement concerning the retention of the money he owed me, PP had autocratically decided to incorporate my money into the purchase of a newly built house in Wiltshire. He had already made a provisional agreement with the construction company in Salisbury, regarding which site he was interested in buying... and all before I was even made aware of his intentions.

So far as he was concerned, the money he had borrowed from me had become his money. There had never been any intention in his devious mind of ever returning it to me. Now it formed part of his assets, and was simply being rolled over, and incorporated into the proceeds from his own house sale. Consequently, it remained completely under his control. If I refused to go ahead with our marriage, I would never see, or benefit, from a penny of it again.

It was a case of heads, and tails he won. From whichever position I viewed the situation, I was still the loser.

The new property he was planning to buy was over two hours journey by car from my home. Not surprisingly, the scheme the silver-tongued Dr Jekyll went to work describing to me, sounded both conciliatory and generous. He claimed he wanted me to be happy and for our relationship to flourish. The Wiltshire cottage would be a permanent holiday home for us, and somewhere we could go every weekend. He intended it to be a place where we could relax and enjoy ourselves after the working week, and troubled by no one.

It was one more example of his ingenious schemes, designed to control assets belonging to me, and a clever move to prevent me from abandoning the idea of marrying him. For a while, I was completely blindsided by the plausible plan. The capacity of this man to invent convoluted schemes to deceive me never failed to take my breath away.

And as he was quick to point out, his financial part of the investment was much greater than mine. He was making this generous gesture to show his commitment to our marriage, and he wasn't even asking me for an equal contribution, or any further cash.

What could I say to such an apparently generous gesture? His sudden, out-of-the-blue, and unexpected open-handedness made me feel awkward and embarrassed. It seemed I had seriously misjudged him, and PP was Mr Nice Guy after all.

But of course, it was still early days in our relationship, and I didn't yet comprehend the real cunning depths of the devious and manipulative character I was dealing with. Without involving me in his plans, he had already considered all the potential permutations of the arrangement... just as, in a game of chess, an expert player anticipates all the potential outcomes, challenges, and future consequences that may arise as the game progresses, before he ever commits himself to making a move.

One serious effect of having a weekend place... and an important factor I completely failed to recognise... was that I would be away from my children between Friday evening and Sunday evening every week. Their inclusion was not part of this weekend arrangement. But naturally, that was something he hadn't troubled to mention. And somehow, caught up in the unexpected excitement, I managed to overlook that aspect of the situation myself.

He already had the entire course of our relationship mapped out, and one of his devious intentions was the process of eventually splitting my children up from me. Isolating the three of us for three nights every week was the way the process began. Every weekend, it was going to be just him and me. I would not see, or be able to talk to my daughters. And the process of isolating us from one another, and breaking down our close relationship was already under way.

There was nothing generous or magnanimous about PP. It was a coldly premeditated cruel plan, which at first, I completely failed to recognise. But that was only the beginning of his attempt to drive a wedge between my daughters and myself.

The notion of a weekend cottage built from mellow limestone seemed at first a perfect dream... the ultimate place to unwind and relax after a hectic working week. The village was delightful, with a narrow river meandering through its centre, flanked by flat grassy borders and shady trees, with places to sit and relax dotted along the quiet waterside. This rural idyll was only a five-minute walk from the site he had very thoughtfully selected for our weekend retreat.

Unfortunately, the reality of the proposed relaxing weekends proved to be very different. Apart from working to cause a rift in my family, the scheme was designed to get me tied up financially, and nothing to do with the romance of Salisbury. Romantic evening strolls at twilight along the riverbanks were not among PP's weekend ambitions.

With his eyes firmly fixed on increasing land values and resale prices, the plot he had reserved was a huge corner site, and incorporated a paddock the size of a football field, along with an immense garden. The paddock could not be built on because there were archaeological remains beneath the ground. Hence it was useless to anyone who did not keep horses, sheep, or chickens. And the large corner garden needed to be planted, and regularly tended, while the paddock required regular mowing.

When the exciting plan had first been described to me, I had completely overlooked these multifarious downsides, and the negative effects my regular absences would have on my children and our family life.

All properties require attention, even those only used at weekends, but I naively imagined that looking after everything would be a shared activity. PP would look after the gardens and the paddock, and I would attend to the house.

He had, of course, carefully avoided discussing the subject of how our weekend visits would be managed. And it came as an unpleasant surprise to discover he had a completely divergent set of ideas from me. His actual plans only became clear after the house was bought, and a lorryload of my furniture was installed there. Then on our first visit, I discovered just how he intended the situation to work.

He had absolutely no intention of doing anything at all while he was there... except relaxing and taking life easy. As he so elegantly put it, 'Ah doan keep a dog an bark mesel.'

It became only too clear from the start of our weekend visits, who had been designated as the 'dog' and allocated the job of doing the barking. The reality of the so-called weekend breaks, entailed my being run ragged with gardening, housework, shopping, and all the other duties needing attention. On top of that, I was constantly at his beck and call from morning to night, producing endless cups of tea and sandwiches, along with three-course meals, and incidental snacks during the night, if he felt peckish.

There was no relaxing, weekend break or rest after the working week, for me. The extended, week in and week out round of never-ending responsibilities soon reduced me to the point of exhaustion.

PP managed to keep himself busy reading the paper, or lying in bed snoring his head off, or watching television, while he waited for his next meal to be served on a tray. My scenario was very different. He made very sure he enjoyed his weekend... 'life of leisure in the country', while I became the dog's body, maid of all work, and general factotum, conveyed there every Friday evening to wait upon him hand and foot. Between Friday evening and Sunday evening, I was kept working until I dropped; there was no relaxing weekend break for me.

Invariably I fell asleep on the homeward journey late each Sunday evening. But he always made sure he woke me up when we reached the London ring road, claiming I had to help him to navigate.

It was so late when we arrived back at my house, I didn't even get to speak to my girls before Monday morning, when I was still exhausted, and we were all rushing to get ready for school. His devious scheme was certainly working to plan, and it left me with no time to talk to my children anymore.

To put no fine a point on the situation, for me, the weekend cottage rapidly became a bloody nightmare, and nothing but a burdensome millstone around my neck. Buying it had certainly been a clever ploy on PP's part, for many cunning reasons. For me, I deeply resented ever having become involved with it. There were no advantages whatsoever for me in going there... just grinding hard work.

If I complained of being tired, and needing him to help me, his reaction was...

'it was of no concern to him how I felt. The fresh air must be doing me good after I'd spent all week playing school, and drinking tea in a stuffy office. If I had to work on a building site, I would soon learn what proper hard work really was. Then I would be entitled to take things easy. He, however, deserved peaceful leisurely weekends. Idle twats like me didn't know what it meant to work for a living. Any spineless cunt who idled her way through life as a schoolteacher or a clerk (which was all he considered I was anyway) was a fucking lazy cow.'

That was his outrageous derogatory, and sarcastic opinion, and he frequently took pleasure in expressing it.

Needless to say, he never lifted a finger to help me in any way... nothing new there.

If I suggested we might go out for dinner on Saturday evening, or have lunch out on Sunday, to give me a break and save me from the endless round of cooking, I was informed, in no uncertain terms that...

'if I wanted to eat out I could fuckin' well pay for it... He wasn't going to... And he certainly wasn't there to make my life cushy, or dance attendance on me. He wasn't my fucking entertainment committee'.

After the disgraceful revelations experienced in our visit to meet his aunt Yvonne, and the way I had been manipulated over the weekend cottage, I sank into an emotional lethargy of hopelessness. His intentions for keeping me tied to him by confusing me over the financial arrangements involved in purchasing the cottage had worked. Once again, he had got what he wanted. Now he was back to being the cocksure controlling chauvinist I loathed. And I was more deeply entrenched in the hopeless state of limbo into which I had been manipulated, and no nearer recovering any of my money from him.

I remained in a state of confused ignorance regarding whatever his eventual plans for me were, but I was increasingly troubled about the forthcoming marriage, which I could now see no way of avoiding. It seemed the more I did for him, the greater his demands grew.

Now the point had been reached where I was continually at his beck and call, even to fetching him the newspaper... and responding to his intermittent gluttonous demands for food, couched as queries... 'ave yer gorra samwich?'

This man never lifted a finger for himself. Everything was my job according to him, and I was being trained to...know my place...That was all I existed for... in his eyes.

During the weeks leading up to the wedding, I felt like I was wandering in a dark confusing maze from which I could find no way of escape. I had a growing foreboding that I was about to be compounding a terrible life-changing mistake. But I was always so tired, and my mind was so divided about what was and wasn't true, concerning the integrity of the man I was imminently due to marry, I was living in a state of permanent confusion. I felt weary to death all the time, and so exhausted I felt myself revolving in a depressing and unsolvable dilemma.

That quiet, logical part of my mind was still busy working overtime, trying to bring me to my senses, concerning the dangers ahead. It was haunting my nights, and making me toss and turn, because of these irresolvable worries and uncertainties.

On the evening before the wedding day, my mental state became so agitated I finally developed a full-blown attack of cold feet. In spite of all PP's elaborate and manipulative plans, the wedding veered perilously close to being cancelled. I spent that evening working myself up into a mental frenzy over how little I really knew about the man I was supposed to be marrying the following day. There were a great many aspects of his character I really didn't like, and nothing about him seemed either sincere or caring.

Eventually my brain became so overtaxed I couldn't decide if he was a genuine, trust-worthy person, or a complete rogue out to defraud and ruin me. With my brain at explosion point, I finally reached an impasse and announced my decision to cancel the entire thing and send him on his way.

Having spent hours alone in my room attempting to put the jumble of crazy jigsaw pieces together... beginning with the conflicting circumstances of our first meeting...I eventually came to the conclusion he had been coldly and callously manipulating me from the start. For the very first time I recognised that the entire course of the relationship had been all about him. From our first meeting, he had been working on bending my mind to manipulate and control me. Everything was always about what he wanted; while he never had a kind word to say about me, or Alan or my girls; and never missed any opportunity to impress upon me how useless and stupid I was; how he despised me, and how desperately I needed him to keep me straight. He was constantly lecturing me that without him ...to take me in hand and keep me straight ...I would be nothing...Well, somehow or another, I had managed without him for most of my life...and it had been a very good one...without anybody having...to keep me straight.

The realisation suddenly came to me that ever since I had known him my head had constantly been bombarded by his orders, and his threats, and stuffed with his devious deceits and lies, and conflicting opinions, until I had no idea just where the truth lay, or even what kind of a man there really was beneath all the lies and aggression.

Suddenly all the disjointed pieces seemed to be dancing into shape in front of my mind's eye like a moving film, and I recognised how he had been extracting money from me, and conning me all along. He didn't have the least emotional attachment to me at all. The truth was I was regarded as nothing other than a means to an end... a woman he could manipulate to get what he wanted... which was everything I possessed.

Somehow, he had succeeded in manipulating me into believing his complex lies. He'd conned me into agreeing to loan him money... conned me into opening a joint bank account with him... conned me into housing him and feeding him. He had even conned me into having all my salary paid into a joint bank account. The whole basis of the relationship had just been one enormous series of deceptions and manipulations...one BIG CON. He had been making a fool of me time and time again... and always for his own gain.

This journey towards the altar had continually been littered by his endless broken promises and manipulations; most recently even over the purchase of the cottage in Salisbury. Lately I had discovered he had arranged a standing order with the bank, so that without being aware of it I had been made responsible for paying the council taxes on it. There seemed to be no end to this man's nefarious lies, deceits and schemes to manipulate me. He was treating me like a fool, and working to financially ruin me.

For some inexplicable reason, on that very significant evening, my mind had been freed from his overbearing presence. And it had cleared sufficiently for me to suddenly recognise a wagonload of undisguised truths. Revelations were pouring in fast, and with incredible clarity.

Suddenly my focus turned to his elder daughter, Mandy, the daughter I had never met. She had been estranged from him, and hadn't spoken to him in over three years since he and her mother had been divorced. The cock and bull tales I had been told about everything connected with his family were all, at best, a collection of distortions and half-truths. Every story I had ever heard always portrayed himself as the victim of manipulative deceitful females. If PP was to be believed, there had never been a good woman among any of them.

It was amazing how clearly my brain was suddenly functioning. All my manipulated confusions and muddled thoughts had suddenly become crystal clear. The more of his plausible twisted stories I recalled, along with the other vindictive stuff that constantly poured out of him, the more inflamed my sense of outrage became. All his opinions, and all his weird behaviours were grotesque perversions... nothing other than malicious fabrications, without any trace of affection or compassion attached to any of them. They were all lies, lies, and more lies.

Now it occurred to me that his relationship with his older daughter, Mandy, was the weirdest one of all. Once I began thinking through the lascivious tales I had been told, about how he felt about her, the more I was struck by what an extraordinary father-daughter relationship theirs had been. As I began putting together the strange, fragmented stories he had personally related, I began to seriously consider whether or not their relationship might have been an incestuous one.

He had certainly expressed some very odd, unfatherly feelings for the girl... feelings that seriously stretched the credibility of innocence to its extreme. He had never made any bones about how deeply emotional his feelings for her were; and how it had always given him pleasure to describe how 'passionately fond' he felt of her. Love takes many forms... but surely passion is an unusual way for a father to describe his feelings for his daughter.

Now the accounts I recalled of this strange obsession, began to strike me as predominantly sexual in nature. His feelings were possessive and controlling in the extreme, and over-laid by deeply seated jealousy. His endless stories always revolved around how passionately he felt about her... that word frequently cropped up in his stories... along with how vindictively he had punished her for leaving him. Were these the usual emotional reactions of an average, normal loving father? I wondered.

She was a young woman after all, not a small child. Yet he had drooled about her wonderful slender figure, and her lovely personality, and about how happy she had always been to sit on his knees while they joked and teased, and spent hours playing intimate games with each other...just the two of them. I recalled his accounts of what wonderful times they'd had going to discos and pubs together, and on intimate holidays to the house in Leicestershire; and the caravan holidays they'd shared when only the two of them were there alone. It seemed the rest of the family, including Beryl, were invariably left behind at home.

This sort of intimate one-on-one relationship scarcely added up to normal father-daughter affection...not where adults were involved. I began to wonder if their entire relationship was a healthy one, or was it one that was inappropriate, and a long way removed from the behaviour considered as normal family affection.

With only nineteen years between their ages, he had been proud to admit it had pleased and flattered him, when they were at discos together, and strangers had mistaken her for his young wife. I had also heard about the numerous social events they had shared at meetings of a club for single and divorced parents, known as, Spice-Life-Up. I recalled how he'd boasted many times about the weekend barbecues, and boozy parties he'd taken her to, more as his girlfriend than as his daughter.

Unfortunately for PP, at one of these events she had eventually met and hooked-up with Joe Jackson. PP had gone berserk with jealousy, and had done everything he could to bully her into ending the relationship, when he had discovered she had become involved with Joe. He even related to me, in detail, how he had forced her to stand in his office, like a naughty child, while he ordered her to break off her relationship, and make a phone call to Joe, telling him their romance was over, and that she would never be seeing him again, because she wanted to stay with her father.

She was nineteen years old for goodness sake; but such had

been his obsessive jealousy, and determination to keep her with him, that he had raged and screamed at her, until she was broken and weeping and bullied into obedience. Eventually she had made the phone call he had demanded.

Within days of the incident she had rebelled, turned the tables on him and left home to run off and live with her boyfriend, Joe. Such an obsessive degree of parental bullying and intimidation rarely works for long. And as a determined young woman, she had finally rejected her father's selfish possessiveness and chosen to be with Joe.

PP's reaction to her leaving went beyond all reason. He considered she had wilfully deserted him, and thrown away everything they had meant to each other. She had run off to be with a man he now hated. Driven insane with jealousy, he had gone to her home a few nights later in an insane drunken rage, and had smashed her car to smithereens to punish her for abandoning him.

Now, as I sat alone with my thoughts, on the eve of what was supposed to be our wedding, everything I recalled about this inappropriate relationship suddenly made me realise he had always regarded his daughter as his personal sexual property. She alone was his passion, his fantasy... his ideal woman. It was a relationship of an entirely different colour, from the normal mundane parental one he had with his second daughter, Liz... or, for that matter, with me. He had desired and wanted to possess Mandy, in the disgusting sexual way only a sick pervert wants to possess his daughter.

My mind suddenly did a backward flip to the incident with Liz, when I first encountered her at the hospital. Something unspoken had been uppermost in her mind that afternoon, when out had come tumbling all the terrible things she had been screaming at her father, concerning his deviant sexual behaviour. I needed no further convincing. The man was, without doubt, a sexual pervert. If even a quarter of Liz's passionate accusations were true, PP was not a man I should ever be considering tying myself to in marriage. He was a sick, mentally twisted degenerate.

At eight o'clock that evening, I announced to my daughters and the guests staying with me that I was not going through with the wedding. I was calling it off.

No one ever knew any details of my decision or my suspicions. But that evening I had finally realised just how far I was from knowing even a fraction of what there was to know about this dangerous and perverse man. The marriage was something I had been rushed into, with no real time to think. Now I could see that I had been bullied and manipulated into agreeing to what appeared to be an ill-advised and dangerous union. I was almost sleepwalking into a commitment with a man about whom I really knew nothing either benevolent, honest... or even sane.

The house was thrown into a frenzy for several hours, until those who were with me persuaded me to calm down... and eventually I was talked around and persuaded I was suffering from pre-wedding nerves. My fears were calmed, and I was jollied along until I was persuaded to relent.

Perhaps I had been panicking? The combined opinion of those with me was it was for the best that I should still go ahead with the ceremony as planned... After all, as it was pointed out to me, everything was arranged and paid for.

Looking back, I can only say what a ludicrous, and totally crazy reason that was to proceed with any marriage. The truth of the matter was, that evening my rational subconscious mind had almost triumphed. My future life, and my family's happiness had hung in the balance, with salvation almost within my grasp. But fool that I was, once again I pushed logic aside and resigned myself to putting the blindfold back across reality. Instead of saying goodbye, I allowed myself to blunder ahead, inadvertently colluding in creating a future of perpetual misery for my children and myself.

The final part of the wedding fiasco unfolded the next day, when I arrived at the church. As the bridal car drew up, I saw Norman, our vicar, hurry from the porch to meet me. He was there to enquire most anxiously if I still wanted to go ahead with the wedding, because there was still enough time to cancel it. All I needed to do was get back into the car and drive off.

In all honesty I was dead tired, and my head was still reeling from the previous evening's emotional tussle with my vociferous subconscious. Eventually, I laughed off his suggestion, and gathering my shaky composure, I finally made my way into church.

Standing there, with my mind still in turmoil, I was struggling against the temptation to turn and flee. Such was my uncertain emotional state, I barely heard the words of the ceremony... not until Norman got to the part of the service that required him to ask PP to repeat his wedding vows: 'I, PP take you, Delia to be my wife, to have and to hold from this day forward, for better or worse, for richer or poorer, in sickness and in health, forsaking all others to love and to cherish, till death do us do part, according to God's Holy law. In the presence of God, I make this solemn vow.'

At that point, reality hit me like a fist in the stomach, when I heard his response. With undignified haste, PP interrupted, and kept on repeating, 'Yeah, yeah, ah will, ah will, vicar. Jus 'urry up an git on wi' it. Yeah Ah'll marry 'er. Jus git it over, will yer. Ah wan the cestificat, an' Ah want me dinna.'

I had burned my boats. The deed was done. Now there was no way back.

But PP's responses had shocked everyone who heard them. The sacred vows he had made actually meant less to him than getting his hands on the wedding certificate, and his nose into the feeding trough. No vows were ever sworn with less sincerity than PP's wedding vows to me.

Taken as a series of strange events, the entire sick saga could scarcely have represented a less auspicious collection of omens for the future success of the marriage.

Twenty-four hours later, and with the wisdom of hindsight, if I could have rewound time, I would certainly have played it all very differently.

Chapter 12

Meet Mr Hyde

It was the evening of our wedding day when we arrived in Sorrento. In the warm twilight the air was sweet with the perfume of lemon and orange trees. Fruit and flowers swayed together among the leaves, and swathes of lights twinkled all around the silhouette of the distant bay. I closed my eyes in silent delight, and breathed deeply. This was how I wanted my future to be, forever tranquil and peaceful.

An immaculate tree-lined avenue swept from the Piazza Emanuel in the town centre, to the palatial Hotel Palazzo Victor Emanuel. All around its lush grounds and terraces lay panoramic views of the Bay of Naples, with the brooding outline of volcanic Mount Vesuvius dominating the skyline. It was the most romantic setting imaginable. A more enchanting golden twilight could never be imagined. And being there in the midst of such luxury, it seemed impossible for anyone ever to be unhappy.

We followed the porter through the entrance hall to the lift. Everywhere my eyes alighted, the walls and ceilings were decorated with frescoes and lavish gilding, and the entire hotel glowed with colour and romantic ambience. Such exotic magnificence more resembled the private residence of an Italian nobleman than a commercial hotel. I closed my eyes, breathing in the beauty of it all. I could scarcely believe it... for two weeks the luxury and pleasure of such surroundings were to be mine.

An ornate gilded-ormolu lift silently carried us to our suite of rooms on the second floor, and we were ushered into a small hallway with three doors. One door opened into a beautiful bedroom with two huge beds; the second, into a spacious sitting room; and the third revealed a large en-suite bathroom, with a white marble bath and gilded fittings. Each room was paved with cool, white-veined marble, and all the furnishings were immaculately coordinated in pale willow-green and gold.

Our luggage was left in the bedroom. And when the porter had gone, I walked through to the adjoining sitting room to enjoy the views from the windows. They were floor-length, and had been left open to let in the cool scented evening air, with just a film of lace screening the balcony beyond.

I stood there for a few moments, gazing out at the dark shining waters of the bay, and breathing in the perfumes drifting in from the gardens, thinking that no place on earth could ever be more tranquil or beautiful.

My pleasure however, didn't last long. Loud noises coming from the adjacent bedroom brought me back to earth, and I turned to see what was going on. PP was not in the least interested in our accommodation, or the view. He was sprawled fully dressed, across one of the large beds, pretending to be asleep, and making the most awful snoring noises imaginable.

It was a deliberate expression of his boredom and intended to bring me to heel.

As soon as he had my attention, he began complaining loudly that he was hungry and wanted to eat. Leaving our luggage to be unpacked later, I followed him to the lift, and down to the dining room.

A small chamber orchestra was playing unobtrusively in the background, and we entered to the romantic sounds of Vivaldi. In keeping with the rest of the hotel, the dining room was truly a feast for the eyes. We were shown to our table, and I sat down feeling relaxed and happy. My uneasy feelings from earlier in the day had evaporated, and I looked around contentedly at the beautiful decor.

No dining room could ever have been more pleasing to the eye. Romantic frescoes encrusted every part of the plastered walls and arched ceiling, while the outer wall, comprising of floor-length windows, presented an incredible moonlit panorama of the curving Bay of Naples and its faintly glowing volcano.

The day had been a long one, but now I felt relaxed, with an inner glow of contentment. Two wonderful weeks lay ahead. I had put aside all my fears and doubts, and I was determined to enjoy every moment of this vacation.

As we waited to be served, I noticed PP seemed to be behaving oddly. He had begun tapping persistently on the table with the handle of his knife, banging it up and down like a child. It was obviously being done to draw attention to himself, and I found it quite irritating. Glancing at him, I saw an angry brooding expression on his face.

I was about to ask if anything was wrong, when the wine waiter came to take our order. For some reason, PP suddenly turned aggressive. I was shocked by his unexpected rudeness to the man. He almost shouted at him, telling him to 'clear off' and roughly refusing to look at the offered wine list, demanding beer instead.

I had no idea why he was causing such a rumpus or behaving so morosely. He hadn't asked me if I would like some wine with my meal, so I smiled and reached to take the wine list.

When the waiter politely bent to hand it to me, PP deliberately intervened. Banging it with the back of his hand, he sent the folder flying out of the man's hands and spinning across the floor. Then he roughly shoved him away to prevent me from ordering. His scowl had intensified as the bemused man retrieved the embossed folder. Then twisting his mouth into a sardonic grimace, he snarled, 'Fuck off. She doan want none. She alus drinks more then is good fer 'er. Can't yer see Ah'm avin ter keep 'er off the booze? Just sling yer 'ook.'

I was horrified. What on earth was wrong with him to publicly insult me like that? This display of crass ignorant behaviour towards me was a side of him I had not witnessed before. And it left me choking back tears of shame from such a public humiliation. I could feel the eyes of the other diners on me; they had all heard him insulting me, and were tactfully averting their gaze, but clearly continuing to listen intently. Such a disgraceful display was unforgivable. But he wasn't done with me yet, and stubbornly continued with his sullen petulant attitude.

I did my best to ignore his vile outburst, and tried to make light conversation to brush the incident aside. But all my attempts at light-hearted pleasantries were ignored. He sat morosely poking and prodding at the food when it was served, as though it was poisoned.

He was determined to create an unpleasant scene, and deliberately persisted in exhibiting his vile mood. Something had displeased him, and he was taking it out on me. He was certainly creating the impression of building up to the start of a terrible row about something, and sat glaring at me across the table with a face like thunder.

Suddenly, with no explanation, he stood up and pushed his chair away so violently it fell over onto its back with a crash. As the waiter hurried over to retrieve it, PP roughly pushed the man aside before storming off towards the lift.

By that point I was so distraught I didn't know how to react. Should I hurry after him, or stay where I was? I had no idea what was going on, so I tried to fix a faint smile on my face while I continued quietly nibbling the delicious food, which by now tasted like sawdust in my mouth.

He already had me conditioned to his unpredictable mood changes, and that I was always responsible for them. For some unknown reason, I automatically felt guilty, believing that in some way, I must have offended him, and was responsible for causing this petulant display of bad temper. Perhaps in all innocence, I had inadvertently said or done something to anger him. But I had no idea what it could be.

He was missing for twenty minutes, and when he returned, he seemed even more irate. He offered no apology or explanation for his behaviour, and continued displaying his outrageous aggression, quite deliberately making himself the centre of attention, very much to my intense distress.

He stood behind his chair for several seconds. Then for no obvious reason, he picked it up and began slamming it around noisily. Such a weird display of aggressive behaviour ensured all eyes were on him, and the room became very quiet. Eventually he morosely slumped down onto it, and resumed glowering menacingly at me. He shouted for more beer and reverted to ignoring me as though I were invisible.

I was finishing my coffee when he finally leaned across the table and said in a deliberately loud coarse voice, 'Wot in fuck's name made yer pick this bloody graveyard fer a 'oliday? It's like 'avin ter spend a fuckin' fortnight in the fuckin' British Museum. The bloody place is stuffed wiv soddin' corpses, and that fuckin' wailin' and scrapin' ain't no sort o' music Ah want ter 'ear.'

The discrete chatter in the dining room died, but there was no shame in him. His loud vulgar comments were deliberately intended to be overheard by the other guests.

I bit my lip and cringed from embarrassment. For me such vile behaviour was humiliating beyond belief. My God! I thought. Why on earth is he doing this to me? What am I supposed to have done to deserve this disgusting treatment?

But before I could find anything to say, he again pushed his chair away from the table, stood up, and announced he was going to bed. 'Are yer comin'?' he demanded loudly. "Cause Ah'm lockin' the fuckin' door if yer doan come now!'

I had already experienced a salutary lesson in his uncouth behaviour some weeks earlier when he was drunk. But this inexplicable outburst of vulgarity, and on our wedding day, appalled me. We were guests in an expensive, exclusive hotel, not ignorant riff-raff in some scruffy downtown bar. Such disgusting uncivilised behaviour was beneath contempt. But it was a close replica of the disgraceful behaviour he had demonstrated at the Golden Lion Pub the evening when his aunt was with us.

This, time however, it was much more public, and in a highly upmarket setting. It was intentionally and deliberately degrading, pointedly offensive, and done for no other reason than to publicly humiliate me. I had never felt so degraded in my life. I choked back tears of revulsion and misery, and wanted the ground to open and swallow me.

Without waiting for my response, he stormed off to the lift. And by the time I had scrambled to my feet and followed him, he was halfway to our suite.

Minutes later when I reached it, the door was locked. He ignored my tapping and discrete requests to be let in, and kept me standing outside for five minutes while passing guests stared at me curiously.

Eventually the door opened. But he framed himself in the opening, deliberately blocking the entrance, and intentionally keeping me outside in the hallway. His ugly mouth was twisted into its sardonic smirk, and he continued looking me up and down, as though he had never seen me before, and was assessing me as a lecherous customer might eye up a prostitute in the street.

Moments later, I realised he was waiting until a group of approaching guests were within earshot, so he could humiliate me further. At the end of the corridor, the lift slid to a halt, the doors opened, and several couples who had been downstairs in the dining room got out. When they were a few feet away, he unexpectedly grabbed my arm and said loudly, 'Are yer the womin Ah told the desk ter send up? Ah 'ope yer clean, an not one o em backstreet prozzies Ah've eared abaat... them wot gives a bloke a dose o the pox. Yer Italian whores are worser than 'em in 'Ong Kong fer syphilis.'

There was nothing I could say. I was being subjected to a totally degrading scene, and stood there with my head down feeling completely mortified, and with tears pouring down my cheeks.

The passing guests turned their heads and glared at me, as though I was a piece of filth. They were still craning their necks watching as he hauled me inside the room, before slamming the door.

Once inside, a cursory glance told me what he had been doing in the twenty minutes he'd been missing during our meal. He had effectively been ransacking my luggage. The room looked like burglars had been at work. Every item of clothing I had brought with me was strewn around; even my makeup case had been turned out, along with my overnight bag.

At first, I wondered if he had been searching for money or jewellery. But I was left with no time to consider either possibility, as he instantly launched into a physical attack on me.

What he had found was a packet of contraceptive pills. His reaction was insane and totally beyond reason.

In the following hour, I learned more about his real, inherently violent personality than I had ever imagined possible in the six the months I had known him. Everything he had purported to be had been a charade... nothing except a cunning well-honed act, deliberately fabricated to deceive me.

From our first meeting, he had set out to convince me he was a 'benevolent rough diamond', a 'kind-hearted gentle giant who would never raise a finger to any woman'. This had been the portrait of himself he had cunningly painted for my benefit. And as liars go, I had never met one who was more convincing. Like a gullible naive idiot, I had overlooked his previous disgraceful behaviour, and allowed myself to be won over by his lies. Now

I was being given plenty of reasons to ask myself why on earth had I ever been stupid enough to trust him.

Now, isolated with nowhere else to go and a thousand miles from home, I was trapped. I was married to him, and face to face with his alter ego... a vicious uncontrollable monster who seemed driven by undisguised hatred of me.

Today was our wedding day, and Dr Jekyll had suddenly been replaced by the evil Mr Hyde. There was nothing kind or benevolent about the real man now facing me. The facade had vanished, and what stood in his place was, in every way, the scum of the earth. I was now legally tied to an emotionless savage brute. This was the real man I had been deceived into marrying.

There had been several slip-ups along the way to the altar, when his true personality had almost revealed itself. But that evening following our wedding, the masquerade finally ended. Now the marriage was legally binding there was no further need for pretence... no reason to struggle any longer with the assumed role of Mr Nice Guy.

Six hours after our wedding, the moment of denouement had finally arrived. He had been planning how my future was going to be ever since he had scraped an acquaintance with me six months earlier.

For a man of his volatile, tyrannical temperament, it must have been a struggle to keep his real demonic personality suppressed for so long. But he had worked hard, and had kept up the deception, continually impressing me with his woebegone stories of his first marriage, and his former wife's madness; along with vows of undying devotion and passion for me... until I had finally weakened and had been persuaded to believe him.

Now it was suddenly clear that I had been nothing more than a needy and gullible idiot ever to have been taken in by him. He had played a part worthy of an Oscar, and had cunningly subdued all my doubts when they had arisen.

But the dress rehearsal was over, and we were into the cold light of reality. Now I was facing the cold-blooded character I had been cajoled into committing myself to, and the full horror of the real man behind the illusion, was about to reveal himself.

The time for lessons in violence, brutality, and intimidation had come. I was about to be shown how he intended to manipulate me, and shape my future.

In disregarding his previous episodes of selfishness and singular behaviour, and persisting in blindly continuing to trust him, I had condemned myself to going into this marriage, like a lamb to the slaughter.

Suddenly with my road to freedom finally blocked, I was face to face with my deceiver.

For six months I had been played like the proverbial fish on a hook... And because of my crass stupidity, and my foolish denial of the warnings from my deeply perceptive intuition, I had effectively colluded in my own downfall.

Now I was terrified that he was about to murder me.

Chapter 13

A Night of Terror

At that moment I was bewildered, and terrified out of my wits, to find myself locked in a room with a total stranger... a maniac with a red face and bulging eyes. Before me, this deranged man was lunging towards me. He clearly had every intention of attacking me and causing me harm. He was coming at me screaming obscene abuse, and cutting off all possibility of my escaping from him.

Suddenly, and before I could do anything to protect myself, he grabbed me by my throat. One large hand was firmly and intentionally squeezing my neck so savagely I felt myself losing consciousness, while with his other, he was rhythmically slapping my face backwards and forwards so hard, I lost all sensation of place or time. My legs gave way beneath the onslaught, and I sank to my knees in a dizzy stupor.

This inexplicable violence had erupted out of nowhere. He had come at me so unexpectedly I was incapable of taking in the full brutality of what he was doing. The situation was surreal. I was rendered incapable of defending myself, and so shocked and emotionally stunned my reaction went beyond terror.

Unexpectedly he laid his hands on a heavy metal tray and began beating me about the head with it. I was already on my knees, and as a feeble attempt to defend myself I cowered away from him and flung my arms around my head. But he never stopped battering at my head for a second, and just went on beating me mercilessly. My head, my arms, any part he could make contact with were battered relentlessly.

Then he paused, and dragging me back onto my feet, he began driving me backwards into the bathroom, constantly lashing at my head with the tray, until he had me pinned against the glazed wall. At that point, he suddenly switched his focus back to my face, and became obsessed with trying to mutilate and disfigure me.

I was completely helpless against this merciless attack. I was scared witless, and convinced he was about to kill me. But there was nothing I could do to defend myself.

Grabbing my nose, he suddenly twisted it so forcefully it felt like he had broken it. Then both his huge hands were once again locked around my neck, crushing my throat, and preventing me from breathing... he was choking me, while he relentlessly went on shaking me. Blood was pouring from my nostrils... I could feel it blocking my throat as I struggled to breathe. Red streams spewed in cascades across the room, hitting the walls and running down the marble tiles, trickling everywhere like little rivers of red rain.

His attack was relentless, and he just went on shaking me, and now battering my head against the door frame and the tiled wall, forcing me into a position of terrified, abject surrender.

I suddenly realised he still hadn't finished trying to disfigure my face, when he forced one of his thumbs into my mouth, pushing hard against my teeth in an attempt to break them; and screaming all the while, 'Ahm goin ter shuv yer fuckin' teef down yer froat, an' choke the sodden life art uv yer, yer fuckin' bitch.'

Having split my lower lip and lacerated my mouth and nose, he turned his attention back to my eyes and began jabbing at them with two thick fingers, clawing at the sockets and the eyelids. He now seemed hell-bent on blinding me by gouging my eyes from their sockets

I was sick from terror and in unbelievable pain; blindly staggering about, nauseated by the blood I was swallowing, and terrified beyond words of this devil who was trying to disfigure me and kill me. My face was smeared in blood, my neck lacerated with scratches and bruises, and I was reduced to a state beyond terror and confusion, with no idea why he was attacking me.

Had he suddenly gone mad? How could this possibly be the man I had just married? He was unrecognisable. For no reason I could possibly imagine, a demon had been unleashed in him. And suddenly he was inflicting unbelievable torture on me and screaming filthy abuse at me, that I was...insane... a whore...a sexual pervert...a thief... He was spewing the most degrading filth imaginable at me...

Why? I had done nothing I knew of to offend him. Yet he was spitting at me, and swearing and telling me how much he hated me, and how he couldn't bear the sight of me and wanted me dead.

Unexpectedly, in mid flow, he suddenly released his grip and gave me an almighty push, which sent me skidding crazily across the floor. I lost my balance and fell, hitting my head hard against the marble bath. My condition at that point was indescribable. I was covered in blood, and I could barely open my swollen eyes. Blood was dripping from my mouth and nose, and I was struggling to breathe, while my bruised face and neck were so painfully damaged from his clawing at them, I believed I would be permanently disfigured.

I lay sprawled on the floor, semi-conscious and in a state beyond hysteria. My clothes were soaked in blood. And I was trembling so much I couldn't stand. In an attempt to escape from him, I crawled on my hands and knees into a corner and curled up like a beaten animal.

Only at that point did he produce my contraceptive pills. He walked over to where I was cowering, glowering at me with total hatred. Then slowly and menacingly, he squatted down beside me, grabbed me by my hair, and began forcefully trying to push the entire plastic packet into my mouth.

As I twisted and turned my head, trying to escape from what he was doing, I realised he must have found the packet in my hand luggage earlier when he had ransacked the room. My brain was churning crazily with wild memories and anxieties, but nothing I could remember made any sense, or explained why he was brutalising me. Nothing I could recall could possibly justify the terrible attack he had just launched on me.

Before I had ever agreed to marry him, I had made no secret of the fact that, at the age of forty-one, I did not want any more children. I had told him all the details of my disastrous medical history, and that a further pregnancy would be highly dangerous and would very probably kill me. He already had three children, and I had two of my own. There was every reason for me to take sensible contraceptive precautions.

If finding my contraceptive medication, had triggered the insane attack he had just launched on me, then without any doubt, ever since I had known him, he had been deliberately deceiving me and concealing his true intentions, along with this violent, insane side of his personality. The subject of contraception had never been alluded to before. He had spent six months cunningly worming his way into my life, deliberately manipulating me into agreeing to marry him, with an entire catalogue of false promises, none of which he had ever had any intentions of keeping.

Now, less than six hours after the wedding, he was demonstrating, beyond any doubt, this was a totally loveless union. He was screaming that he hated me and wanted me dead... and all seemingly because I was unwilling to submit to becoming pregnant.

Cowering from him in terror, on the floor of that bathroom, I realised there was no way I could possibly continue with the relationship. Confronting me was a dangerous and unpredictable man, who had the strength and the malevolence to kill me. I needed to escape from him as soon as I could. If I valued my life, I had to leave him. And I must do everything I could, never to become pregnant by such a monster.

I spat bits of plastic from my bleeding mouth. But now, suddenly, he was upon me again. Grabbing my hair, he dragged me across the floor to the lavatory to perform some new form of torture that had formulated in his deranged brain. I screamed, as more pain hit me, this time from the swath of hair he was gripping as he dragged me along. Then my face was being rammed into the lavatory pan, and he was attempting to drown me.

With one foot pressed hard onto my neck, he forced my face right inside the porcelain, and began flushing and re-flushing the cistern until I couldn't breathe. My nose and mouth were submerged by gallons of water; it was suffocating me...drowning me, and I was again fighting for breath...for my life.

Through my swollen eyes I saw my pills disappear in the swirling bloodstained water, along with the last remnants of any trust I might ever have imagined I could feel for him.

Moments later, warm water was pouring across the back of my head and neck. It made the cuts on my face and neck sting, and soaked my hair. All my struggles were futile. His foot remained clamped firmly on my neck, and I couldn't escape. Then some of the warm liquid trickled into the corners of my mouth and I realised, with nauseating revulsion, he was urinating on me.

'Eat shit and die, yer fuckin' bitch,' he snarled. 'No fuckin' cunt will iver stop maa kids from be'in born... not yer, not any fuckin' twat. Jus' try pullin' this fuckin' trick agin, an Ah will kill yer. Yer 'aven't seen the arf yet of wot Ah kin do. 'Ave yer got tha' frew yer thick fuckin' skull? Ah'll kill yer, and that's a promise. One way or anover, yer'll be dead.'

He gave my head one extra hard thrust into the lavatory pan. Then I heard him zipping his trousers, and laughing to himself. He found what he had just done to me insanely amusing. After flushing the cistern again, he stormed out of the room.

Gasping for air, my terror went beyond words. I was left coughing and choking, and fighting back my fear and revulsion as I tried to ease myself into a sitting position beside the pedestal... praying to God that he had gone, and I would never see him again. Then suddenly, to my horror, the door burst open and he was there again, pointing malevolently at me and glaring ferociously. His eyes, still wild with fury, focused like brands of fire on where I was still crouched on the bathroom floor.

I shrank back from him, automatically fearful and shrinking from another attack. But he just stood there watching me, pointing at me, a satisfied sneer distorting his ugly mouth as he nodded his head meaningfully.

'Yer goin' 'ome pregnan' from this fuckin' expensive caper, or Ah'll fuckin' want ter know why,' he snarled. 'An jus' fink on. There'd bettra be no more fuckin' pills, or Ah'll tek yer fuckin' 'ead off yer neck. Yer know naw I'm capible ov enyfink, doan yer? So fink on. One way or anover, Ah will kill yer.'

After that, he left, slamming the outer door behind him and leaving me paralysed by fear of what he was intending to do to me when he came back. He had made his intentions very clear. His plan was to force me into a pregnancy by raping me. I had been given my first lesson in the degradation and insane brutality he could inflict on me. I was left with my brain spinning in fear, and petrified in a torment of grief...terrorised beyond reason.

But deep inside, my emotions were very much alive and burning with a hatred I had never before known in my life. My thoughts were in total confusion. In the few, short hours I had been married to this monster, I had been humiliated, and vilely abused by him, informed that he hated me, and reduced to a quivering pulp.

I could not control the trembling that seemed to have taken control of my battered body. But hatred of him blazed like an inferno in my mind. One thought was uppermost. I have got to get away from this bastard. This marriage is the most terrible mistake of my life. This brute is a sadistic maniac, a total fiend. Somehow, I must get back to England and arrange for this insane fiasco of a marriage to be annulled, before he rapes me or kills me. In God's name, no normal sane man would ever behave like this.

Eventually as reason returned, I gradually regained control of my thoughts. I was in terrible pain, but I struggled to my feet and managed to fill a glass of water, intending to swallow some painkillers. But my throat was too painful to swallow them, and my hands trembled so much I was unable even to hold the glass with both hands.

My terror remained overwhelming, and I lay down for a while. With my swollen eyes too painful to properly open, and my mind in state of turmoil, I just lay there shivering and trembling.

Just before dawn, my shaking steadied and got up. I remained traumatised, but realised I had to pull myself together and plan how I was going to escape from him.

There were things to be done before he came back., and I had to tidy up the blood-splattered bathroom before the maid came in and discovered its wrecked state.

Only then did I examine the state of my face. One glance in the mirror confirmed what a mess I was in. I bathed my swollen, battered eyes and mouth, and did what I could to disguise my injuries with make-up.

My nerves were shot to pieces, and my hands were still shaking so much I could scarcely hold anything. Unbidden tears persisted in trickling down my cheeks, washing grooves in my carefully applied camouflage, and I had to begin again, attempting to patch myself up.

He was still missing at eight o'clock when I rang reception and asked for a breakfast tray to be sent up. I ate and drank slowly, tearing little pieces from the croissants I had been brought. My battered lips and jaw were too painful to deal normally with any food. When I had eaten what I could, I packed my suitcase. Everything was a struggle, but I was making resolute efforts to stay calm.

At nine, I contacted the holiday company rep and asked her to come to my room. I didn't go into any details just explained I urgently needed to arrange a flight back to the United Kingdom as soon as possible.

We were still talking when PP walked in. He instantly sized up the situation. Suitcase and bags by the door, my face heavily made up; dark sunglasses; company representative with documents spread on the coffee table; coat over a chair... clearly, I was making imminent plans to leave him.

Having so recently experienced the full force of his undisguised evil persona, I found it quite a revelation to watch how easily he was able to slip back into his well-practised Dr Jekyll routine. Within seconds, he was all smiles for the young lady visitor... once again assuming the benevolent if rough-and-ready character of that all-too-familiar, regular Mr-Nice-Guy, who I'd previously succumbed to. In a heartbeat, Dr Jekyll was performing his practised affable act on another gullible woman. Only this time, I sat watching his performance, quietly bemused and cynical, and able to observe his techniques and mannerisms without being directly subjected to them.

The secret of his rough disarming charm lay in the way he was able to assume an affable, easy-going, jovial, and familiar manner towards any woman who appeared on his horizon. Not a word or gesture betrayed the vicious personality of his gross alter ego. He was completely in control of the situation... not a trace of anxiety or anger. and as calm and chatty as he had been with me when we first met. Within moments of entering the room, he had smoothly and easily slipped back into the winsome coaxing character he delighted to portray.

He didn't need to enquire who she was. Her name badge and the company logo on her lapel said it all. And after a brief glance at the table, littered with the remains of my breakfast, along with her company files, he had instantly assessed the situation. Taking the friendly hand she offered him in greeting, he hung on to it, drawing her seductively towards him, eyeing her breasts approvingly, and peering closely at her name badge.

With a resigned boyish grin, he said, lugubriously, 'Naw, Jennifer, luv. Wot's all this abaat?'

I saw her glance nervously in my direction as he went on.

'Wot's she bin sayin' ter yer? Ah'll bet she's bin tellin' yer a convincin' pack o lies abaat uz, like wot she allus does ter iverybody? Well, Ah 'ope yer tek no notice of 'er. She does 'ave er little tantrums, like a big kid yer know. Meks up fairy stories abaat uz. Ah've gorra lot ter put up wiv yer know…'er an 'er tantrums an''er constan' lyin'.'

He sighed despairingly. 'Ah've brought 'er ter this mos' lovely place, wiv no expense spared, an all she duz is complain and moan. She abused uz sumfink rotten las' night, carried on summat kronic, hittin' uz , an bad-mouvin' uz, till Ah walked out an lef 'er ter calm down. Screamin' she wants ter go 'ome. Wot can a bloke do? Ah'm the kindest bloke ony womin cud wish fer. Ah reelly don' no wot ter do wiv 'er, an' that's a fac.'

The puzzled woman glanced from him to me, while I maintained a horrified stunned silence.

He kept eye contact, gazing at her sorrowfully before leaning towards her and whispering conspiratorially. I heard odd words.

"istory of madness', 'bin secshund'... And I recognised, in disbelief, how quickly and cunningly her manner towards me was being modified. I saw her expression change, as she finally succumbed to his rough charm, and accepted unquestioningly, the lies he was spinning about me.

While I had been distressed and agitated during our brief conversation, PP was now on the scene taking charge, and calmly spinning her a yarn about how he was the long-suffering husband of a deranged madwoman, who was attempting to run away from him... escaping again. Something in his twisted, weirdly charismatic personality always facilitated this plausibility, and made it possible for him to spin his outrageous lies to make them sound completely truthful and convincing.

'Well,' she began, clearing her throat nervously. 'I've been explaining to your wife that it's impossible to arrange a flight back to the United Kingdom. There are simply no empty seats available. I'm sorry you're not enjoying your holiday, but I'm afraid you're stuck with the reservations you made.'

PP turned a tortured expression towards me, and shook his head as though he was dealing with a perverse child. 'Wot on earth meks yer fink we're goin 'ome? Wot a silly womin yer are. Weear would yer be wivout uz ter keep yer straight? We're 'avin a great time 'ere. Yer sed so yerself only las' night.'

Turning back to the rep, he shrugged in despair, and gave a deep sigh, followed by a mournful, helpless poor-me look. Tapping his head significantly he said, 'She ain't right in thee 'ead. It runs in 'er fambly. She gits these moods on 'er, weer she meks up lies and tells weird stories abaat uz. Tells folk Ah does bad fings to 'er...beats 'er up an such which. Well, as yer can see, it's all bloody lies and 'er mad fancies...stories inside 'er 'ead. Ah'm the mos' kind-'earted bloke yer cud ivver meet. She'll 'ave ter see the docter agin wen we git 'ome. May ave ter go bak inter the mad'ouse agin. It's a terrible struggle, but Ah puts up wiv 'er.'

He pulled a sad face, and wagged a chastising finger at me. 'Yer 'aven't bin takin' yer pills agin, 'ave yer?'

I was rendered speechless by this convincing, and totally conscienceless performance, along with its pack of incredible lies. My heart sank, and I realised I was not going to be allowed to escape from him. I was trapped. And now he had worked out what I had been planning, he would make sure I didn't get away from him until he was good and ready to get rid of me himself.

He had already told me what his plans were for the following two weeks, and silent tears began to trickle down my face again. His every intention was to ensure that, when I did go home, I would be pregnant with his child. Now it seemed nothing could stop that from happening, except for an act of God.

The rep looked embarrassed. I could see from the look on her face that he had already convinced her I was certifiably mad, probably psychotic. She avoided looking in my direction and said nothing further to me.

I continued watching dumbly, as she gathered up her files and papers as quickly as she could, mumbling an apology for not being able to help. Then PP walked her to the door, muttering things I couldn't hear, but assumed were more lies concerning my alleged insanity. And I saw her nodding sympathetically, as she momentarily rested her hand on his arm before she left.

So, this was his new game. If I disagreed with him over anything, he intended to paint me as a hysterical mentally deranged woman... a psychotic and a pathological liar.

It was unbelievable. I just couldn't understand what was driving him to do such wicked things to me. But his degrading behaviour triggered memories of some of the stories he had told me. I recalled some of the terrible accusations he had made about his first wife. He had regaled me for hours with his fanciful stories of Beryl's crazy behaviour; even describing in gory detail how she had been sectioned for three long periods in psychiatric institutions. Now he was busy reinventing the same line in fantasy tales about me... this time, to beguile another gullible female into believing I was mad.

Suddenly his perverse deceptions became much clearer to me. This was an insane mind game he played, where he made the rules, and only he knew it was a game. He actually enjoyed making fools of the women he abused. In his twisted brain it proved how superior he was to all of them.

'Dear God,' I whispered, 'please help me. Somehow, I have to escape from this diabolical bastard.' I remained immobile, sitting where he had left me, and silently suffocating in fear of what was going to happen to me next.

He had no capacity to have any sort of genuine feelings for me... or for any other woman for that matter. But he had made it abundantly clear he intended to force himself upon me repeatedly, and without mercy, until I was pregnant. The very thought of him ever touching me again, and forcing me into an unwanted pregnancy, repelled me beyond endurance. I felt my hysteria returning.

He closed the door once Jennifer had gone. Then ignoring me completely, he stormed into the bathroom and began slamming things about. I guessed he was planning to take a shower before going to bed. Where he had been all night was of no interest to me, and if he decided to sleep all day and ignore me, that would be a relief. I just wanted to keep as far away as possible from his evil presence.

For a while, I stood on the balcony, trying to calm my mind. It was a beautiful morning, and the warmth of the early sun felt soothing on my ravaged face. As I gazed out towards the darkly smouldering volcano, its brooding power and concealed violence reminded me of the man in the next room, and I prayed urgently for divine help. There was nowhere else for me to turn.

Perhaps I was mad. Alan's death was again uppermost in my mind. Ever since he had died, I had been desperate to find respite from my grief. I had done all I could to try and put my mind in neutral, so that I didn't have to endure living with the unbearable pain which refused to leave me. Had I been unconsciously looking for some sort of support to help my heartache to heal? Or was I simply in need of someone to offer me some degree of compassion... someone to empathise with my despair... or maybe just offer me a kind shoulder to lean on?

I most certainly had not been looking for a substitute husband. I'd just wanted basic kindness and friendship I suppose... nothing permanent or complicated... just another human being to be a compassionate friend.

Whatever it was my soul had cried out for, as a result of my confused state of mind, I had somehow ended up getting myself involved in marriage to a virtual stranger. This vile wretched product of the devil himself, had inveigled his way into my clouded mind, playing a cunning manipulative part. And now, with the marriage a legal certainty, he had revealed himself for what he really was. I needed legal help as soon as possible, and a permanent way of escaping from him.

I stood, silently praying to the clear, empty, blue-sky for help.

It was a desperate cry from my heart. I stood there in wretched contemplation and self-loathing, castigating myself for the senseless bad judgment I had been drawn into.

Moments passed in this state of deep despair. Then slowly and unexpectedly, a sense of calmness settled on my mind. I realised my frequently disregarded inner guide was still with me. This time it was advising me to make a record of everything that had happened. I was being prompted to write down all of PP's abusive, and manipulative behaviour towards me, and keep a careful record. Spoken memories and mental recollections, are no substitute for written records made at the time of the events. If I kept to my legal intentions, such evidence could be vital.

At my first opportunity on returning home, I must take my notes to a solicitor and begin the process of having the marriage annulled. For the present, I needed a safe space, well away from PP... somewhere I could hide myself and quietly begin writing.

This time I heeded that wise voice of sanity. Very stealthily, so as not to be overheard, I took a sheaf of headed notepaper from the drawer of the writing desk and stuffed it into my handbag. Then after arranging a large floppy sun hat and oversized sunglasses to hide my battered face, I grabbed my jacket and let myself out of the room

Waiting downstairs at the reception desk, I found it impossible to avoid the curious stares of the guests who had witnessed PP's behaviour in the dining room the previous evening. But I got what I wanted, a duplicate key to the bedroom suite.

Then I set out to find sanity in Sorrento. I needed to escape from PP's overpowering presence. But I also wanted somewhere secluded to calm my traumatised mind and organise my thoughts, while I recorded the shocking experiences of the past twenty-four hours.

The hotel's people carrier took me to the centre of the town and left me with a list of pick-up times for the return journey. I was temporarily free of the man. For the entire morning and afternoon, I was at liberty to spend as long as I wanted wandering along the shopping streets, thinking and planning, or sitting in a bistro drinking coffee and writing.

In the ten months since Alan's death, the memory of what peace of mind had always felt like had vanished from my life... crushed into oblivion like a lovely butterfly beneath the boot of a Neanderthal.

Had it been possible, I would never have returned to the hotel, or the vile man lurking there. To me, he was nothing but a monstrous predator... a destructive cold-blooded python, existing only to crush all hope from me and destroy me. He gloried in his own savagery, and clearly achieved some sort of sadistic pleasure from his remorseless brutality. I had just bound myself to a man who gained satisfaction from humiliating and manipulating me, a monster who planned to see me dead. PP was something unnatural, a creature with no conscience, and incapable of human emotions. It was beyond my understanding how any human being could be so unfeeling and so evil.

After wandering around for a while, I found a quiet backstreet bistro and settled myself in a corner to clear my mind and write. Sitting there alone, nursing my painful injuries and my remorseful indignation, I began to review the events of the past six months, which had brought me to the appalling predicament I now found myself in.

There was no hiding from the facts that I was partly to blame for my present situation. My bereavement had left me emotionally vulnerable, frightened of being alone, and convinced I was about to die. Unexpectedly, my normally perceptive brain had gone into an overdrive of self-doubt, where I had drifted, like a rudderless boat, into the very murky waters inhabited by a cunning predator...the malevolent python, PP. He was a man to whom no sensible woman should ever allow herself to fall prey.

But it was too late for self-recriminations. Unfortunately, I was now his wife. And after just twenty-four hours, I was already bitterly regretting that commitment. Learning that he despised and hated me, had come as a terrible shock. But having quickly absorbed those facts, I was not someone who would easily fall to pieces over his distorted opinions of me. My only way forward was to take positive action, and legally get him out of my life as soon as I could.

I remained in my thoughtful solitude for several hours, lingering over coffee and salad, while I compiled my notes. Getting rid of him was not going to be easy. But no matter what else might happen, I must keep my resolution to escape from him foremost in my mind.

I sat for a long time, mulling over my disastrous predicament, but ended still nowhere nearer understanding the full horror of his twisted behaviour, or how divergent from normality his sadistic brain really was.

Behind my sunglasses, my eyes involuntarily began to overflow again. I was emotionally desolate, and physically so bruised and battered I felt close to mental implosion. I was attempting to deal with so many terrible things inside my head all at one time, I just couldn't cope with them all.

In my heart and mind, waves of yearning for Alan constantly overwhelmed me. The terrible pain of losing him had never left me, and more than anything else, I longed to feel his loving arms suddenly wrapped around me, cradling me tenderly, and reassuring me everything would soon be all right. Alan had always been there for me, with endless loving support and encouragement. Surely none of my current terrible experiences could be real? They must all be part of a nightmare, and surely when I awoke, they would all have disappeared

I would have given the world if only that could have been true. But I knew, in reality I wasn't asleep. My injuries were real. They were painful; and the rest was just a bereaved woman's foolish fantasy. I was conscious, wide awake, and not wandering inside a waking nightmare.

The reality was, I was battered and bruised, and sitting in an Italian bistro with my record of events stacked neatly in front of me, wondering how on earth I was going to survive the situation I now found myself in. The rational part of my mind reminded me Alan was dead; he couldn't help me.

When I eventually completed my notes, I folded them into my bag. They were smeared and smudged by tears. But I had done what I had set out to do, and made a written record of my night of hell.

It was almost six when the chauffeur took me back to the hotel. I dreaded having to see PP again, but forced myself to return to the suite. I let myself in, feeling deeply apprehensive.

It came as a surprise to find the entire place in silence. I made some coffee, relieved to discover he was missing, and happy to think he must have gone out.

Unfortunately, he hadn't. And on hearing me moving about, he began bellowing at me, demanding that I must come to the bedroom immediately.

My feelings of terror returned instantly. I didn't trust him and had no wish to see him, so I hung back, trying to ignore his demands. But he persisted, shouting that he was ill and needed help. The bellowing continued, and eventually, out of curiosity, I opened the bedroom door and looked in, determined not to go anywhere near him if I could avoid it.

My mind was already made up. That night I intended to sleep on the sofa in the sitting room, fully dressed if need be, and with a heavy metal pole from a patio sunshade beside me, so I would at least have a fighting chance if he attacked me again.

I found the curtains were closed, and the room smelt foetid and sour. He was rolling about on the bed, his fat face pallid, and glistening with perspiration. I could see he was feverish. He was sweating, retching and vomiting, writhing about, and making an outrageous fuss about the level of his abdominal pain.

I stood watching him silently, hovering in the doorway for a minute or two, feeling strangely detached and emotionless. I might have been watching a movie. Not a flicker of empathy or even pity for him registered on my emotions. In that moment I knew he would always be a stranger to me, and not even a tiny part of me felt remotely sorry for him.

He was genuinely ill, having gone down with an unpleasant infection... something akin to gastritis or gastric flu, which was affecting his entire digestive system.

It almost seemed like an answer to my prayers, and I felt a surge of relief, and stirrings of exhilaration, knowing his vile plans for the next two weeks had unexpectedly been cancelled.

Instead of raping me daily as he had been planning, he was confined to bed with his condition. For the rest of the holiday, he enjoyed nothing except drinking boiled water and eating boiled rice, while the bacteria played havoc with his system.

There he remained, confined to bed, continually moaning and complaining about everything, while I kept away from his infection and slept safely on the sofa.

But every day, and totally without any feelings or compunction, I abandoned him to his miseries, and let the people carrier take me into Sorrento. My two weeks were solitary. But for me that time of aloneness was a respite and infinitely preferable to his despicable company, and his never-ending demands.

That solitary time came like a gift from heaven. It liberated me temporarily, and created a space from the fears and apprehension that had haunted me since Alan's death. The terrible pressure lightened, and the fear that I was about to die eased.

I realised I could make my way in the world alone, and that whatever happened as the result of my ill-advised marriage, I needed to hang on to that thought. I even came to terms with the fact that there was no one I could appeal to for help, because there was no one in the world to ensure my survival except myself.

The very last thing I had ever needed in my life was a manipulative brute like PP. He would never show me any compassion. All he would ever do would be manipulate me, and plot and scheme to drag me down into despair. I needed to steel myself to survive.

In that short space of time, enough common sense returned to make me realise there were far worse things in life for me than being alone. I could and would survive. But how I was ever going to reach my intended destination of freedom from this terrible man, I still had no idea.

PP's sudden illness was an unexpected gift... a temporary pause in his plans, which made it possible for me to enjoy Sorrento, and the beautiful Bay of Naples, in ways I would otherwise never have found possible. My spirits were raised to find temporary respite from his controlling brutality, and to find myself released from any possibility of returning home pregnant.

Above all else, my two weeks alone gave me time to think... time to consider the mindless stupidity of what I had done, and time to consider my survival as a single woman, should I ever find my way out of this mockery of marriage to which I had committed myself.

Those few golden days in Italy were to be my last opportunity to savour the precious feeling of freedom for a very long time to come.

What I blanked from my mind was that my foreseeable future was still going to be lived with him. The brutal PP would always be close by, forever menacing me, and constantly controlling me. I entirely failed to predict that in the life which lay ahead of me, nothing would ever be happy or peaceful again.

Chapter 14

Master of the House

For PP the expensive holiday in Sorrento, which he had funded, became a bone of contention, and a bitterly resented waste of his precious money. For him, no part of it had gone to plan. He had been forced to spend the entire two weeks in bed alone with a stomach infection.

However, for me, it became a memorable holiday for an entirely different set of reasons. I had experienced the shocking and violent denouement of the evil man I had married. I had been humiliated, beaten, and abused beyond belief, by him. But I had learned one significant fact... that without any shadow of doubt the marriage had no prospects of success, and at some point, I already knew it was destined to end in disaster.

As I travelled home from Italy, I had plenty of time to consider my options, and face the fact that I needed to bring the marriage to an end as soon as I possibly could. A swift divorce was the best way to resolve the fiasco, and the sooner I could achieve that result, the happier and healthier I would be.

From the moment we left the hotel to the time we arrived back to my house on the Sunday afternoon, he barely spoke to me, except in angry grunts and petulant monosyllables. He was ridiculously peevish and unpleasant, and childishly determined I should know how furious he was with me. He refused to be seated next to me on the aircraft, or even tolerate standing beside me while we waited in the airport. Whatever lay at the bottom of his vile mood, he was making a public spectacle of demonstrating to me that he was working himself up into another mammoth rage about something, and I was being held entirely responsible for the foul temper he was in. Whatever was going on in his convoluted malevolent brain, it was my fault, and I was going to be made to pay for it.

I had no idea what was currently bugging him, and I had no intention of stirring him into further spontaneous violence by enquiring. But I was nervously aware he was building up to some sort of outburst, and I spent the entire journey completely on edge. Sitting in the car, alongside his seething hulk hunched over the steering wheel, my stomach turned to liquid acid. It felt like I was sitting next to a constipated gorilla with a grenade stuck up its arse, and being put through mental torture while I anticipated its imminent detonation.

I felt nauseous and fearful all the way from Gatwick to my front door, and I just wanted to get inside quickly, and hide from whatever he was planning to do to me once we were behind closed doors.

As soon as the car pulled to a halt in the drive, I grabbed my cases and headed off to open the front door. I had reached the foot of the stairs before he caught up with me. Grabbing me by the shoulders, he roughly swung me around to face him.

'Not so fast, womin,' he snarled. 'Ah got sumfink ter tell yer afore yer run off 'idin upstairs. So yer'd better lissen up, an tek notiss, cos wot Ah 'ave ter say, Ah mean.'

My mouth instantly went dry, and I began to tremble all over, as fear once again gripped me. I felt my heart speeding up, and the pounding inside my chest thumping like a machine. But I remained silent, wondering what I had now done to displease him.

Standing on the second step of the stairs, I was on eye-level with his intimidating glowering face. I sensed his rising fury, and I knew he was preparing to attack me.

Suddenly, his left hand shot out and grabbed my throat, restricting my breathing and forcing my face over to one side. Then he began jabbing with the index and middle fingers of his right hand, aiming first for my left eye then my right one. It was a familiar replay of what he had previously done to me in Sorrento now starting all over again. He had me painfully immobilised by my throat and was launching another attack on my face.

After savagely gouging at my eyes, he repeated his trick of pushing his thick fingers beneath my lips, pressing hard against my teeth in a renewed frenzy to break them. Then suddenly, he changed back to attacking my face with the slapping technique I had also previously experienced... a hard slap left, followed by a hard slap right, first the palm of his hand and then the back of it, backwards and forwards, knocking my head from side to side almost rhythmically, while he continued choking me with his other hand.

All the while this abuse continued, his evil face was grinning maniacally, and his glaring eyes were boring into my head. I could see he was enjoying the agony he was inflicting on me. He was deriving sadistic pleasure from it. Without any shadow of doubt, this pervert enjoyed watching me suffer and enjoyed seeing my terrified reactions to what he was doing to me.

The choking and the pain were intolerable, but I knew if I cried out or tried to struggle, his game could change in a moment and become even nastier.

Suddenly he transferred both his hands to my neck, with the thumbs pressed hard against my windpipe until I couldn't breathe. Then he forced me from the steps and down onto the hall floor, on my hands and knees until I was cowering in front of him while he towered over me. I was in a position of subservience before him, and that made him happy. He kept one foot pressed hard down onto the fingers of my right hand, gradually constantly increasing the pressure. It made escape impossible, unless I was prepared to break my own fingers in a frantic struggle to extract them.

'Naw! Air yer lissenin' womin?' he snarled. "Eers wot yer goin ter do termorra. Yer goin ter git daan ter the solicitor an git this 'ere 'ouse put inter my name. Cos Ah'm master 'ere, an this 'ouse an evryfink innit blongs ter me naw. An then yer'll git ter yer bank an git me fifty fowsan pouns in cash. Ah've married yer, an' naw ah wants yer dowry. Ah reckon payin' me fifty fawsan fer marryin' yer is a bargin fer an ol' whore like yer. Yer gorra bit ov a bargin gittin a big 'ansom bloke like me. Wimin yer age doan git decen' blokes like me nokkin on ther dor ivvry day, not decen men wots willin' ter marry 'em. Ah shud axe fer more, bu' Ah'll settle fer the fifty fowsan.'

'What?' I gasped in disbelief. 'Don't be so ridiculous. I'm not going to do any of that. You must be mentally deranged. Is this some sort of sadistic joke?'

The pressure from his foot eased slightly, and I finally wrenched my fingers from beneath his size elevens, and struggled to my feet.

'You are an indescribable brute.' I gasped. 'We're not living in the dark ages, or in some primitive Far Eastern feudal state.' I was still coughing and gasping from his strangulation efforts, and struggling to recover my breath. 'This is my house.' I choked, deeply distressed. 'It's got nothing to do with you. You must be mad. No one has a dowry anymore. That archaic tradition disappeared into history with the Victorians, and I'm certainly not handing any sort of dowry over to you. I'm giving you nothing. You owe me thousands already.'

He gave a sneering half grin. 'Yer talkin' a load o shit, an' fuckin bollocks, womin. Av ah not git frew yer fuckin' thick skull yit. This is mah 'ouse naw. An Ah'm not askin'. Ah'm tellin yer. Git it signed over inter me ritful name, an' get uz tha' dowry. Ah've married yer. An' from naw on yer'd better do wot Ah'm tellin yer, yer fuckin twat, or it'll be the werse fer yer. Doan say Ah did'n' worn yer. Yer'll soon fin out wot sort uv a joker Ah am if yer try defyin' uz.'

His entire demeanour was terrifying, and his bloated face had turned scarlet and contorted with rage. I watched in a mixture of disgust and terror as he ground his teeth, and frothy white spittle began foaming at the corners of his mouth.

Suddenly the violence erupted again, and he unexpectedly lashed out at me. I had no time to avoid the unexpected blow, and his right fist landed directly beneath my chin.

The experience was incredible. I felt myself lifted from my feet and sent spinning through the air, amid cascades of bright blue stars. The incident could only have lasted for a brief couple of seconds, but momentarily, I experienced something I had never seen before... exploding fluorescent blue star-lights bursting all around my head.

Reality, in the form of terrible pain overwhelmed me, when I suddenly came down hard on the solid corner of the brick hearth in the hallway. The tender area directly beneath my left kneecap took the full impact, and the terrible pain I felt, left me convinced I had been crippled. Blood was pouring from my tongue, which I had bitten in the attack, and I was in so much pain I couldn't get up. I lay stunned and bleeding on the hall floor, sobbing my eyes out in unbelievable pain and distress.

But true to form, the unspeakable wretch never paused or offered to help me. His intention had been to hurt me, and he didn't do remorse. He just turned on his heel and walked out of the open front door, got into the car, and drove off.

Another significant lesson had just been delivered for my enlightenment by this devil I was now shackled to. My pain was unbearable and I was left in abject despair. But there was no other recourse open to me, except to lie bathed in tears and blood until I was able to drag myself onto my feet and upstairs to bed.

I was still sore and bruised from the beating I had taken in Sorrento, and now I had good reason to believe he had permanently crippled me. My face and my tongue were already swelling, and my knee was so painful I couldn't stand. The knee injury did eventually leave me with permanent problems, which still continue to trouble me.

But violent criminal behaviour such as PP inflicted on me, was not at that time recognised by the law of our land. There was little point in my attempting to complain to the police about his violence. I was not some stranger he had attacked in the street. I was legally his wife. And so far as the law appertained, (at least at that time,) he could treat me however disgracefully he chose… with legal impunity.

I believe he would have had to kill me before the police would have become interested. They did not consider domestic violence serious enough to be a reportable crime however brutal or damaging the injuries might be. A man attacking his wife was dismissed as just another 'domestic fracas'. And there was no legal protection for any woman to prevent what PP was doing to me from happening again and again.

I was understandably terrified of him, and I had no idea what other injuries he might suddenly feel motivated to inflict upon me. But I was forced to accept that until I could find some way of escaping, I was completely at his mercy… especially now I had resolved never to relinquish my home to him, or hand over my finances.

His evil personality had no redeeming or altruistic side to it. He was exactly what he looked… a coarse and brutal, vile, manipulative animal, of whom I needed to be constantly very wary and very afraid. Marriage had made me his prisoner and his victim, and I was only at the beginning of what might very well be a life sentence of tyranny.

Until Alan's death, my only experience of men had been based on his personality, which was caring, loving, and compassionate. I had imagined deranged brutes like PP only existed in fiction, or living among the lower criminal classes, or locked up in Broadmoor with the criminally insane.

But for the duration, I was legally condemned to remain the victim of this violent man. Not by accident, but by design, I had been selected for what I had, and what he wanted. He was never going to let me go until he had coerced and stolen everything from me that I owned... or was dead. There was nowhere I could turn for help.

That night, I was kept awake by the agonising throbbing of my injured knee. As I lay unable to move, my distress went beyond words. Every defensive emotion I felt was outraged by his sadistic criminal brutality.

How could I ever have allowed myself to be hoodwinked into marrying such a brute? It was clear all my earlier suppressed suspicions had been well founded. But his devious play-acting and cunning charades had well and truly fooled me. A vicious swine like him didn't have it in him to feel any genuine concern or affinity for me. Nor would he ever deal kindly with my children if he was left in charge of them.

I thanked God for the foresight I'd had before the marriage to draw up my legal will; if I died, it would stand. And if he eventually engineered my death, by one means or another, he would find his plans for getting his thieving hands onto my daughters' inheritance well and truly thwarted.

It was obvious there was no way I could physically fight him without some significant weapon in my hands. But I made up my mind to defy him and never comply with his demands, even if he killed me in the process.

All that night my mind was in a state of turmoil. I was sick from pain, and terrified. But lying there in the darkness, I decided the only way I could handle the ludicrous demands he was making on my home and my money, was to do all I could to avoid the subject ever being mentioned again.

In dealing with a warped mind like that of PP, my idea of ignoring his demands was never going to succeed. He was inflexible, brutal, and resolute... totally focused on getting exactly what he wanted... and by using whatever brutal means he deemed necessary. This had been his original objective from our first ill-omened meeting. And he had gone to some trouble to demonstrate to me that he was someone who always achieved what he set out to do. My refusal to comply would achieve nothing. My idea of playing at being an ostrich with this man was naive.

Everything he was doing to me was part of the scheme he had devised long before we had ever met. I had been on his radar for five years before he had actually inveigled an entrée into my life. Hearing of Alan's death had been the catalyst that had set matters in motion again. With my imagined assets of millions, and no relatives to speak of, I had been lined up as a very desirable and easy target to satisfy his avaricious ambitions. What madness was that?

Having already made so much progress with his long-term plans, he had no intention of giving up. For a scheming, relentless psychopath, like PP, no scheme is ever abandoned until it has been successful completed. And until he finally had his thieving hands on all he coveted, he had no intention of letting me escape simply because I refused to cooperate with him.

He had given me an order, and I would disobey it at my peril. My persistent refusal to hand over my house, and fifty thousand pounds, unleashed a year-long convoluted campaign to break me, and compel me into submission with his will. It was a relentless violent vendetta he intended to carry out, and one such as I could never have imagined.

During the following twelve months, he brought to bear not only extremes of physical violence, but also excruciating mental and psychological torments as well... each one a calculated malevolent intention aimed to drive me to the edge of suicide, or into insanity, or both. The convoluted repertoire of sadism that PP enjoyed using on me was so terrible I could never have imagined one human being would deliberately inflict such sick brutality upon another.

He made no threats, just got on and carried out his barbarous programme, with never a solitary compassionate thought ever entering his brain.

For me, there was to be no let-up in his campaign, and no respite to my misery and despair... not before I had either capitulated or been destroyed by him.

Chapter 15

A Year to Break Me, Part I: Father and Son.

There were still several weeks of the school summer holidays left, and within a couple of days of our arrival home from Italy, PP had brought his son to live in my house. There had been no preparatory discussions about how we would arrange the coming together of the two sets of teenagers, and I had never been consulted about the arrival of the youth. Neither did I have any idea regarding what PP had said to the boy to prepare him for living with a family he didn't know.

I had anticipated some initial difficulties, at least while the boy learned to adjust to life in someone else's home and got used to different family rules and ways of doing things. Based on the brief encounter I'd had with him months earlier at his father's house, I was anxious about his initial antagonistic attitude towards me. His disobedience and rudeness on that occasion had been appalling, and I couldn't imagine how I would ever get along with such a difficult youth.

I soon discovered my fears had been well grounded. From the day his father brought Steve to live with my family, the boy was determined to cause trouble. The pair of them were living in my home and at my expense, yet their behaviour was immediately abominable. Neither of them showed me any courtesy or even respect at all. Neither of them even attempted to be pleasant.

From day one, PP had wasted no time in making it abundantly clear that I must never attempt, in any way, to exert any authority over his son, or correct him for any reason. I was not in charge of him, and the boy was aware of that.

'Mess wiv ma lad, yer bitch, an'yer'll git a basin fullo'wot yer diserv. Keep yer nose arta moi lad's busniss, an doan go frowin yer wait abaat tryin ter tell im wot's wot... Ee alriddy nows ee dusnt av ter tak ony notis iv yer. Ah'm the only won ee as ter lissen ter'.

Consequently, the boy was aware he had carte blanche to do whatever he chose. He had been given the power to cause untold mischief for me. It was an intolerable position to have been placed in within my own home.

Within days, the pair of them began actively taking over control. I rapidly found I was increasingly being treated like an incidental nuisance, who was tolerated only to make their lives comfortable. My function in my own home was reduced to that of a servant. It became increasingly apparent that my life, and my authority as the owner, were being invidiously usurped.

The first significant indications of how things were going to be for me, living on a day-to-day basis with my two new residents, came on the Sunday morning, the day after Steve moved in. I was downstairs in the kitchen when PP finally emerged from bed.

My experiences in Sorrento had speedily awakened me to the truth about the man I had married. He was far from being any kind of 'rough diamond'. He was, in fact, a ruthless, vicious deviant, with long-term plans to take over my life. This two-faced monster had wasted no time in demonstrating that his secret agenda in marrying me had always been to control and manipulate me, and ultimately rob me of everything I owned. Several deeply worrying and seriously unpleasant things about him had emerged... the first being his unpredictable, aggressive, and physically abusive personality. The second was his tyrannical determination to be obeyed. And the third was that he was the laziest and greediest person I had ever had the misfortune to encounter.

In the short time they had known him, my daughters already detested him, and had begun spending as much time as they could upstairs in their bedrooms to keep out of his way. That was where they were that Sunday morning when he sauntered into the kitchen.

I had set five places at the table with the usual crockery, glasses, and so on and put out the three breakfast cereals we normally ate. There was a large jug of milk and another with orange juice in it. The toast rack was in place, waiting for the toast I intended to prepare when the family sat down. There were also egg cups and a bowl with uncooked eggs in it, along with a bowl of bananas, as well as marmalade, sugar, salt, and such. Everything was ready for our normal Sunday breakfast.

PP glared at the table the moment he walked in and then slumped down on a chair, scowling ominously. 'Wot's fer brekfas?' he demanded aggressively through clenched teeth, as he eyed the boxes of cereal.

'What we always have,' I replied mildly. 'There's muesli, Rice Krispies, or Weetabix. Or I can make some porridge or boil some eggs and make toast; I've put the marmalade, orange juice, and butter out all ready.'

The words were barely out of my mouth when he let out a horrible roar; leapt to his feet; and, with one almighty swipe, sent everything from the table crashing onto the floor. The contents of the cereal packets went flying in every direction, while the glass jugs were smashed into smithereens, with lethal shards scattering everywhere, mixed with milk, orange juice, and eggs. Everything was instantly splattered across the tiled floor, together with the marmalade jar and everything else that had been on the table. The mess was unbelievable.

I stood speechless, looking at the appalling chaos he had deliberately created. My little dogs were instantly terrified, and tried to hide under my dressing gown to escape this bellowing monster that had descended upon them. They were trembling and shaking and trying to climb up my legs. Shards of glass and china were strewn everywhere, and it looked like a bomb had just exploded in my kitchen, while I remained frozen to the spot from shock.

Before I could remonstrate with him, he barged over to where I was standing and grabbed me by my throat, shaking me like a rag doll and screaming into my face. 'Yer fuckin' hore, 'ow dare yer put that chicken shit in frunt ov uz an' expek uz ter eet it? Yer ain't deelin wiv yer soft twat Alan no more. Ah'm a reel man, an Ah wont proppa fud. Yer ain't deelin wiv a fuckin mouse no more. Ah wan a proppa brekfas. Doan yer ivver dare put tha' sorter shit in frunt ov uz agin, or Ah'll stuff it daan yer fuckin froat, brokin glass an' iv'ryfink.'

He kept on shaking and choking me, while tears flooded down my face. Then he violently threw me down among the mess he had created, and kicked me hard in the ribs.

My knee was still swollen and very painful, and I struggled to get back onto my feet; but as soon as I did, he pushed me down again among the broken glass and china, and kept me there with his foot on my back. My hands and knees were already bleeding, but he continued to loom over me, red faced and furious, maintaining the pressure with his foot, and screaming repeated threats and insults at me.

Then dragging the tablecloth from the table, he threw it over me and screamed, 'Naw, git yer fuckin pans an' git cookin' uz sum proppa grub, yer lazy fuckin' twat. Ah wan bacon, eggs sunny side up, sossiges, fried bred, beans, mushrooms, and termaters. An' ah wan it naw! Git moovin, yer lazy cunt, or Ah'll top yer! An' git this fuckin' mess cleend up while yer at it. Yer keep this fuckin' place like a fuckin' pigsty.'

The savage reality of what I was facing is impossible to explicitly describe. He removed his foot, and stood glaring at me, grinding his teeth. I was bleeding and in pain, and rigid from terror. But he continued menacing me, leaning on the table with such a terrible expression of hatred on his face I really believed it was more than my life was worth to utter a single sound… convinced if I did, he would kill me.

Terror was his stock-in-trade. I had already learned that in Italy. And that Sunday morning he appeared so full of hatred, he really seemed to be anticipating some trivial excuse to kill me.

There was nothing I could do except empty the fridge and

cook what he was demanding. As I put the piled-up plate of food in front of him, he snarled. 'Wier's the ketchup? Ah allus 'as termata ketchup wiv a fry-up. Tha's summat else yer'd betta rememba in fucher…if yer doan wan anovver slap.'

Watching the obscene pig shovelling food into his ugly mouth was more than I could bear, and as soon as he was slurping and belching and covering himself in grease, I began attempting to clean up the mess he had created.

He was still belching and farting when I went upstairs to the bathroom to attend to my injuries. My hands and my knees had splinters of glass in them, slivers I needed to pick out with tweezers. When I had finished disinfecting my injuries and patching myself up, I quietly went downstairs into the study, to keep out of his way. I was struggling to keep myself calm by focusing on some schoolwork I needed to complete. But I was trembling and in such a state, I couldn't hold my pen to write.

From across the hall, I could see the back of his head, and I was only too well aware of the continued noise of his obscene belching. Then he moved from the kitchen into the drawing room, and sprawled across the length of the sofa with the newspaper.

Very quietly, I closed the study door.

At half past eleven, the door suddenly burst open.

'Oi you! Wot yer sulkin in 'ere fer?'

'I'm working,' I said quietly, biting my lip and trying to maintain a placid non-confrontational manner.

'Well Steve's jus gorrup, an' ee wonts 'is breakfas'.'

I gave him a withering look and quietly replied, 'I'm not

cooking anything more this morning. My hands and knees are very sore. And, as you can see, I'm working. Steve's fifteen, and you've already made it very clear he's your son; he doesn't need a nanny. He must have made his own breakfast plenty of times before, and he knows where the fridge is. I have more important things to do than dance attendance on him. In this house, nobody is a servant.'

He crossed the floor to where I was sitting at my desk faster than I would have believed possible. Grabbing me by the hair, he dragged me from my desk and frogmarched me into the kitchen, where his son was already sitting at the table grinning maliciously and holding a knife and fork in his fists.

With an almighty push, I was sent sprawling into the middle of the floor.

'My lad wan's 'is breakfas',' he shouted. 'An yer fuckin' well 'ere ter mek it fer 'im naw, yer lazy cunt.'

'No! I won't,' I said angrily, getting unsteadily to my feet. 'I'm not here to dance attendance on him. You've brought him here. He's your son, not mine. You've made that very clear. So why don't you see to him yourself!'

Brave words indeed. Or a foolish attempt at defiance?

He came and stood right up against me, pushing me into retreat with his huge belly, until I was pressed against the sink. Then he commenced jabbing at my chest with his clenched fists, much as a boxer might jab a punch bag. His face was scarlet, and he was breathing heavily, working himself up into a fury at my refusal to obey his order to feed his son.

Meanwhile the odious youth continued sitting at the table, enjoying the scene. It was clearly very entertaining for him, and he was grinning excitedly and pounding the table with his cutlery, watching his father's furious display of aggression, as he continued battering me in my stomach until I vomited into the sink.

Finally, PP gave me a really hard blow, which knocked me to the floor. Then placing his foot firmly against the middle of my ribs, he stood grinning down at me. I'd seen that sardonic look before, but I was struggling to breathe because of the weight pressing down on me. He ignored my distress and continued shouting at me. Then moving his foot, he began kicking me in my stomach. I was helpless to fight back, and overwhelmed by the nauseous urge to vomit again.

'Yer'll git back ter tha' cooka an' mek me lad 'is breakfas', yer bitch, or Ah'll chuck yer aou in the street weir ye b'long an' lock the fuckin' dor. 'E wan's 'is breakfas', same as wot Ah 'ad. So ther's yer fuckin choice womin. Feed 'im er yer goin aout on yer arse'ole. Jus' see if Ah really mean it er not.'

While this terrible scene was being played out, the youth sat at the table grinning and laughing, and shouting encouragement to his father. The humiliating performance had been put on for his son's benefit, and was meant as to demonstrate to him who now ruled the roost in my home. It must have convinced the pair of them their takeover was going very well indeed.

That morning's humiliation left me seething, with an inexpressible, deep and silent hatred for that pair of indescribable brutes, both of whom had been installed like loathsome leeches in my home without any invitation from me.

I was being deliberately humiliated by PP... beaten to a pulp by him and torn apart, both physically and emotionally. And to add insult to injury, he was sponging off me, contributing nothing to either his own, or his abominable son's maintenance. My appalling situation left me with a burning desire for revenge.

As the weeks passed, I became increasingly depressed by my invidious situation. I now realised this controlling behaviour was part of PP's scheme to establish his dominance, and keep me paralysed by intimidation and fear in order to coerce me into relinquishing my home to him.

I had chosen to dig in my heels, and refused to comply with his grotesque demands. Consequently, he was resorting to a campaign of total brutality and degradation to break me to his will, and drive me out of my own home.

One evening, a week or so after the breakfast incident, I returned home from work to discover Steve upstairs lying on my bed. He claimed to have a bad cold. However, germ ridden or not, he had managed to ransack my bedroom and turn it into something resembling a bomb site. He was sprawled across the bed surrounded by the contents of my dressing table drawers.

It was obvious he had skived off school, with the excuse of having developing a bad cold, and returned home to entertain himself in my bedroom, ferreting about to see what he could find to amuse himself with. His ransacking of my private possessions had produced a collection of letters from various deceased members of my family.

I walked in on him to find my property strewn everywhere across the room. The entire collection of correspondence between my father and mother from before their marriage, was now strewn about, all screwed up and scattered over my bed and the floor of the room, like so much wastepaper.

I was outraged.

Among the debris were letters written to my mother by her father when she was a small child. Those letters were family history, and had been written to her from the trenches of the Somme during the First World War. There were dozens of love letters written to me by Alan, all dating from before our marriage, along with every kind of personal and intimate document imaginable.

Now everything I treasured lay torn and scattered about the floor and the bed. My family's private and sentimental correspondence had been rifled because of the prying curiosity of the vile teenage yob who had ransacked my room to find it, read it, and destroy it... simply to amuse himself.

Now he lay sprawled on my bed, arrogant and shameless, surrounded by the scattered evidence, with not a shred of embarrassment. I had caught him, red-handed, ripping stamps from the envelopes and crumpling the correspondence, tearing much of it into shreds. The mangled evidence of his unspeakable prying and vandalism lay everywhere around him.

I was so incensed by what I found that afternoon my first instincts were to attack him physically. But at six feet tall, he was much heftier than I was, and I realised I would stand no chance of even scratching him, if I gave way to my outraged feelings.

Controlling my anger, I said quietly, 'I think you had better go to your own bedroom. If you are ill, you shouldn't be spreading your germs about in here. This isn't your room, and we have to sleep in here tonight.'

He slithered off the bed slowly and insolently, with a self-satisfied sneer. Then he deliberately turned, picked up a pillow, and wiped his snotty nose on it, before throwing the filthy thing at me. After that, he slowly sauntered along the landing to his own room, coughing and spluttering as much as possible, and for maximum effect.

When he reached his bedroom door, he turned to face me and demanded, 'Ah want sum paracetamol an a 'ot drink. Yer'd betta go an git thim fer uz naw, or Ah'll tell me dad.'

'If that's what you want, then you can go and get them for yourself,' I replied coldly. 'It appears you've had enough energy to ransack my bedroom this afternoon, poking about, and prying into things that are none of your business. If you want anything...then go and see to yourself, you disgusting boy. I am not running about after you.'

As I turned and went back into my own bedroom, I heard him slam his door in a peevish fit of temper. I was quite sure his father would get some distorted version of the incident when he arrived home.

After surveying the scene-of-destruction he had left behind, I took three deep breaths and began the task of rescuing my vandalised documents. Inside my mind I was burning with outrage; but I struggled to keep calm and gathered up the torn crumpled pages, and did what I could to piece them together.

Never before had I ever experienced such tangible and growing hatred for anyone. But now this new overpowering emotion was very much alive inside my mind, and directed towards the two disgusting pieces of filth currently usurping my home.

I constantly feared for my own and my children's safety, but could find no solution to my invidious situation. It seemed I had become impaled upon a proverbial, beds of nails and trapped there, with no realistic or practical way of escaping from the constant abuse.

I couldn't even be sure I would survive my current situation. But I knew, come what may, I would never hand my property over to the two monsters I was currently being forced to house.

My home was being turned into a madhouse by two perverted lunatics, who had no intention of leaving. I was being terrorised by the pair of them, with no means of defence against either of them. Before any of us had realised what was happening, this awful pair had descended on us, hell-bent on taking over our home, along with everything in it.

Suddenly my daughters and myself had become incidental unwanted occupants, and my position had been relegated to being the provider of whatever the usurpers demanded. I was ignored and disrespected at every opportunity. And nothing I said or did mattered a jot to either of them.

I didn't know how to handle the situation I'd become enmeshed in. My girls were increasingly unhappy, and I had no way of getting the intruders out of our home.

Steve was the same age as Samantha and a year younger than Nathalie. He was a large youth, heavily built, and of the same mental disposition and physical appearance as his father. And he had no interest in school. All I had been told about the situation was, for his last year at secondary school, his father would be driving him there each morning and collecting him each evening.

My own children were talented and bright, with every prospect of obtaining good academic grades, and eventually moving on to university places, without any expectation of serious problems arising to prevent their success. All my concerns were focussed on my daughters' future. The increasingly disruptive effects the two miscreants were having on their education was worrying me sick, and I was painfully aware that my girls were becoming increasingly unhappy.

An endless succession of horrendous changes was continually being forced upon the three of us. Now I was increasingly being forced to accept PP and his son weren't living with us. We were being relegated to living with them.

I had anticipated the situation of having two strangers living in our home would gradually settle down and become more normalised, once we all got to know one another. But it had quickly become obvious that was never going to happen. This pair of aggressive conscienceless guttersnipes was intent on taking possession of our middle-class family home... while laying claim to everything in it we possessed and dominating and destroying our lives There was no denying it... they were determined to drive us out.

Chapter 16

A Year to Break Me, Part II: Gateway to the Maze

$\mathfrak{I}$ was in despair, and constantly having to remind myself that it wasn't yet a year since Alan's death. Before I'd had had time to come to terms with my sudden devastating bereavement, I had fallen into the hands of PP. Now with the arrival of his diabolical son in my home, my family's life was being destroyed piece-meal on a daily basis.

I was in an invidious and vulnerable situation, both of mind and body, and stressed beyond belief. I was permanently living on the knife-edge of PP's outrageous mind-blowing behaviour.

Inside the monstrous skull of this man, there was no Mister Nice Guy, although his earlier highly plausible tactics had been cleverly designed to convince me there was. The truth was I had been cunningly, and very rapidly manipulated into marriage, before I had time to regain my ability to differentiate the truth from his cunningly developed fiction.

Marriage to him had instantly cancelled out all the rubbish he'd spun me about being 'a diamond geezer'. And I had woken up to discover I was married to a foul-mouthed, loathsome bully, whose fixed intentions were to steal my property and destroy my life.

My vulnerable teenage daughters, Samantha and Nathalie, were helpless to defend themselves. They were too young and inexperienced to help me combat the pair of criminal delinquents we were now housing. Very soon, they too were destined to become victims of PP's malevolent behaviour. They were already being forced to accept their normal family way of life was systematically being altered beyond recognition, by the appalling usurper who was manipulating their mother into becoming someone they no longer recognised.

They had no insight into what I was actually being subjected to. All they saw was my apparent personality change, as I was turned into an erratic woman, who appeared to be running herself ragged trying to please the horrible man who had moved in on them, along with his delinquent son.

Perhaps a psychiatrist might have had an explanation for my confused, personality disintegration. I only knew I was floundering, like someone who was drowning, with no help at hand. I was barely surviving, and in a state of constant confusion, unable to swim against the force of the current dragging me into the depths of despair.

Very soon, my children began to feel rejected by me, as the destruction of our family unit got under way relentlessly orchestrated by PP. Whatever the strange mental influence PP was exerting over me, it was akin to the perverse charismatic miasma Hitler had used to hypnotise the German masses. Such an evil, overwhelming, mesmeric, psychopathic power lay completely outside of logical explanation.

It was the relentless charismatic insanity of a madman, and something I still do not fully comprehend... although I am well able to recognise the crazy parallel.

When I had refused to sign my home over to him, I had no idea of the level of brutality he would resort to in order to bend me to his will. My previous experience of ruthless brutality was non-existent, and it had never occurred to me that this was how his twisted brain worked. In truth, I barely knew anything about PP's real character or his twisted psychology.

How could I have guessed that, before he ever met me, I had been selected as the objective which he intended to pursue relentlessly?

His deranged brain rendered him an intuitive master of psychological propaganda. He had intentionally inveigled his cunning way into my bereaved mental state to prey upon my emotional vulnerability. It was a cold and calculating process, carried out with the sole intention of convincing me he was the strong, dependable, pragmatic person I needed to get me through my distressing grieving process.

Now, with his son in residence to reinforce his brutal behaviour, he had begun to push forward his intentions of destroying my mind, by a clever system of brainwashing. He intended to destroy my rational senses, and bring me to a state of confused despair, verging on hysteria and mental breakdown.

But breaking me mentally, still had not been achieved. I was most certainly terrified of him, and deeply confused by his erratic behaviour. But my powers of reasoning still persisted, and I was not so totally dominated by him that the fundamentals between right and wrong were completely suppressed in my brain.

I was entirely inexperienced in the controlling mind games he was playing. But he knew they worked, because he had already played them with his first wife, Beryl. She had endured twenty years of his vile intransigent behaviour, and now he was endeavouring to use the same methods to control me.

His perverse game plan was aimed to establish the idea that I must accept everything unpleasant he was doing to me; because as he enlightened me, 'ahm ere ter put yer rite, cos it's the only way ter mek yer inter a betta persun...neebody kin live wif the selfish kindo bitch yer ere.'

He claimed he wasn't treating me badly, and I was frequently reminded...

'The punishments my outrageous behaviour was forcing him to carry out on me, were corrections I deserved, because I was disobedient, and lazy, greedy, selfish, and spiteful; and in need of systematic sound thrashings, to sort me out, and force me to see the error of my ways, as he struggled to turn me into a better person.'

He was hell-bent on convincing me that I was deranged. So he set about endlessly lecturing me, that unless he could see some signs of 'improvement in my attitude and my behaviour' very soon, he would have to begin the process of having me sectioned under the Mental Health Act, and committed to a psychiatric hospital... just as he had done with Beryl.

He claimed the evidence of my mental derangement was my 'bloody ridiculous behaviour' since he had married me. I was a stubborn, opinionated, unpleasant, and selfish...a madwoman it was impossible to live with.

This was the constantly repeated mind-bending propaganda I was forced to listen to both day and night.

I was continually reminded that it was necessary for me to be....

'moulded into a different behaviour pattern, because all my life I had gotten away with behaving badly. I was a stupid selfish child, who needed to be brought into line. I had been spoilt and indulged all my life, and had never learned how to relate to other people... especially where a relationship with a decent, normal red-blooded man was concerned.

'My arrogant behaviour was all my 'stupid mother's' fault. She was the silly cunt who had caused my problems. She had spoiled me rotten and allowed me to get away with my demanding selfish behaviour, all my life. The best thing she had ever done for me was to die five years ago. She was at the bottom of my problems, and it... wuz a fuckin good job she wuz naw ded.

'For years I had been married to a stupid brainless twat, who was nothing better than a soft stupid bugger... a pathetic excuse for a man and a brainless mouse who was too weak and useless to take my outrageous behaviour in hand and teach me what any half-decent bloke would expect of his wife. And that was obedience.

'Alan had been a useless ignorant bugger... a feeble excuse for a fucking man, happy to let me run everything, and give me and his fuckin kids whatever we demanded...

'Fuckin Alan wuz a dickhead, as thick as pig shit, an 'appy ter let yer treat 'im like a fuckin doormat... a fucking twat content to live quietly under yer fuckin control'

'But he was dead now, as well as my fucking mother, and his place had been taken by a proper man... a man who lived in the real world, not some fairy-tale pretend place. In the real world, a woman had to be taught to know her place. My place was under him now, and he didn't take orders from a stupid cunt like me. He wasn't there to dance attendance on me, and I'd better get my thick brain around the fact that I was there to do as I was told, not give orders.

'My outrageous, selfish, self-centred behaviour meant I needed a few slaps at regular intervals to keep me in line, and force me to face the truth about what a brainless cunt I really was. I needed to remember I was now married to a real man, who was not prepared to put up with anymore of my nonsense. So, the sooner I got my thick skull around those facts and accepted how the future was going to be, the better it would be for me. Or I'd find myself ejected into the street on my earhole, or confined in a madhouse.'

Such was the substance of the invidious and relentless brainwashing and mental conditioning I was constantly subjected to. It was a daily non-stop tirade, and went on... and on... and on... like a loop recording that was endless. He was determined to condition me into the belief that his obscene behaviour was normal and entirely acceptable; while my behaviour was that of a mentally unbalanced and insanely selfish and opinionated child.

There was no valid excuse, nor any justifiable reason for this abusive and bullying behaviour. Nor was there any excuse for the insulting collection of vile insults that he directed against my husband and my mother... neither of whom he had ever known. Having to listen to his tirades of abuse against people whom I loved dearly was, in many ways, worse than enduring his physical violence. I couldn't defend them, or prevent him from spewing the disgusting filth he enjoyed expressing about them.

The mental and emotional pain he was deliberately inflicting on me was shredding my deepest emotions into little pieces.

This scheme was being carried out relentlessly and systematically, with the intention of breaking down my mind, and implanting in it the acceptance of his superiority and dominance over me.

Next on his agenda, in his psychological plans to undermine me, was to attack my professional qualifications, and the validity of my career and my work.

The entire fabric of my life had to be rubbished, and everything I had ever achieved reduced to worthless trash to debase and humiliate me, and destroy my self-esteem.

He had decided I must to be convinced that everything about me was worthless and wrong... I had no opinions worth listening to, and I was just a stupid numbskull idiot. Very rapidly, I found myself being continually harangued with vile denigration regarding my academic qualifications.

Among the endless litany of derogatory, brain-washing lectures I was now forced to listen to, I was informed...

'The ony reason yer ivver git bummed up ter becumin' an 'ead teacha wuz 'cause, the powers wot be wuz tekkin any rubbish ervailibil, an jumpin' em up ter mek eejits like yer look importan... an' cos nuffink betta wuz ervailibil jus then. Ony Tom, Dick, or 'arry as more brains in ther likkle fingas an yer... Yer jus pig-igoran, and nuffink betra van a road sweepa, er a low-daan scrubba oos 'ad a lucky break... Oonvarsety is jist sumweir ova privliged rich rubbish loik yer gan ter play silly buggas fer a few yers, an git laid. Bluddy wais uv space...bluddy oonavarseties... full uv bluddy twats loik yer.

'Ah've git aal th powa aah need in me 'ands, ter git yer sacked ony time ah wont. So womin, if yer wont ter to keep yer fuckin stoopid job, yer'd betta buck yer ideas up, and dee evryfing ah tells yer in fucha...er aal git yer fancy job tekken orf yer, an then yer'll be aat on yer eer 'ol wiv nuffink.

Every day, and by every disgusting means he could invent, this evil man's deranged, hateful behaviour towards me was screaming the undeniable truth into my face.

This man is my enemy. He is working to demoralise and destroy me by brainwashing me. He is continually endeavouring to undermine my self-confidence and self-worth. His intention is to do his utmost to denigrate, and annihilate my past, and undermine my self-esteem. He is working to condition me into accepting his physical and emotional violence as though it is normal behaviour. He is endeavouring to convince me that he is all-powerful, and I have no choice other than to accept what he has decided I deserve. I am being trained, as he would train a dog, by beating me, and intimidating me into submission.

I couldn't handle the excruciating awfulness of my situation, and I had no realistic way of blocking it. There was no place where I could escape from him... I was trapped, with no one to turn to for help or advice, or even minimal physical protection. Consequently, as I could achieve nothing in my own defence, he was left with free rein to systematically continue eroding my life more and more, as the days passed.

It gave him pleasure to see me crumbling beneath his violence and abusive onslaughts. Everything he found fault with was always my fault, and nothing to do with his deranged psychotic personality. His behaviour, in every respect, was beyond question and always justifiable, and it was persistently being impressed upon me... that I was forcing him to beat me... in order to make me see sense, and mend the errors of my ways.

Propaganda is only as effective as the people who are persuaded to believe it. And PP was an expert at creating malevolent propaganda to suit his own ends. Plus, he possessed a cunning tongue, and the determination to see that his plans succeeded. By using every devilish scheme his twisted brain could devise, he intended to dispossess me of my home, along with everything else I owned... including my self-worth and my family.

Driving my children away from me was an important part of his evil plans. He intended to isolate me from them, and eventually turn them against me. He had decided they must both be driven out of the house.

His divisive schemes had worked with Beryl. Now he meant to use the same alienating methods to drive my children from me. What had worked once would be made to work again. And this time, my children and myself were his victims.

Once he had me totally isolated, he would decide how to dispose of me... time, place, and method to be decided later. But first he needed to completely break me.

I feel certain that any perceptive, rational person viewing the situation from the outside, would have been able to identify this man as a sadistic emotionless predator... an aberration of humanity, devoid of all normal human emotions. I meant nothing to him, except for being the victim he had selected to manipulate, rob, and destroy.

Looking back on that terrible time, I have no idea how I managed to blank these realities from my normally stable, pragmatic brain. I was fighting just to survive, and to hang on to the last vestiges of my mental rationality.

Bringing his delinquent son to live in my home gave him additional physical support, and helped reinforce his determination to gain the upper hand, not only over me but also over my daughters.

It was a time of particularly severe distress for them. They were young girls, teenagers, already struggling to come to terms with the sudden death of their beloved father.

To them, my behaviour appeared crazy, and beyond anything they would ever have expected from me. It seemed as though I had suddenly become a different person, and turned into someone they no longer knew. I had allowed this terrible man into their home, and I was doing nothing to prevent him from destroying their fragile happiness and security. Tragically, his aggressive intrusion into their lives left my children with indelible emotional scars.

I still regard all his behaviour as wicked and unforgivable. But I will always castigate myself for my weakness in failing to prevent the situation from happening in the first place; and even more, for allowing it to continue as it did, to the detriment of my children's welfare. I still believe I should have been able to find some way of stopping him.

Perhaps I should have killed him... I have sometimes thought a more violent woman would have done. I doubt if the law would have vindicated me, and I know I would have been imprisoned. But he had me trapped as his prisoner in the isolation of invidious abusive and emotional persecution. It was a truly terrible place; and one from which, even with the passing of time, I could see no escape, except by death.

The appalling events PP increasingly inflicted upon my daughters began one Saturday morning during that first October. Samantha was musically gifted and identified as such when she was just six years old. She played the piano, the oboe, and the violin. That month, she was preparing for her imminent grade six violin exams, as well as for an important music festival.

That Saturday morning, she was in the drawing room practising her violin pieces when PP came down for his breakfast. All the internal doors were closed, and very little sound was escaping from her practise session. He slumped down at the kitchen table, expecting his usual cooked breakfast to be served immediately.

Then he suddenly shocked me by leaping onto his feet and bellowing through the adjacent serving hatch at her, 'Shut the fuck up, wi' tha' fuckin' catawallin'. Ah wan' me brekfas' in fuckin peace'. Go an stick yer bluddy fiddle daan the fuckin lav. It's bluddy murder. Its mekkin the fuckin' milk go off. If yer doan stop tha' fuckin' racket Ah'll fuckin smash the soddin' fing over yer hed.'

My defensive parental hackles instantly rose at this outrageous outburst of aggression directed towards my child. But I recognised by the glowering look on his mean face this was no joke. I had bought Samantha the expensive Van Dolling violin after her father's death. It was not her first instrument, and she played it beautifully.

In the other room, Samantha suddenly stopped playing. Knowing PP's unpredictable volatile behaviour, the idea of him smashing the instrument over her head had scared the living daylight out of me. However, for some inexplicable reason, Samantha treated his threat as a strange sort of joke, and as he sat down again, she pushed the serving hatch open, stuck her head through and pulled a face at him. 'Ner naw, ne ner naw,' she chanted playfully in response.

Within seconds, I saw her expression change to one of terror. The thunderous look glaring out of PP's livid face was no idle warning. And the truth suddenly registered with her... His words were no joke; he really had meant exactly what he had threatened. Within a heartbeat she rapidly scrambled to escape from what she now so clearly recognised as imminent danger.

With great presence of mind, she darted out of the drawing room, her violin tucked under her arm. And acting on a commendable self-preservation instinct, she ran to the interconnecting door between the kitchen and the hall, where she shot the retaining bolt into place, before haring off for her bedroom to lock herself in.

He, meanwhile, wasted no time in getting out of his seat and heading for the kitchen door to grab her, clearly intent upon carrying out his threat to destroy her instrument, and launch a physical attack on her. From the vile look on his bloodshot face, I was left in no doubt he intended to thrash her and smash her instrument to matchwood. But he found his progress blocked by the bolted door.

His insane rage, and violent aggression towards my child had terrified her, and it had also scared the life out of me. I felt my heart thumping alarmingly as my adrenalin surged, and I was instantly provoked into defensive mode to protect my child. Enraged by his obviously intended violence towards her, I was instinctively motivated to act in her defence.

I gave no outward sign of my enraged reaction, just silently and resolutely picked up a large carving knife. With my heart pounding madly, and every nerve in my body and mind inflamed, I waited resolutely, ready to strike and gripping the knife behind my back, with the fully focused intention of using it to kill him.

If he laid so much as a finger on my child, I would stab him in the back, with all the force I could muster and then telephone for the police. This monster would never be permitted to attack either of my children, without receiving instant retribution from myself. If I had to kill him to protect them, I was ready to do it.

I was trembling like a leaf with emotion, but wired and ready to act. My mind was resolute. If he succeeded in his intention of breaking through the door to attack my daughter, I was psyched up to react. Every nerve and fibre of my body was fully prepared to defend her against him. Despite the violence he constantly visited upon me, and disregarding whatever faults he had persuaded me to believe about myself, I was a mother, and I would never stand by and allow this deranged brute to lay a finger on either of my children.

That morning, my resolve to take defensive retaliation was never eventually tested, and the knife remained concealed harmlessly behind my back. Thwarted by the secure bolt, he set about attempting to kick the door down to get at my daughter. Fortunately for everyone, the bolt continued to hold. But he was so insanely enraged he didn't stop his crazy efforts to demolish the door until he had succeeded in kicking a huge hole in the lower part of the wooden panelling.

Then, true to form, as in the aftermath of all of his previous physical attacks, he stormed out of the house and drove away. I can only assume he spent the hours of his absence scheming and designing new ways to punish my children, in order to increase their fear and unhappiness, and as a means of driving a deeper wedge between them and me than he was already causing.

The following day, he calmly informed both of them that they were henceforward not permitted to display any photographs of their father in their bedrooms or anywhere else in the house. If he found they had disobeyed him, the pictures would be burned, and they would be punished by being deprived of food for twenty-four hours, or longer, until they came to him on their knees to humbly apologise for offending him.

Any other family photographs he could lay his hands upon would be torn up and binned immediately. I took this threat as being directed at me.

Just how demonically sadistic, this new example of his savage behaviour was for the three of us, cannot be adequately described. Nathalie and Samantha were distraught by his outrageous spiteful ban. Suddenly, every last visible trace of their dearly loved father was to be obliterated from their everyday lives, and from their father's home. This monstrous man was changing the normal structure of all our lives, and I constantly castigated myself because it was all my fault. I had allowed him into our home, and now he was taking from our lives the last vestiges of all our remembered happiness and normality.

Later that day, I quietly gathered up all the family photographs I could find and smuggled them out of my house to school, where I kept them safe in the locked security cupboard in my office.

His next vindictive attack on my children came when he announced the end of their monthly clothing allowance. They were to be deprived of something we as a family had decided on two years previously, when they were twelve and thirteen years old. Nothing this tyrant did was ever in consultation with me, and each new edict came as a complete shock to all three of us. Their monthly clothing allowance had been agreed to replace their weekly pocket money, and had come about quite reasonably when our daughters had asked to be allowed to choose and buy their own clothes.

Now because PP was making it his business to scrutinise the joint bank statements every month, he had found the regular withdrawal I was making for my girls' allowance and had decided to use it as another vindictive means of causing them grief. Henceforward, we were all informed, their allowance was cancelled.

In future, if they wanted money to waste on clothes, they would have to take Saturday jobs and earn it for themselves. He was no longer going to provide them with funds to fritter away on rubbish.

I was, once again, left furious and totally emasculated by such an unbelievably vindictive, mean-minded exhibition of control and power. I immediately retorted that he had no authority over my children, or authority to prevent me from continuing with the arrangements that predated his advent into our home. He had set out his rules regarding my lack of authority over his son, and reciprocally, my children were my business, not his. What I did with my salary each month was down to me to decide, not him. My children were my responsibility, and they were not going to be forced by him into taking Saturday jobs.

As for the so-called, joint bank account, there had never been so much as one cent of his money ever deposited in it. I actuality I was funding everything connected with the household expenditure, while he, and his son, were, in fact, both living off me.

I was outraged by his unreasonable, autocratic diktat against my children, and I demanded to know exactly when was he going to begin contributing financially to the household maintenance, and to the cost of feeding himself and his son... along with all the other household outgoings he took for granted.

I told him in no uncertain terms that I had never imagined anyone could invent such spiteful malicious punishments against my children, and that he had no authority over anything to do with my daughters. I would continue to make all the decisions concerning their welfare, not him. They already had enough to occupy their weekends, with their homework and music lessons, and they were never going to be forced by him into earning money to pay for their own clothing... not while I had breath in my body.

I recall watching as he slowly got up, staring at me with that familiar menacing leer on his ugly face. Then he suddenly lunged forward and grabbed me around my throat with both hands, before launching into another violent attack. He was foaming at the mouth with rage one moment, and battering my head against the wall the next. Then, he was punching me in the face, all the while screaming that... 'if he found one fucking picture of Alan displayed anywhere in the fucking house, my lazy fucking kids would find themselves thrown into the street, with me alongside them. This was his house, and he decided what happened in it. And as for the breath in my body, well he could soon arrange to have it terminated.'

Moments later, he released my neck, and turned his attention onto my body, punching me in the chest and stomach with his fists and screaming at me. 'Yer fuckin' kids an' yer... the lor of yer... is only livin' in this 'ouse under maa suffrance, cause the 'ole bloody place naw b'longs ter me...ter me...git it? Ah won lissen' ter any more uv yer moanin' an gripin'. Yer talkin a load uv bollocks. Ah'm boss 'ere naw. So larn yer lessons, womin, and do wot yer telt ter do. Yer ain't got no money. Wotivver yer 'ad is naw mine. So git the fuckin' deeds signed over ter me, or Ah'll boot the lorra yer out wivart a fuckin' cent.'

My attempts to argue with him were finished. I was defeated, beaten, and left with two cracked ribs and a black eye. When he had finished, he threw me onto the floor and stood over me. Supporting himself against the sink unit, he stamped down onto my rib cage and then continued pressing his foot hard against my painful ribs until I could not breathe. With his other foot, he ground down onto the palm of my right hand.

I remember screaming for him to leave me alone, to let me get up, gasping that I couldn't breathe and that he was killing me... until eventually I passed out.

When I regained consciousness, sometime later, I found the kitchen in darkness, and he was gone. Once again, I was left in terrible pain, every breath I took an agony. I struggled upstairs to the bathroom and lay in the warm water for ages, going over and over in my mind the constant problems I was facing. How, in God's name, was I ever going to get rid of him? I had nowhere to turn for help, and he had me totally at his mercy.

Persuading me to agree to a joint bank account had been a very cunning move. It was one of the first subtle and manipulative actions in his master plan to control and dominate me. His promised equal monthly household contributions had come to nothing, as he had always intended would be the case. And I had found myself left in the invidious situation of receiving nothing from him at all, except abuse.

Now each month, he took possession of my bank statements as they arrived and studied them. Then he quizzed me on each line of expenditure. Having discovered one outgoing every month was for my daughters' clothing allowance had made him see red. Cancelling an arrangement that impinged on him not at all was a hateful way to penalise my children and something that caused not only resentment, but also my growing venomous hatred of him.

He hadn't counted on me speaking up to defend them as I had done. Clearly this had proved I was not yet totally under his control. I still had some fight left in me.

I had done my best to defend them, even though I had failed.

As I lay in the bath, I kept asking myself if I really was losing my mind. Was I genuinely mentally sick, as he kept on insisting? To my way of thinking, my mind was perfectly lucid, and not confused in any way, and I had never suffered from any form of mental illness before I met him.

Then I recalled how he had spent hours impressing on me, when I first met him, the grim details of how he had previously been married for twenty years to a woman who was mad... someone who had needed to spend long periods of time as a sectioned patient in various psychiatric hospitals.

What terrible persecutions had she endured at his hands? I wondered. What part had he played in her descent into mental illness?

Despite all his persistent vile accusations about my current mental state, was it perhaps nearer the truth that I was totally rational, and having to struggle to survive in a situation of permanent torment? I began to realise what he was attempting to do to me. He had already made me his victim, and now he was deliberately working to break my mental and physical health.

He had already succeeded in driving one wife into episodes of mental breakdown. Why not play the same games with another? This time round, there was much more at stake. I knew I was, in no sense out of touch with reality, and well able to recognise how I was currently being manipulated and kept confused by his extremely erratic and insane behaviour.

This man was a terrible, violent and unstable character. And he was enjoying carrying out his full range of sadistic entertainment on me... forcing me daily to endure unbelievable and diabolical physical and psychological abuse, in his determination to coerce me into humble obedience and capitulation.

It seemed no stretch of the imagination to identify his behaviour as insane and, at the very least that of a seriously mentally abnormal person. Surely, he could not continue doing what he was doing to me for much longer?

Chapter 17

A Year to Break Me, Part III: A Pair of Sadists

The shocking experiences of my first year of marriage to PP were only the beginning of a long and desperate journey into abject misery and despair. His vicious behaviour did not comprise occasional random violent outbursts of bad temper, or unexpected aggressive activities, emerging first as one thing and then another. This man had tremendous persistent, versatile energy, along with the relentless determination to cause me grief in innumerable vicious ways, all carried out simultaneously. His sadism was coldly calculated, and he was well prepared to invent and carry out an incredible variety of psychological torments, alongside his physical attacks on me.

I realised he had a distorted brain that was capable of producing multi-layered, ingenious, and creative persecutions, with an incredible variety of targets. Some were aimed to harm me on a physical level, and some on an emotional level. Some were directed at my children, and some, at my pet animals. Many others were just an inexplicable mixture of all kinds of horrible things... all intended to distress and persecute me, and cause me deep psychological damage.

I was enduring a reign of terror, carried out by a seriously perverse and depraved character, who was completely ruthless and focused in everything he was doing to me. It was his frequent boast that nobody could read his mind, and nobody knew what he would do next. It remains my belief that no sane person would, or could, ever invent or sustain the terrible abuse he conjured up.

A few days after forbidding me from giving my daughters their personal allowance, and ordering them to find weekend jobs to pay for their own clothing, he went out and spent several hundreds of pounds buying his son a 50cc Vespa motorcycle.

It was a deliberately callous demonstration of his power, and his deranged cruelty was intentionally aimed at my children to demonstrate how he was in charge and would do whatever he wanted. It was also intended to show all three of us that he despised us, and would manipulate and control us in whatever way he chose. We were three insignificant nothings in his eyes... just encumbrances standing in the way of his taking over our property.

His son was never obliged to have any sort of weekend job to pay for maintaining or running the machine he had been given, or for buying his own clothing, for that matter. Steve was given unlimited amounts of pocket money by his father. And under PP's sadistic rules, the youth was allowed to live in my home under a completely different set of rules from those he had set for my own children. Steve was encouraged to do whatever he wanted, with no parental authority at all exercised over his activities. He was at liberty to ride around the town on his new machine without any restrictions, and return to my house as and when he chose to gorge himself on whatever food he wanted to take from my refrigerator.

PP had quickly made it clear that he had no intention of contributing anything to the household expenditure. He kept all his money to himself in his business account, and invented whatever rules suited him concerning the running of the household; while I was treated like an unpaid servant, who existed only to provide the pair of them with whatever they demanded.

The situation was intolerable. I was savagely intimidated into silence, out of fear of what he would do to me if I raised any objections. But in no way was I ever complacent about any of his activities.

With the arrival of PP and his son, my food bills had become astronomical. I had never before had to spend so much money on filling and refilling my fridge several times every week.

Then one day he informed me of a new decision...

'In future, I must provide the two of them with a different roast dinner every evening at seven o'clock. He had worked out a menu that I must abide by. The meals must comprise a joint of beef, pork, or lamb or a whole chicken; occasionally, prime steak was acceptable, or pork or lamb chops. Added to this, there must always be three different vegetables, plus Yorkshire puddings and potatoes... roasted, baked, or mashed... along with gravy. This dinner must be followed by a homemade pudding of some description, served with custard.

'I would be instructed each morning what meat he wanted served that evening. Furthermore, my kids would eat at school, and I would only continue to be tolerated in the house for so long as I obeyed these instructions and kept my "big mouth shut." It was my choice... stay and obey, or be thrown out of the house with nothing.

'Minced meat was prohibited. Sausages were breakfast food only. And no variety of meat was to be served as cold cuts on the following day, or in any shape or form on two successive days. All joints must be served fresh from the oven. Frozen vegetables were not acceptable, only fresh ones, hand prepared by me. Or I could expect to have them thrown at me, along with the dishes they were served in.'

I had now been reduced to the level of an unpaid housekeeper in my own home. And so far as these catering demands went... I was forbidden from buying a microwave oven to make my life easier.

'His orders were that everything must be cooked in the gas oven. Furthermore, if I did not spend at least three hours each evening in the kitchen cooking this meal, dire consequences would result.'

His latest demands now gave him the greatest of sadistic pleasure by ensuring he was making my working life as hard as possible. Any attempt to contradict or question his orders was met with a new display of violence for daring to oppose him.

My function now was of waiting upon the two of them hand and foot. And every miserable day that dawned saw me dancing attendance on the unbelievable demands of this pair of thugs. Each morning I had to be up early to make them cooked breakfasts and pack two enormous lunch boxes. They simply rolled downstairs after eight o'clock, ate their breakfasts, collected their flasks and lunch boxes, and left the house.

This incredible preoccupation with food was compounded by Steve, who had quickly developed the disgusting habit of emptying my fridge each evening before I got home. When I arrived, complete with armfuls of shopping bags, I would find him seated in my wooden rocking chair in front of the open door of my fridge-freezer, rocking backwards and forwards snatching whatever took his fancy from the shelves... packets of ham, the cold remains of a joint of meat, the remains of a chicken, a packet of chocolate rolls, a tub of ice cream. Anything and everything that took his fancy, he was at liberty to scoff and simply throw the rubbish, or half eaten food, onto the floor for me to clear up.

But I remained under dire threats never to utter one word of reproach to this delinquent youth for anything he did. Attempting to remonstrate with his father was pointless. My efforts to curb his son's outrageous greed were met with more threats of violence, along with a sickening rebuke. 'Ee's a growin' lad. If ee's 'ungry, he kin 'ave wotivver ee wants ter eat, an' yer'd better not try stoppin 'im. Yer'll av ter lern ter git more in. Then yer'll not run short. Ah'm sick and fed up wi' yer mean selfish carryin' on ova fud. Ee's maa lad, an' Ah'll not see a selfish mean cunt like yer try an' starve 'im. Shut the fuck up. Or Ah'll give yer anovver good 'idin'.'

This constant insane preoccupation with food became their daily norm. It was beyond reason, and I just could not keep up with it physically or financially. It felt like I was feeding some obscene Gargantua and son, and could do nothing to stop them.

At that same time, my personal domestic situation had become so dreadful I scarcely ever saw my daughters anymore. They ate their main meal at school and then bolted straight up to their rooms at the end of each day, to keep out of the way of PP and his son.

The advent of Steve into my household had also introduced the brutal reality of his delinquent personality. With a psychopath for a father, his behaviour should not really have come as any great surprise to me. But at that time, I was still unaware of the clinically abnormal psychology of the deranged character I had married. I had never read about, nor had reason to investigate the irreversible condition of psychopathy. Why should I? The only people I had ever known were normal.

It did not take me long to discover Steve was just like his father... and with a far from normal mentality. Everything about the youth's behaviour was perverse and delinquent; and his attitude towards me, my children, my home, and my pets, was viciously sadistic and beyond any level of civilised behaviour.

Sadistic cruelty is not accidental. An innate vicious disposition must exist to drive the perpetrator to derive pleasure from acts of cold and calculating sadism. In neither PP nor his son did I ever see the slightest trace of conscience or compassion... only egocentric selfishness and relentless cruelty. With the pair of them, anarchy and violence certainly ruled the world they occupied.

Right from the time when PP first brought Steve to live in my house, terrible things began happening. Within days of having him living under my roof, our pet animals started to die. Alan and I had always believed that our children should grow up loving animals and taking an active interest in their welfare. And since they were toddlers, both Samantha and Nathalie had grown up surrounded by a variety of pets. These little creatures had all lived long and happy lives... until the arrival of PP and his son.

Their slaughter began only days after the youth moved in. We had two large heated-vivaria, kept in the conservatory. One was the home of four red-eared terrapins. The other was a nursery tank for five young tortoises. The baby tortoises were the progeny of our adult pets, Garfy and Petra.

Alan and I had supervised their hatching and had watched over them since the day their mother, Petra, had produced her eggs. We had been on our way to church one hot Sunday morning in summer when we'd noticed Petra busy in the garden laying a clutch of eggs and carefully covering them with soil.

When we came home, she had disappeared into the shrubbery. Rather than leave the future of the eggs to the vagaries of nature, we carefully excavated them and incubated them in the airing cupboard. There were six in total and five of them hatched successfully. They had been given every care and attention, and now the young tortoises were almost two years old.

One morning, when I went to feed the tortoises and terrapins, I found Steve in the conservatory ahead of me. He was silently examining one of the little tortoises. He had lifted it out of its glass tank and was holding it upside down, and jabbing its flat fragile basal carapace roughly with his fingers. I could see its little legs flailing as it was struggling to get free.

'What on earth are you doing?' I said, hurrying to remove the little creature from his rough curiosity.

'Wot yer got vees crabs 'ere fer?' he retorted, swinging his arm away to evade my efforts to retrieve it.

'They are not crabs,' I replied. 'And please put that one back where it belongs. You have no business to be handling them. They don't belong to you.'

'Are kin 'andle 'em if Ah wont,' he snapped back insolently, still continuing to poke and prod the little creature. 'Yerve go no bizzness, tellin' me wot Ah kin do. Theses jis slimy fuckin' crabs yer keepin', it's disgustin'.' He roughly threw the little creature back into the mossy tank, where it landed on its back, struggling in helpless panic.

I pushed past him and picked the little tortoise up, carefully placing it on a rock under the overhead sunlamp. I was biting my tongue and doing my best to ignore his insolence and stay calm. Then I began feeding all the inhabitants of the tank.

Steve had already moved on to the tank housing the four little terrapins.

'Don't you dare to touch them,' I said. 'Leave them all alone. They're still babies, and you haven't a clue what you're doing.'

He deliberately ignored me and began pushing the little terrapins around, as though he was stirring dishes in a washing up bowl. 'Doan yer give me orders. Ah'll fuckin' do what Ah wan. Anyways, yer diddlo,' he announced. 'Keepin fuckin' stinkin' vermin in thee 'ouse. Somebody shud flush the fuckin' lot daan the drain.'

'Well you had better not try,' I said angrily. 'The RSPCA will hear about it if you try anything like that.'

He came and stood right beside me. 'Yer defnitly diddlo, yer stoopid cow. Bu' Ah'm not.' He sneered meaningfully. 'There's uvver ways o doin fings, ain't there? Ah doan like 'em... An yer doan 'ave ter shoot a dog ter kill it.'

The following morning when I went to feed my little tortoises, one was dead. It was lying on its back, with blood coming from the centre of its flat basal carapace. Something very sharp had been forced through the plates and into its abdomen. The other four died in a similar fashion during the next ten days.

I was shocked and deeply upset. I knew without a shadow of doubt who had been responsible for killing them, but I could prove nothing.

The four young terrapins all came to similar ends, and within a month, both my vivaria were empty.

I cried buckets over all those little creatures. I had nurtured them with care and affection, but I was helpless to do anything about the senseless cruelty done to them by the vicious youth now installed as a second despicable resident of my home. Steve's father approved of everything he did, and all the wanton tricks the boy knew he had learned from his sadistic parent.

Next to meet their ends were our beautiful doves. We had brought six of them with us from our home in the north five years earlier. They had settled happily in the dovecote Alan had made. The summer before Alan died, they had produced two young squabs. It was lovely to see them flying gracefully around the garden, and watch them cooing and posturing on the roof of the dovecote. They were snow-white fantails, and the most beautiful and graceful creatures anyone could imagine.

But before the first anniversary of Alan's death, they were all dead. Their necks had been broken, and their wings torn off... one after another. When I went looking for them, I found first one and then another, dismembered, their broken bodies hidden behind bushes or pushed into plant pots. Six adults and two young squabs were all murdered by the vile youth who was now tormenting our lives on a daily basis.

I soon learned that, when PP was intending to do anything underhand at my house, he always ensured I was out of his way at school. He had made it abundantly clear, right from the start, that he did not do any kind of gardening or any other sort of work about the house... not even at the weekend cottage. Those things were all part of my responsibility.

How surprising it seemed when I discovered he had developed a secret interest in making fires in the garden. But these weren't fires for burning garden waste or household rubbish; he only enjoyed burning things he took a dislike to or felt maliciously driven to destroy. Without a shadow of doubt, he was responsible for cremating my pet tortoise Garfy alive, by trapping him in one of those destructive bonfires he enjoyed making.

He called it an accident, but I knew that was another of his evil lies. Poor little Garfy would never have accidently crawled into a fire PP happened to have made that afternoon and foolishly rolled onto his back so that he burned to death. He may have been a tortoise, but he instinctively knew when a situation was dangerous, and he could move quickly when he wanted to... that is, unless he had been deliberately trapped.

And that was exactly how I found him when the flames died out... deliberately trapped inside a constructed pile of bricks that had been carefully arranged in the centre of the fire. He had been deliberately placed there, on his back, with no space to struggle or to right himself and escape. It was quite obvious what had happened. One or other of the sadists had deliberately placed him there and left him to suffocate and die in the flames. The bonfire had, in fact, been constructed around him to incinerate him.

My poor Petra simply vanished and was never seen again. I have no doubt that pair of savages knew exactly what had happened to her. In a five-foot high brick-walled garden, there was no way she could have simply gone missing.

All these innocent creatures had been our pets for years, living happily and healthily without mishaps of any kind... until the family from hell arrived. Within three months of the arrival of PP and his son, all we had left, apart from my four little Yorkies, were two rabbits and four guinea pigs.

My little dogs were as dear to me as children, and I foolishly believed they were safe from his evil plans. He would not dare to harm them. But I knew I had to do something to save the lives of the rabbits and guinea pigs. I took them to school and housed them there safely. The children learned to take care of them. And thanks to the devotion of my caretaker, Greg, and his wife, Alison, they survived happily for many years, away from the destructive devils that were infesting my home.

However, even after his mass slaughter of our family pets, PP still wasn't satisfied. Nineteen animals were dead, and he and his son had only been living in our home for less than three months. Now all there was left to turn their devilish spite against were my four little dogs. They were left at home all day while I was at work, and now they too were at his malevolent mercy.

It was early October, and PP persisted in lounging around the house every day, doing absolutely nothing except eating and sleeping. It seemed strange to me how easily he could take days on end away from his working responsibilities, without receiving complaints from his two fellow directors.

Theirs was a working partnership, where each partner had specific on-site responsibilities. I knew PP was supposed to be overseeing an important million-pound council contract, which the company had been awarded, for the construction of a large block of community housing units. Why was he never there? I wondered.

Then one afternoon, I came home expecting my four little dogs to come bouncing out to greet me as usual. Only that day, they weren't there. What I found in the kitchen, when I went looking for them, was a devastating mess but no sign of my little dogs. What I did find was the kitchen floor littered with wood shavings, and shredded newspapers. The built-in furnishings, and even the walls and the tiled floor, along with the table and chairs were splattered everywhere in bright blue gloss paint. And the floor had been left swimming with water. In my absence, my kitchen had been turned into an unbelievable tip, with lumps of timber, blobs of tar, screws and nails, and pieces of roofing felt scattered everywhere. A can of paint thinners had been spilt all over the top of the table, leaving a long dull scar indelibly etched into the surface. The sight that met me looked like a bomb had exploded.

As I stood gazing around in horror, I saw there was an ominous gap in my kitchen units, where my recently installed dishwasher had been. A pipe from it was still dangling in the gap, with water dripping from it. PP had spent the entire day wrecking the room. And worst of all, my little Yorkies were nowhere to be seen.

I was gutted by the sight, and in wretched disbelief as I tried to make sense of the mess he had deliberately created while I had been at work. It was wonton spiteful vandalism to destroy my modern architect-designed kitchen, and tears poured down my face as I stood stupefied by the mess surrounding me.

Eventually I found my voice. 'What on earth has been going on here?' I yelled. 'Where's my dishwasher? And why is there water everywhere, and all this paint and wood? And where are my little dogs?'

I turned to face him, infuriated beyond words to have come home to such a deliberate vindictive act of vandalism. 'Why have you done this to me, you evil devil?' I choked helplessly. 'Are you sick in the head or just a deranged sadist?'

He was standing quite still, quietly watching my reactions, waiting to see what I would do. He was enjoying my distress with obvious amusement... a smug self-satisfied smirk on his ugly face. There was clear perverse pleasure written there, and not a trace of remorse or shame. For his own sick reasons, he wanted to observe how I would react to what he had done in my home.

I realised with an overwhelming surge of contempt that the evil swine was actually getting his kicks out of seeing me so devastated and unhappy. My voice suddenly failed me, and I broke down in sobs. I could not believe any sane person would do such unbelievably awful things out of sheer malice... And what had he done with my little dogs?

I went over to the gap where my dishwasher had been. 'Where is it?' I demanded. 'What business was my dishwasher of yours?'

'Oh, that ol' fing.' He grinned maliciously with a menacing lunge towards me. 'It 'ad a 'ole in it, an' it weren't no more fuckin' use. So Ah chucked it daan the tip. Better fer all uv uz if yer start washin' up by 'and. Only lazy cows use fings like tha'. An oi ain't avin no woman in vis 'ouse startin' ter git lazy.'

He produced another of his malevolent grins, which fired my outrage so much I wanted to attack him... to hit him in his ugly mouth and cut out his vile tongue. He was mocking me and parading his blatantly 'aren't-I-clever' sneering attitude callously and deliberately to cause me distress.

'What?' I yelled back. 'That's another of your bloody damned lies. Alan bought that for me, and it's not three years old. It works perfectly well, and I want it brought back. You've stolen it, you evil devil. I don't believe you've thrown it away. It wouldn't surprise me if you'd sold it, you unbelievable despicable swine. You had no right to rip it out and dispose of it. You didn't own it. It has never belonged to you. And where are my little dogs, you insane brute? What have you done to them?'

Suddenly, he lunged forward at me, his face only centimetres from mine, his heavy jowls leering at me with the inevitable clumps of frothy white spittle at the corners of his thick flabby lips.

I already knew from bitter experience another attack was imminent, and I shrank back.

'Well it doan belong ter yer no more. Wierivver it is, yer doan 'ave a fancy dishwasher no more. So git used ter the idea. Yer goin ter be the dishwasher roun''ere from naw on. So, git yer 'ead aroun that, cos it's a fact. Yer'll be washin' dishes from naw til kingdom come, yer fuckin' whore.' At that point, he lifted his heavy fist and cuffed me hard across the side of my head.

'Arsk no questchuns, an' yer woan be teld no lies. An' doan yer ivver raise yer fuckin' voice ter me agin, yer cunt. Fings in this fuckin' shit'ole is goin' ter change. Ah'm in charge 'ere, an' yer goin ter 'ave ter look arter uz proper. So shape up. Yerve ad an eezy life so far, an' naw it's time ter git used ter roughin' it. From naw on, yer'll wash up by 'and, or Ah'll knock yer fuckin''ead orff yer fuckin' neck an stuff it daan thee 'ole.'

Breathing heavily, hc turncd away to look out of the window, towards the garden.

My head was reeling from the blow he had just dispensed, but I refused to back down... not until I knew where my little dogs were. 'Where are my little dogs?' I shrieked. 'What have you done to them, you evil bastard? If you've injured them in any way, I'll call the police and the RSPCA and have you arrested.'

He came back to where I was standing, the evil grin still fixed on his big slobbering mouth, and began slapping me across my face rhythmically... first the left and then the right cheek, reciting with a sing-song stupid voice. 'Ah-ain't-dun-nuffink-ter-them-fuckin'-dogs. Not yet. Ther wier-ther-b'long...outside-i-the-fuckin'-gardin. Ah-ain't-livin-i-this-shit'ole-wiv-em-no-more. So-mek-yer-mind-up-womin. Eyver-ther-go-or-Ah-go!'

I was at breaking point. I'd had enough. I wanted him to go. And if he had walked out at that point, I would have been totally relieved to see the back of him. But of course, he had no intention of leaving. He had manipulated himself too far into my life to lose control by walking out. He was almost at the winning post.

I was in floods of tears... humiliated, distressed, and furious beyond caring where he went. 'If you're forcing me to choose,' I sobbed, 'you can leave now. But if I find you have harmed any of them, you know what I will do. I've never been more serious.'

I slammed out of the room and raced into the garden to find them. Poor little innocent creatures, I found them tied up out of sight at the bottom of the garden. He had fastened pieces of clothes line around their necks in noose-like sliding loops. The more they struggled, the tighter the nooses became.

How long they had been left like that I never knew, but in another half hour, I believe they would all have been dead. He had them all tied to a blue painted wooden monstrosity he must have spent all morning constructing. They were terrified, and gasping for breath when I found them. Cowering and trembling, with not an inch left to move, they were all hanging by their throats, with their tongues turned blue and lolling from their mouths. But when they saw me, all their little tails started wagging feebly. Their fur was matted with bright blue paint, and they were trembling so much they couldn't stand from weakness and thirst. All they could do was whimper weakly.

It broke my heart to see what he had done to them, and to witness the terror in their eyes. They were just four tiny miniature Yorkshire terriers. Little Sheba and her sister Tina each weighed no more than three pounds. And Ralphie and Roxy were no more than six pounds each. They weren't mastiffs or Alsatians. They couldn't hurt a fly. And they would never have had the stamina to live outside.

The evil monster had kept them trapped and terrified all day, tied up by their necks and left struggling and choking from exhaustion and thirst. Thank God I had discovered them before he had killed them too. The devil had deliberately tied them up like that, and he had done nothing to help them. He'd just abandoned them to die horribly.

Inflicting pain was a joy to him. Compassion was a sentiment he neither cared about nor understood.

Why would a twenty-stone man want to terrorise four tiny little creatures? I believe he was doing it from pure evil motives. He liked hurting animals, and he enjoyed seeing them suffer. And of course, there was the other appalling motive. He wanted to inflict immeasurable grief and pain on me. Killing them would really have fulfilled that intention.

My hands were shaking, and tears were streaming down my face as I gently untied the nooses strangling them. I scooped the four of them up into my arms, thanking God I had found them in time and was able to carry them home alive. They were weak, but doing their best to wriggle happily in my arms... ecstatic to see me, and panting for breath, but still doing their best to lick my face with their hot little tongues.

It was an episode I can never forget, and the grief of it will never leave me. As soon as they saw him, still looming like the monster he was in the middle of the chaos he had created, they refused to let me put them down on the floor for a drink, but clung to me like terrified children while I gave them water, as I held them on my knees.

I never left them alone with him again. And their fear of him never died away. They refused to go anywhere near him again, and hid if they saw him.

The blue painted, wooden monstrosity he had wrecked my kitchen to make had been planned as a way of forcing them out of the house. He had actually intended to make them stay outside in it all year round, summer and winter alike. Constructing the outdoor kennel had been his way of challenging me to attempt to defy his authority over my little dogs.

Presented with another fait accompli, would I dare to challenge him, knowing the level of abuse he would use against me? He had already gotten away with treating my children abominably, and with allowing his dreadful son to murder our other pets. Dealing with my little dogs must have seemed easy to him. He had never considered I would stand up to him over them, or threaten him with legal action.

His terrible bullying and intimidation of me were issues I still hadn't found a way of dealing with, and his brutal success had come as the result of my personal grief, my emotional weakness, and my plain ill-advised stupidity in ever allowing him into my life. His appalling behaviour towards me was something I was struggling with, and it was a situation I would need to face up to at some future point when I felt strong enough to openly do battle with him. But until I was able to regain my emotional strength and defend myself against his tyrannical dictatorship, my only surviving instincts were to protect my dependants. Any attempt he might consider making to actually injure my children or harm my little dogs were issues I was still prepared to fight him over.

Whether my threat to involve the police, and the RSPCA did actually have any lasting effects on him, I do not know. But never in my life had I been more determined about anything. The blue kennel remained in the garden until it rotted; but my little Yorkies continued to live their lives indoors, safe from any further attacks on them.

However, PP was a man who always found ways of revenging himself against anyone who dared to defy or oppose him. With his malicious sadistic mind constantly at work conjuring up new ways to cause me pain and grief, he soon had a new plan worked out to take his revenge on me.

So far as he was concerned, my stubbornness in ignoring his claims on my home, and his demands for a huge dowry had not been broken. I was blatantly defying him, and my stubborn will had to be broken. Very rapidly, he initiated a new and terrible campaign against me. But this time what he decided to do was more covert, and aimed at breaking my mind, as well as my body.

 Chapter 18

A Year to Break Me, Part IV: The Lunacy Continues

After many years of enduring life without Alan, I still know of no cure for a broken heart. Losing one's beloved life partner is akin to a double death... because your broken heart, and your emotions, lie in the grave alongside your lost love.

Only the return of a calm peaceful mind, after an adequate period of grieving, ever allows for a gradual coming to terms with your loss. Anyone who has found themselves walking through that terrible valley of the shadow of death, after the loss of someone dear to them, needs time to mourn. Acceptance is only achieved gradually, as mental and emotional adjustments are made. Acceptance of the inevitability of death is at best, a slow and unhappy process. And although the soul-wrenching grief may fade in time, the process cannot be hurried, and the sorrow of the deep loss, never really departs.

Perhaps like the graceful faithful swan, genuine everlasting love comes into our lives only once, to show us that we have been truly blessed. I know, from my own perspective, one true and lasting love was all I could ever have hoped for. And for the life that had been lost, there could never be any substitute.

From my devastating experiences with the monster PP, I had learned that committing to a second marriage is a very risky business, and the equivalent of handing your half-used life into a virtual stranger's keeping, and trusting that stranger will respect everything you treasure, along with the precious memories that still tie you to the past. My own devastating experiences taught me that there is a great deal more to a successful second marriage than picking up the pieces with someone new, and attempting to begin again.

With three weeks to go before the first anniversary of Alan's death, I no longer felt I was living. Everything meaningful in my life had been destroyed, or turned into ugliness by the vile presence of PP and his son. The pair of them had set about destroying everything of value left from my marriage, along with anything that reminded me of my beloved Alan. Their callous machinations ensured I was constantly kept in a state of absolute misery and unbearable mental torment.

Day after day, all the things that were invested with happy memories for me, were systematically and deliberately being stripped away, by a hateful man who did not have any capacity for genuine love in him, or even the ability to understand what love was. He was unfathomably envious of something he could recognise, but was incapable of either giving or receiving. Therefore, his only recourse was to destroy all that he had no ability to comprehend. That was why he set about relentlessly destroying everything that linked me to my happy past with Alan.

Alan's body had died, but no part of my love for him was dead. That was as strong and enduring as ever. And my memories of our life together kept him alive in my heart and my mind. In some strange way, I believe PP knew that. He had recognised my emotions would never belong to him. It was Alan I still yearned for, and only Alan. Nothing relating to that emotional bond would ever die. The monstrous PP could never be Alan's substitute; and whatever evil plans he made to harm me, he would never destroy my memories, or my feelings for my one true, ever-loving, and loyal husband.

There was simply no point of comparison between the two of them. Ever since the bleak day I had married PP, I had been discovering, at first-hand, the wisdom of the saying, 'Marry in haste, repent at leisure.' He had nothing to offer me except misery, violence, and subjugation. And in his twisted destructive character, there was nothing I could ever find to like, or respect, much less love.

It gave him a perverse kind of pleasure, knowing how unhappy he was making me. He obviously derived some sort of sick kicks from causing me endless pain, as he worked to destroy my life, and everything tangible that connected me to the past, and to my memories of the happiness I had previously known. With only weeks to go before the first anniversary of Alan's death, I had become desperately low and despondent.

A couple of days after the episode of the blue kennel, PP got up early and began barging around the bedroom, creating a tremendous racket. He was in a vile temper and wanted me awake and on the receiving end of it. As always, he needed someone as the conscious target for his insane outbursts, and that unenviable position, as usual, fell to me.

While I had been asleep, he had begun emptying all his clothes from the wardrobes. It was barely six thirty, and as intended, the noise he was making startled me awake, along with the weight of the boxes and clothing being roughly dumped on top of where I was lying. He had all the lights switched on, and there were half-filled boxes strewn everywhere around the bedroom.

I eased myself up in bed and sleepily asked what he was doing.

At first, he ignored me and just continued storming around, refusing to answer my question. I could see from the furious glowering expression on his face he was working himself into a rage for some reason. His mouth was pursed and tight-lipped. His eyes were glaring. And his face was set in the familiar furious expression I knew only too well. But I had no idea at all what had gone wrong this time to trigger his aggression.

With increasing anxiety, I pulled myself into a seated position and wrapped my arms around my knees, watching in silence while he slammed around the room, grabbing things and throwing them into one or another of the large boxes. I knew with an overpowering feeling of dread, his mood would eventually erupt into a violent outburst, and I began looking about nervously for some way of escape.

But I was already too late. Within moments, he launched himself at where I was sitting and grabbed my throat, shaking me like a rag doll. 'Yer fuckin bitch,' he screamed. 'Yer know wot's wrong. It's all abaat yer, ain't it? All abaat yer an' yer fuckin' soddin' kids. This fuckin' place ain't moy 'ome. An' it ain't Steve's niever. Ah ain't goin' ter stop wier me an me son ain't welkum. Yer kin keep yer fuckin' 'ouse and yer fuckin' money. Ah'm leavin' yer.

'Wot yer did wiv them soddin' dogs ain't ackcep'ible. An' wot yer did ter moi lad the uvva week ain't ackcep'ible niever. Goin' on like a mad fing coz ee wuz lookin' fer sum tablets in yer fuckin' draws, cos ee wuz feelin' right pooly. Jis coz ee dropt sum o yer fuckin ol' papers on the flor. Wot yer fink yer ol bits a fuckin' paper er werf beats me. Yer wudn't 'elp my lad, yer bitch, wud yer? Yer told 'im ter look arter hisself.

'Well, me an 'im er orff. Ah'm tekin me stuff wiv uz. Yer kin stuff yer fuckin' 'ouse, and choke on it fer all Ah kair. Good riddance ter yer, ah sez. Yer a fuckin' whore. Ah made a big mystek ivver marryin' yer. Ah no naw ah marreed the wrong womin. Yer jus' a fuckin' soddin' greedy cow. Ah 'ope yer die o cancer or sumfink jis as 'orrible.'

He suddenly stopped shaking me and pushed me back into the horizontal position, then bashed his fist into my face, then stormed out of the room. I was left coughing and choking, and a trickle of blood had started running from my split lip, while my mouth felt numb. Slowly, I pulled myself back into a sitting position. I was shocked and dazed and bordering on hysteria, unable to comprehend what had actually triggered such an aggressive outburst before dawn.

Then I recalled the bedroom incident with Steve, weeks previously. So that was what had prompted this revenge attack. PP had wrecked my kitchen and stolen my dishwasher, and made his vile attempts to kill my little dogs. But all of that was somehow my fault? Now I was being punished again because of the story Steve had told him.

It was insane... just another crazy example of his primitive vengeful agenda. Here was another warped, sadistic, sick demonstration of the way his mind worked. Like everything the pair of them ever did, it was savage and inhumane, and beyond all reason.

Up to that point nothing had been said to me about Steve's bedroom escapade. But the arch troublemaker had obviously been working on an elaborate story to wind up his ever-volatile father into launching another hate attack on me. Presumably, he had finally got the reaction he had been planning in order to get even with me. The youth was a nasty malicious piece of work... At the fleeting thought that I might finally be seeing the back of him my spirits rose quite unexpectedly...But the feeling vanished in moments.

As I wiped the blood away from my mouth, I suddenly found myself overwhelmed by a flood of mixed emotions. I began to shake uncontrollably. It was barely daylight, but somehow the sudden shocking events were triggering a deep emotional reaction in me.

The sad anniversary of Alan's death, was very much uppermost on my mind, and PP's vindictive attack that morning exploded inside my head as a kind of ghoulish climax to the horrors of the entire year.

My emotions, and my repressed thoughts had always been very much with Alan. Each day, I had found myself clinging to the fond memories that I found I needed, just to keep myself functioning, while each day of marriage to PP carried me ever deeper into grieving my unbearable loss.

Suddenly I was overwhelmed by a desperate sensation of divine retribution... as though I had been condemned by heaven to live in torment and endless punishment, forever reaping the awful harvest of my ill-advised remarriage... Greater comparisons between two men could never be imagined... Yet somehow, I had allowed myself to replace my loving Alan with a monster beyond human imagining.

I was confronting, face to face, the terrible reality of what I had done; and into accepting the responsibility for turning my own life into this current living nightmare.

As the pain and feeling returned to my face and mouth, I began experiencing an overwhelming sensation of anger and resentment following PP's latest violent outburst. A mountainous jumble of mixed emotions and terrible reality seemed to be fermenting inside of my head, until unexpectedly my crazy emotional roller coaster began spinning out of control, and I found myself somewhere outside of reality, trembling and silently tearful. The never-ending unremitting grief of bereavement, along with the uncertainty of every moment I now lived... the endless pain, the violence, the despondency, and the confusion... suddenly everything climaxed, like an enormous explosion inside my brain, and it all became too much for my mind to carry... Suddenly I fell apart.

As I listened to the noise of PP leaving, my body began to experience violent spasms of shivering. I wasn't cold, but as he continued dramatically and violently banging around downstairs, throwing things onto the floor, and barging his way through the rooms carrying his boxes out to the car creating as much pandemonium as possible, I just could not control the shaking. My mind had gone beyond my control. The sensations grew worse as he chivvied his son to hurry up. The racket only ended with the sound of the car driving away and the return of total silence in the house.

At that point, my shaking and the tears morphed into a deluge I couldn't control. I couldn't pull myself together. Some part of my rational brain was asking...Why was I so distraught?... I had no idea... I knew I should have been celebrating the relief at seeing the back of the pair of them. My tormentor and his son had finally left... So why would my tears not stop? Something seemed to be blocking all reason from my brain, and all I could do was shake and cry like an abandoned child.

The lingering remnant of my intelligence was telling me I should be delighted they were going. But for some inexplicable reason, I had lost control, and become hysterical. This was some kind of uncontrollable, demoralising, grand climax to my life, and I was shaking and crying my eyes out as though someone dear to me had just died.

PP had no emotional involvement with me at all. But he was counting on the certainty that I had a vulnerability that he could manipulate. His intention that morning to push me over the edge and break me, was as malicious and calculating as ever.

That late October morning, as he drove off, he left me so overwhelmed and sick with confusion, over the incomprehensible situation I found myself in, that I collapsed in hysteria. My head felt like it was exploding... and I had completely lost control of my emotions, and had to be sedated by the doctor.

I now realise that was the point when I should have called time on the destructive relationship. The only functions PP had ever occupied in my life were to be my abuser and my tormentor. He had achieved very little financially. None of his grotesque demands had yet been met, and by and large, my finances were still intact. His petulant leaving was a heaven-sent, once-only chance for me to escape from him.

After three months of diabolical marriage, during which time he had devoted all his efforts to creating his own perverse version of hell on earth in my life, he had suddenly decided to abandon me, because, so he claimed, he had married the wrong woman.

That awful day should have ended the relationship...I wish to

God it had... but for some insane reason it didn't. It brought me to my knees in a confusion of grief and despair, and called back into life the incomprehensible chemistry involving abandonment left dormant inside my temporarily distraught brain since Alan's death. All that unresolved grief, and the despair overwhelmed me again, brought back into focus by this new shameful act of wanton cruelty and desertion by PP.

Even now, I do not properly understand my reactions. I was like a drug addict who desperately wants to abandon drugs, yet is constantly drawn back to them, knowing in the end they may well kill her. A clouded mind rarely sees reason, and my golden opportunity that day was missed, for reasons I have never understood.

The two of them were gone all day; and I spent it in a half-drugged stupor from the sedatives the doctor had injected into me. At six thirty that evening, my phone rang, and a voice spoke. It was not a voice I immediately recognised, until eventually the penny dropped in my fuzzy brain, and I realised it was PP using his Dr Jekyll voice. He was back in the character he had portrayed when I had first met him, and sounding all sweetness and light, as he set about performing a first-class act to convince me of his remorse for his diabolical behaviour that morning. He was suddenly almost grovelling in his apologies.

Of course, I should have immediately suspected his motives and hung up...But my brain was still addled... and I was struggling to figure out what on earth was wrong with me.

This man always operated on a hidden agenda of one sort or another, and could instantly switch to any persona necessary to achieve whatever he intended. I had already experienced almost six months of his amenable assumed Dr Jekyll persona before he had switched to his natural deplorable character of Mr Hyde on our wedding day.

Suddenly on that October evening, Dr Jekyll was on the phone, cajoling me, and bamboozling me into feeling sorry for him. He had beaten me that morning, and said all manner of vile things about me, concluding the tirade by telling me he had married the wrong woman and was leaving me. He had said that, after three months, he considered the marriage was over and finished. Now, like the cunning and talented actor he was, he was attempting to turn the tables by seducing me over the telephone, and producing a convincing show of remorse in order to re-establish his devious manipulation of me.

It must be said he was a supremely accomplished and plausible liar, and I was still an incredibly gullible fool... far too unworldly and naive for my own good. After I had been cajoled into listening to him and not hanging up, he succeeded in capitalising on my vulnerability. Eventually, still in my stupefied, woozy state, I let him convince me he really was sorry for his disgraceful earlier behaviour. I even extracted a solemn promise from him never to hurt me again, and keep Steve in check, and to begin contributing towards the housekeeping expenses and the joint bank account...all as he had originally promised he would do.

His telephone act was humble and seriously convincing, and he readily agreed to all my conditions and terms... swearing that he would do anything and everything I wanted if it would make me happy. He swore he loved me and that all he wanted was the opportunity for another chance to make things between us work.

My drug-induced gullibility in falling for this unbelievably monstrous cunning pack of lies, is something about which I still castigate myself. After everything he had been putting me through for months, and all the terrible things he had done to my children, how could I ever have been persuaded to allow such a villainous two-faced liar to return to my home? How could I have accepted the return of his awful son?

In all my dealings with PP, I remained an incredibly gullible, and naive slow-learner. Of course, I should have known better than to ever permit his return… But that evening my addled brain was dull, and unable to query the reality behind his sudden change of heart, or his blatantly unscrupulous manipulations.

Perhaps deep-down, in some inexplicable way, I had always nursed the hope that he would recognise what a terrible person he was, and decide to change his ways. But that was merely hiding from the truth… In reality I already knew him well enough to know he never felt remorse or sorrow for anyone except himself. That evening I should have recognised Dr Jekyll's plausible, mealy-mouthed apologies were only being made because he had a new ulterior plan in his mind with which he intended to manipulate me.

In truth, he would have agreed to anything to get himself and his son back into my home.

Promises…what were they to this man? Just a set of meaningless and easily forgotten words that would be vehemently denied later. Pie-crust promises, only made to be broken. There was neither truth nor honour in anything he ever said. His promises were of no more significance than messages written on sand, instantly blown into oblivion by the winds of inconstancy.

The genuine truth, concealed behind his volte-face, had I known it at the time, was an entirely different story. That morning when he left me bleeding and hysterical, he already knew where he was going. His plans had been made the previous day, when he had organised accommodation for himself and Steve, at the home of Val Evans, the woman he had once planned to marry.

I guess she was as foolish and as gullible as I was. In any event, and for whatever reason, she had been happy to hear from him again, and had offered the two of them accommodation in her small house. He had even promised her that, later on, they would talk about re-establishing their relationship... once he had sorted out the enormous mistake, he claimed to have made in marrying me.

Having successfully organised somewhere for himself and Steve to stay, a comfortable compromise with Val had very swiftly been established. And later that day, PP had phoned his daughter Liz to tell her the good news. He knew she liked Val and would be really pleased to hear he had left me and gone back to live with her.

Unfortunately for me, Liz had some news of her own to relate to her father... news that had been much less welcome. She was in the process of being dishonourably discharged from her military service with the WRAF, for gross insubordination and refusing to obey orders.

It came as a shock to hear that after only six months service, she was being kicked out of the air force. The following weekend she was expecting him to provide her with a place to live.

It was the moment when he recognised that in walking out on me so dramatically, he had burned his boats. He needed to do some tactical, quick repair work to sort out their accommodation problems, if all three of them were no going to end up homeless.

Of course, at the time, I was told nothing about the real reason motivating his plan to establish a rapprochement with me. Naturally, Liz and her problems, were never mentioned.

Had I been asked if I would be willing to accommodate her, I would have refused, and suggested the girl should contact her mother and go and live with her. That was the most feasible and practical solution to the problem. However, I was deliberately kept in the dark. And as usual, told nothing about the latest manipulative scheme he was busily concocting.

Once I had been sweet-talked and cajoled into accepting his glib apologies and promises, and had been persuaded into agreeing his return to my home, Dr Jekyll disappeared overnight... along with his worthless pack of promises. Mr Hyde and son were back with a vengeance, and I was quickly relegated into being an insignificant nobody in my own home once more. Only this time, the family from hell was about to increase in size.

The following Monday morning, as soon as I had left for school, he began a frenzied attack on my box room, with the intention of turning it into a bedroom for his daughter's occupation. I went to school that morning entirely in the dark regarding his surreptitious plans and with no idea of what he had organised in my absence. It was business as usual for PP. Whatever he decided to do was considered, in his usual high-handed fashion, to be none of my business.

Without telling me anything about his conversation with Liz, he had arranged for a driver to bring a wagon from work that morning. Together, he and the driver spent all day loading everything from my box room into the wagon. Then without so much as a... by-your-leave, my property was carted to the municipal dump.

When I arrived home, and demanded to know what was going on, he announced his fait accompli. Liz was coming to live with us the following weekend. Every last piece of property stored in my box room, apart from a spare bed, had been disposed of so that his loud-mouthed daughter could take up residence in my home.

He was back in the same old familiar controlling mode as ever. All the wheedling and the promises to be a kinder more considerate person towards me had meant nothing. They were just another pack of convincing lies, invented to fool me all over again, and manipulate the situation to facilitate the arrival of his daughter in my home, along with the return of himself and the abominable Steve.

My personal stupidity and mental impairment at that time still appal me. This shameless individual took my compliance for granted in everything he did. I was expected to stand aside in my own home and give him free rein, making no objections to anything, however offensive or unacceptable it might be to me.

In any event, every objection I ever raised about anything was simply ignored, and I was invariably severely punished for raising it. Once again, my authority in my own home had been disregarded. And this time, things for me were destined to be getting a great deal worse than they had been... very quickly.

If I had imagined, for one moment, he had ever seriously intended to change his ways to fit in with me, I was now told, in disgusting and explicit words, to dream on. Or as I was informed more and more frequently as time passed, I was ...

'diddlo just a crazy madwoman who nobody took any notice of, or ever bothered listening to. I was a stupid bitch who would not be surviving for much longer if I didn't stop complaining, and giving him grief.'

Certainly, none of the family from hell ever took any notice of my feelings. Once they had all moved in together, their joint intentions to take over my property came with the united determination to succeed. This was now their house, and my children and myself mere incidental nuisances to be gotten rid of ASAP. We were to be driven out, by every means possible and with no holds barred, just as soon as they could arrange it. Their intentions now were focused upon making the lives of the three of us so difficult we would want to leave.

Chapter 19

A Year to Break Me, Part V: The Family from Hell

With the ever-bolshie Liz now residing in my home, along with her aggressive father and malevolent brother, the situation in all areas of life rapidly became much worse than it had been previously. I now had three disagreeable, disruptive, and determined intruders to contend with.

Within a matter of days, I realised that whatever demands Liz or Steve made of their father, he condoned and agreed to them. Particularly as those demands invariably came at no personal cost to himself, and were always made to my detriment. Their wishes had become his commands. I was consulted about nothing, and whatever the two of them wanted they got.

Matters eventually came to a head over my car... Liz was almost four years older than Nathalie and five years older than

Samantha. My girls had never met anyone like her before. She was loud and lairy; drank pints of beer, went to all-night discos, and stayed out all night, whenever she chose; and did pretty much whatever she wanted with the blokes she picked up in pubs and discos. And she was as cocky and ignorant as her brother. Six months in the WRAF certainly hadn't improved her morals.

The prospect of having her living in my home filled me with dismay. I viewed her as an appalling role model for my young teenage daughters. However, being at an impressionable age they found her outrageous behaviour, and her streetwise erratic lifestyle, fascinating, and something to be admired.

When she had left home and joined the WRAF, her father had forced her to sell the car he had bought. Her dark green Morris Minor had been a gift with strings attached... bought for her a couple of years earlier when she had passed her driving test and was still living at home looking after her brother and himself. This had been in the wake of the divorce, and following Mandy's departure to get married.

But in PP's world, nothing to do with money ever came without strings. That meant the recipient of his goodwill must always pander to him, and never displease him, if the said beneficiary wanted to keep him sweet. Motor vehicles were things he liked to use as major rewards for his children. In exactly the same way as he had provided Mandy with a car, Liz had been given the Morris, and recently Steve had been bought the Vespa 50cc motorcycle. No doubt, in two years' time, he would be next in line for a car, as soon as he passed his driving test.

However, each daughter in turn, had seriously displeased him by leaving home and, as he saw it, had wilfully deserted him to do what she wanted. He regarded such behaviour as deliberately defiant. And in each case, that had triggered the penalty of having their vehicle taken away. He could legally do that, because he had cannily retained ownership of each girl's vehicle. They were only the nominated keepers, not the owners.

In Mandy's case, he had gone to her new home and smashed her car to smithereens. In Liz's case, she had been made to sell hers, and return the money. Now that her days as a military cook were over and she had returned to him, she was carless, and eager to get back into her father's good books.

From the stories he had previously told me, I knew she had always been academically challenged, and was nothing to speak of in the intelligence stakes. The only employment she had ever been qualified for was kitchen work. Now that her days of military service were over, she had found herself a job in a local bakery.

However, unskilled work did not pay much, and she couldn't afford a replacement car. But that didn't stop her from feeling entitled to have the use of one whenever she wanted. After all, she had come back to dear old dad, so she felt she was entitled to the usual family mobility perks. The following week after she came to live with us, while PP and I were away at the weekend cottage, she took my car on the Saturday evening, along with my impressionable daughters, and drove sixty miles to an all-night disco... having said nothing to me about any of these plans.

After all, PP had instructed both Steve and Liz, that I was nobody of any importance, and everything connected with the house already belonged to him.

From our first encounter, I had already found Liz an ignorant, loud-mouthed piece of work. Having her living under my roof had simply endorsed that opinion. I found her total lack of courtesy towards me beyond belief. She was certainly not cerebrally gifted. But her lack of intelligence was no excuse for her lack of consideration and common decency. I considered her to be as deliberately cunning and devious as her father and brother. But I had never suspected she would ever have the gall to misappropriate my car, or take my children joyriding.

To take and use my property without permission was, in my opinion, dishonest and unforgivable. But to provoke my children into disobeying me was beyond the bounds of common decency and bordering on criminal. When I uncovered the awful reality of what had gone on, it made me want to ban her from ever setting foot in my home again.

Her only excuse was that she had asked her dad if she could use my car, and take my daughters with her. He had happily obliged, and secretly found my keys and handed them to her. PP had been falling over himself to be indulgent because she was back with him after her WRAF fiasco. It had flattered his ego that she had not chosen to go to live with her mother, and had chosen him instead. So as there was no cost involved in handing over the keys to my car, he had readily agreed that she could use it. Yes, of course she could take my car. It was nothing to do with me what he did. And in any event, I need never know. They would never tell me, would they?

This cavalier attitude was typical of his I'm-in-charge mentality. Liz was his daughter, and it was no business of mine if he gave her the use of a car. After all, I was now regarded as having no more relevance than an incidental blip in the household, so far as any of them were concerned. He'd told both of his children many times that the house and everything in it now belonged to him. And it suited their own selfish purposes never to question the truth of anything he ever said.

The first I knew about what had gone on in my absence came on the Monday morning. That Sunday evening, I had returned from Salisbury just as my girls were getting ready for bed. It was already quite late, and as usual, we had no time to say much more to one another than... good night. I asked them if all was well and if they'd finished their homework? But apart from that, nothing was mentioned about anything untoward that might have happened during my absence.

As the owner-driver, I was the only person insured to drive my car, and I would never have condoned anyone else using it. I most certainly would never have been persuaded to allow my teenage daughters to be driven anywhere by the feckless Liz... and certainly not during the late evening to an all-night disco sixty miles away, at the opposite end of the county.

The following morning, I was left to discover the state of the vehicle, without any cautionary word or any apology ever being said about it. It was parked outside my house in its usual place, but not in its usual condition. When I went to look, I discovered it was seriously damaged and dangerously un-roadworthy. One entire side was wrecked beyond belief. And the vehicle was clearly a write-off.

Hardly surprisingly I was furious to find my car in such a state, and I demanded to know what had gone on behind my back during the weekend. Liz was still in bed, and for a long while, she refused to get up and come down to talk to me.

Eventually she appeared, and I was informed her version of the truth, in an abrupt offhand manner, which was very clearly a pack of lies. She sullenly admitted to having taken the car, along with my daughters. But there was not a shred of truth or remorse, or even an apology, in anything else she said about what had happened. Everything was justified in her ignorant dissembling mind, because her father had given permission for what she had done.

The sense of outrage I felt was incandescent. A girl for whom I had no liking or responsibility, and who was no concern of mine, had taken my car along with my children, and gone joyriding behind my back, and without any permission from me. For these dangerous and illegal activities, her only insolent excuse was… her dad had said she could.

Subsequently, she had returned my car as a total write-off. Yet the previous evening when I had arrived home, she had not had the common decency to even bother to tell me about it. And neither had her father. In their typically cavalier fashion, I had just been left to discover the damage for myself, in daylight the following morning.

To add insult to injury, she clearly felt no guilt whatsoever, nor any need to even explain what had gone on behind my back. The words I'm sorry, never passed her lips. Nor did she offer me the weakest of explanations. It seemed her father's permission exonerated her from all blame, and my wrecked car was nothing further to do with her. It was 100 per cent my problem… not hers.

As for PP, words failed me. During that weekend, while I had been gardening, cooking, and cleaning, a hundred miles away at the cottage, to keep him happy, he had never seen fit to mention one word about what was happening in my absence back at home. It was, apparently, none of my business that he had loaned my car to his daughter.

Suddenly, nothing concerning my family or my property, was any longer any concern of mine. In his high-handed opinion, any private arrangements he might make with his daughter relating to my property, or my children, were no longer deemed to be any concern of mine.

The feckless woman could have killed them, miles away from where I believed I had left them safely at home; and I would have remained in ignorance of their whereabouts or their fate, until I arrived home.

PP always considered, that I was a mere nonentity, and he was in charge of everything. It had never been intended for me to know the truth about the arrangement. The matter had been between him and Liz. If the wretched Liz had returned my car unscathed, then in all probability, I would never have been told. And she would have gone on using my car, as and when she wanted. After all, PP was making it increasingly clear he was now in command of my possessions, and I was just a piece of surplus baggage he had acquired, someone who no longer had any significance whatsoever.

Naturally, I felt an immense sense of relief knowing my children had not been injured in the accident. But I was furious about the disgraceful way I was being treated by this family from hell. They had move in on me like squatters and had taken over my home and my life... and all with never any by-your- leave.

When I was eventually given an explanation for what had happened, it was nothing but a cock-and-bull pack of lies, invented by Liz to exonerate herself. She was totally unabashed, and clearly disinterested in ever revealing the truth. Why should she be in any rush to explain, or apologise, for what had really happened? It was just my car. And so-far-as she was concerned, I was a woman of no importance at all... a despised nonentity, to whom she owed nothing, not even the truth.

When she did eventually saunter downstairs that Monday

morning, seemingly without a care in the world, I immediately challenged her about the damage. All I got by way of a reply was the insolent answer that her dad said she could use the car. And if I had anything to say about it, he had told her to refer me to him, and he would... 'deal with me.'

My furious response to such insolence was cold and to the point. I instantly left her in no doubts that she was an adult, and had to answer for her own misdemeanours. I informed her that she had no business going behind my back to use my car. She was living as a guest in my house, and had no permission to purloin or take possession of any of my property. I said that when I'd had a better look at the damage, she might well find herself in serious trouble with the police. She had taken my vehicle without permission from me, the legal owner, and driven it without any valid insurance, then returned it wrecked. And there was also the very serious matter of her driving away my two underage teenage daughters without my knowledge or permission.

In typical family style, she immediately set about an aggressive shouting match, yelling obscenely at me and calling me names. Her ignorant guttersnipe attitude closely echoed the experience I had witnessed at the hospital the first time I had ever laid eyes on her.

She even had the gall to deny the accident was anything to do with her, and claimed she had found the car bashed up when she came out of the disco, early that Sunday morning. Her fanciful lie was, that some unknown person must have caused the wreckage by ramming the car into a wall when she wasn't there. And as the accident had happened on private property, the police would not be interested.

I strongly suspected that piece of blatant fabrication had been constructed at her father's instigation. I could almost hear him speaking. In some devious way, they had already discussed the matter. And he had instructed her what she should say when I began asking questions. I already had enough experience of their devious feral behaviour to identify a clear family tendency towards automatically lying, and dissembling about any situation when questioned. Whatever genetic criminal mentality PP had inherited, was also very clearly evident in his offspring. Lying was clearly a talent inherent in their blood, and they were all as devious as each other; not one of them was to be trusted or believed in anything they ever said or did.

I waited until she had finished her rant. Then I calmly said she would probably have to explain her argument to the police. She was legally an adult, and as such, she was responsible for her actions. No matter what sort of excuses she tried to make, there was no getting away from the fact she had taken my car, and my children, without my permission, driven many miles without insurance, and then brought the vehicle back wrecked.

Her insolent, self-justifying attitude infuriated me. Having wrecked my car, she was persisting in hiding behind the feeble excuse that her father's permission gave her carte blanche to do whatever she wanted with my property. But I was also left facing the disastrous facts that my car was now a write-off, and there was no insurance to cover it, as I had not been driving.

The whole episode was sickening. And as soon as they came downstairs, I began questioning my daughters to find out what light they could shed upon the events. Both Nathalie and Samantha looked extremely sheepish, but they both simply repeated the cock-and-bull lies I had already heard from Liz.

That distressed me more deeply than the wrecked car, because I knew instinctively that they were both lying to support her and cover up the truth behind what had gone on. I had never known my girls to look more sheepish and guilty. My gut instinct told me that she had put them up to deceiving me. It was something neither of my children had ever done before. They weren't perfect angels. But in such a serious situation, I knew they would not readily choose to lie to me. They knew how important my car was to me. And beyond that, I knew they actually loved me.

The deep disappointment and shock I felt knowing they were lying to help Liz, caused me deep distress. I had a feeling of dread that they were falling under her devious influence, and lying because she had persuaded them to back her story up against me.

I had never expected such disloyalty from either of my children, and their attitude grieved me. Now the whole situation we were enduring, with the advent of this terrible family, was tearing me apart emotionally. My children were being influenced, and perverted, by the monsters living with us. I was at a loss to know how I was ever going to get to the truth.

If Liz stuck to her lies, and my girls persisted in supporting her, what could I do? The awful dilemma was threatening to create a terrible wedge between the three of us, and I felt I was losing everything... even the loyalty of my children. It was one of the darkest points of my life. I spent that evening in absolute misery.

Then just before bedtime, Samantha came to me and said she wanted to tell me the truth about my car. She said she understood how important it was to me... how I relied on it for work and shopping, and a lot of other necessary things. She was in tears, and full of remorse for having deliberately lied, and promised she would never do it again.

Shortly afterwards, Nathalie joined her, and together they explained what had actually happened. As I had suspected, there had been no mysterious unidentified car-park miscreant responsible. The damage to the vehicle had been sustained while they were on their way home. Liz had consumed several pints of beer in the disco, and her reckless driving had been responsible for everything. The story I had been told had been a pack of lies invented to hide her guilt and her responsibility.

I already knew from stories her father had previously told me that she was a totally erratic, and irresponsible driver. It had even come as a complete surprise to him when she had passed her driving test.

In every way she was thoughtless and wilful, and her attitude to driving in particular, reflected her mental attitude. She already had a history of accidents going back over the two years she had held a licence... There had been one incident, after she had been drinking, when she had abandoned her car, bonnet-down in a ditch.

Yet, this vile man had seen fit to give her permission to use my car, and to take my two young daughters with her, knowing that I would never have agreed to any of it. Being a well-practised, cajoling, and natural-born liar, like her father, she had prevailed upon my girls to back up her lies about what had actually happened, so she would not be blamed or held responsible.

I guess the fact that I was their mum had finally trumped her dubious and short-lived friendship... along with the fact, that my girls were naturally more inclined to be truthful.

The fact was, my car had been hit by a heavy goods, TIR, (Transports Internationaux Routiers, or... International Road Transport vehicle, in English), when Liz had been driving home.

She had been driving too fast, and in the wrong lane when they had come to a roundabout. Luckily for all of them, the driver of the oncoming heavy-goods vehicle, which had joined the roundabout from an intersection, had managed to squeeze past them, and had avoided what could have been a devastating, and fatal, head-on crash. As a result, my car had been flung aside by the larger vehicle, and sent skidding along the roundabout's stone retaining wall, virtually tearing one side of the car's body work almost off, and resulting in major irreparable damage.

The crazy girl had never even bothered to stop; she had just carried on driving like a maniac, running away from what she had done, half drunk, and heading for home. The accident had never been reported. The insurance details clearly were an irrelevance... she had none, and in any event, she could not have exchanged document ownership details with the other driver, as she had no rights of ownership. I was amazed not to have already had the police banging on my door.

So now I had the truth... In one respect alone, I considered myself lucky beyond belief... I still had my two live, uninjured daughters. But it was little thanks to Liz, or her father. Between them, they could have been responsible for the deaths of my children.

I hugged my girls, and followed up with a stern warning that I never wanted them ever to go anywhere with her again, unless first asking my permission... which I made very clear I would be highly unlikely to give.

After that, Liz went her own way and left my daughters alone.

Meanwhile, I was left with a wrecked vehicle that was not roadworthy, and for which I could make no insurance claim. Late the following morning, I was standing in the drive, glumly surveying my wrecked car for the umpteenth time. I had just provoked a blazing row with PP about it. My outburst had completely taken him by surprise and had been so verbally aggressive he had not had time to go through the usual process of winding himself up to violence, in order to silence me. I remained outraged by what had happened, along with all the lies and dissembling that had gone on. My anger had not been so much about the wrecking of my car, as the dangers my daughters' lives had just been subjected to.

We were standing beside the wreckage in the drive; and the angry verbal attack I had just delivered had caught him on the back foot. I accused him, in no uncertain terms, of the ultimate responsibility for wrecking my car. I blamed him for setting about to deceive me, just to please his own daughter, and said that his crass dishonesty could well have resulted in the death of my children.

I was really furious, and had left him in no doubt that I knew Liz had been lying to me; and I accused him of putting her up to it. His daughter was not only a liar and an irresponsible driver, but she had also been drinking, and had no insurance to cover her. Everything about what the pair of them had done had been illegal and despicable, and she hadn't even stopped at the scene of the accident.

My unplanned outburst, and my unexpected surge of courage in tackling him, surprised me. But my defensive feelings for my own children's safety had left me more enraged than I realised; nor was I prompted to hold back from speaking my mind, regardless of any consequences I might be creating for myself later.

I remember saying that I believed that he and his two appalling children were manipulating me, and disrespecting me in every way they could. This was still my home, it belonged to me; and he did nothing to respect the fact that I was now housing all three of them. He was not even putting his hand in his pocket to pay for the food they ate.

I said he seemed to think he could do whatever he liked without consulting me about anything, and that he made no efforts to control or correct the disgraceful rudeness, and unacceptable behaviour of either Steve or Liz. I held him responsible for what had happened, and it was now up to him to sort the situation out, or I would involve the police.

His response to my anguished outburst was so ridiculous I would never have credited him with such infantile behaviour had I not witnessed it. He stuck his fingers in his ears and began to yell, 'Blah! Blah, blah, blah, yah, yah, yah, blah, blah, blah,' over and over again at the top of his voice, in an attempt to drown me out.

For so long as I continued voicing my complaints, he continued his counter-attack of infantile noises... and all at full throttle, and for the benefit of a number of curious passers-by. Then he rushed off, got into his car, and drove away, leaving me standing speechless alongside my wrecked vehicle.

When he eventually returned, I was sitting on the window seat inside the drawing room, trying to work out what I was going to do, and how best to deal with my current situation. I noticed he was unloading several tools, some cellulose filler, and several cans of white cellulose spray paint from his car.

However, during his absence it was obvious he had been working himself up into a rip-roaring, towering revenge-rage against me. No doubt what I had said to him had given him enough motivation to want to tear me apart. I could see from the black fury written on his face, what was uppermost in his twisted mind.

I watched without any real interest, as he set about hammering and banging the damaged bodywork. It looked as though he was revenging himself upon me by making an even bigger mess of my car. His efforts to straighten the unyielding bent metal, with its multitude of dents, folds, splits, and grooves, improved nothing. And as I cast the occasional glance from the window to see what he was doing I observed the mess was becoming steadily worse. It was obvious he was attempting to save the expense of garage repairs. But he had neither the skill nor the patience, to achieve anything remotely acceptable.

My car didn't need hammering and bashing to put it right. It needed a whole range of expensive new body parts... To reinstate it, even cosmetically, it needed two new doors, replacement body panels the length of one side, and two new wings, as well as replacement headlamps, a new bumper and windscreen, and a new bonnet, plus replacements for the two buckled near-side wheels. What other unseen, additional, damage lay out of sight in the chassis region, I had no idea. But to my mind the car looked beyond the economics of repair... with everything twisted and out of alignment. It was just an irreparable heap of junk and needed to be scrapped.

He spent several hours on his efforts, sweating like a pig, and turning the air blue with his expletives, as he rolled and pushed cellulose filler into the wide gaps and deep dents, before smoothing the result off with his stubby fingers. I thought he resembled a fat unpleasant child, making sausage animals out of clay.

Eventually he sprayed the resulting bodged mess with the cans of white paint. The result was an unbelievably awful mess.

'There,' he snarled, when I eventually came outside to inspect his efforts. 'Ah've sortid it.'

I looked at the resulting wreck scathingly. 'You've made it into an even bigger mess than it was,' I said quietly. 'I've seen better cars at the scrapyard after they've been through the crusher.'

'Well, it's drivable,' he retorted spitefully. 'It wuzn't in no showroom condishun afore.'

'If you think it's drivable,' I said angrily, 'then you drive it. I'll take the car I paid for... that one standing over there.' I pointed to the smart gold-coloured Mercedes. 'And you can have this one you and your daughter have just wrecked... the one you claim is drivable. If you want to kill yourself, then go ahead, be my guest. Or else give me back the money you owe me, and I'll buy a new one.'

'Yer kin fuck off,' he yelled. 'Phone yer soddin insuras an' tell 'em yer've 'ad a fuckin' aksiden an' wan ter mek a claim. It's no big deal. Mek them pay fer it.'

That twisted suggestion made me even more outraged. 'I'll do no such thing,' I said quietly. 'I have no intention of shouldering the blame for an accident I was in no way responsible for. And I am not getting involved in lying about it for you, or bloody Liz. This entire episode is all down to you and your crazy daughter.

'I've given you the options. Make your choice. Otherwise, I'm going to the police about her. And I will have her arrested; you can be sure of that. What you are suggesting is that I should dig a pit for myself by telling a load of lies, to support her criminal behaviour. She took my car without permission and without insurance, and she wrecked it. Her crazy behaviour could have killed my children.

'Either you give me back the money you owe me, or I will do what I say. I need a reliable car for work before next Monday, and I am not risking my life driving that wreck. I absolutely refuse to tell lies and get myself into a whole load of legal trouble on her account, just to satisfy you.

'You brought her to live here without consulting me, and I owe her nothing. She's never been anything but an arrogant, rude, insolent brat, who does exactly as she pleases. I will never forgive her for what she's done, and for getting my girls to lie for her. You already owe me the cost of that smart Mercedes standing over there, and I want my money back. Or I will take the Mercedes to replace the wreck the pair of you have left me with.'

His loud-mouthed backup team had joined him during this argument, and they were noisily butting in, typically swearing and calling me names and voicing offensive things about me, in support of their father... all of which I chose to ignore. My own children were standing inside the hall saying nothing, just listening quietly.

I had said what I believed needed to be said, and saw no reason to prolong the argument further, so I walked back indoors.

With some insistent prompting, he chivvied his glowering offspring into the Mercedes and drove off in high dudgeon. In my heart I hoped they would never return. But sadly, we all experience unfulfilled hopes and dreams in our lifetimes.

As soon as the car was gone, Nathalie and Samantha came and sat with me in the drawing room.

'Will you really go to the police, Mum, if PP doesn't give you your money back?' Samantha asked.

'I never make idle threats,' I said. 'Liz is just like her father. She thinks she can get away with anything she wants, so long as he says it's all right. She has been insufferably rude to me ever since the first time she laid eyes on me, and I'm not putting up with her insolence and terrible behaviour any more.

'The three of them are all the same... just greedy grasping guttersnipes. Well they can't come here taking over our home and our lives, just because he tells them they can. There is such a thing as showing respect for other people's property, and they've shown not a shred of concern for any of us, or even how I might feel about what they are doing. This is our house, not theirs. They all need to learn respect and stop taking liberties.'

'PP looked really mad when they left,' Nathalie said. 'Do you think he's planning something else to get even with you? I don't trust him, Mum. I really wish you'd never married him and brought him here.'

'Oh, my darling, so do I,' I said wistfully. 'But how do I get out of it now? I honestly didn't know what he was really like until after the wedding. I thought he was a decent sort of man... a bit on the rough side, but I hoped we could all get along together. Now I've seen how they all operate, and I know they're like a feral street gang. I never know what's going to happen next. His family are awful; the lot of them are nothing better than violent, loud-mouthed, ignorant yobs.'

'Well we said from the start he was nothing like Daddy, didn't we?' Samantha said tearfully. 'But we didn't want to upset you by saying what we really thought about him. He really is a nasty horrible man. I just wish he would go away and leave us alone... What are you going to do about Liz?'

'Oh! I meant what I said about her,' I replied. 'I intend to get my money back to buy a replacement car. I'll have to let the smashed-up car go, and just write its value off. He's never going to give me any money to compensate me for that. But I want the return of the money he borrowed from me, and I'm determined to get it back. He deliberately set about conning me out of thousands to buy that fancy Mercedes. That beastly man owes me a huge amount of money.'

'Will you really go to the police about Liz if her dad doesn't pay you?' Nathalie said.

'Yes, I will,' I said resolutely. 'I want that awful girl out of my house. She has a mother of her own she can go and live with. I certainly don't want her living here. She was never part of the agreement I made with her father. If the air-force couldn't control her mouthy petulance and wilful disobedience, and turn her into a reasonable person, why should I have to put up with her? She's less than nothing to me. I've already got her wretched brother making my life hell. I don't need her here as well.'

'You really don't know half of what Steve gets up to while you're away at weekends, do you?' Samantha said quietly. 'Now he's got that Vespa motorbike, he thinks he's grown up. It's really awful being here at weekends with him when you're away. We both think he's heading for a load of trouble, Mum. He's started drinking, and there are other things he's doing that should be stopped. His dad should do something about him before he gets into serious trouble with the police.'

'Well he's no concern of mine,' I said sharply. 'Whatever trouble he gets into, his father can sort it out. He's made it abundantly clear what Steve does is none of my business. So, you just keep away from him, and his infernal sister. They're both trouble with a very big T.

When father and son eventually returned after their dramatic departure, Liz wasn't with them. She had gone to stay at her mother's house to keep out of my way. Nothing more was said to me about any plans PP might be hatching concerning their future, or about returning my money. But I knew instinctively something unpleasant was afoot.

A few days later, as nothing more had been said following my ultimatum regarding my car, or the return of my money, I began steeling myself to carry out my threat of going to the police. School was due to recommence the following Monday, and I was still left without any means of transport. It was a really worrying dilemma, and I was unsure how I should act.

He had realised my threat about involving the police was not an idle one, but he was still determined to pull every trick he could invent to avoid repaying me what I was owed. Where money was involved, PP always ensured he organised the odds in his own favour. He was as cunning as any low life member of the criminal class could be, and I never had any real hope of recovering the debts he owed me. Without my knowledge, the man had already worked out his next move to thwart me. But never in a million years had he any intention of ever returning one penny of my money.

On Thursday afternoon, a caller came to the door asking to speak to PP. The man didn't give me his name, or any business card, he just asked to see PP. As we were speaking, I glanced over his shoulder and noticed he had parked his car halfway onto my driveway. It was a low-slung, bright scarlet, two-seater sports car. It struck me as being a young man's car, and looked very cramped and difficult to get into and out of... not the kind of thing I would have expected an elderly man to be driving.

However, I gave a mental shrug and took the visitor into the drawing room and then called PP.

When he came in, I turned to leave them, but he stopped me and told me to sit down. For some inexplicable reason, he was switched into his Dr Jekyll mode, and was chatting amiably with his visitor as though they were old friends.

'Ah allus sez nuffinks too good fer mah wife.' I overheard him gushing to the stranger. 'She's got me woun' rowand 'er likkle finga. An Ah'm putty iner 'ands. Ah no Ah'm stoopid. Me kids tell me tha' aal the time. Bu' she gits evryfink she wan's aouter me. Ah jis can't 'elp mesel'.'

I stared at him in disbelief, wondering what on earth had triggered the need for such a silly performance. He wasn't impressing either his visitor or me with it.

The stranger had his briefcase open and was busy rummaging about in it, pulling out a sheaf of papers. He wasn't paying any attention to PP's farcical performance. Then I realised the act was intended for my benefit, to impress me, and soften me up for some new and devious trick he was about to pull. At that point, my mental radar swung into action.

I watched the man spread his papers on the coffee table before he produced a pen. He looked up smiling. 'Now, sir, what name shall I put on the ownership documents for the registration?' He paused and looked expectantly at PP, waiting for a reply.

After a moment of shifty hesitation PP said, 'Ah... wot thee 'ell diffrence does it mek? Yer kin stick mah name on 'em.' And he began spelling out his own name.

Suddenly it dawned on me that he was in the process of pulling another of his diabolical con tricks on me. Ownership documents? Vehicle registration?

The proverbial penny dropped, and I realised what was going on. In a final attempt to forestall my threats of going to the police about Liz, PP was about to replace my wrecked car with something he had arranged to buy, but about which he had never said a word to me.

However, this was no act of benevolence or generosity. Nor was it even a genuine way of making good for the recent wrecking of my car. This was his crafty way of writing off his debts to me, and he was about to go through the motions of presenting me with a new replacement car, only with the covert intention of fooling me yet again.

Whatever the car was, I had not been invited to choose it. And I felt sure it would be a vehicle worth many thousands of pounds less than the amount he owed me for the Mercedes. Now, to crown that cunning subterfuge, he was intending to register whatever it was, with himself as the legal owner. In any future ownership dispute, the car would not legally belong to me at all. He was craftily setting up a situation whereby he could take it away from me with impunity whenever he saw fit, and give it, or loan it, to whoever he decided.

I recognised it was just another of his scams, another trick intended to defraud me. He had gone about making all the underhand arrangements in complete secrecy, while I had been told nothing at all. I hadn't even seen the car, much less approved it. His intention had been downright deceitful. And he had planned to spring the arrangements of buying it on me, hoping the surprise would delude me into joyfully accepting the deal without question, as his flamboyant and ostentatious way of rectifying the current unpleasant situation.

However, this time I had assessed his underlying intentions quickly. He had been at it again, inventing ways to trick me, making plans behind my back, and pretending to be generous and doing the right thing. But there had never been any genuine or honest intentions at all. This time, my intuitive suspicions were working flat out, and I saw through the ulterior schemes already designed in his dirty little brain, relating to the vehicle.

'Hold on a minute,' I said loudly. 'Would you mind letting me see those papers, please?' I held out my hand to the salesman.

PP's jovial manner froze, and he gave me a hard, intimidating stare as the salesman passed over the, as yet incomplete transaction documents, for me to examine.

After a cursory check, I threw them down on the table. 'Do these documents refer to that sports car standing outside?' I demanded.

The salesman looked at PP and then slowly nodded.

'Then you can take it away,' I said curtly. 'What use do I have for a squashed-up, cramped sports car, with an enormous 1800cc engine? I'm not a boy racer, and I don't want it,' I said. 'I'm about to call a taxi, because I'm on my way to the police station.'

I continued glaring back at PP, before adding tersely, 'Did I not make my feelings clear enough? I hold you and your daughter responsible for wrecking my car. I emphasise the word my car, because I have never in my life driven a motor vehicle I did not own. And I have no intention of starting now. I refuse to be fobbed off like this by you, and I will not drive something I do not legally own. If it's registered in your name, then it's your car and not mine.

'You owe me the price of that expensive Mercedes automatic standing in the drive, and I want my money returned. You also owe me for my wrecked vehicle...I want the return of my loaned money, and the additional cost of replacing the vehicle which you and your daughter have written off...I want a car suitable for my own lifestyle, and something of my own choosing.'

I looked at the bewildered salesman. 'He's trying to pull a fast one on me,' I said angrily. 'I don't want this car he's brought you here to deliver, so you can take it away. I've never seen it before, or driven it, or even been involved in choosing it. And I sure as hell won't own it. But he will, and he'll be at liberty to take it away whenever the fancy suits him, and give it to his son or his daughter, or anybody he chooses. I want a car that belongs to me, or the return of the money he owes me, to purchase a vehicle of my own choosing.'

The salesman was looking totally embarrassed and perplexed. He clearly had no idea what was going on and turned towards PP for an explanation. 'I was under the impression that we had agreed on this sale,' he said nervously. 'When you and your son test-drove the car yesterday, you were both delighted with it. Your son said it was exactly what he had always wanted, and he was over the moon with the gift. You led me to believe you were buying it for him. You didn't mention your wife was involved.'

I stared at PP. 'So that was your devious plan, was it?' I said. 'Pretend to be giving the car to me to repay the £25,000 you owe me? Make a fool of me by letting me drive it for a couple of years, and then as soon as Steve gets a licence, I would suddenly find it taken it away from me and given to him... all because you had craftily seen to it that the bloody thing was never my legal property in the first place. You really are a filthy conniving swine.'

PP was, by that point, furiously red in the face and grinding his teeth. For once I had caught him out, and humiliated him publicly as the double-dealing shyster he truly was. Clearly my words had struck home, and I returned his glare as he sat biting his lips and clenching and unclenching his fists to restrain himself from leaping at me, and striking me down in front of the salesman.

The scene was volatile. But the fact it was being played out in front of an independent witness held him back from attacking me.

The poor salesman clearly felt extremely awkward to be caught in the middle of such a highly contentious family dispute. He fiddled nervously with his pen and then coughed. 'Well I came here under the impression the transaction had been fully negotiated yesterday,' he said, clearly embarrassed. 'We gave you an exceptionally good discount of £4,500, because you agreed to accept delivery and settle the account today. Do you or don't you want me to leave the car? And if you do, whose name shall I put on the documents?'

After once again firing evil and threatening looks at me, PP suddenly blurted out, 'Ah! For fuck's sake. Let 'er 'ave 'er own way. Put the bloody fing in 'er name. If Ah doan agree Ah'll nivver 'ere the end of it. She's fuckin' money mad. The bloody cow finks o' nuffin but money.'

So that was how the situation concluded. I had been fobbed off with a cramped, fancy two-seater sports car, which I did not want. Instead of a safe and spacious five-door saloon car, I now owned a soft-topped, red sports car, with no room to carry children, or shopping, or anything other than legless dwarfs on the rear parcel shelf. There was no boot-room for luggage, and it was entirely unsuitable for my lifestyle as a working mother with two teenage daughters.

But of course, the car had never been intended to become my property.

Fortunately, I realised in time that if I refused to accept it as my replacement vehicle, PP would rapidly decide he did not owe me anything at all, and I would be unlikely ever to see any other replacement car, or the return of my money either. I never did receive any of the remainder of the money I was owed. It was all conveniently forgotten…rolled up into property deals, as invariably, were all his debts to me.

But my timely reactions had thwarted his cunning plans to eventually deprive me of ownership of the car, and hand it to his son. In any event, I only kept it for ten months before I got rid of it.

Fortunately, I had kept in mind the shameful stories I had previously been told, of how disgracefully he had treated Beryl. When he decided to divorce her, she had been sent packing with all she owned in black plastic sacks, and he had refused to even loan her a car to move her things. Legally she owned nothing, because everything was in his name. Beryl had been forced to endure the humiliation of leaving their family home by public transport, on a bus.

PP had never experienced any guilt over what he had done. Remorse was just another emotion he never felt. But he considered himself extremely clever to have left Beryl stranded, after twenty years of marriage with no means of transport. It was just as I had previously noticed. He had no capacity for real emotions, like love, or guilt or shame. This was a man who had no soul, and no conscience.

But I am a good pupil, and I take note and absorb the lessons I am being taught, even if they are intended only as incidental stories. Fortunately, I also hold to the belief that 'forewarned is forearmed'.

My insight had come from previous lessons learned during moments of PP's cocksure, bragging bravado. In future, so far as motorcars went, he would never be able to do to me what he had so hatefully done to Beryl... and Mandy... and even Liz. For once I had outwitted him. But it was a hollow victory, and one for which I would be made to pay... later.

Chapter 20

A Year to Break Me, Part VI: The Delinquent Arsonist

Following the chaos Liz had caused in taking my car, wrecking it, and lying about it, she now made sure she kept out of my way as much as she could. She had already made her dislike of me completely obvious. But that was a two-way street so far as I was concerned. For a variety of good reasons, I resented her being in my house, and now it seemed, she didn't want to be there either, which suited me perfectly. The result was she made arrangements to live part-time with her mother, and she also began spending a lot of her free time with her married sister, Mandy.

I felt relieved she was now largely out of my hair and, thankfully, leaving my girls alone. But if I imagined things with her had quietened down, I was living in cloud-cuckoo-land.

Meanwhile her brother was acting like an unbearable, vile hooligan in his usual delinquent fashion. Like his sister, Steve's behaviour towards me had never been pleasant. But following the car episode, he became deliberately and insufferably even more rude and disrespectful. He had been seriously peeved over the way the planned future ownership of the red sport's car had gone wrong. He had anticipated that, on his seventeenth birthday, the car would be taken from me and handed to him. Everything had already been covertly arranged, and his father had even let him choose the make, and his favourite colour, bright red, for the bodywork.

Now he was behaving like the spoilt brat he had always been. Because I had acted intuitively and insisted on the car being legally registered in my name, my foresight meant he was never going to get his hands on it. As a result of being deprived of what he had been promised, he played up appallingly and was as obnoxious and as peevish as he could be towards me.

Every weekend my enforced obligations at the cottage meant Nathalie and Samantha continued to be left at home with him. And while they now both worked all day on Saturdays, he was at liberty to tear around the town on his Vespa moped, and get up to whatever mischief he wanted... including smoking, and developing a fondness for alcohol.

Without doubt, his behaviour was seriously delinquent and totally out of control. He was just going on sixteen; but so far as his father was concerned, 'the lad was jus' behavi' like eny normal kid 'is age, an lettin rip wiv 'igh spirits.'

My girls had tactfully tried to warn me about Steve's behaviour at the time of the car incident, but I had been too preoccupied with my other worries to take much notice of what they were trying to tell me about him. In any event, I regarded him as a lost cause, and no concern of mine. There was nothing I could do about him. His father had already threatened me with violence over the youth, and forbidden me from correcting him for anything he did. Consequently, he had carte blanche to go his own way. My position in his life was merely to house and feed him, and nothing more. My opinion was, if the awful boy was running wild, he was his father's problem and nothing to do with me.

In a manner of speaking, PP's chickens first began coming home to roost one Sunday night in late November, when he and I arrived home from Salisbury. As soon as we were indoors that evening, I sensed something awful had gone on in my absence, and I was seriously alarmed. I could smell petrol fumes, and the strong odour of burning; in fact, the whole house reeked of it.

If PP noticed anything was wrong, he chose to ignore it. But it alarmed me sufficiently to make me hurry around the rooms checking to see if anything had been damaged or burned. Eventually, I took a torch and went outside to search the garden and the outbuildings.

Outside, the stench was even stronger. The pungent smell of petrol was unmistakable, and I knew something really bad had gone on in my absence. Naturally, I was determined to get to the bottom of it, but it was too dark for me to find the source of the stench, and there was nothing I could do until the following morning.

As soon as it was daylight, I took my little Yorkies outside for their morning run, and while they were busy, I began searching the garden. The aroma of petrol was still evident, although an overnight breeze had cleared some of it away.

At first, I found nothing. Then as I came back towards the house I saw, near our upturned sailing boats, two huge circles of burned grass, each two metres in diameter. They had been carefully constructed within half a metre of the conservatory, but out of sight of the kitchen windows which overlooked the garden. When I looked closer, I could see the circles were broad grooves that had been excavated about six inches deep into the turf to create a continuous circular channel. Both channels were blackened and charred, and appeared to have been filled with petrol and set alight. A swathe of the surrounding grass had also been badly scorched, and I was alarmed to see that, only by some incredible luck, the conservatory and the boats lying close beside it, hadn't caught fire and sent the entire house up in flames.

In the middle of one of the circles, something appeared to have been cremated. The only remaining evidence was a pile of ashes, with no immediate way of telling what had been burned there. After gently raking the ashes with a stick, I found two metal shoe buckles from a pair of sandals. They were blackened and badly scorched, but still identifiable...this evidence instantly told me who had been responsible for the outrage.

Steve had been moaning during the previous week that he wanted a pair of leather sandals. To make him happy, I had gone out and bought him a pair. Now all that was left of them were the fire-tarnished buckles.

There was no point in asking his father to take the boy to task. He would have instantly gone on the defensive and aggressively denied the boy was responsible. But I knew for certain he was the culprit.

Very conveniently he was currently missing from the house... supposedly staying with a friend, and consequently not available to question. All I could do was ask my daughters about what had gone on. I was sure they would tell me exactly what they knew.

Their account did not come as a huge surprise. They had come home from work at five o'clock on the Saturday afternoon to find Steve busy digging in the garden. When they asked what he was doing he told them to, 'fuck off and mine yer own bisniss'.

They'd guessed he was up to some sort of mischief, so they had watched from indoors as he finished digging the two large circular trenches. They then saw him bring a can of petrol from the garage and fill the channels he had excavated. After that, he placed the pair of sandals I had bought him in the centre of one circle, poured petrol over them, and began cavorting around the circles in a crazy wild dance, shrieking and shouting curses about me, and calling for the devil to come and kill me.

They had been alarmed by his outrageous behaviour, and the awful curses he had been chanting and shouting in his efforts to summon up the devil to help him. At first, they felt too intimidated to attempt to intervene, but they had kept watch while he kept his crazy performance going for about an hour.

When he eventually poured more petrol over the sandals and set fire to them, they became seriously scared. By this stage he was shrieking and laughing insanely, as he continued his crazy efforts to invoke the devil. Then, before they could stop him, he suddenly ignited the two large circles already filled with petrol.

At that point, my girls threw caution aside, ran out to tackle him and attempt to put out the flames. Their efforts led to a battle, with him violently wrestling them over possession of the hosepipe. As all three of them fought for it, Steve suddenly darted away and turned off the water tap. He had a sharp craft knife in his hands and was lashing out at both of them in a determined battle to keep his arson efforts going.

After a set-to lasting several minutes, the girls eventually managed to overpower him, and prevented him from slashing the hosepipe with the sharp knife. He was acting like someone crazy in his determination to keep the blaze going. Eventually, they got the water turned back on, and in the ensuing scuffle, he was soaked to the skin.

Leaving the fires blazing furiously, he ran off, got onto his motorbike, and rode away. He hadn't returned all weekend.

With Steve gone, the girls had turned the hosepipe full on and spent the next hour or so soaking everything they thought was in danger of catching light, as they battled to extinguish the flames, and prevent them from growing any higher and spreading. It hadn't been easy for them. A wind was blowing towards the house, and the burning petrol was floating on the water and spreading the flames onto the surrounding lawn even as they continued struggling to control the blaze.

The two of them had been in a state of panic, because they could see that the house was at serious risk of catching fire, and there was no adult around to help them. They were both wet to the skin, but they had continued giving the boats and everything else which the hose could reach, a good soaking, until eventually they had managed to put out the flames. Thankfully their efforts had prevented the flames from spreading to engulf the sailing boats and ultimately saved the conservatory and the house from incineration.

Their story horrified me. But the clear evidence of what had gone on still remained for anyone to see, along with the smell. It was only by a fortuitous chance that Nathalie and Samantha had both come home when they did. Any later, and there could well have been a total disaster, with the house ablaze.

I was shocked to the core by this latest malicious criminal activity of the dreadful youth I was housing. His crazy delinquent behaviour could easily have led to both of my daughters being severely burned, and our house burning down.

My girls had been extremely frightened, but they had been commendably quick-witted and brave. The volatile fumes and the smell must have been a terrible experience for them to deal with. I had no lingering doubts, that everything Steve had done had been deliberate malicious and dangerous, and disgustingly and cowardly.

There hadn't been any time for my daughters to leave the hosepipe and go indoors to telephone the fire brigade. But they had acted bravely on instinct, and in sheer desperation to save our home in the only way they could think of.

Once again, I was faced with the lethal potential and the delinquent malicious behaviour of one of PP's obnoxious brats. This time, it had been his wretched son who had deliberately put the lives of my children in danger, along with potentially destroying my property.

So far as I was concerned, it now appeared Steve had the twisted inclinations of a psychopathic arsonist, and I was left incandescent over his criminally wilful behaviour. Equally disturbing was the callous way he had run off like a pathetic coward, and left my daughters to cope with the results of his flagrant behaviour. His father had certainly raised him to be a total shit... a conscienceless, vicious scumbag, just like himself. There was no denying it... the depraved youth had made a deliberate arson attack on my property, then run away from his crime, and left my young daughters to deal with the fire he had started.

I told them both I was deeply sorry I had not been there to prevent what had happened, but I thought their courage and presence of mind had been amazing.

The results of this trauma left me in a state of mental turmoil. How was I ever going to bring an end to all these terrible things that were happening to us? PP and his criminal family were turning our lives into a living nightmare.

Not one solitary word was ever said about the incident by PP or his son. They just blanked what had gone on that weekend, and PP never asked or attempted to find any explanation for how two huge, burned circles had appeared in the lawn, so dangerously close to the conservatory, or how all the paintwork on my family's sailing boats had come to be blistered.

It crossed my mind to wonder if he might have had some prior knowledge concerning the entire incident. I even considered the possibility he might have even put Steve up to setting fire to the house. He had already threatened me with burning my boats if I didn't dispose of them.

In my recent experience of this man, nothing was beyond his evil mind. He already knew I was paying a substantial insurance policy on my house, with cover worth one million pounds, should the house be destroyed by fire.

It could be no accidental coincidence how close to the house the fire had been. And I considered it highly suspicious that such a dangerous incident had been allowed to pass without any comment from PP. No normal parent would so easily have ignored the evidence of a significant fire being caused that close to his home, without at least making enquiries about it, or carrying out some kind of investigation into who was responsible. But PP did absolutely nothing and took no steps whatsoever to punish the culprit.

To my mind, the evidence spoke for itself. I guessed he and his son probably found it secretly amusing, and even laughed about how close Steve's arson attempt on my property had come to succeeding. I remained convinced that PP was fully aware of exactly what his son had been up to. The scars on the lawn, the burned shoe buckles, and the scorched and blistered paintwork on my boats were unmistakable evidence of an arson attempt... and facts that no right-minded person would ever have avoided investigating.

I made a point of asking a couple of times where the expensive sandals I had recently bought for Steve were. Lost... was all the explanation I ever got.

This delinquent youth was almost sixteen, but he was already experienced in every sort of vice and perverted behaviour imaginable... including drinking, sadistic animal cruelty, and highly dubious sexual behaviour. And now it appeared his criminal inclinations also included malicious arson.

From his father's own boasts, since childhood he had raised Steve to copy, and follow, whatever he himself did. And the boy had been brought up to consider himself some sort of 'son of god'. PP certainly considered himself and everything he did beyond the law, and outside of normal conventional restrictions of any sort. Nothing was prohibited to him. And as such, he could do and say whatever he wanted with complete impunity.

Months earlier, I had been forced to listen as PP had bragged how proud he was of the way he had raised his son. It had given him some sort of paternal glow to regale me with wild stories of how he had trained his boy from childhood to copy his own behaviour in every way.

He proudly boasted how he had removed the child from his mother's control and influence, from the age of two, and taken him everywhere with him... including on pub crawls, and staying overnight with women he had picked up in pubs. This shameless recital had included stories of how he'd educated his son in smoking, swearing, fighting, setting fires, and destroying property, and generally denigrating and abusing females of every creed and colour.

Without a flicker of shame, he claimed he had raised Steve to hate his mother, and to ridicule and ignore anything she ever did or said. He spitefully insisted this was justifiable, because his son had been rejected at birth by her, and that she had always refused to care for the boy.

Since their divorce, any gifts she had sent Steve were returned to her, along with insolent notes addressed to 'the Haggis Bag', a derogatory nickname encouraged by his father, and invented out of a sick desire for spiteful revenge.

Was it any wonder that I now found the youth had such an appalling attitude towards me? Their family ethos was, without a shadow of doubt, highly complex, and dangerously dysfunctional.

From the arson episode onward, each weekend when I was away from home, I worried myself sick, wondering what devilment the awful youth might be getting up to, and what new mischief he might be creating in my absence, involving my daughters.

As things turned out, I was absolutely right to feel such concern. Samantha and Nathalie had very gently tried to warn me about Steve's feral behaviour weeks earlier, but I had chosen to ignore their warnings. However, his lawless activities were about to catch up with him. The police were not likely to ignore his delinquent and public antisocial behaviour for very long.

One Monday morning, several weeks after the fire circle episode, I had a phone call at school from the police. The officer enquired if I had a son called Steve. I said I didn't, but I did have a stepson of that name, and enquired if there was some sort of problem.

I wasn't given a direct answer. But after checking his full name and age with me, the caller insisted it was the boy's father they needed to speak to, face to face. The police caller stated that they considered the boy was running wild and needed serious parental discipline. An interview had been arranged at the police station, and both father and son were required to attend. Otherwise, they would pick the boy up and bring him into the station to be interviewed and officially reprimanded. That was all I was told, and the conversation ended with a polite request that I should relay the message to his father, and ask him to attend the station and bring his son with him.

I wrote down the name of the senior officer who would be conducting the interview and the time and date of the appointment. When PP came home that evening, I explained what had happened and that there had been a phone call from the police requesting he should take Steve with him and attend the office, to receive an official reprimand.

His instant reaction was aggressive and threatening as usual. He turned on me, shouting and swearing, and began slapping my face and poking me in the mouth and accusing me of going to the police behind his back to make trouble, telling lies about his son concerning the fire rings.

It was the first time he had made any reference to the fire rings. Up to that point, he had totally blanked the damage that had been caused. Suddenly, he was acknowledging that he knew about the arson attempt, and was now accusing me of going behind his back to the police about the incident.

He categorically refused to attend the police interview, and said as I had caused the trouble I could go and sort it out. There was no reasoning with the man. I said I had no idea what the police wanted to interview Steve about, but the fire rings were nothing to do with it. He ended the situation by aggressively threatening me, and refusing to be involved. I was left with no choice except to attend the police station with Steve myself.

Throughout the interview, the boy sat alongside me morosely slumped on his seat, tilting his chair backwards, rocking it to-and-fro, and glowering at everyone. His behaviour was diabolical throughout the interview, and he sat glaring at the officer with a belligerent, aggressive and sullen face. I doubt if he could have behaved more rudely, and insolently...and his responses to all the questions put to him were no more than surly monosyllabic grunts.

Whatever he had been up to, he demonstrated not one fragment of remorse. And being in the police station didn't seem to intimidate him at all. I was surprised the officer conducting the interview did not take a much more severe approach, and make the interview a great deal more intimidating than he did. The boy was nothing to do with me, but I felt absolutely ashamed of him.

It was made very clear during the course of the proceedings that he had been called there for two reasons, neither of which had anything to do with the fire rings. The first issue related to complaints that had been made about his intimidating sexual behaviour. Several complaints had been received relating that on the past two Saturday evenings, he had been reported for stalking a series of solitary young girls as they were walking home alone, along quiet roads in the town. He had deliberately terrified them by following them, and then concealing himself before jumping out from behind bushes to grab hold of them, whereupon he had wrestled them to the ground and attempted to overpower them in some form of attempted sexual attack.

Having failed in that, when they had escaped and run off, he had pursued them, yelling sexual abuse and disgusting threats. He had been using obscene language and threatening to rape them and perform a variety of highly unsavoury acts on them, such as pulling off their underwear, with the intention of stuffing the garments down their throats. This was seriously worrying, and highly intimidating, perverse sexual behaviour, and the girls who had reported him claimed he had smelt strongly of alcohol.

The second complaint came directly from the police and related to his Vespa moped. I wasn't too familiar with the engineering of the bike, but I managed to follow the general reason for the police complaints against him.

Because of his age, the machine required some sort of mechanical governor fitted to the engine, to prevent it from producing more than 50 ccs of power, or going at more than thirty miles per hour. He had removed this mechanical restriction, along with a noise suppressor fitted to the exhaust. Subsequently, he had been caught speeding around the town at more than thirty miles per hour and creating the devil's own racket with the modified exhaust.

I found the hour-long interview an entirely embarrassing experience. Steve spent the entire time lounged morosely in his chair, wearing an insolent, detached expression the entire time we were there. And his attitude towards the officer in charge was intentionally provocative and confrontational. He grunted and shrugged throughout, in a couldn't-care-less series of monosyllabic responses to all the questions he was asked.

I did my best to apologise for his behaviour and emphasised he was not my son, and that I really had no control over him. I had neither provided him with his motorbike, nor sanctioned the modifications he had carried out to it.

The interviewing officer was obviously sympathetic towards me in my awkward situation. He wanted to know why the boy's father hadn't attended the interview, and I had to make up some excuse about his work commitments preventing him from being there.

I don't know if I was believed or not, but eventually, because I was a local head teacher, and said I would do my best to see nothing similar occurred again, they let the boy go, with nothing more than a stern warning.

Steve merely regarded the situation as hilarious... a huge joke. And later that day, both he and his father turned the entire episode into a farcical charade. Steve performed a crude parody, for his father's amusement, mimicking both the police officer and me, as he ridiculed how each of us had behaved at the interview. Neither of them showed the slightest regret, and not even any appreciation for my help. And a month later the boy was again in trouble with the police over his activities, and his motorbike.

This time, his father received an official letter, which obliged him to attend an interview. I have no idea what came of that, as I was never told. But there was no subsequent comedy act following it.

I feel absolutely sure PP would have spun an incredible tale of pathos to the officer interviewing them... unhappy divorce, mother mentally deranged, unhappy at home, stepmother who didn't want him. Plausible lies were, after all, his major talent. I had heard them all myself months earlier. Believing them had got me into the mess I was in.

At about the same time, as Steve's antics were coming under police scrutiny, Liz re-entered the avaricious family arena, intent upon bringing me a whole new set of problems.

She still hadn't succeeded in obtaining a replacement car, but now she wanted a house... not a rented house or even a flat. She was nineteen, and she wanted to own her own house.

She felt entitled, as usual, because she wasn't happy living with her mother or with me. And of course, that was all my fault.

Very soon, and without my ever being aware of their new convoluted scheme to defraud me, I was about to be inveigled by her father into providing her with what she wanted. It was their latest nefarious plot to con me out of money, and once more demonstrated my gullible stupidity.

# Chapter 21

A Year to Break Me, Part VII: Fraud, Insolence, and Attempted Rape

There was one very good reason I was never informed of any of the devious plans, PP and his malignant brood were continually plotting. It was because their schemes were always made to my detriment, and to benefit themselves. And invariably, the acquisition of money was involved... money they intended to defraud from me.

Their meetings were akin to a secret cabal. And I only ever found out about their plots once they had already become faits accomplis. After the business with my wrecked car, and the arson attempt on my house, the plotting and scheming that went on between Liz and her father and brother was never spoken of.

But going on beneath my radar, there was a new sinister plan afoot to manipulate more of my assets to their own advantage.

PP's family was a devious malicious lot. All were greedy and self-opinionated in the extreme. And each of his children had inherited the twisted criminal mentality of their father.

It eventually came to my knowledge that he had told them all months earlier, when he first met me, that I was a millionaire and the ideal candidate he had been looking for to marry. He had assured them that I meant absolutely nothing to him but promised that when he had eventually extracted every penny I possessed, he would use all my assets to make each of their lives comfortable. Each of them would get everything they wanted... including a house and a car apiece.

The only problem was they would have to be patient and give him time to put his plans into action. Consequently, there was always some scam or another going on that involved trying to screw money out of me.

One afternoon, I came home laden with the usual half-dozen bags of groceries to find my driveway blocked. Eight low cc motorbikes were strewn untidily across all the parking space on my driveway. I recognised the red one as belonging to Steve. All the others were of a similar restricted engine type, but I didn't recognise any of them and had no idea who they belonged to.

With double yellow lines on the adjacent roadway, I had to risk parking my loaded car there while I went indoors to find out what was going on. I found my kitchen in chaos and full of strange youths I had never seen before. The din and the smell were unimaginable. They had the radio turned up full blast and were shouting and jumping on the table and the workbenches like so many crazy monkeys. The place was choking with cigarette smoke, and they were all swigging bottles of beer, while the door of my fridge was standing wide open, with the contents, or what remained of it scattered everywhere on the floor and work surfaces. The place was an absolute tip.

I was livid to have come home from work to find such pandemonium going on, and the place full of half-drunken juvenile louts. Shouting above the noise, I asked them to remove their bikes and give me access to my driveway. But my voice went unheard above the din they were making. They didn't even seem to care that I was standing there quivering with rage. Not one of them had the courtesy to even glance in my direction.

I stormed over and turned off the radio and then shouted above the remaining racket that, if they didn't remove their machines from my drive and clear off, I was calling the police to have them arrested.

They continued to ignore me as though I was invisible... until I picked up the telephone and began to dial. The noise abated slightly.

Then I heard Steve's mocking voice loud and clear. 'Aw tek no notice uv 'er,' he sneered drunkenly. 'She's only the latest fuckin' owld slapper wot sleeps wiv me dad. She finks coz ee lets 'er live 'ere wiv us, she kin behave like she owns the bloody place. Bu' she's not in charge o diddly-squat. This in me dad's 'ouse. Ee sez wot's wot 'ere...not 'er. Ah kin do enyfink Ah wonts, and bring enybody 'ere I fancy. Jus' ignore 'er. She counts fer nuffink. She's jus' the fuckin' skivvy round 'ere.'

To emphasise his outrageous misogynistic insolence, he waved a bottle of beer in my direction, shook it, and squirted the contents at me... before sticking up two fingers to show his contempt.

Such disgraceful insolent behaviour from anyone was incredible. But from someone so young, who was living in my home and at my expense, it made me furious. I gestured back at the crowd of youths, by waving the telephone receiver at them. 'Well, we'll see whose house this is when the police arrive,' I said quietly.

'If you, idle yobs aren't out of my house in the next ten seconds, I'll have the lot of you arrested ... including you, you disgusting oaf,' I said, pointing the handset towards the chief miscreant.

There was an instant lull in the racket, followed by a noisy scramble as chairs were overturned in their rush for the door. Bottles of beer and cans of lager went flying in all directions as they dashed past me. Seconds later, I heard their engines roaring into life, and they were gone... thankfully, never to return.

I turned to look at the remaining cocky individual, who was still insolently lounging with his feet planted on the table, slurping from a two-litre bottle of beer and leering at me menacingly. 'Now, let you and me get one thing straight, right now,' I said. 'This is my house, and I won't have you bringing that lot of tearaways here again.' Then after a pause I added, 'And as you are now free, I would like some help to carry the groceries in from my car, please. You and your mates appear to have eaten everything that was left in the fridge, and the replacement supplies need to be brought in.'

He didn't move a muscle, just gave me another insolent stare and sneered. 'Then fuckin' do it yerself! Ah'm busy. Ah doan fetch an' carry fer yer. Yer jus a nuffink roun' 'ere. An yer doan gi'e me orders. Me dad sez yer jus' the skivvy ee keeps ter cook an' clean up... and fuck. Me dad's the boss 'ere. It's 'is 'ouse naw, wotivver yer try ter pretend. This place doan b'longs ter yer no more. So fuck off.'

I suppose what the cocky, foul-mouthed oaf was rehearsing was no more than a repeat of what he had been trained to say by his disgusting father. He had just expressed a clear unambiguous picture, illustrating exactly how the pair of them actually viewed me. They were satisfied that, by some strange and inexplicable act of submission, I had already surrendered my family property to them. And everything they planned to do with it was their God-given right as the new owners.

I knew I had already been outrageously abused by the lot of them for far too long. I had scarcely been married to PP for five months, but with the advent of his insolent son and his loud-mouthed manipulative daughter, my misery seemed set to be continually compounded. All three of them were hell-bent on abusing me and taking advantage by every means they could devise.

I had no idea what I could do to bring the situation to an end. And I was only too well aware that PP would injure me further if I ever attempted to correct his son or complain about his behaviour.

As a married couple, our relationship was meaningless and built on nothing but the shifting sands of lies, intimidation, and manipulation. I was at my wit's end to find some sort of satisfactory solution to my problems. And I desperately wanted a way out of it.

Some days after this disgraceful incident in my kitchen, PP decided he wanted to talk to me. His approach was highly amenable, chatty, and concerned for my welfare. He was using his best and most concerned Dr Jekyll manner. In fact, he was all sweetness and light when he opened the subject of finding somewhere else for Liz to live.

It was unforgivably stupid of me, as well as a serious miscalculation of judgment, not to have instantly suspected his motives. But he opened his conversation so innocently and mildly, and set about manipulating me so cunningly that I really believed he was trying to find a solution to help me.

My recent experiences involving his manipulative talents, so far as anything to do with money was concerned, should have instantly put me on my guard and made me suspect his intentions. In fact, anything to do with his family and money, was always going to be against my best interests.

The story he had concocted this time was made to appear motivated by his sympathetic concern for my seriously injured feelings, over the recent behaviour of Liz and Steve. The plausible proposal he brought to me was cleverly presented, and intended to play right into my hopes for getting Liz, permanently out of my home. It was a masterpiece, of fiendishly concocted lies; and so well structured and rehearsed I was completely taken in by it. As usual he was playing on my emotions, manipulating my mind, and claiming to have my feelings and my best interests at heart.

He began by telling me he understood how difficult it must have been for me, having to accept Liz living with us, since she had left the WRAF...

'Ah naw it wuzn't eesy fer yer, me bringin' Liz ere wivaaut no werd afor 'and... Then we aal got muddld up wiv tha bit of a misunderstandin ova yer car... Ah naw it med fings more arkwad atween us. Bu' ah've bin finkin fings ova, an'givin thim a lorra fort, an' ah kin see naw ow it wud be fer the best, al roun' for both 'er and yer, if she ad somewheir else ter live. She disn't wont ter to live permnantly wiv 'er muver... it's ova fer er ti travel ti werk... An uvcors jis yet she disn't 'ave a car...

'Naw... gittin a flat wudn't reely suit 'er. Wot she reely needs ter settle 'er dawn, an mek 'er act sponsibly, is an ouse uv 'er own.'

This was the cunning plan he outlined to me, making sure he stressed how he believed it would resolve the residential problems for me, as well as for her. ...It now appeared that Liz had already been looking around, and had found a small three-bedroom terraced house she liked, at the east end of the town, in Stevenson Street. He had already been to look it over and check it out. It was small and a bit old-fashioned, but it was structurally sound and big enough for her needs.

In fact, quite a lot had been going on without anything ever being mentioned to me...It seemed quite a number of enquiries had already been put in hand...If my thinking hadn't been so clouded, and I had been given more time, I certainly would have been asking a lot more questions than I did. But time was never a commodity PP ever gave me...FOR THINKING.

He had the whole project cut and dried, before ever I heard anything about it.

Because of her age, and her poor job prospects, a mortgage was out of the question; so, he was proposing to help get her sorted, by mortgaging the Salisbury cottage, to raise the purchase price. If he purchased the little house in his name, she would then pay the mortgage costs each month as rent... right up until the loan was repaid. It would all be done properly, and be legally arranged all above-board. She would have a weekly rent book, and pay the loan from her wages.

The house was a snip at £45,000, and it had vacant possession. There was only one snag... In order to close the deal, the money needed to be forthcoming immediately, or she would lose out to another interested buyer, and have to return to living with us (a clever psychological point, which he stressed).

However, as he most calmly and logically went on to explain, the entire matter could be easily settled. All we had to do was go to the bank and arrange a temporary bridging loan for the whole amount. That would get things moving quickly, and afterwards everything could be smoothly sorted out. Once the house had been secured, he would arrange a mortgage on the cottage, and the bridging loan would then be redeemed and the bank loan paid off. He was certain it would all go smoothly...The entire plan was fool-proof... as simple as ABC.'

Of-course it was fool-proof, the biggest con man in England had designed it. But I alas, was the gullible fool being taken for yet another financial ride by this expert con artist.

Loud-mouthed Liz got her house... exactly as planned. But without my knowledge, or consent, there were drastic unexplained changes made to the original plan into which I had been manipulated to agreeing. Most significantly, the deed-of-ownership, was put into her name, not her father's. He had originally promised her a house, paid for by me ***once we were married...*** And now she had it.

Too late, I learned I had been duped by their cunning deception and false promises, into committing myself to a huge bank loan for the purchase of a property I had no legal claim on. PP had never had any intention of raising a mortgage on the Salisbury house. Nor did he ever pay any money into the joint bank account to offset the loan. I was simply left to discover I had been manipulated into full responsibility for Liz's huge financial debt, plus all the interest that rapidly began to accrue at fifteen percent, on the bank loan.

There never was any attempt to take out a mortgage on the

Salisbury house, and Liz never paid me one penny in rent, or bank loan, or the eventual mortgage repayments I became saddled with. The truth was, neither of them made the least effort to pay off a penny of the loan into which I had been cunningly manipulated.

Why should Liz be troubled? Legally the house belonged to her. The debt for its purchase had been fraudulently dumped onto me. Another diabolical financial deception by PP had been successfully achieved.

These two low lives had successfully saddled me with a large bank debt, which I could ill afford, simply to satisfy Liz's greedy demands. She wanted a house, as promised by her father from the start of his involvement with me.

I feel certain the pair of them were highly delighted by the cunning con they had succeeded in playing. Getting one over on me had become the family game with which they amused, and enriched, themselves.

Unfortunately, at that same time, there were other things going on relating to PP's delinquent family that added even more to my burden of distress.

Following the episode involving Steve's thwarted efforts to burn down my house, I was becoming increasingly unhappy about leaving my daughters at home unchaperoned every weekend, with him still in residence. Samantha and Nathalie had struggled to control him during his arson episode. And each weekend they were out doing their Saturday jobs, while he was left with free rein to run riot in our home. I had no way of knowing just what malicious plans he would come up with next. His perverse mentality and his deviant sexual inclinations ran strongly in his blood. He was a large six-foot tall youth, and much stronger than either of my daughters.

A couple of weekends after Liz had moved into her new residence in Stevenson Street, I came home on the Sunday evening to find my girls barricaded in Samantha's bedroom. When they eventually unlocked the door and let me in to talk to them, they insisted they didn't want PP or his son to hear what was being said. The story they had to relate turned my stomach, and inflamed my anger against the horrible youth yet again. Now I discovered terrible perversions had been going on during my absences from home... things I feared but had hoped would never happen.

The problems with Steve's increasing drunkenness had been going on for quite some time. But what sent me into a white fury was hearing he had been attempting his sexual perversions on my daughters, ever since his last brush with the police.

Two weeks previously, Nathalie had been woken during the Saturday night to find him in her bedroom. He had been drunk, and in a highly aroused state, demanding that she must let him get into bed with her and have sex. He was so forceful and brutal he had terrified her. He wouldn't take no for an answer, and she had begun screaming at him to get out of her room. But instead of leaving he had become threatening and refused to go, even attempting to force himself on her... until a battle had rapidly ensued.

Hearing Nathalie's terrified yelling had brought Samantha rushing into the room to find out what was going on. Between them they had tackled him. The youth had been raving and lashing out at them with his fists, frothing at the mouth and grinding his teeth like someone quite mad. Eventually the pair of them succeeded in forcing him back into his own bedroom, after threatening to call the police if he didn't leave them alone.

After that incident, they decided not to say anything about it to me because they knew it would only lead to much worse trouble and retaliation if I complained to his father.

Unfortunately, that vile episode had not been the end of his sexual perversions. That latest Saturday night during my absence, he had made another serious attempt at rape. This time he had picked on Samantha. My younger daughter had been woken during the night to find him climbing, stark naked, into her bed, and making determined attempts to sexually force himself on her. He had pressed his hand over her mouth to prevent her from screaming, and violently held her down with every intention of raping her.

To her credit, my daughter was a really feisty girl, and she had fought him tooth and nail, repeatedly hitting him with the only weapon she could reach; the bristly side of her wire hairbrush. It had dented his intentions somewhat, and scratched his skin quite severely, but it hadn't stopped him, and he had persisted in refusing to leave her room. At that point, she had picked up a heavy winter boot and launched a counter-attack on a delicate part of his anatomy. That had finally sorted the situation, and he had retreated, swearing he would get even with her.

I was deeply relieved to hear nothing more serious had come of the attack, and that she was uninjured. But the following night, before I arrived home, both of my girls had felt sufficiently uneasy about his perverse inclinations, and they had locked themselves into Samantha's room, just in case he tried his aggressive sexual tricks on either of them again... this time, using more force.

The entire situation we were all facing due to PP and his unhinged sociopathic family was intolerable. I had to find a way of putting an end to Steve's sexual abuse of my daughters, before something more serious happened. My immediate parental instincts were to tear the young devil limb from limb. But there was no way I would have ever succeeded in such a vengeful attack.

Instead, I decided to confront PP with the shocking details of his son's flagrantly perverted behaviour. I intended to give him an ultimatum... if he didn't do something about the boy and get him out of my house, I would go to the police and lay charges against him for the attempted rape of both my daughters. Steve had already been in police trouble for attempting to molest young girls in the street, and had been interviewed by the police as a potential sexual pervert.

His father's reaction surprised me. I had anticipated roaring denials and a vengeful physical attack... much like all the others I had experienced at his hands. But for some unknown reason, he remained cool. This time, there was no aggressive shouting or lashing out at me.

He talked to his son alone. I never heard what was said. But within a week, the delinquent youth had moved in with his sister, and was no longer living under my roof.

However, PP always had a driving need to seek revenge for anything he didn't like. And consequently, from that time on, whenever he flew into one of his interminable rages, one of his favourite accusations was to scream at me, 'Yer fuckin' bitch, yer frew me little kiddies out inter the street, like the whore yer are.'

What a strangely convenient, but illogical kind of memory the man had! There was not one accurate, or truthful, fact among this string of frequently repeated expletives. I was already aware that his mind worked in very strange and convoluted ways. And spinning convincing lies came as second nature to him.

But there was one very odd side to his predisposition for

manufacturing lies...if he liked the sound of any story he had invented, no matter how outrageous or far-fetched, then magically he turned it into THE TRUTH. Thereafter, he would argue tooth and nail that whatever the story was, it was now unquestionable fact, not fiction. In his distorted view of reality, all lies became the truth if they were repeated often enough. It was another dogma he had taken to heart, from studying the propaganda of the Nazis...particularly the perverse philosophies of Joseph Goebbels, who was one of his personal heroes.

For me, it was a welcome relief that PP's daughter and son were now out of my home. But they were living in a house I had been fraudulently manipulated into financing. It was the vilest deception PP had played on me...a deceit for which I would never bring myself to forgive either father or daughter.

I was never sure why PP bought a BSA 250cc motorbike shortly afterwards. Maybe it was some kind of consolation prize for Steve... to compensate him for the loss of the red sports car. But it was never insured for him to use, and well beyond the legal engine size for someone of his age to drive. Whatever the truth of the matter was, it wasn't long before Steve decided to take possession of it during our interminable weekend absences.

This time, he got himself involved in a much more serious police incident. He was caught driving at seventy miles an hour, with no driving licence and no insurance. When he was flagged down, he refused to stop and drove on, as fast as the machine would go, in an attempt to outrun the police car that was chasing him. In his warped feral brain, he imagined, if he ignored the blue flashing lights, and just keep driving flat out, he would outrun the police and escape. He was cocksure the coppers would eventually give up their pursuit, and let him get away.

Surprisingly, that proved not to be the intention of the police at all. And he was eventually caught when he drove into the rear yard of a pub some twenty miles away. He tried to hide the bike behind some outbuildings and run away. But his plan failed. The police had him in their sights, and they pursued him until there was nowhere left for him to hide. He was unceremoniously dragged from his hiding place and arrested.

This time he was taken into custody, and a uniformed officer called at the house in person to inform PP of his son's arrest, and request his father's attendance at the station at once, where his son was in custody. The boy was quite clearly out of control, and so far as the police were concerned, no more road traffic infringements would be tolerated from him. He would go up before a magistrate for juvenile sentencing.

Unfortunately, the trivial slap-on-the-wrist punishment he received from the magistrates had no effect whatsoever in terms of bringing him into line, or of making him less belligerent and more law-abiding. He had been born to be an obnoxious shameless lout. And in appearance, personality, and behaviour, he was his father's adolescent double.

Some weeks later, he announced he had found himself a girlfriend at school, and her family said he could stay with them at weekends.

Knowing his precocious sexual inclinations, I felt some concern for the girl and her family, and wondered if they knew what a troublesome, and sexually promiscuous character they were welcoming into their home.

I guessed they had probably been taken in by Steve's well-honed cunning charm offensive, performed for their benefit... just as his father always did when required. This ability to turn on the deceptive smarmy charm was a frequent ploy the youth used whenever useful, and something he had learned from his reprobate father.

Steve had no need of any further lessons on how to ape his father's behaviour, or how to deceive naive individuals less streetwise than himself. He was a guttersnipe already, and well skilled in the arts of barefaced lying and all other forms of manipulating the truth.

I had no doubt that, given time, the family he had battened on to would eventually discover what the real Steve was like. How long would it take I wondered, before this new, innocent family realised they were harbouring a potential juvenile rapist?

I felt moderately sorry for the young girl involved... But I was very glad he was no longer any concern of mine.

Chapter 22

A Year to Break Me, Part VIII: Relentless Brutality

One evening in January of that first year, I came home from school early. I had developed a raging temperature and was aching everywhere. I was so dizzy I felt I was whirling about on a merry-go-round and couldn't see straight. I knew from the symptoms that I was coming down with flu. It had been a real struggle to get home, with my head burning and throbbing so much I could barely focus to drive my car.

The prospect of having to spend the next three hours cooking a mammoth meal for PP was out of the question. I scribbled a brief note explaining that I had come home ill and gone straight to bed, and left it on the kitchen table, telling him there was prepared food in the freezer. All he had to do was thaw it first and pop it into the oven for half an hour.

I felt so sick I didn't even have the energy to get properly undressed. I just took off my outer clothes and curled up under the duvet still wearing my yellow polo-necked sweater and my underwear. With my head swimming and feeling delirious and nauseous, I was glad to just huddle in the dark room. I think I must have fallen asleep straight away.

At about six thirty, I was suddenly awoken by crashing and banging coming from downstairs, followed by heavy feet pounding up the stairs. Suddenly, all the bedroom lights were switched on, and PP was in the room, shouting and bawling at me, ordering me to get out of bed.

My head was still throbbing, and the sudden glare of the lights was very painful to my eyes. I tried remonstrating with him, and croaked hoarsely that I had come down with flu and was too ill to get up.

But he took no notice of me at all. 'Ah wan me dinna, yer lazy fuckin' cow,' he yelled. 'Wier's me dinna? Yer've dun nuffink abaout it, 'av yer, yer fuckin' bitch. Ther's not even any meat in the uven cookin. Weir's the vegibles? Wot the fuck's yer game? 'Ave yer bin doin nuffink aal artenoon, jus' lyin' 'ere fuckin' asleep? Git outer tha' fuckin' stinkin' pit an' git daanstairs inter the fuckin' kitchin an git uz me dinna.'

Without listening to one word I was trying to say, he stormed over to where I was lying, and began slapping me hard across the face. Then he grabbed the polo neck of my sweater, dragged me bodily out of bed, and dumped me on the floor.

Standing with his legs astride my body, he towered over me menacingly, and continued his tirade. 'Git up, Ah say, git up yer lazy fuckin' bitch.'

My throat was raw, my painful head was spinning, and I felt

violently sick. I could hear the stream of abuse he was shouting thundering through my head, but I felt too ill to move and far from able to stand up.

To encourage my efforts, he aimed a really hard kick at my ribs, which made me double up in tears. 'Git up, yer idle cow. Ah wan me dinna. Weir's me grub?' he yelled. 'Yer've dun nuffink excep' lie 'ere aal arternoon, yer idle trollup. Wot the fuck der yer fink yer playin' at? Cryin' crocodile tears ain't goin' ter change nuffink, an' they doan cut no ice wiv me. Yer ain' sick. Yer jus play-actin'. Ah doan care 'ow much yer blub. Yer 'ere ter mek me dinna. There ain't nuffink wrong wiv yer, excep' fuckin' bloody laziness. If yer doan git down them stairs rite naw, and inter that fuckin' kitchin, Ah'll fuckin' well frow yer daan em, an brek yer fuckin' neck if Ah need ter.'

And throwing me down the stairs was exactly what he proceeded to do. He had not one shred of sympathy, or any compassion for how ill I might be. All he cared about was himself and his own immediate selfish demands. Grasping me by the hair at the nape of my neck, and the back of my sweater, he dragged me, still unable to stand, fifteen feet along the landing to the head of the stairs, from where he hiked me half onto my feet, and physically threw me down the stairs, head first.

There was no way I could save myself, and I crashed down every stair, hitting my head and face on each one, until I landed in a heap on the half landing, head first. I was barely conscious, and in a terrible state, but he was still not done with me.

Lying with my head foremost and sprawled the length of the flight of stairs I had just been thrown down, I was verging on hysteria. But my distressed state meant nothing to him. He never left any violent attack unfinished. While I was groping around blindly to find something to grab hold of to pull myself up, he came storming down behind me, deliberately stamping his way down the length of my awkwardly sprawled body, his heavy work boots ploughing right across my hips and spine. He even made a point of putting his full weight onto the back of my head, all twenty stones of it, forcing my face hard down against the woodwork. Then standing on the half landing, he turned and again grabbed me by the back of neck, before dragging me, staggering and half-conscious, onto my feet. Seconds later, I was again pushed, violently and headlong, down the second longer flight of sixteen stairs, and so down into the hall.

How my neck was not broken as the result of this violence, I will never know. I finally lay in a crumpled heap at the foot of the stairs unable to move, as he came charging down after me, his fury still unabated. To complete this grotesque vicious attack, once again he grabbed my hair and the neck of my sweater, this time forcing me onto my knees. Then dragging me behind him like a sack, he thrust me through the kitchen door and precipitated me across the floor towards the cooker, with his boot in the small of my back.

I could do nothing to help myself, as I skidded bodily across the tiled floor and hit my head on the cooker, finally coming to rest in a collapsed heap in front of it.

By that stage, the ligaments in my left wrist and ankle had been torn, and the bridge of my nose, gashed and broken. I was in an indescribable agonising physical and emotional condition. Apart from the high temperature I was already running, my nose was bleeding profusely from the gash, and I was in a state of collapse. But he couldn't have cared less.

'Naw mebbe yer'll fuckin' well do wot Ah tell yer womin. Git cookin'. Ah'm sick uv yer bloody stoopidity and yer play-actin'. Yer 'ere unda suffrance from me. If yer doan wan chuckin' aout in the street, do wot yer 'ere ter do, and git uz me dinna. Naw.'

It is impossible to adequately describe the state I had been reduced to. But there was terrible pain, deep humiliation, tears, hysteria, fury...and hatred... all mixed together... to season every mouthful of the food I eventually prepared for that evil monster. I am not a vindictive woman, but I believe, if I had been given access to some deadly poison, it would have gone into the gravy, along with the ocean of tears I shed as I cooked that unbelievable monster his meal.

Somehow, I got myself to the hospital the following day. The dislodged bone fragment, was put back into place, and my nose was stitched. But I was black and blue across my entire body for several weeks afterwards. My torn wrist and ankle ligaments eventually healed, but the strength in them never returned fully... just another permanent injury I had to learn to live with.

PP, of course, with typical self-induced amnesia, immediately blotted the entire event from his mind and showed no shred of concern or guilt at all.

Years later, when accused in court, he denied everything and swore with his usual vehemence that he had never, ever laid a finger on me. He even accused me of inventing the entire episode to make him appear to be a man of violence and a liar.

None of the suffering he ever inflicted upon me was any concern to him, and he always conveniently wiped from his mind the truth that his flagrant brutality might easily have killed me.

No doubt, that day I was thrown down the stairs could very easily have broken my neck. But I know for sure, that had I have been found dead, he would have written the incident off, claiming I must have tripped and fallen down the stairs before he returned from work.

How the mindset of any man is capable of feigning total denial for his own brutal behaviour is beyond my comprehension. But the mind of PP was capable of denying anything, and everything he did. No matter how inhumane his behaviour was, he invariably claimed voluntary amnesia, and simply deleted the event from his brain, in much the same way as pressing the delete button on a computer deletes an electronic memory.

In any event, he later insisted that the injuries I sustained when I fell downstairs, had come about,

'... because I had flu at the time, and had experienced a dizzy turn as I'd started to walk down the stairs to the hall. He had taken no part in inflicting any injuries on me, and he wasn't even there when it had happened.'

Without my being aware of what he was doing to me, he had already begun attempting to condition me into believing I was losing my mind. To do this he deliberately rejigged the facts of any unpleasant situation he ever caused, and then attempted to persuade me my mind was playing me tricks.

Time was passing, and I was becoming more and more terrified and intimidated by the man. I was also aware that he had me increasingly under his control and at his mercy. No act of violence against me was ever taboo.

As that first winter turned into spring, I was becoming more deeply depressed. I was constantly confounded by his twisted, contradictory, and perverse mentality, and his vicious behaviour towards me. I had never known anyone remotely like him before. And I was still doing my best to cope with his increasingly erratic black moods which changed like the wind. There was always an undertone of menace, and threat, about everything he said, and did.

That first year of marriage to PP was the worst year I had ever lived. Every day he increased his pressure on me, and not a day went by without some form of abuse and coercion being perpetrated upon me. This insane behaviour of harassment and abuse was relentless, and continued verbally and physically by day and night.

Even when I was at work, he never let me be, and constantly telephoned demanding to speak to me... to make more accusations and demands, and issue me with an endless stream of threats and orders.

I became so depressed I didn't want to be anywhere near him. At the end of each working day, I often just drove around the town, or sat for hours in a car park on the sea-front, even during the coldest of the winter weather, because I dreaded going home to more of his persecution. The constant violence and sleep deprivation to which I was being subjected had physically weakened me. Together with the unrelenting levels of emotional and psychological abuse, I had been rendered utterly exhausted. I didn't care if I lived or died. I just wanted to find a way of escaping from him.

When he wasn't physically abusing me, or ranting and threatening me with more violence, he found an infinite variety of demands for me to fulfil... endless jobs to be carried out and messages to run. I was never allowed any time to myself. It seemed I had become just someone he owned... a mindless creature or an automaton, with no human rights, and who never deserved a moment of freedom, not even to sleep.

When he was not of a mind to physically abuse me, he frequently kept me awake at night to endure a seemingly endless recital of disgusting filthy stories, which he took pleasure in relating, about his sexual exploits before he ever met me.

Everything about the man disgusted and nauseated me. I began to understand that there were some people who were born for no other reason than to turn every life they touched into misery and despair. PP was such a person. His morals were totally despicable. He was incapable of love, or any other caring emotion. But he was insanely jealous and suspicious... forever accusing me and questioning me about my faithfulness to him; and suspicious of every one I ever spoke to. He suspected every man I ever met, no matter how innocently, of being my lover. So unhinged was he that, at one point he even accused me of running a brothel at my school. I believe that, if he could have gotten away with it, he would have chained me up and never let me out of the house.

The effect of this cumulative and never-ending controlling behaviour was increasingly driving me deeper into fear and loathing, of him. But I could find no acceptable means of escaping from him.

So far as his personal morals were concerned, he had a completely different set of standards, and took the greatest of pleasure in recounting the details of the sordid past he had lived before, during, and after his former marriage. And it soon became apparent that the accusations heaped upon him by Liz when I had first encountered her at the hospital, had not been exaggerations of the truth. The criticisms she had screamed at him had been statements of fact... not malicious fantasies. His idea of faithfulness in marriage applied only to the female partner in any relationship. There was, it seemed, in his twisted version of reality, a different set of standards for men.

He wanted to reduce me to being a mindless creature, like

something hatched from an egg of oblivion... a woman with no past before he came along. My enduring, deeply loving, and passionate relationship with Alan was anathema to him. He couldn't bear to think about the life Alan and I had shared or that, even after his death, I would never stop loving him. Our relationship was something of which I never spoke, but for some intuitive reason PP was haunted with an obsessive and destructive jealousy. He was unable to endure the thought of how much a part of my internal, emotional life Alan still remained. And this raging jealousy found expression through his violence towards me, and his obsessive drive to control me.

I was regaled, ad nauseam, with horrific threats of the punishments he would inflict upon me if I ever tried to leave him or divorce him. At all levels, I was made aware that I was never going to escape from his clutches, alive. 'There's only wun way yer'll ivver git away from me, womin, an' that's in a wooden box.'

Marriage to PP had nothing to offer me except endless mental and physical pain. I frequently found the situation ramped up, for no reason I could fathom, into periods of unrelenting terror, which then continued twenty-four hours a day and seven days every week.

His daily abuse revolved around his determination to keep me under his control by threatening, intimidating, browbeating, and coercing me into relinquishing my home and my assets to him. He wanted me reduced to being nothing, owning nothing, feeling nothing, and totally submissive to his power.

His endless intimidating threats were monotonously repeated daily diatribes, which continued without end, until one day I could finally bear the ranting and the intimidation no longer. He was in full voice, yelling obscene threats of how he was going to kill me if I didn't obey him, poking me in the face, and slapping me around the head to keep me in a state of tearful distress… threatening me, yet again that he would never cease to harass me until I eventually capitulated and signed my house over to him.

Unexpectedly, my emotions suddenly reached a point where I could stand no more, and I suddenly snapped. I began screaming back at him that I would never relinquish my home to him, no matter what he did to me.

My self-control had reached emotional meltdown. I remember screaming that he would never benefit from anything I had left… In my blazing fury I screamed hysterically… 'Nothing I have will ever become yours…I already made my will months ago, in anticipation of this marriage. It's signed and sealed and completely legal… everything Alan and I owned will legally pass, upon my death, to the girls… All you will get is what you deserve…NOTHING.'

Between anguished sobs I continued screaming… 'If you kill me, you will still get absolutely nothing, and you will serve years in prison for my murder. Nothing you do will ever make me surrender my home to you. Everything Alan and I spent our lives working for will go to our children…never to you, you bastard. You are a disgusting, filthy devil from blackest hell. You have set yourself to terrorise me day and night since the day I was foolish enough to marry you. I loathe and detest you with every part of my being, and I will never surrender my home to you.'

For several days afterwards, he stayed away from the house. I guessed he had gone to lick his imaginary wounds at Stevenson Street, and discuss the unexpected turn of events with his support group living there at my expense. I knew something bad must be brewing, but I had no way of knowing what new scheme of torment he and his backup team had been busy hatching.

When he came back, he appeared to have developed a keen interest in the cost of the household outgoings, and demanded to know exactly how I was wasting every penny of our money.

As none of his money had ever been involved in any of the household expenses (because he had never contributed anything), along with the fact that I was now having to bear the cost of the substantial bank loan I had been inveigled into securing, for the purchase of his daughter's house, quite naturally, his outrageous nit-picking of my bank statements made me deeply resentful. I was angered by his autocratic third-degree interrogations, and pronouncements on how I spent my money.

It didn't take me long to realise this was his new tack, and had a different set of ulterior motives driving it. Right up to the time when his son and daughter had moved out, he had been relentless demanding I must put my house into his name. Suddenly this had changed. Now I had to listen to his revised demands, which were suddenly focused upon inveigling me into selling my house, and buying somewhere smaller, so that HIS name could be on the deeds. Suddenly, I became subjected to endless lectures on how the time was coming when there would only be the two of us living there, and we wouldn't need such a big house. More and more, his new propaganda was focused on dissecting the costs of maintaining my present home, set against the economics of selling it.

To that end, he started a new campaign, which began with nagging me upon how a smaller property would be cheaper to run. And it would have both our names on the deeds. It would be his home, instead of 'this shit'ole', which didn't belong to him, and where I was forcing him to live.

Constant carping and complaining, became his new tactic. His malicious determination was still to wear me down and demoralise me. But now his focus had morphed, from transferring my home into his name, into selling it and buying another, which would be his, because both our names would be on the new title-deeds.

As I saw his proposal, this revised version of the saga, meant any house I might subsequently be manipulated into buying, would still be totally funded from my assets. He had no intentions whatsoever of contributing anything, either towards the purchase, or the maintenance.

But I could see very clearly what he was now trying to manipulate me into doing. By selling my family home and moving to a new address, I would effectively negate the prenuptial will I had carefully drawn up to protect my children. With PP's name on the new deeds, he would legally be the joint owner. And in that way, all possibility of my daughters' rights being safeguarded would be cancelled. If by any mischance I were to die, he would become the only surviving beneficiary, and my children would receive nothing.

Only the year previously, before I had agreed to marry him, he had given me his word he would never ask me to leave the home I loved. Now he was denying he had ever made any such promise.

It seemed that every day I was learning new things about the man I had been manipulated into marrying. I had already learned I was married to a pathological liar and a violent aggressor... a man who would say anything, and agree to anything while it suited his purposes, and then turn the tables just as quickly, and reverse everything to which he had previously agreed.

These were all seriously significant facts that I ought to have ensured I was well aware of, long before I ever agreed to any marriage taking place. PP was never going to change. He had been born to be a manipulative liar, and he would always remain obsessively egocentric, and relentless in his intentions to dominate and control me.

What might become of me, or my children, was of no concern to him. We were merely dispensable collateral damage in the resolute war he was waging over acquiring my assets.

Chapter 23

A Year to Break Me, Part IX: Gaslighting and Mental Torture

After Liz moved into the house in Stevenson Street, it very quickly became a convenient bolthole for PP. It provided him with an insulated space to think... a place to go to moan about me, and somewhere to make plans for his next devious campaign against me. It was obvious I had been cunningly conned into providing my enemies with a private meeting place. And I am quite sure its delinquent occupants contributed in every way they could in encouraging him as to how he could attack me next.

Running away from the difficult situation you have caused is an easy get-out, especially if you don't want to hear your opponent's version of the argument. Beginning with his first violent attack on me in Sorrento, PP had always used this tactic.

After his physical attacks on me, he would very rapidly leave... just as Liz and Steve had both done at various times.

Now, instead of sitting brooding in a pub somewhere, or driving off in high dudgeon after attacking me, PP could disappear whenever he felt inclined, to plot and sulk at the house in Stevenson Street.

As his victim, I was naturally kept in the dark regarding all his covert intentions. And at the beginning of that first New Year of the marriage, he had already decided on a new sinister tactic... this time he was concentrating on malicious psychological games, all intended to bring me to my knees, and drive me to a mental breakdown.

His ownership plans for my house had changed. Now he intended to manipulate me into selling it, and buying a different property. It was a cunning move that would give him the legal inheritance right to ownership, should I die. I suspect somewhere along the line he had spoken to a solicitor, and been disabused of his original notion that marriage confers ownership of a wife's property upon her husband. Such an archaic idea was positively medieval, and had no factual legal foundation. But in whatever way this revised knowledge concerning legal enlightenment had been obtained, and from whatever source, his plans had now changed.

Learning about my pre-nuptial will had come as a shock. I feel quite certain he would have legally checked it out, and found it was lawful. It had now forced him into a rethink, and into adapting his tactics. Now he was hell-bent on coercing me into selling my home, and buying something else... with his name jointly on the deeds to ensure his inheritance rights.

I continued to refuse his ludicrous demands, and resisted his efforts to manipulate me into doing what he wanted. I was endeavouring, as best I could, to defend my children's legal rights. My daughters would always be my first concern, and of far more importance to me than this manipulative beast of a man would ever be.

A year had passed since Alan's death, and my natural perception and emotional balance were gradually returning to me. I had begun putting together some of the pieces of my current deeply depressing marital jigsaw. I had finally woken up to the realisation that, time and again, this treacherous man had cunningly set about manipulating me...lying to me, and persistently deliberately cheating and deceiving me... always for his own benefit and self-enrichment.

Apart from his calculated brutality, I now knew he was nothing but a pathological liar, who considered truth to be a convenient variable, and something he rarely indulged in. Nothing he ever said could ever be believed, and promises were just throw-away air-bubbles. For me, his latest confidence trick over the bank loan for the house in Stevenson Street, had been the final straw in this shocking saga.

Consequently, I continued to refuse to do as he wanted and sell my house. It was my daughters' home, and their only security for the future.

However, after having ruthlessly tried for six months to break my resistance, PP changed his tactics as the result of my continued stubborn refusal to comply with his revised demands.

Now he decided to make psychological changes to his methods. Instead of concentrating on battering my body, he would go to work on my mind and my emotions. He was determined to bring me to submission by whatever means he could devise.

By breaking my mind, he would achieve the same results as he had with his first wife, Beryl. I knew her history, because he had often told it to me... or his version of it. And it was nothing but a disgusting saga of violence, manipulation, and sexual brutality, beyond that of any normal man. Beryl had experienced three full-scale lengthy mental breakdowns during their marriage. And each one had resulted in long-term periods of confinement as a sectioned patient in a variety of psychiatric hospitals. Eventually, after twenty years of abusive marriage, she had been happy to walk away with little more than the clothes she stood up in.

But of course, Beryl had come to their marriage empty-handed. She was a girl from a poor Scottish background, with nothing of any value to her name. I was a professional woman, recently widowed, and the sole owner of a large mortgage-free property; along with other enviable assets PP lusted after. Some of these assets were real, and others were total figments of his twisted imagination.

Now with his new campaign of emotional abuse in mind, the first subjects he turned his evil attentions upon were my four little Yorkshire terriers. He knew how much they meant to me, and how dearly I loved all of them. One morning, out of the blue, he issued me with an ultimatum, announcing the youngest one, Tina, had to go. He would not tolerate her presence in the house any longer.

Tina was the smallest of my little dogs and had done nothing to offend him. Nevertheless, he calmly announced that, if I did not get rid of her within the next ten days, he intended to kill her. His manner was completely unemotional. There was no reason or logic in what he was saying and no consideration for how I might feel about such a vicious ultimatum issued against one of my little pets. That was just the way his evil mentality worked.

I knew without any shadow of doubt that he meant it. He would kill her. She was a lovely little creature, gentle and loving and full of life, and just three pounds in weight. I pleaded with him, and implored him not to be so cruel. But he was coldly and immovably resolute. He didn't care if I gave her away or sold her, or had her euthanised. I had ten days to get rid of her, or he would strangle her while I was at school.

I already had plenty of experience with regard to what he could get up to while I was missing from the house. Parting with my dearly loved little pet broke my heart. But I knew only too well how cold-hearted and ruthless he was, and that he would have no compunction in killing her if I refused to obey him.

That was the opening salvo of his new plan to persecute me psychologically. After bullying me over Tina and forcing me into the heartbreak of rehoming her, he wasted no time in finding more ways to attack me through my emotions.

Next on his targeted list was the destruction of items for which I had deep sentimental attachments. If I treasured and valued something, it was destined to be burned.

He derived some strange sense of power from burning things. It gave him a perverse and sadistic sense of pleasure to see things I put great store by, and which were linked to my past, going up in smoke. It was a particularly nasty destructive power game. And he loved to play it for his sadistic enjoyment and in order to watch me suffer.

He was aware my beloved father had died from cerebral cancer when I was just six years old. One childhood toy that was more precious to me than anything else from my childhood, was the large doll's house my father had made for me while he had been terminally ill. With my dad's encouragement and help, I had designed my dream doll's house, which he had then built in secret, and as a surprise for me. It was the last Christmas gift I ever received from my beloved father before his death, and an enduring reminder of our last family Christmas together.

While I was at work one day, PP took it into the garden and burned it, along with every other toy he could find associated with my childhood.

Next into the fire went the various precious things Alan had made for our children... their large doll's cot; the lovely doll's bungalow he had built for them, along with all its furnishings; and their easel/blackboard, which converted into a desk. Everything PP could lay his evil hands on that was connected with my children's emotional past, and with Alan, was incinerated.

Every object he destroyed had been made by the caring, loving hands of men in whose shadow he was not fit to walk... compassionate and loving family men who were so different from himself he seemed not to have originated from the same strata of humanity.

But whatever he destroyed... and the pain he caused was excruciating... he could never obliterate our lost loved ones from our hearts, or from our memories. No matter what vicious senseless things PP did, no fire could ever erase the enduring memories or the love we had known. In that respect, no matter what evil he perpetrated...he could never win.

By these despicable acts of wanton cruelty, he was demonstrating his sadistic power over my daughters and myself... forcing us to watch in silence as our precious possessions were burned. Every single thing he ever did was intended to cause deep pain. But in fact, these actions served only to reinforce our clear vision of what a cruel and spitefully insane vindictive monster he was.

My hatred of him grew by the day.

But in spite all these outrageous and senseless acts of destruction, I stubbornly continued to refuse to sell my home. Eventually, he decided upon a plan he was convinced would drive me to a mental breakdown.

This plan, which he began very suddenly, was intended to persistently deprive me of sleep. He intended to cause me so much mental confusion and despair, that my desire to go on living would be destroyed, and I would rapidly be reduced to thoughts of suicide. At the same time, he intended to work on implanting in my mind the belief that I would never escape from him, unless I killed myself.

By day and night, I became subjected to a campaign that ensured I never got any sleep. He planned to cause me such severe disorientation and confusion that I would welcome death as my only possibility of escaping from him.

I quickly found myself living in a continual knife-edge situation where at any moment of the day or night, I would be attacked by him for one distorted and illogical reason or another. Nothing PP did had ever made any sense. But now he was endeavouring to keep me in a permanent state of anxiety, which he had every intention of continuing until my stubborn will to survive was defeated.

It started with him making up rules about everything he could think of, which I was then ordered to obey. However, even when I did my best to comply, I found the rules had already been changed into something else. Consequently, I was then accused of deliberately setting out to anger him and into forcing him to physically punish me for my obtuseness and disobedience.

If he said black was white, then this became a fact that I must accept… or suffer the consequences for disagreeing with him. If he said the freshly-cooked food I put before him was inedible and stone cold, and threw the plate at me, I must meekly return to the kitchen and cook him something else.

The situation increasingly became more and more bizarre, and I was beaten across my head with any object he could lay his hands on, for not cleaning up the mess he had created quickly enough. I was constantly accused of hiding things belonging to him… his car keys, his shoes, his tape measure, or his wallet. Anything and everything became part of this perverse game of accusation and punishment. I was ordered to produce the items he claimed I had hidden, and not allowed to sleep until I did. I had no idea where any of the missing things were, but he would keep me searching for them right into the night.

There were days when he would arrive home with his feet quite deliberately caked in animal faeces, and immediately tramp about the house, upstairs and down, leaving excrement everywhere. Then he would accuse me of laziness, and of encouraging my little dogs to foul the house… all to initiate another excuse for a physical attack on me.

I was constantly forced onto the defensive, and endlessly made to apologise, continually cleaning and scrubbing carpets. And as I did so, I would be screamed at and harassed… accused of 'keepin' the fuckin' house like a shit'ole'. All of this was because, according to him, I encouraged my pets to 'piss and shit iveryweir'.

I soon realised he was working his way towards forcing me into getting rid of them. That was something I would never have tolerated. I had already been put through enough torment over his diabolical activities regarding little Tina... along with all our other pets, which he and his son had viciously slaughtered months earlier.

I believe if he had persisted in his abominable attempt to deprive me of my precious little Yorkies, he would have pushed me beyond endurance. I honestly believe I would have eventually been provoked far enough into making an attempt to kill him.

I was being deliberately and maliciously manoeuvred towards my breaking point. His intention was to have me removed from the house and placed into a psychiatric establishment... diagnosed as mentally deranged and in need of treatment.

Without any doubt I was trapped as his victim in the crazy games he was playing with my mind. These games had no constant rules, only the variable ones he invented as he went along. Everything he did was deliberately planned to wrong-foot me, and keep me confused. He was working towards accusing me of being a crazy neglectful wife, a mentally unbalanced woman, and entirely deserving of confinement in a psychiatric unit.

I had no means of defending myself. And with nowhere to turn for support or help, I became deeply worried about my mental resilience and powers of endurance. How long could I withstand his persecution before I snapped? I was already living in permanent dread of what he was going to do to me next. Everything he contrived was intended to make my behaviour automatically wrong.

In this way the persecution continued, as I was brainwashed and intentionally manipulated into believing I was losing my mind. I frequently found myself grovelling before him, and forever being forced into apologising for my endless mistakes and stupidity. Day after day I was pushed to the ground and forced to kiss his feet to show my humility.

My life had become an endless routine of mind-bending abuse. I was constantly repeating, 'I'm sorry. I'm sorry.' While he persisted in forcing me into admissions of guilt, even when I didn't have a clue what my supposed failures had been, or even what I was being forced to apologise for.

My life had descended into an unbelievable hell on earth, invented by this devil I was supposed to call my husband. Night after night, right through the worst of that cold winter, I found myself woken in the small hours, with all the lights switched on, along with the radio tuned into some foreign station, to blare out discordant noise at full power... all to ensure that I would get no sleep.

Then there were the times when I was suddenly grabbed and dragged bodily out of bed half asleep, to be thrown onto the floor as he screamed senseless accusations at me. I would be forced onto my knees, and into making grovelling apologies for a variety of incomprehensible provocations he claimed I had done earlier to offend him.

Some nights he would pursue me around the bedroom, battering me about the head, or banging me against the walls, haranguing me, and accusing me of the most outrageous misdemeanours. I was accused of carrying on affairs with different men, stealing his money, putting poison in his food, telling lies about him, or hiding his mail or his car keys or his spectacles. Any fantasies he cared to invent gave him fresh cause to abuse me.

I was beaten and cross-examined for hours over accusations I was concealing dozens of secret bank accounts, each stuffed with millions of pounds, thereby depriving him of what was, '...rightf'ly moine'. His crazy justifications for these insane accusations all returned to his original claims... that he had married me and was, therefore, legally entitled to take possession of all my assets, those which were visible, such as my home, and those he claimed were secretly concealed. I was habitually called, a devious greedy bitch... guilty of constantly lying to him and refusing to hand over the huge amounts of money which he claimed I was hiding.

At one point, he even began accusing me of putting black magic spells on him! The list of crazy and mind-blowing accusations he invented against me was endless.

Some nights the excuse to keep me awake was because he felt hungry. I would be woken and ordered downstairs at three o'clock in the morning to cook a meal he was demanding. The food had to be served on a tray, and I was instructed to stand by the bed and watch while he ate it. I was not allowed to sit down or fall asleep during any of these ordeals.

The variety of terrifying situations he invented was insanely creative, and inescapable. I had no defence against any of them. A refusal to comply with his demands was not an option, unless I wanted another vicious beating.

Another of his frequent and brutal activities was to rape me. If he thought I had fallen asleep, I would quickly be brought back to consciousness, either by being brutally sodomised or raped. Then when he was satisfied, he would commence upon a tirade, accusing me of doing something to prevent myself from becoming pregnant.

There were other nights when he suddenly switched into his violent mode and began screaming terrible threats against my children. Or he would man-handle me into a chair, and tie me to it in the early morning, then lock me in the bedroom to prevent me from going to school.

Grabbing me by the throat was one of his well-practised forms of attack. Whenever he worked himself up into a rage, he took sadistic delight in squeezing me by the throat. He would place his thumbs against my windpipe and throttle me savagely, until I began to choke, or even lose consciousness.

In those days I was rarely seen at school without a scarf securely placed around my throat to cover a welter of purple bruises.

And of course, gouging his fingers into my eyes was another of his favourite sports. I was convinced he was actually trying to blind me. And the force he used in jabbing his thick fingers into my eyes left terrible bruises. Scarves and sunglasses both became normal parts of my every-day working attire.

All his methods of terrifying me were creative and brutal, and every attack was carried out relentlessly, and for his own sadistic pleasure.

There were frequent occasions when I was shocked awake, at one or two in the morning, with the room in total darkness, and the pillows suddenly and violently being pulled from beneath my head, before being quickly pressed hard down over my face, and held there until I couldn't breathe.

I remember only too well, thrashing about, and struggling against the full weight of his body pressed down on top of the pillow. His arms and elbows securing the pillows at either side of my head to cut off my air supply and my breathing, and prevent my escape, while he carried out his determined attack, of trying to suffocate me.

Then suddenly, he would stop his murderous game, and abruptly leave the room. Moments later, I would hear his car drive off. But for the remainder of the night, I would lie awake in terror, my heart pounding in the darkness, choking and coughing, and too afraid to allow myself to fall asleep, in case he came back, intent upon finishing what he had begun.

One of the favourite persecutions which gave him pleasure on really cold wet winter nights, was a particularly vicious way of terrorising me and attempting to induce hypothermia. I would wake during the hours of darkness, shivering and frozen to the marrow, to find the bedroom icy, and the air damp and moisture laden.

All the windows would have been opened wide to let the wind and rain blow into the room. The curtains would be flapping noisily, sucked outside into the wet night, and I would be lying on the bed, numb from the cold, with all the bedding stripped from me and removed from the room.

When I staggered downstairs, icy cold and shivering, I would find PP asleep on the drawing room sofa, snugly wrapped in the duvet, with the gas fire blazing, and all the bedding he had removed from me strewn across the floor.

Following these, and many other equally terrible nocturnal activities, it pleased him to know I had to get up at dawn and get ready to go to school. It was his perverse pleasure knowing how constantly exhausted and tired I was, and how disorientated and ill I was becoming. It all went to prove his plan was having its intended effect.

He, of course, being self-employed, could spend the day as he chose, lying in bed and catching up on his missing sleep, while I had to attempt to maintain the normality of my working day.

The situation became so mentally destructive and unbearable, I was being driven deeper into depression, and recurrent suicidal thoughts. To escape from many of these depraved attacks, I began fleeing the house in the middle of the night.

After enduring weeks of these endless night-time tortures, I had reached the end of my tether, and was desperate to escape from his relentless abuse. Often, in the early hours, I would drag on my dressing gown, run downstairs, and drive... in blind panic and floods of tears... to the cemetery gates. I knew they would be locked, but it was the closest I could get to my beloved Alan. And more than anything, I desperately wanted to be with him, just to find peace and freedom from PP's never-ending abuse.

I lost count of the number of nights I sat there in the darkness, frozen to the bone and broken by despair, sobbing my heart out until dawn came. Sometimes in my blind grief, I became so mentally agitated and overwhelmed by suicidal thoughts I felt a compulsion to drive down the motorway at full speed, and ram my car full tilt into one of the road bridges. Ending my miserable life seemed the only way I would ever escape from the remorseless persecution I was experiencing at home.

Only one thing ever prevented me from ending my desperate life. Somehow, shreds of sanity lingered. Something inside me persisted in urging me to cling onto life. The quiet guardian inside my mind kept reminding me I could never abnegate my responsibility for my children.

There had to be another way to overcome my dilemma than by suicide. I prayed in desperation, and meditated all through those bleak hours, seeking some form of spiritual help. But like the cemetery gates, the gates of heaven seemed closed against me.

When I did eventually calm myself enough to drive home, I would always find PP in bed, snoring his evil head off, and not in the least bit concerned about my absence, or the devastating effects his cruel torments had inflicted on me. For him, the effects of these vile episodes were of little significance... just successful results in the deranged game he was enjoying playing with my mind and my emotions.

As this period of persecution continued, I felt my powers of endurance, and my faith being tested to breaking point. Eventually my despair became total and abject. I could not understand why a loving God would lead me into such a bedevilled cruel relationship, after depriving me of my loving husband. I felt that my faith was being eroded and tested to breaking point. And I often asked myself... How many more times must I go on turning the other cheek, to this man who is determined to destroy me?

For me, the first two years of life without Alan, were degrading and terrible... an endless saga of diabolical, savage schemes, all remorselessly carried out against me. They were beyond anything I could ever have imagined any man would intentionally plan, and carry out against his wife.

I came to believe that the man who was controlling my life had originated from some dark strata of creation... a hellish underworld of which I knew nothing. His cruel and vindictive activities were concepts I had never met before...and had never even imagined might exist anywhere outside of hell.

But by far the worst thing he ever did to injure my mind and my emotions was a pernicious lie he invented, with the sick intention of alienating me from my daughters. Everything else I was forced to contend with during that first brutal year of marriage was invidious, and intended to undermine and destroy me. But he was also maliciously intent on causing devastating damage to my children, and to the close bond between us.

I recognised I was fighting to hold on to my sanity, and I was doing all I could to protect them.

My daughters were young teenagers, and I barely understood how betrayed they felt, and how totally confused my strange behaviour was making them feel. They saw only my unbelievable change of character, and my crazy slavish behaviour towards PP. They never saw, or understood, any of the sadistic reasons that lay behind it. They felt they had lost their father, and now it seemed they had also lost their mother... It was all part of PP's demonic plan to alienate us from one another, and to drive us apart.

I hid my injuries, or made excuses for those I couldn't hide. I kept my arms covered, and wore high-necked clothing. I covered the injuries to my face with make-up, and hid the bruises that covered my body under bulky clothing. The livid marks constantly around my neck vanished under scarves, just as oversized sunglasses concealed my bruised and swollen eyes.

My odd choice of attire often drew curious comments from my staff at school, and there were numerous comments made about my rapid weight loss since my marriage. I had become so thin that everyone thought I must be on a strict diet. Or perhaps I was ill with some awful wasting disease, because I always seemed to be so exhausted.

But I kept my problems to myself and confided in no one. I was simply too ashamed to admit what was going on behind closed doors.

PP was extremely devious and cunning, and always made sure none of his violent behaviour ever had witnesses. Not even my daughters heard or saw anything. To the eyes of the world, he kept up a good pretence of being the benign 'rough diamond' he claimed to be.

My daughters judged me by my out-of-character behaviour, and thought I had turned into someone they no longer knew. I seemed to have undergone a personality replacement. I never seemed to have any time for them, as I was always too preoccupied... busy dancing attendance on PP... forever fetching and carrying for him... cooking food for him... buying him clothes, and chasing off to Salisbury every weekend, leaving them to their own devices. I appeared to be totally obsessed with PP, obeying his every whim to try to please him. Samantha and Nathalie became convinced I had rejected them, and no longer loved them, or even wanted them anymore. All I appeared to want from life was to keep PP happy.

He was very effectively making his evil scheme a complete success, and bringing about the total destruction of my family's life. Along with all his other diabolical plans, he had always intended to alienate my children from me, and reduce me to a position of complete isolation and total dependency on him. Then having achieved his full ambitions, he would arrange my death... by one means or another.

It was a matter of sick pride to him that he had alienated his own children from their mother. He had often boasted how he had raised his son to hate Beryl, and had done everything in his power to prevent her from having any influence over any of her children... until finally he had succeeded in driving her from their family home.

Now this evil bastard was trying to achieve the same atrocious results with my children and myself. He actively intended to drive a permanent wedge between us, and turn us against each other. To this end, he invented the malevolent evil story already alluded to. It was a major part of his insane attempts to alienate me from my children. A more malicious, and evil product of his deranged brain would be difficult to imagine. But the scurrilous story he invented was intended to poison my mind against my daughters, so that I would finally reject them, and force them to leave home.

One evening, he slyly informed me that he had been having a conversation with Nathalie and Samantha about their father's death… He was using his Dr Jekyll tactics, and being very smarmy and chatty. But I recognised it as one of his contrived ploys to soften me up for some new plan he was concocting. According to the story he began to relate, my girls had approached him and asked if they could speak to him, in confidence, about their father's death.

The idea that my girls would ever consider talking to him about their father came as a massive shock. After the disgraceful ways he had previously treated them, it was incredible to me they would ever actually approach him to talk about Alan. Normally, they had as little to do with him as possible.

After forbidding my daughters from displaying photographs of their father in their bedrooms, it seemed incredible that my children would actually want to talk to him about Alan, or ever discuss with such a despicable monster, the terrible events surrounding their father's death.

However, I suddenly found Dr Jekyll was seeking to fill my head with a tale, which he claimed my daughters had brought to him, and related in confidence, concerning their father and me.

According to his malicious story, Samantha and Nathalie

had asked him if they could discuss their deep resentment of me, and my wicked behaviour surrounding the circumstances of Alan's death. They both wanted to ask his advice upon what they should do about me.

In this poisonous revelation he explained how my daughters had tearfully told him of the deep hatred they felt for me. He gleefully related their alleged account of how much they loathed and despised me, and how both of them considered me no better than their father's murderer.

When I heard such a terrible indictment made against me, and attributed to my own children, I was horrified beyond words. I simply couldn't respond. To even contemplate that such a terrible conversation had ever taken place was a heart-wrenching, and soul-destroying shock, and I burst into tears of despair. I felt stabbed in my heart by this cold-blooded revelation... incredulous that my children would tell him, of all people, such a revolting lie. The concept was more than I could bear, and I felt faint.

But the worst part then followed, as he proceeded to tell me they had sworn him to secrecy, before confiding they wanted to go to the police about me because they both held me entirely responsible for Alan's death. He claimed they had told him that I'd had Alan cremated for one reason only... to hide the fact that I had murdered him. According to his sick fantasy, I had cruelly and callously walked away, and left their father to die in agony, while I had deliberately and cold-heartedly done nothing to help him, when he was experiencing the agony of a massive heart attack, and lay dying in terrible pain.

This malicious fabrication went even further. He claimed my girls had told him I had refused to call either a doctor or an ambulance, and left their father to die, while I calmly went off to take a shower. Now they were both secretly consumed with so much hatred of me, and filled with such deep resentful fury they felt they should go to the police with their accusations and have me arrested. He claimed it was their belief that if I had behaved properly, and made more efforts to summon help for their father, he would never have died, and would still be alive.

Then he added, with a sly sadistic grin, that they had sworn to him they would never to forgive me for my wicked neglect and cruelty. They both despised me so deeply that as soon as they could, they intended to leave home and never return, or ever speak to me again so long as I lived. In their eyes I had never been a caring wife, or even a proper mother to them. I was a cruel, heartless woman, who had never shown either their father or themselves a scrap of affection.

He ended this monstrous fabrication of lies, by sardonically informing me that they both hoped I would soon be dead... and preferably if I killed myself.

By the time he had finished his appalling recital of hatred, knives pushed into my heart and brain would have been a welcome release from the terrible anguish he had inflicted upon me. I was heartbroken and distressed beyond words. It was unbelievable that my own flesh and blood would have said such terrible things about me. In my heart, I would never have imagined either Samantha or Nathalie capable of expressing so much virulent hatred for me. Why either of them would say such wicked and untrue things was too much to bear, and I began to think it would be better if I were to die.

The acute pain this caused me was unbearable. My daughters knew I loved Alan more deeply than words could ever tell. And they knew I had done everything in my power to keep him alive. They were there when it all happened... They knew the truth...

and it was nothing like the story he claimed they had told him. Now my heart was being broken for a second time, to hear this terrible malicious account PP was ascribing to Samantha and Nathalie. His despicable accusations left me prostrate and emotionally destroyed. I felt completely destroyed by it, and as though my heart and soul had just been wrenched from my body for a second time... by my own children.

My daughters meant more to me than anything on earth. But it was a long time before I could summon up the emotional courage to confront them with this horrific tale, and ask them to explain how PP had become involved in such an appalling catalogue of lies.

It was, in fact, several years before I eventually found the courage, and the composure, to relate the incident to my daughters.

When that moment eventually did come, it felt as though I was baring my anguished soul. I could barely speak the words because of my own unresolved grief. The anguish I had been forced to carry for a long time had been unbearable, but I had held it inside me in silence.

Their instant reactions were as horrified as mine had been when the tale had originally been related to me... shock, horror, and disgust... along with a renewed outpouring of grief for the loss of their father.

There had never been any such conversation about Alan. The entire account which had been recited to me, had been nothing more than another of PP's vile and malicious fabrications. Another of his sadistic evil fantasies intended to cause maximum grief, and hopefully permanent alienation between my children and myself.

Apart from their undisguised horror, the response from both of my daughters was instant disgust; and each in her own way expressed what amounted to the same heart-felt comment, 'Why on earth would we ever talk to him about our Dad? PP was a vile, devil-man, and we loathed him.'

However, I still have no doubt that when he poured his toxic venom into my ears, he believed it would be enough to create a lasting hiatus between my daughters and me, which nothing would ever erase.

How very wrong he was.

Chapter 24

A Year to Break Me, Part X: Moving House

After many long and tormented months of living with PP, my home had become a place of dread. It held no joy, or even peace of mind for me anymore. It was a place where I endured endless pain, violence, and abuse of mind and body; a place where I was constantly interrogated and castigated, and violated by my cohabitant's remorseless persecution.

I was paroled on Monday mornings, and permitted to go to work... because, he claimed, it amused me. The reality was I had to work to earn the money that kept us. My salary paid for everything, domestic and personal. Now it had to stretch to cover the payments for the bank loan on Liz's house, along with the local council taxes, and domestic outgoings on both my home and the cottage, and everything else that he refused to contribute anything towards.

One Monday evening when I arrived home, he was waiting for me in a foul temper, and greeted me by waving the latest bank statement in my face, yelling at me that I was… 'up ter yer ol tricks uv, 'iding money from uz agin'.

The weekend had been terrible from beginning to end, on account of his manic preoccupation with money. As usual, we had been at the cottage. But he had spent the entire weekend railing at me to provide him with the funds to buy a ride-on motor mower to cut the grass in the paddock.

We had driven around various suppliers of ride-on mowers within a thirty-mile radius of the cottage, until eventually he had selected the machine he wanted to own. It was an eight horse-power, ride-on motor mower, which I was then instructed I must buy for him. I hadn't enough money left in the so-called joint bank account, so he ordered me to sell my holiday caravan and use the money for the machine he wanted.

That morning, while I had been at school, my bank statement had arrived. And in his rigorous inspection of it, he had discovered the small amount of pension I received each month from Alan's pension fund trustees. It was a family benefit for me to spend however I chose, to support our children. I had never touched this money, and each month, a standing order immediately transferred the amount into a savings account. My intention was to let the money accrue, and then divide it between my daughters when they went to university. The money was nobody's business except mine, and had nothing at all to do with PP. How I disposed of it was my business.

Now he was raving mad… raging at me that I was cheating him and hiding my secret income from him. I was being threatening with more violence, and he was demanding to see the savings account. The situation gave him another excuse to launch an attack on me, and he began throwing his fists about, calling me vile names and slandering Alan shamefully.

'Ah ain't keepin' that fuckin twat's lazy fuckin' kids,' he screamed. 'The bugga can keep 'is own soddin' brats hisself. Yer kin git tha' money and gi'e ma lad sum uv it. 'Ee diserves it arter yer fuckin' well frew im owt on the fuckin' street, yer bloody bitch. An eny more muney 'ad betta git put straight inter the bank, cos as long as those two fuckin brats live unda maa roof, Alan kin feed 'em, an keep 'em hisself, cos Ah ain't.'

His venomous outburst was shameful, and naturally I jumped to the defence of Alan and our children. I defended myself as best I could, reminding him that I worked and maintained my children myself, and that he had never spent a penny on them.

But PP was someone who refused to allow any opposition to anything he did or said, and he set about his usual tricks of battering me around my head.

Still, I refused to be silenced and continued telling him some home truths about himself. I told him he was the meanest and most selfish man living, and that he had manipulated me into providing for himself and his despicable offspring, and had brutally manipulated and coerced me into supplying all their never-ending demands. I enraged him even further by goading him to answer me... How much had he ever contributed to the housekeeping budget since I had known him? And what had he ever paid for since I had married him?

My questions were answered by a welter of blows, rained down across my face and head. But I stuck to my guns and kept repeating the questions. Why did he imagine Alan's pension funds had anything to do with either himself or his son? The money was from Alan for our children's future. It came from their own father, and it was nothing to do with either himself or Steve.

Within seconds, he once again had me by my throat, choking the breath out of me to shut me up. Eventually I slithered down onto the floor gasping for air.

The following lunchtime, I was driven to the bank, under vile threats of what would happen should I attempt to refuse his demands. He had Steve alongside him. And under dire threats, I was intimidated into withdrawing everything from the savings account and closing it. The two of them stood alongside, watching intently to make quite sure I counted the money equally into three piles. Then, without even a brief word of thanks, the young oaf snatched up one pile of cash and stuffed it into the pocket of his jeans.

A week later, without ever consulting me, PP towed away my caravan and sold it. I never saw the proceeds, or even knew how much he had sold it for. He claimed to have used the entire amount to buy the ride-on mower he wanted.

Increasingly, with every day that passed, I was learning to hate this terrible man more and more, with every fibre of my being. There were no limits to what he would do to defraud my children and myself. Anything he wanted he simply took from me.

But the cumulative toll of all the abuse and violence, and the resulting stress, I was experiencing at his hands, was already seriously undermining my health. The longer I persisted in resisting his demands, the more physically weak I was becoming. Being subjected to relentless day and night abuse, and unbearable psychological stress, was damaging my physical and my mental health. I knew I was crumbling beneath the strain, even before I began to suffer from blackouts. These incidents began to happen at increasingly frequent times... when I would suddenly lose consciousness and fall senseless for several minutes.

When an attack began, I would become very dizzy, with the room spinning wildly around me, before I felt myself rapidly disappearing into a kind of black vortex, as I lost consciousness. The incidents were potentially dangerous, and deeply distressing for me, but they were becoming increasingly frequent as the months went by.

One such incident occurred at the cottage, after he had sent me upstairs to fetch something for him. As I climbed the stairs, I seemed to be descending into a deep dark well. The higher I struggled to climb, the deeper and blacker the well became, until eventually the well just swallowed me up.

When I regained consciousness, I was lying in a heap at the foot of the stairs, and he was standing over me slapping my face and haranguing me, accusing me of laziness and play-acting, and ordering me to get up from the floor because my dramatics didn't impress him in the slightest. I heard his voice coming from what seemed a long way off, informing me that my act would win me no sympathy from him.

Then another problem began troubling me. During the episodes when he was persisting in waking me during the night, I began experiencing a terrible loud pounding noise, akin to a steam hammer throbbing inside my head. A terrible sensation of pressure seemed to be pushing on my brain from the inside of my skull. This pressure was so painful and severe I felt compelled to hold on to the sides of my head; this experience became so bad I was fearful my brain had swollen so much my skull was imminently about to split open.

Each time this happened, I spent the remaining dark hours supporting the sides of my throbbing head, convinced it was the only way I could prevent my head from fracturing and my brains from pouring out. I seriously began to believe, that at any moment I was about to fall dead from a stroke.

Eventually I was forced to consult my doctor about my health problems. But even then, I could not bring myself to confess the full facts of what was going on in my life, to him, or to anyone else. I felt too ashamed to admit exactly what I was continually experiencing at home every day, or the terrors every night of my life now brought.

My blood pressure was critically high, while my weight was plummeting drastically. The doctor could not understand why I was in such a stressful state, and prescribed a course of diazepam.

I had the prescription filled... but I never took the tablets... I was anxious they would cloud my mind, and I knew I needed to keep all my remaining wits about me to survive what PP was so relentlessly doing to me.

Somehow my life staggered on. I seemed to have become the frail incompetent ghost of the professional woman I had always been before Alan's death. But no one ever knew what was wrong with me, or even suspected the abuse I was being forced to endure at home.

My eventual surrender over my home came so suddenly and so unexpectedly, I was stunned by my own unintentional admission of defeat. Without making any conscious decision to capitulate, some part of my subconscious simply decided for me that I'd had enough, and had reached my breaking point.

Consciously, I still remained as determined as ever never to surrender to PP's demands... until that other part of my mind made a decision in its own inexplicable way, and threw in the towel. Perhaps it was working to save my sanity? I really don't know.

What I do know is my final defeat came about as the direct result of one of PPs horrendous night-time attacks on me. At two o'clock that morning I was suddenly awoken by him. He was kneeling alongside the bed, bellowing into my ears, and beating the underside of where I was lying, with a blackthorn walking stick. The stick, which had originally belonged to my grandfather, was four feet long, and had a solid iron rod running inside the length of it, and a round lead-filled handgrip. It was a sturdy and significantly offensive weapon, and had originally been intended as a gentleman's defence against Victorian footpads in the days before electric street lighting.

However, like everything else I owned, PP had taken charge of it. And for months he had been using it to terrorise me... threatening to beat me with it. I am convinced that, had he used it on me, he would have broken my back, because it was totally rigid and very heavy.

Most recently it had become his implement of choice to prevent me from sleeping. It was long enough to reach beneath the bed, and he took sadistic delight in banging hard and rhythmically directly beneath where I slept. He could keep this game up as long as he wanted to, and always until I was wide awake and in a terrified state of mind.

That was how he woke me on that particular occasion. Bang! Bang! Bang! came the hammering from beneath me, with the accompaniment of his voice bellowing, 'Fuckin' shitty dogs. Gerrout yer buggers, gerrout, afore Ah kill the lorra yer. Ah know yer 'iding unda there. Come aout afor' Ah breaks yer fuckin' 'eads. Fuckin' sodden shitty buggers. Come aout or Ah'll smash yer ter pulp.' A torrent of these obscenities was being yelled, without pause, together with the thumping and battering going on directly beneath where I was lying.

As soon as he was certain I was wide awake and trembling from shock, he intensified the attack. Beating on the bed like a madman, and yelling abuse at me about my little dogs, and how he intended to kill all three of them as soon as he could get his hands on them.

'Them fuckin' dogs is up 'ere 'idin and shittin' under the fuckin' bed. Ah ain't sleepin' in this shit'ole wiv them bloody dogs pissin' and shittin' ivvry wear. Gerrup, yer lazy bitch, and mek 'em come aout. Ah'm goin ter finish the fuckin' lorra them orf. Ah've 'ad enuff of yer fuckin pigsty an yer soddin animals.'

There were no dogs beneath the bed. My dogs did not sleep in the bedroom. My little Yorkies had never slept upstairs. They had always had their beds in the kitchen, which is where they had been all night. He was simply using the excuse as his latest reason to harass me and cause me severe distress. It was all just a continuing part of his relentless determination to break my nerves and my spirit.

This time, it was the last straw, and his aggression against me suddenly pushed me beyond endurance. For some inexplicable reason, that night I suddenly crumpled. It was too much to withstand... I could take no more of his relentless persecution.

Before I even realised exactly what I was doing, I burst into tears, and began screaming at him, 'Stop it! Stop it! You're insane. The only pig here is you, you evil monster. My little dogs are downstairs. I've had enough of your torments; I can't take any more. Stop! Stop! In God's name stop this. For God's sake, stop! I've had all I can take. I give in. I surrender. You can sell the house. Just leave me alone. For God's sake, leave me alone. Give me some peace. Let me sleep, you maniac. I can take no more. Just leave me be.'

That was exactly what he had waited twelve months to hear. Finally, he had broken me. Now he had achieved what he wanted... my capitulation. He knew he had finally won. And I knew I was beaten... broken...defeated. I watched a smug self-satisfied grin spread across his ugly face as he put the blackthorn stick down.

His campaign had finally been successful, just as he had always intended it would be. He had relentlessly delivered his campaign, and my surrender had finally been achieved. He had done what he had set out to do... He had finally broken me.

I was left in a kind of stupor... physically exhausted, and emotionally fragmented. I was numb from grief and despair... and from twelve hellish months of struggling against him.

At nine o'clock that morning, and before I had time to change my mind, I was marched into an estate agent's office, and my house was put on the market. He took charge of the entire business, and named a price far below its market value, informing the agent, 'Weir lookin' fer a quick sale.'

I had already descended into a state of shocked torpor, and abject misery. He had successfully overseen the disintegration of my resistance and smashed my confidence to pieces...This evil bastard had turned life as I knew it into an unrecognisable wreckage. Now I had lost everything... all because the devil who had insinuated himself into my quiet, bereaved existence had finally broken me, and had taken complete control of my life.

I had known this awful man for only eighteen months, and over that time, he had successfully manipulated me into the marriage made in hell, battered me into submission, and concluded the destruction of all that was left of my happy marriage to Alan. I had finally been emotionally pulverised. He had won. He had achieved his brutal intentions of destroying me, in order to take away my family home and usurp my children's inheritance.

Amazingly, now he had defeated me, he suddenly lost interest in the entire affair. He wanted nothing to do with finding us a new place to live. His main objective had been to get me out of my home, and ensure the proceeds from it were under his control.

Whatever new place I bought would now have his name on the title- deeds. Half of it would belong to him. And should, I die he would become the sole owner. That was his idea of success. My spirit had been broken, and financially, he was the winner. His daughter had a house, as she had been promised. He had a new Mercedes car. And he was now well on the way to owning my property.

None of these successes had cost him a brass cent. Small wonder he was cock-a-hoop, and very well pleased with himself.

However, my devastating capitulation sent me crashing even deeper into despair, as the matter progressed. I was like someone half-alive and living in a drugged stupor. I couldn't believe I had actually surrendered to him.

At that time the property business was a sellers' market. The ridiculously low price he had stipulated for my home meant it sold to the first family who viewed it. They knew they had secured an amazing bargain, and It was gone in days.

That completed his smug satisfaction. He'd gotten what he

wanted, and now he just wanted to get me out of my home, and the assets secured for himself ASAP. Finding a replacement place to live was a horrendous undertaking. In the booming market, all I could now afford for my money was a cramped modern detached new build, on a small estate. I had been financially fleeced of the spacious, architect-designed mortgage-free home I loved, to end up with a run-of-the-mill modern house, a third of the size. And all was because a cunning malevolent villain had inveigled his way into my life with the intention of defrauding me.

After being terrorised and coerced into selling my family home for £100,000 below its market value, I now needed to arrange a mortgage on the new property, to pay off the bank loan I had been left paying for the earlier purchase of Liz's house. I was at a point beyond despair, with my life reduced to ruins.

It pains me more than I can say, to recall the events surrounding that part of my life.

It seemed almost impossible to believe that, since Alan's death less than two years earlier, this evil manipulative character had inveigled his way into my life and engineered so many devious and duplicitous crimes. The entire sordid experience had been a criminal scheme from the start, designed only so that he could rob me, and endeavour to destroy me.

But the sadistic malevolence of PP was not yet concluded. He had something else in mind, and another crime to perpetrate against me, already planned and waiting just around the corner. His evil intentions against me were still not fully played out.

On the morning of the removal day, he switched on the bedroom lights at 3 a.m. and shook me awake with the announcement, 'Me guts is rumblin'. Ah wan summat ter eat. Git yersel daan them stairs to the shit'ole an' mek me summat ter settle fings daan.'

Not wanting to compound my troubles ahead of the incipient removal, I got out of bed and obediently went downstairs, returning with a tray of cooked food. From his morose manner, I sensed some new trouble was brewing, and I stood nervously by the side of the bed, watching as he shovelled the food into his mouth.

When he had finished eating, he wiped the back of his hand over his greasy mouth, belched several times, and then folded his arms across his distended belly and announced, 'Well, yer mite as well know naw, Ah'm not cumin wiv yer. Ah've dun wot Ah set out ter do. Ah've got yer out've this fuckin shit'ole. An Ah've got wot's righf'ly mine. So Ah'm not cumin. Ah'm orf.'

For what seemed like an age, my brain seemed to be frozen. I had heard the words... but the space between my ears did not seem to be functioning. My brain felt numb, and it was refusing to process what I was hearing... and for a while, I failed to actually comprehend what he was telling me. I continued dumbly watching him in uncomprehending silence, staring at him in disbelief. The words were vicious... cruel... and gloating, and I simply could not correlate his actual intentions with the words he had just said.

He had spent months persecuting me, resolutely determined to break my resistance, and force me out of my home, claiming it was his property. But now he was revealing that he had never had any intention of living anywhere with me... All he had ever wanted was to have his name on my house deeds, to prove HIS legal ownership.

The only thought that came into my head was the question...

If it had always been his intention to leave, why had he not simply gone months earlier, and left my daughters and myself peacefully in the home we loved?

He had turned the entire year of our marriage into an inescapable nightmare for me from its outset, while he had planned and executed what he now claimed had always been his evil, sadistic intentions.

I had been treated as his enemy, persecuted as his constant victim, and made to suffer unbelievable physical and psychological coercion and torture. Every activity he had undertaken had been orchestrated to be the height of cruelty, and designed to cause me maximum grief, as he had striven, and worked, with every fibre of his vicious being to drive me into eventual capitulation over my home.

After months of carrying out his relentless persecution, his diabolical campaign had brought me to my knees. Now he was calmly sitting in bed informing me he was walking out, abandoning me at the worst possible moment, on the morning the removal vans were imminently due to arrive.

It was too much for my mind to deal with. He had done no end of sick, viciously evil things to me, during the past twelve months; but this was the most malicious one of all. How was it possible he could be so calm and complacent, so unemotional and totally detached about his despicable premeditated intentions? He had even had the heartless audacity to order me to cook his breakfast, and watch while he ate it.

Eventually I found my voice, but it was a broken one, which I didn't even recognise as my own. 'I don't understand. Why you are doing this to me?' I croaked. 'The removal wagons will be here at eight to start loading my furniture. You've been going on about moving for months... doing everything you could to force us out of our home... constantly bullying me all the time into selling. Why? Why have you done such terrible things to me if you knew all along you had no intention of coming?'

He leered at me smugly, and pushed the greasy remains of his breakfast across the bed towards me. 'Well naw yer know. Ah nivver 'ad any intenshuns uv goin' enyweir wiv yer, yer fuckin' cow. Bu Ah'd married yer so wot was yers cud becum righf'ly mine. Bu'bein' a greedy selfish whore, yer wudn't 'and it over. So this is 'ow Ah decidid ter mek yer coff up. Ah'm orf, cos Ah've finerlly got wot Ah wonted. Yer an' yer fuckin' kids kin moov on yer own. Ah've 'ad enuff of the lorra yer... aal airs an' graces, an fuckin' lar-dee-dah eydeas. Ah ain't comin'. 'Ave yer go tha'? It's ova. Ah've go wot Ah wontid. Ah've 'ad ter settle fer arf yer bloody 'ouse, when Ah shud a copped fer the lot. Naw all yer've got is the uvver arf. Enjoy it, and Ah 'ope yer soon die uv cansa Then Ah will cop the lot. Yer caan stop uz naw.'

Suddenly, my head, my world, and my home... everything... seemed to explode into tiny fragments. Nothing around me any longer seemed to possess any solid shape. It was all just a swirling chaotic mass of pieces that made no sense, and none of it was real anymore.

I ran blindly from the room in hysteria and locked myself in an outbuilding in the garden. For the next five hours, I was incoherent and suicidal. I hacked at my wrists with a knife, and huddled in a heap under a blanket.

That terrible day, my despair reached annihilation point. I wanted to die to escape from the life I was enduring. He had maliciously and deliberately persecuted and manipulated me right up to those final moments, in order to maximise the intensity of my despair.

What kind of devil out of hell does that? He had even wished a horrible death upon me. There was not one shred of remorse, or even a blush of shame in the bastard.

At eight o'clock, two huge removal vans arrived to begin emptying my spacious family home. At the same hour, PP got into the Mercedes, threw his possessions into the boot, and calmly drove off. He had already secured himself a bolthole in preparation for what he had been planning to do. And that was where he went... to the house I had been manipulated into buying for his daughter Liz, the house in Stevenson Street.

Five hours later, while the men were still busy emptying my home, he came back in high spirits and lit one of his destructive bonfires in the garden. He hadn't yet quite completed putting the final finishing touches to my annihilation... not yet. He still had a couple of nasty tricks he wanted to pull before he could enjoy the satisfaction of knowing he'd completed the job of destroying me.

He had a wagon and two of his workmen with him, in order to load the stuff belonging to Alan that he intended to remove and keep. This primarily comprised of all Alan's engineering tools and machinery, along with our large aluminium-framed greenhouse.

After asking my girls where I was, he broke down the door of the outhouse and dragged me outside to witness what he was about to do next. I was covered in blood and locked into a state of irrational hysteria... lost beyond reason, in grief and despair. But he wanted to hurt me even more. He wanted to see me fully destroyed, and gloat over what he had been capable of achieving. He'd been planning it for months, and he had no intention of allowing me to escape, without one final twisting of the dagger he had already pushed into my heart.

While he had been ransacking Alan's workshop, he had discovered several large boxes of correspondence written to me during Alan's service days in the Royal Air Force. Alan had lovingly and faithfully written to me every day during the five years he had served his country. There were many hundreds of letters, and every-one was intimate... filled with private sentiments and tender declarations of love.

I was the only person who had ever read that correspondence. And no one had any business, or any right to tear those letters from their envelopes and publicly display them. Now, in the middle of the most terrible ordeal possible, I was forced to bear silent witness as PP took possession of the entire correspondence. I came outside to the appalling sight of my letters being wilfully being scattered all over the garden, while he and his two workmen were laughing and joking as they read sections of the personal contents.

His latest torment was to force me to watch, as he burned them.

Our two sailing boats were already alight, and he was jumping about like a lunatic, flinging handfuls of Alan's precious letters into the flames. I was already deeply traumatised, and beset with hysteria. Yet he dragged me to the fire, laughing in my face, and forced me to witness what he was doing. It felt like I was being forced to watch my entire life being incinerated.

That day, I truly wanted to die. But I was forced to stand silently by, drenched in tears and in deepest distress, and watch while he burned my family's boats, along with those precious love letters, and piles of family photographs of people he had never known.

It was an act of incomprehensible insanity and heartless vindictiveness. These things had to be destroyed simply because they were deeply personal to me. Because they belonged to the most significant and meaningful part of my life... a happy loving youthful life that had existed long before I had ever heard his hateful name... they had to go. His motivations and the evil brain that had invented them were beyond comprehension. He wanted to destroy my past, negate it, ridicule it, and wipe it out, as though it had never existed.

The things he destroyed that day had nothing whatsoever to do with him. And the emotions expressed in every loving word Alan had ever written to me, lay a million miles beyond PP's deranged mentality... the grief he was causing me was beyond traumatic.

However, after a while, even in my distress, it did not escape my notice, that the two workmen he had brought with him had fallen silent, as they witnessed the depth of my pain. I saw their shamefaced disgrace as they stood looking on, while he carried on with his diabolical destruction of my emotions and my life. I feel sure they were both decent family men. But neither of them dared to say a word, or object to what he was doing to me. He was, after all, their employer.

Nevertheless, their demeanour, and their down-cast faces spoke for them. Even in my grief, I could see how appalled and totally disgusted they were by what they were having to witness, and by his gloating behaviour towards me.

And so, on that terrible day Samantha, Nathalie, and I moved house. That evening, we found ourselves in the cramped new place, distraught, and at our wits' end.

I named it 'the Rathole'. To us, it wasn't a home. It never would be. Our familiar, well-loved furniture was randomly dumped in two garages, stacked in crazy piles, and squeezed into the small rooms wherever it would fit, just to get it under cover, in the cramped living space we now had to occupy. It felt like we had been condemned to live in a permanent jumble sale.

I soon discovered the previous owners had owned a very dirty cat. The place stank of cat urine, and it was impossible for me to get rid of the stench.

Finding places to fit my possessions was akin to attempting to pour a gallon of water into a small teacup. Eventually, we were left to contend as best we could with both garages, crammed to their ceilings with our furniture. Precious antique pieces were stacked one on top of another, with many items balanced on top of the grand piano.

Samantha fell through one of the bedroom ceilings as she attempted to haul boxes of our belongings up into the loft, and her accident left one of the bedrooms out of action, with a huge hole in the ceiling and the bed smothered in lumps of plaster. To make matters even worse, she had hurt herself quite badly in the accident.

The place was in chaos, and I could never imagine how, even in a thousand years, it could ever be organised to be anything else. It was just somewhere we had been callously dumped, and abandoned. Our lives had been reduced to ruin, and it felt like we were uprooted refugees from some terrible war, with our belongings muddled up all over the place in boxes and cupboards.

There were two very smelly rooms downstairs, comprising a tiny kitchen, where you could not sit down to eat, and the dual purpose, living-room-cum dining-room area, where you could. Upstairs were four minute, and very basic bedrooms, each of which held nothing more than a bed and a cupboard. The last room was a small basic bathroom, containing a blue plastic bath and a lavatory. There were seven small cramped rooms in total, plus two garages, now crammed to the ceilings with the contents of a large seventeen-room detached house.

That night there was no sleep possible for me. I lay awake desperately trying to formulate some way of organising our lives in this hellish situation. We had been cruelly manipulated into an unbelievable mess, and I knew I was entirely to blame for ever having allowed such a vile creature as PP into our lives.

Chapter 25

Denied Justice and Confounded by Religion

That first night in the Rathole, I tossed and turned all night, overwrought by so many conflicting emotions, it felt like I would never sleep again. Then sometime before dawn, my tears suddenly stopped. Completely unexpectedly, my distraught mind suddenly became calm. A new energy had found its way into my distress, and something wonderful was illuminating the bleak misery crowding my unhappy mind.

An amazing bright light had been switched on. It was the light of reason. And it was blazing a trail through all the confusion, distress, and misery that had been choking my thoughts and my psyche for the past year. For the first time, the entire invidious plan PP had been plotting against me, stood out in clear details. At last I understood. It had always been his cynical intention to reduce me to this level of despair.

Alan and I had never been millionaires, nor anything approaching such affluence. Our home had been the result of our combined professional success, and gained from our joint endeavours. It wasn't something we had won by good luck, or been given, or even inherited. We had jointly worked hard for everything we had. But our relationship had always been based on love and united goals, and on supporting one another in every possible way.

PP was a sick mockery of a man. He lacked any capacity to understand the loving loyalty that Alan and I had always shared. He was incapable of giving or sharing anything. His entire sick existence was constructed from greed, jealousy, and malicious vindictiveness. He had a driving sense of entitlement, to take for himself whatever I had. And he had been determined from the outset to snatch away and destroy, everything I valued and held dear, from my life with Alan.

Our home had always been his target because of what it represented. Whatever PP envied, and was incapable of achieving by fair means, he had always intended to appropriate by foul ones.

Now, unexpectedly because my mental illumination had come as a wake-up call I understood everything. It was a Heaven-sent warning to take immediate action to prevent any more of his sadistic plans from coming to fruition.

Perhaps the unexpected enlightenment was a warning message from heaven; or maybe it was just good old-fashioned intuition at work.

Either way, it came as a revelation, and it saved me from even further grief. I was left with the absolute certainty that I must not waste a single moment once the daylight had returned. The summer holidays had only begun, and my salary for July and August had just been paid into the joint bank account.

My traumatised brain revived, and my physical energy suddenly went into overdrive. At nine o'clock, I was standing in the street outside of the bank, waiting for the doors to open. At five minutes past the hour, I was sitting in the manager's office, relating my problems, and arranging to transfer my entire salary for the next two months into a new account, in my own name. At ten minutes past nine, a cashier rang through to say PP was at her till, demanding to empty the joint account and close it.

Had I ignored my inspirational guidance that morning, and remained depressed and immobilised, licking my emotional wounds in despair, what would have become of my children and me that summer? PP had already laid his plans to visit the bank that morning, with every intention of completing his pernicious activities, and callously leave the three of us penniless and destitute.

Only twenty-four hours earlier, he had happily reduced me to such depths of despair I had wanted to kill myself. His calculated cruelty had rendered me so emotionally desolate I could see no further reason to go on living. Then to round off that unmitigated outrage, he had intended to leave my children and myself destitute as well.

Of such a degenerate bastard, what more can be said?

But hope springs eternal, so the saying goes. And I was never born to be a quitter or a coward. Now, under the influence of my strange inner revelation, I was fighting back. He had nailed his colours to the mast, along with his dastardly intentions. Now I was resolved to rid myself of him permanently... and as quickly as possible.

I had finally been forced to face the bleak, undisguised facts... a creature like him had no soul, no remorse, no conscience, and no compassion. There was nothing good in him. He was one of the devil's own... a cold-blooded monster with no human feelings or emotions inside his evil head. I needed to get him out of my life as quickly as I could. This time, there could be no going back.

Over the course of a year, he had viciously manipulated me beyond all sense and reason, to achieve his own malicious intentions, only to abandon me in the most heartless possible way.

Now he was gone, having never set foot in the new house which I had been harassed and manipulated into buying. And he was living only a short distance away, in Stevenson Street... in another house I had been coerced into providing.

A few nights later the harassment began again. This time, it was a new regime of terror, conducted from a distance, and intended to keep me aware that I still remained under his surveillance and control. Such continuing insane and obsessive behaviour was just so much further proof of his deranged distorted mentality.

His new controlling tactics were intended to cause me continuous stress, and loss of sleep. This new programme of harassments were all carried out under cover of darkness, and included waking me by repeatedly slamming the garage doors during the small hours; then there began persistent weird, nuisance telephone calls at 2 a.m., when a lunatic voice would scream obscene abuse into my ear; or sometimes it was the blaring noise from a foreign radio station tuned at full volume, and set slightly off-channel, for maximum effect, being piped down the telephone.

It took no great stretch of the imagination to guess who was behind this crazy harassment. After enduring endless nights of these, and other weird persecutions, I began to ensure I took the telephone receiver off the hook before I went to bed.

But that didn't stop him. He simply varied his tactics. Instead of using the telephone to provoke and frighten me, someone would hammer loudly and insistently on my front windows, or persistently kick the front door to waken me, before disappearing into the darkness, as I struggled, in panic, to get downstairs to see who was there.

Large quantities of soil and stones were tipped onto the driveway, to prevent me from getting my car out... The catalogue of persecution was relentless, and the variation in tactics constantly disruptive and distressing.

In spite of this relentless crazy behaviour, as my days of solitude ticked by, I found time to begin straightening out my mind and my life. I had long yearned for a return to the normality of a quiet solitary life. But with his persistent vendetta constantly going on in the background, I was not destined to find very much peace.

However, the upside of my being removed from his overbearing physical presence was that it gave me some space to clear my mind, and evaluate just what he had been doing to me ever since our first encounter. Very slowly, during that summer, I began to put the fragments of my life back together.

Following his unsuccessful attempt to clear out my bank account, I soon began to plan the action necessary to extricate him from my life. My first practical act was to visit the local car showrooms and strike a deal with a sales manager. I had wanted rid of the frivolous red sports car ever since it had been purchased. What I needed was a conventional saloon car... a vehicle that would carry my daughters and myself, along with three small dogs, in some comfort, and provide boot space big enough for my shopping and my briefcase.

Eventually we agreed on a direct exchange. The garage took back the red sports car they had sold ten months earlier, and I came away with a new, white four-door, saloon car.

Having been freed from the continuous overbearing presence of PP, I had some quiet time to begin evaluating the malicious emotional damage he had been inflicting on me. I needed time to recover my normal lifestyle, and even time to grieve properly for Alan; and I needed time and space to get myself back to the normal functioning of my daily life, and my work.

As I recalled the horrors I had endured, there was no solution possible, other than to get my abuser permanently out of my life. His unsuccessful attempt to clear out my bank account really had been the final straw. I made an appointment to consult a solicitor, with the intention of seeking an immediate divorce, on the grounds of PP's unreasonable behaviour, and his eventual desertion.

I took with me the large box file containing all the evidence I had been compiling. It was a full record of his unrelenting brutality, from the first day of the marriage in Sorrento. Everything was there... with every attack recorded, including the brainwashing, and relentless persecution he had used to coerce me into selling my home, followed by his cold-blooded desertion. There were lists of dates, and all the debts I was owed by him. I had recorded everything in diary form. To my mind, there was no possibility any reasonable fair-minded judge in the land could refuse my divorce petition. I believed the evidence I had gathered was indisputable and damning.

I wanted my freedom from his oppression, and never to be forced to endure one moment more of his insane sadism, violence, jealousy, and greed... along with the restitution of everything that had been so viciously coerced from me.

Believing I would soon be legally rid of the evil man gave me hope for the future.

At that time, I still remained oblivious to the fact I was contending with a seriously deranged, high-scoring psychopath. I had only ever recognised him as an extremely brutal, unpredictable, controlling, and violent man... someone who was a pathological liar, and did all he could to viciously manipulate me and rob me.

'Psychopathy' was something I still knew nothing at all about. The threats he had made detailing what he would do to me, if I ever attempted to divorce him, had sounded like wild talk... akin to the foolish threats aggressive adolescents make when they are frustrated and angry.

I had no idea that psychopaths, such as PP, are ruthless, single-minded individuals, who always resolutely carry out whatever threats they make. In the world of the psychopath, idle threats do not exist. For PP, his reactive behaviour ran in straight inflexible lines... cause and effect being his sadistic mantra.

You do this to offend me, and my response will be to do that to revenge myself against you. Only I will hit you much harder, to make sure you know I am taking maximum revenge on you.

His form of revenge was always the extreme of, tit for tat. And no offence, however trivial, ever went unpunished by some outrageous, calculated, and savage reaction.

He had a whole range of vindictive punishments already planned. These were remorsefully fixed in his mind, and unalterable. And he was resolute in carrying them out systematically and implacably, so as to cause maximum harm to whoever happened to be his victim. There were no exceptions to this doctrine. His abnormal brain was always preoccupied with perverse get-even schemes, and every one of them focussed upon extracting excessive revenge.

His malice was enduring. He was capable of bearing a grudge for years, in order to eventually exact sadistic retribution. Revenge gave him a deep satisfaction and pleasure. 'No bugger ivver gits the betta o me. Ah allus gits even wiv ivry last one of 'em in the end. Mek 'em suffa. That's maa motto.'

I had frequently heard these boasts concerning the damage he had inflicted on others. So why would I foolishly imagine he would not carry out his malicious threats made against me?

The bottom line was, he was such a convoluted and malevolent individual, it would have taken a hundred years to know the dark depths of his febrile mind. After only one year of marriage, I really didn't know him well enough to recognise the true parameters of his extreme potential for evil.

Mr Trevor Snelling, the solicitor I consulted about my divorce, listened to my tale of woe, and eagerly took possession of my box of evidence, along with a substantial cheque for his anticipated services. But our initial meeting left me feeling deeply uneasy. Something I couldn't quite identify about Snelling made my flesh creep, and I took an instant, intuitive dislike to him.

Something about his personality struck my senses as... untrustworthy. He was just too unctuous and smarmy to be likeable. In fact, I found everything about him off-putting, from his appearance, to his repellent mannerisms. He struck me as somewhere between the character of Dickens' Uriah Heep, and a cunning little ferret. But I had no logical reason to suspect his integrity. He was, after all, a lawyer. He was taking my money and, consequently, legally bound to have my best interests at heart... or Did He? With an effort I pushed my suspicions aside...I was employing him to organise my divorce, not impress me with his riveting personality.

Whatever my intuitive radar was trying to tell me, I silenced it, and decided I was duty bound to trust this man, in order to obtain my freedom from PP.

I am quite sure that as a solicitor with many years of experience, Mr Snelling was well versed in the laws relating to divorce. And had he been an honest lawyer, he could have told me at our first meeting exactly what my prospects for obtaining the divorce I was seeking, were.

But he did not. He merely said he required time to study my paperwork carefully; and made a subsequent appointment to see me again in a week's time.

Another week came, and another cheque was handed over. All I got in return were more excuses concerning the length of time he required for his perusal of my paperwork. And of course, his taking his time to read my extensive submissions was costing me money.

At the end of our third appointment, I was left distraught. He flannelled for a while, and then informed me that, as the current law stood, divorce could not be granted to any person who had been married for less than two years. Surely, I thought, he must have been capable of telling me that at our first meeting, and without spending time running me up a huge bill from wading through all my paperwork.

However, his shocking revelations did not end there. He calmly went on to tell me that, since PP now had his name on the house deeds, he could come and go as he pleased. There was no legal recourse to prevent him from demanding the reestablishment of conjugal rights, or even his rights of occupation.

Even though this dreadful man had abandoned me, and had never set foot in the house, these were still his legal rights within the marriage laws. If I attempted to change the locks to keep him out, I could be prosecuted.

The bottom line was, there was no legal possibility of getting the violent beast out of my life... not until at least another year had passed. Irrespective of anything he might do to me during that year, I must remain married to him. The worst part of his concluding summary was that I must allow PP to cohabit in the house where I now lived, should he decide to resume the marriage.

I remonstrated that surely, taking account of all I had already endured at PP's hands there must be some law that could be invoked to protect me from him?

Mr Trevor Snelling remained adamant. The law would not protect me, or allow me to divorce this man who had tricked, and manipulated me into an abusive marriage. And he re-emphasised that, if I refused to allow PP entry to the house, I would open myself to prosecution.

The police were not interested in cases of so-called domestic violence, such as I was complaining about. And neither was the justice system... unless he actually killed me, which I was only too well aware he had frequently threatened, and even tried, to do.

On that issue, I was informed, the law regarded threats, as mere words; and accusations of violence without witnesses, carried no weight as evidence in a court of law.

In due course, I received his final bill for the pathetic, unhelpful, so-called legal advice I had been given. But Mr Trevor Snelling retained all of my paperwork, with the excuse it would be on file when I next returned, in a year's time, to pursue my petition.

I was devastated by the puerile advice I had received, and the duplicitous way my money had been taken. I had no intention of ever approaching the man again on any legal matter. I felt the law had trapped me mercilessly in an invidious situation. It seemed English law was deaf and blind to people in my predicament. Unless PP actually murdered me, there was nothing to be done, and no one was interested. But illogically, if he did eventually murder me, then any application for a divorce would be rendered irrelevant. My life and my terrible experiences seemed to be nothing but arbitrary incidentals, and of no consequence to the law.

I really did not want to die to prove my point. To my mind, such legal disinterest was a terrible indictment of the whole system of Justice.

One night, three weeks later, after my daughters had gone to bed, I was sitting on the sofa reading, when the living room door suddenly burst open. I was terrified out of my wits to find myself suddenly confronted by PP. I had no idea how he had obtained a front door key; but by some illicit means, he had surreptitiously managed to gain entry and without my hearing a sound.

Suddenly, there he was, confronting me, yelling terrible abuse at me, and launching himself upon me in a savage attack. By some inexplicable means, he had discovered I had consulted Trevor Snelling the solicitor, to make serious enquiries about initiating a divorce.

How he had gained such privileged information I never knew for certain, although given time, I did formulate some well-founded suspicions concerning the professional integrity of the solicitor involved.

But by whatever devious means he had obtained the information, PP was now there in the room with me, and determined to carry out his threats to get revenge for my intentions to divorce him. I had no idea how he had gained entry, but he had come to the house determined to show me he was still in control of me, and to let me know there was never going to be any divorce.

He set about battering me around my head and face, until I was dizzy. Then he flung me down onto the sofa, and leapt upon me, and began ripping my clothes from me. I was pinned beneath him, held completely immobilised and unable to defend myself, as he violently ripped the blouse I was wearing into shreds in a calculated act of defilement, and savage domination and humiliation.

Almost surreally, I can still recall hearing the buttons go pinging against the television screen... before he brutally raped me, savagely biting my breasts until I bled.

In one terrifying moment, I was back to where I had been during the previous twelve months... terrified, humiliated, beaten, and violated. I had been deliberately and maliciously attacked, and emotionally destroyed by him, yet again, in an act of disgusting and brutal revenge.

I tried to remain silent, biting my lips, and not daring to scream or call out, for fear of terrifying my sleeping daughters.

If they came stumbling downstairs half-asleep, and discovered the semi-naked state I was in, I knew they would attempt to attack him. But at what cost to themselves and to me?

Snelling, the solicitor, had already told me that I had no right to prohibit PP's return to the house whenever he chose to appear...But this was a brutal violation, not a condoned return... And his sudden brutal attack left me paralyzed from terror, and in a state of sickening trauma and revulsion.

In every respect, PP had proved he still had the whip hand over me, and I was without any means of defence against him.

Before he left, his final act was to jab my face with his thick fingers, and inform me...

'he would be back whenever it suited him, to fuck me again. If I needed constant reminders that he owned me, he would see I got them. I was nothing of any significance, other than the slut he had married, and the whore he fucked, whenever he felt the inclination.'

When he had gone back into the darkness where he belonged, I curled up in a heap on the floor like a whipped dog, and cried until I had no more tears left to cry.

There was no escaping from him. And according to the law, as Trevor Snelling had explained it to me, there was nothing I could do to defend myself against him. He could come and go as he pleased; and it seemed he also had carte blanche to attack, and violate me with impunity, whenever he chose. I was condemned to remain a victim, completely at his mercy, and emasculated by the Law.

Unbelievably, all this was happening in a civilised country where I had always believed our system of Justice existed to protect the weak and defenceless.

Several days later, I had a security chain fitted to the front door, along with a suspended warning bell. Trevor Snelling had expressly forbidden me from attempting to keep PP out. But law or no law, I had no intention of allowing him to ever make any sickening repeat visits to violate me. Neither would I meekly condone his future entry into the house, without making some attempt to defend myself against him.

As an additional defence precaution, I started to keep my grandfather's blackthorn walking stick with me at all times, and wherever I happened to be in the house. If he ever returned, and I had to defend myself against him, I would... with every ounce of energy and determination I could muster.

Strangely enough, he never repeated his rape episode, nor made any further attempts to break in. He merely reverted to his former tactics of psychological persecution throughout the summer and into the autumn.

At the beginning of September, we all went back to school. Nathalie was now in the upper sixth, studying for her GCSE, A levels, while Samantha had taken her GCSE, O levels, and was in the lower sixth. They were both beautiful, intelligent young women, and I was very proud of them.

Nathalie had seen a few boys, and had gone on several dates... flirtations I suppose... but she had never become involved in anything really serious. None of the prospective boyfriends ever came up to her high expectations, or adequately resembled her father in looks or personality. At the same time, Samantha had found herself a presentable, intelligent young man from within their circle of friends.

Max was more of a 'special friend'. He would be going to university soon, and if the two of them had any serious intentions,

I felt it was much too early to be of any concern to me. She was just sixteen, but legally of the age of consent.

I hadn't laid eyes on PP since the rape episode, and I had no wish to hear anything further from him. His night-time prowling and intimidating activities were still going on, and still causing me grief. But my only intention, so far as he was concerned, was to wait out another year and divorce him as soon as I could.

One morning in early October, I was in my school office when my secretary rang through to say I had a phone call. Was I free to speak to the Reverend Norman Forester?

The call came as a complete surprise. I hadn't seen or spoken to Norman in a year, and never since my disastrous marriage to PP. Coincidentally, and as a direct result of what had been going on in my life, neither had I been in church during that time. It had bothered me that Norman had never tried to contact me. Alan and I had always been loyal church members; and as a family, we had all been involved in many of the church's religious and social activities, until the events immediately following his death. For years, the Foresters had been part of our local friendship group.

However, since my disastrous remarriage, not one of our former friends had shown the slightest interest in enquiring how things were going. They had all, quite suddenly stopped contacting me and dropped out of sight.

Norman's call that morning came as a surprise. But I said I was happy to speak to him, and asked my secretary to put the call through.

Everything that came tumbling into my head to say to my old friend was instantly silenced when Norman's curt voice said, 'Delia, I need to see you. This is urgent. We need to speak...

and I mean really speak. There are things I need to say to you that cannot be left unsaid. I've been hearing seriously shocking, disgusting things about you… things that have really sickened me. Are you free this evening? And will it be in order for me to come to your house at about seven?'

I had no idea what he could be talking about, and I was left puzzled by his coldness. It struck me as very odd for him to be suddenly contacting me at school. And I felt confused to hear him speaking to me in such a brusque and unfriendly manner. 'Whatever's wrong, Norman?' I said. 'You sound quite offhand. Is something the matter?'

'Yes! Something definitely is the matter,' he replied coldly. 'Something is very seriously the matter. I just cannot credit the disgusting things I have been hearing about you. Your disgraceful behaviour has to stop. It's completely unforgivable in a woman like yourself.'

'I honestly have no idea what you are talking about,' I said.

'Well you damned well should have,' he retaliated. 'In your position, you are responsible for the lives and morals of young children, and you ought to be fostering Christian ideals, not encouraging flagrantly wanton behaviour. I would never have credited you with having such a catalogue of hidden vices lying beneath your carefully constructed moral exterior. I am shocked beyond words to discover you are raising your own daughters to be whores. Such disgusting, flagrant behaviour is completely inexcusable, and in someone who pretends to be Christian, it's unforgivable. I'll see you at seven.' Then without saying goodbye or anything else, he hung up.

If he had just rattled off half the New Testament in Greek, I could not have felt more confused. I didn't have a clue about what he had been talking about. Could it be some sort of offbeat far-out kind of a joke? Whatever it was, I would have to wait until seven o'clock to find out.

Norman turned up that evening, dead on the dot at seven, carrying a large Bible, and with a stern face that spelled business. I invited him to sit down and offered him some tea, which he declined. He seemed exceedingly agitated, and in a hurry to get to the nub of what had brought him to my door.

Without waiting to exchange any of the usual niceties about family and work, he launched straight into a shocking diatribe against myself and Samantha. Nathalie wasn't mentioned.

'You are despicable beyond words,' he snarled at me, waving his Bible in my face. 'The whore of Babylon has nothing on you, you deplorable woman. I have never had the misfortune to ever encounter such a sinister perverted creature as you in all my life. You certainly had everyone in the congregation fooled. It's to my shame that I ever welcomed you into my church, or countenanced giving you Holy Communion at the Lord's table. You are spittle from the devil's mouth, and should be publicly shamed.'

I was so devastated by this horrifying verbal onslaught, and so shocked I couldn't speak. I just sat staring at him, open mouthed in disbelief.

My silence provided him with renewed energy for his continued slanderous attack. 'It's bad enough the vile things you get up to with your own salacious sexual activities. But raising your younger daughter to be a whore is unforgivable. Such perversion is evil beyond belief.

'But to add to those evils, I am horrified to learn of the wicked and pernicious way you treated poor Alan when he was dying.

Your behaviour was nothing short of criminal, and should be answerable in a court of law. You are a monster. How could you ever deliberately and callously murder such a kind, loving man in cold blood, you spawn of Satan. What kind of woman denies her devoted loyal husband the medical help he desperately needs, and turns her back on him when he pleads for her mercy? You are the scum of the earth. Such vile acts are abominations... demonic sins that will see you damned for eternity.'

He was so enraged and red in the face, he looked about to burst a blood vessel, while I continued to sit aghast and white faced. My pounding heart felt so painful I thought it was about to stop beating... But he wasn't quite finished with me yet.

After hastily gasping for breath he said, 'That I ever agreed to sanctify your second marriage in my church will be on my conscience forever. May God forgive me.'

His rant was ended, and he fell to his knees, crossing himself in contrition, his Bible clutched to his breast, as though it was some sacred defence charm against me, and all the evil accusations he had just levelled at me.

I was stunned by the catalogue of filth he had just spewed about me. But slowly, in my mind, a penny of enlightenment was beginning to drop. I sat in shocked silence for several minutes, as my mental cogs worked to unravel exactly what could have prompted the terrible verbal assault which he had just levelled at me. I could find no words to defend myself, and the silent room seemed to be waiting ominously, as he continued to pray... for what solution I had no idea.

'I think you had better tell me exactly what agency lies behind all of these terrible accusations,' I said eventually. 'You have known me for years, Norman. How could you come to see me and abuse me so diabolically? Whatever is it that has suddenly motivated you to come here and attack me like this? ...And what evidence have you brought to actually support these vile accusations? Could it possibly be that someone I know has been filling your mind with this disgusting poisonous filth, and firing up your righteous indignation to come and insult me?

'I am quite certain such a vile pack of lies would never have come at the instigation of the Almighty. So far as the conduct of my life is concerned, HE knows the truth, and that I am totally innocent of every accusation you have just made against me. It seems to me that PP has somehow or another, been filling your mind with these poisonous lies. I'm sure, if he could, he would have you burn me at the stake, or drown me on a ducking stool, as a witch.

'I have no intention of reducing myself to the disgusting level of your accusations... except to say that not one word of anything you have come here to repeat, about either Samantha or myself is true. Give me your Bible, and I will swear upon it.'

I took a deep breath, fighting very hard to hold back the deluge of outraged tears already stinging my eyes. Finally, I choked out, 'I have always understood that bearing false witness is against the church's teachings? Does it not say in Matthew 5, verse 11, "Blessed are ye when men shall revile you and persecute you, and say all manner of evil against you, falsely"?'

He placed his Bible on the coffee table thoughtfully, then got up and walked around for a few moments. When he sat down again, he began speaking in a completely changed tone. The fire and brimstone in his manner seemed to have died. Speaking quietly and remorsefully he said, 'PP was at my house all last night. He came to me in a terrible state, completely overwrought, and crying like his heart would break. Please believe me when

I say his behaviour was entirely convincing. I have never seen a man in such a state of distress. He claimed to be in desperate need of spiritual help and guidance, and pleaded with me to hear him. He said he had been driven to consider killing himself because of all the vile things he had discovered about you, since your marriage.

'I listened to him all night long, while he wept and sobbed, and told me heart-rending stories that were entirely convincing, and soul destroying. There was an endless catalogue of incidents, and terrible accusations, concerning what he claimed was the truth about your evil behaviour towards both himself and Alan; God rest his soul.

'He maintained you were insane, and a sexual pervert beyond redemption. He said that you were encouraging Samantha down the same evil path to whoredom as yourself... actively teaching her to make a living by sexual activities on the streets.

'I have never listened to a more convincing series of stories in my life. They genuinely had the ring of truth to them, and I was completely persuaded that he was telling me the truth. His whole demeanour was that of a man who had reached the end of his tether... He spent the entire night sobbing and weeping to me about your wickedness. It tore my heart. Never in my life have I seen a man so distressed. It was seven this morning before he left.'

Norman looked at me ashen-faced, suddenly stunned into silence.

'Well, far be it from me to respond to you with more lies, Norman.' I said. 'But if you are at all interested in hearing the facts...the real truth...then maybe you would like to listen to my side of this story?

Norman nodded silently, then sat with a lowered head, as I spoke...

'PP is an evil twisted pervert, without any vestige of conscience,' I said quietly. 'He is a very creative, skilful, and totally convincing pathological liar. The devil gilds his tongue with elaborate, highly convincing deceptions. I have spent a whole year, living with him, as his victim, and experiencing the full force of his convoluted lies, and his vile brutality.

'You aren't the first gullible person he has deceived. Look at me... Look at what he has done to me. For my sins, I am the most foolish and gullible one of all. He deceived me with his pretence of genuineness, only to brutalise me every day since the day I married him. Look around you. Why do you think I am living here, with all my possessions crammed into two garages, instead of in the lovely spacious home Alan and I shared? Why do you think I look so frail? Why do you imagine my body is continually covered in bruises?

'Who do you imagine has done all this to me? I certainly didn't do any of these things to myself. My injuries came from PP; he alone is responsible. He has spent the last twelve months humiliating and degrading me, bullying and brutalising me with his endless violence and coercion, and his mind-bending torments. His one driving ambition has been to dispossess me of everything I own, and ultimately drive me to suicide. That is what the man who fired you up to come here to castigate me is intent upon achieving ...He wants to see me dead, and my children left as destitute, homeless orphans.

'Our marriage has been a mockery from the start. That vile man you came here to defend, has quite deliberately coerced and manipulated me into this situation. And on the day, he finally forced me from my home, he abandoned me. Look around. Do you see him anywhere?

'PP began this violent persecution process on the day of our marriage. You weren't there to witness his brutality. This man is a deranged animal, without any vestige of conscience…He is a mockery of a husband, and someone who has no capacity for remorse or love. I can only guess why he came to you weeping about the situation he himself deliberately created. He has already done something pretty similar to his first wife, claiming she was mad and a sexual pervert. And now I am being given the same treatment… a repeat performance of his special brand of devilment, intended to destroy me.

'This man you have been entertaining all night, is no Christian. He mocks religion, and believes in no god. Nor does he adhere to the teachings of any church. He is truly one of the devil's own. But he can walk the walk, and talk the talk, when he wants to. He's a vicious deviant, and an expert in deception. And like the devil himself, he is a cunning liar and a skilful actor. It's all a game he plays, telling convincing lies, and deceiving gullible people with his glib tongue. It makes him feel clever and superior. He derives enjoyment out of making fools of everyone, and despises their vulnerability. I would guess that he is probably with his family right now, laughing about how cleverly he has managed to draw you into his latest vile scheme, to persuade you into helping him to persecute me.'

I took a deep breath, before I added sadly, 'You knew our happy family before Alan died. You visited our home, Norman. We were contented and deeply in love. I would have given my own life if I could have held Alan back from death. And in that, I call upon God as my witness.

'There is only one evil-tongued cruel monster I know of who would ever persecute me, and intentionally try to harm me, or say such terrible things about me. And you spent last night empathising with him, listening to him, and believing all the vile lies he was inventing about me.

'He has always sworn he would vilify me to everyone who knows me, and destroy my good name, if I ever attempted to divorce him. And he has done exactly as he said he would, targeting you first because you knew me as a friend, as well as a priest.

'Last night you were in the presence of a dangerous and evil man; open your God-Fearing eyes, Norman, and see how you have been deceived. PP is that vile piece of devil's spittle, not me. A more plausible convincing liar does not exist outside of hell. Vice of every description is what he excels in. That is how he knows so much about it.

'Why didn't you question his claims? What convinced you to believe all the slanderous, salacious garbage he was spouting about me, instead of sending him away? You gave him your hospitality, and you chose to listen, and believe...you allowed him to convince you. He must have left your house this morning feeling triumphant.

'Did it never cross your mind to wonder? Hang on a minute... I've known Delia and her family for years. This vile account doesn't sound like her at all? No... You let him pour his venomous poison into your ears... and you believed him.

'May God forgive you, Norman, because I never will. You have destroyed my faith in Christian charity. Perhaps you ought to go home and read that Bible you are hugging. Read it, Norman. Matthew 7, verse 1, clearly says, "Judge not, lest ye be judged".' After this, how can I ever respect your views on Christianity, or even count you as my friend?'

After he had left, I sat thinking deeply unhappy thoughts,

while I remained totally overwhelmed by misery for hours.

I had never previously spoken to anyone about the unbearable circumstances of my marriage. But the shock of Norman confronting me with the monstrous lies PP was now spreading about me, left me utterly humiliated and sickened. Every last one of his fabrications had been carefully constructed to cause me maximum personal and professional harm.

His intentions had always been to vilify me. And he had always emphasised that intention if I attempted to divorce him. He had no qualms about what he would do... he planned to destroy my good name, and ruin me professionally. I had been well warned that he intended to poison the minds of everyone I knew against me, until no one would ever want to acknowledge me, or ever again have any respect for me.

I had chosen to give those threats little credence. They had seemed just wild vicious words, intended to control and coerce me. I had never seriously believed he intended to do the terrible things he had threatened. But now I was facing the reality of what this vicious man was capable of. He fully intended to carry out every threat he had ever made against me.

A slander once spoken is hard to ever fully eradicate. Mud sticks.

I suddenly went cold from terror. I was staring into an abyss. What if he were to worm his glib way into the education offices, and inveigle an interview with the CEO in order to repeat the filth he had already impressed upon Norman? That thought made my blood run cold.

I was the victim of a man who believed himself to be both omnipotent and undefeatable. He was vindictive and aggressive in the extreme, and sadistic and remorseless in extracting revenge. Nothing he ever did was kind or altruistic, and his every action was calculated to benefit himself. He was a man without a conscience, who fully intended to destroy me if I went ahead with my intention to divorce him.

My very first impressions of him, upon our first meeting, had been both intuitive and accurate.

One of his well-rehearsed threats had always been that he would eventually succeed in having me dismissed from my headship if I tried to end the marriage.

Oh, my God! I thought. I don't know what I can do to stop him.

There was no denying it, PP was, by instinct and intention, evil and venomous to the core. I had a marriage certificate with both our names on it, but he had never really been my husband. He bore me no genuine feelings of affection, kindness, or even respect. The religious service of marriage, had been a mockery, a ritual carried out to make me his legal victim, not his wife.

Now I suddenly understood, for so long as we both lived, this man would be my relentless, heartless, and utterly vindictive enemy.

How was I ever going to prevent him from completely destroying my life? He had degraded, abused, and humiliated me; cheated and defrauded me; beaten me; and forced me from my family home. He had lied to me and slandered me. Now he was fully prepared to actively work to have me dismissed from my post, and professionally ruined.

How in God's name could I ever prevent him from destroying what was left of my life?

There was only one solution I could think of that would stop him. And it was the last thing I ever wanted to agree to.

Chapter 26

Between a Rock and a Hard Place

After my deeply distressing meeting with Norman Forester, I was left with no lingering doubts about PP's intentions. The bastard meant everything he had previously said. He was never going to allow me to escape from him. He had seriously meant it when he had told me that I belonged to him. My personal feelings were irrelevant. The only thing that mattered was his ownership of me. He had totally convinced himself I was a millionaire, and the only way to ultimately take possession of my assets was to ensure I stayed married to him until my death. In his twisted mind, I was a piece of property, and something he could manipulate in any way he decided. It was a philosophy of madness.

The sick episode that he had played out at Norman's home, had been deliberately contrived with only two intentions... to blacken my character, and to convey an intimidating message back to me. It was a sinister message designed to blackmail me back into the loveless situation, where he owned and controlled me.

His manipulative behaviour, from the beginning of our relationship, had always been intended to progress to diabolical cruelty, and to keeping me as his terrified captive. It had never been his intention to end the marriage. All his strange vicious behaviour had merely been working demonstrations of the unrelenting power he exerted over me.

Finally forcing me out of my family home, and abandoning me in the process, had been intended to reduce me to grovelling subservience, and to force me into pleading with him to come back and resume the marriage. He had planned the entire scenario of my downfall. And he anticipated my tearful and prostrate capitulation, along with my abject despair, and promises never to oppose him in any way again.

Such grotesque behaviour was totally outside of normality, and it illustrated that he was incapable of seeing the situation through any eyes other than his own manipulative vision. This man was mentally incapable of understanding another person's feelings.

The truth was he really didn't care, so long as he achieved what he had set out to do. But it did signify that he was entirely out of touch with any aspect of real, or normal, human behaviour, and mentally devoid of anything approaching genuine emotions of his own.

He operated on the fixed idea that in brutally terrorising and persecuting me, lay the only hopes he had of keeping me tied to him. It had only been by a fortuitous stroke of insight, that I had pre-empted him from emptying my bank account. Collectively his malicious behaviour went beyond sanity. And his current malicious attempts to turn public opinion against me, and ruin me professionally, were nothing short of malevolent.

He had tested the water by deceiving my priest into believing a collection of the most disgusting filth he could invent. His every abusive word and action was intentionally designed to slander and denigrate me. The extreme plan he was still intending to put into action, if I refused to return to the marriage, would effectively blacken my credibility and ruin me professionally. He wanted to isolate me further, and turn me into a social outcast.

His trial run had been successful. His schemes were being enacted as though we were living in the Middle Ages, and I was deserving of being tied to a ducking stool as a witch, or burned at the stake for my alleged misdemeanours against this 'innocent and grief-stricken' member of the male gender.

If I had needed further proof of the distorted evil mechanism PP had for a brain, I now had it. This man was totally unhinged. He was a remorseless devil, possessed of a poisonous and plausible tongue, and a convoluted cesspit inside his skull which facilitated the invention and delivery of such pernicious behaviour.

I knew I could never again respect anything Norman ever preached about the all-embracing charity, love, and brotherhood of Christianity. He had once been my friend. But he had been prepared to accept every vile accusation PP had made against me.

PP's intuitive psychological skills had calculated that Norman would waste no time in confronting me. And he had felt certain that, within days, I would be sufficiently distressed, humiliated, and terrified, to be pleading for forgiveness and begging him to return.

I doubt that it would be easy for any normal grown man to produce floods of tears, and cry all night long, in order to reinforce the veracity of an incredible pack of lies he was inventing. Even an Oscar winner would find that performance seriously challenging.

Norman was an honest, intelligent man of God, but he had been totally duped and manipulated by PP's melodramatic overnight drama. And right on cue, the following day, his message had been delivered to me as anticipated.

If I did not capitulate to PP's latest manipulations, and take him back, his covert message was clear:

'If you dare to attempt to divorce me, these are the stories I will spread about you to everyone who knows you. I have every intention of seeing you disgraced, and dismissed by your employers. I will drag your reputation through the dirt, and leave you penniless. Don't underestimate what I can do. I've demonstrated I can convince your priest. I'll convince your employers next. The choice is yours. But think on… you'll never get away from me alive. You belong to me, and no other bugger will ever take you from me. I'll kill you first. I won't warn you again.'

He had no intention of allowing me to escape alive… by divorce or any other means. And had I not pre-empted his visit to the bank, when he had intended to empty the account, he expected I would have already been on my knees pleading for his return, under any terms he cared to make.

I realised, if I was ever again forced to share a roof with him, I would never be able to relax my guard, or ever trust him. He had proved beyond all doubt what a perfidious wretch he was. Any future relationship with him would, for me, be nothing but a knife-edge test of endurance.

A couple of days later, Norman rang me again to tell me PP had been back in contact with him...to enquire if I was showing any signs of being sorry, for the terrible things I had done to him.

Our conversation was amicable but strained. I said that, given the circumstances, I was surprised he had even agreed to speak to the man again. We had a very short chat, which sadly was the last time I ever spoke to Norman. He apologised for bothering me, but wanted me to know he had refused to have another meeting with PP, and had merely reminded him of the solemn nature of the sacred wedding vows he had made to me in church.

I never saw Norman again. And a short while later, I heard he had requested transfer to another parish, over a hundred miles away. After that, and within the space of a couple of years, I was saddened to read a report of his death in the local paper.

Following his second conversation with Norman, PP rang me. He seemed to be under the impression that, after manipulating Norman into paying me a visit, pumped up with the vicious pack of lies he had invented, his own recent behaviour was now a thing of the past. This vile man's ability to disregard his own appalling behaviour was deeply worrying; the way that he could vindicate himself of all the evil and wickedness he spewed, was incredible. Now he obviously took it for granted that I would be chastened, grovelling, and overjoyed to welcome him back into my life.

I found his ability to produce such voluntary amnesia nothing other than further evidence of his sick mind, and the fact that he was out of touch with reality. I chose to treat him with the disdain he deserved, and was deliberately cool towards him.

He might imagine he had me over a barrel, with his covert blackmail threats to destroy my good name and my career; but

I had no intention of weakly conceding, and giving him what he wanted... certainly not without first extracting some serious concessions in return.

Dr Jekyll was speaking, and as an expansive gesture of goodwill, he suggested I might like to visit Kew Gardens, just outside of London, to discuss our future.

I said I might be prepared to consider it. But I needed to think things over carefully. If he cared to ring back the following morning at ten, I would give him my answer. For effect, I added that I was about to go on holiday, so if he didn't call back, I would be away for a week. Quite intentionally, I made my conversation, and my manner, sound blasé and detached. I hoped he had caught my implied meaning... that the continuation of our relationship was of negligible priority to me, and I couldn't care less if I never saw him again.

The following day he rang at 10 a.m. That was unusual for him, as he was never prompt to do anything. His manner that morning was still much more Dr Jekyll than Mr Hyde.

I had already decided I would accept the proposed visit to Kew. It would at least give me the opportunity to air some of my own grievances, without risking being physically attacked in public.

Fundamentally, nothing had changed. Being, the obnoxious character he was, PP was incapable of being emotionally affected by anyone else's feelings.

I already knew I could not run the risk of allowing him to cause more damage to my good name. And to put an end to his threats, I was going to have to accept the continuation of the marriage... at least for another year, and until I could find some feasible way to extract myself from it. But I had no intention of letting him imagine the outcome was going to be a fait accompli, or any victory for him… not without first attempting to extract some significant concessions of my own.

When we met, he seemed under the impression that the entire matter was settled, and began the outing in high glee, joking and making stupid puns, and generally behaving like an elated idiot, all the way to Kew.

This infantile aspect of his personality sometimes became apparent when he felt he had pulled off a clever con trick, and was feeling smug and self-satisfied. I viewed his manic behaviour as symptomatic of a bipolar condition which he frequently exhibited, when he wasn't being vicious or downright nasty.

Right up until we finished eating lunch, I let him carry on with his expansive plans, and his flippant exaggerated talk about what we were going to do when we got back together. I saw no reason to ruin a good lunch, which he happened to be paying for.

He was talking loudly and arrogantly, as if I was responsible for all our problems… throwing his kiddies out into the street… and banishing him to live with his daughter, and on and on. And now here he was generously meeting me in a forgiving mood, after all the terrible things I had done to him… The depths of his voluntary self-deluding amnesia was incredible.

While I was drinking my coffee, I casually said, 'How is Liz getting on with the house in Stevenson Street… you know, the one she still hasn't paid me for? The one I'm currently having to pay a mortgage on? Has she decided yet when she's going to start paying back what she owes me?'

My question took the grin off his fat face, and he had to admit she currently didn't like the house anymore, and was planning on selling it. She now wanted to buy something different… somewhere more upmarket… and had set her sights on a bungalow close to where her mother was living.

Well! Well! What a coincidence that was. So now his real motivations in coming to meet me were becoming much clearer. He couldn't prevent her from selling the house, because she had cunningly insisted on having it registered in her own name. But when she did move, it would leave himself and Steve homeless again.

So, Liz was planning on deserting him, again. And this time she was in control of the situation... She had a house in her own name to sell.

Consequently, after his summer-long absence from the marriage, residing with her, our getting back together, was just the latest convenient way of sorting out the problem of where he and Steve would be taking up residence next... and who the fool of a woman would be who would be lumbered with looking after the pair of them.

There was no apology and no remorse. Nor was there any intention, or even mention, on his part, of working to repair the marriage. The primary motivation for re-establishing our relationship was exactly the same as it had previously been... for his convenience, and to give him and Steve somewhere to live.

It looked as though I was currently in the process of being manipulated back into becoming their skivvy, cook and general servant. Well, I had been there before... I had been the weak woman who had provided the pair of them with a home, and everything else they wanted. And I had no intention of going there again.

I shook my head. This was unbelievable. He actually did take me for a gullible feeble-minded idiot.

'You seem to assume some agreement has been reached about our continuing with the marriage,' I said, 'when in fact, I actually mean to divorce you ASAP.'

That seemed to surprise him, and he floundered for a reply.

I took advantage of his unexpected silence to continue outlining my prepared intentions. 'There is no way I would ever again consider any reunion with you,' I said quietly, 'not unless you were first, seriously willing to agree to abide by certain conditions.'

'Wot condishuns?' he snarled...Mr Hyde was back... 'I ain't 'ere ter mek condishuns abaat uz livin' tergitha. Yer nivver sed nuffink on the phone.'

'Oh! Didn't I?' I said mildly. 'Well, I'm saying it now. You would need to make some very serious changes in your behaviour before I would ever dream of agreeing to live with you again. Otherwise, I promise you, there will be a divorce as soon as I can sort the matter out.'

'Yer not forcing me 'and inter agreein' no condishuns,' he retorted angrily. 'Cos if yer do, Ah've got plenty Ah'll say ter yer bosses abaat yer. Doan try threatenin' me, woman, cos threats doan work agin me, as yer'll soon fin' aaut.'

I took a deep breath, knowing exactly what he had in mind. 'And I don't take kindly to you making threats against me, either,' I replied. 'Neither do I take kindly to being robbed by your daughter.' I gave him a weak smile and then added quietly, 'Try me. I'm prepared to go directly to the police about her, if you try any more of your tricks.'

He fell silent for a few minutes, and I knew he was rapidly assessing if there was some means by which he could quickly stymie my unexpected tactics.

When he spoke again, it was in a less aggressive tone. 'So, whot's these crazy condishuns yer arter? Worram ah suppos'd ter do ter git uz back tergiver?'

I kept him waiting several minutes for a reply, as I slowly sipped my coffee. Then I said quietly. 'First off, you had better know, I will never consider resuming the marriage, unless you agree to see a psychiatrist.'

I paused to let my words sink in. 'There's something seriously wrong with your brain, and I refuse to live with you and your atrocious sick-violence, and abusive control, ever again. Unless you see a specialist and get yourself sorted out, our next meeting will be in the divorce courts.'

He was up and on his feet in seconds, and shouting belligerently, 'Ther's nuffink rong wiv uz. Yer the mad cow 'ere, not me. Ah'm seein no edd banger...not unless yer agree ter see 'im as well, an' see wot ee as ter say abaat yer.'

Without a moment's hesitation I said, 'That's fine by me. I will happily agree to be examined by a psychiatrist. I have no problem with that.'

'So worra vese ovver condishuns?' he asked, slightly more cautiously.

'The house is far too small and cramped,' I said. 'If you want us to live there together, then you will have to agree to enlarge it. You're a builder. You built a luxury house for Beryl, so you can easily build a two-storey extension for me.'

That made him smile sardonically. 'If yer wan an extenshun yer'll 'ave ter git sum plans drawn up. Ah'll build it, bu' Ah ain't payin fer no plans.'

'That's fine,' I replied. 'So long as you are in agreement to extend the house, I'll happily organise the plans.'

'So... wot uvver condishuns, an loony complaints 'ave yer got agin uz?' he demanded.

'Quite simply, I want my money back...ALL of it, from both you and your daughter,' I replied. 'Whatever price she sells the Stevenson Street house for, that money belongs to me, and I want it returned. She has never paid me a penny of the money she borrowed to buy it, and I've been left paying a mortgage, with interest, on her account, just because of her greedy deceptions. I want my money returned... plus all the profits from the sale. That is no more than fair and just.'

'Yer can't 'av it,' he said emphatically. 'The kid's done well outta tha' 'ouse, an it'll mek double the price she paid fer it. It's 'er money, and she'll be byin anovver 'ouse wiv it.'

'Then I shall go to the police about her,' I said. 'She's a criminal, a cold, calculating fraudster. Legally, she owns nothing. She's just a kitchen hand who has never had two pennies to rub together in her life. What evidence can she produce to prove she bought the house? Remember, I have all the paperwork, and the financial evidence. She has never had any money of her own. Whatever she makes by selling it, she has scammed every penny of it from me. Rightfully the entire asset belongs to me, and she's been living there rent-free. You had better believe me, I intend to charge your dear Liz, with fraud.'

After some angry chuntering, he half-heartedly agreed he would sort the matter out, and would see I got my money back... I didn't actually believe one word of anything he was saying... But that brought us to my final two conditions, and I made no bones about these intentions. My conditions were not negotiable.

If he thought for a moment, I would continue to keep him, without being given any housekeeping contributions... as he had originally promised he would do... he could take a running jump. And so far as his son was concerned, I would never accept the return of the horrible youth to my home. If they ever imagined I would be taking the two of them back, they could think again.

I was adamant, and I left him in no doubt of the strength of my feelings. 'Let the boy go and live with his own mother,' I said. 'I will never agree to have him living under my roof, ever again. He is not my responsibility, and he is never again sharing my home. That's it... I've said my final word on the subject. You can accept my conditions, or we'll meet in court.'

After a highly melodramatic act of grief, and a sudden deluge of crocodile-tears from him, which I ignored, I resolutely continued to stand my ground.

His incredible rainstorm of grief, over where his son would live, along with his impassioned pleas for me to relent... all intentionally designed to soften my heart and manipulate my emotions... had no effect upon my attitude towards his son at all. I had endured enough perversion and venom from that youth to last me a lifetime, and no power on earth would ever make me change my mind.

The day ended with PP in a sullen, morose sulk.

Eventually he drove me home in a silent fury, and I wondered if that would be the end of our prospective reunion. Perhaps I had finally pushed him too far. No doubt, he would find one way or another to exact some perverse form of revenge for my rejection of his vile son.

But somehow, I just didn't care.

In the three months, and more, that he had been missing, I had begun to get a grip on my situation. I had tasted freedom and independence. Now I knew I would be much happier living alone. I'd had the time and space to begin coming to terms with my bereavement, and for the first time since Alan's death, I had started to regain my quiet peace of mind.

So far as my present tormentor was concerned, I was now certain I neither wanted, nor needed him in my life. If I couldn't have Alan back, then I certainly didn't want him.

Chapter 27

A Psychiatric Consultation

I have never considered myself to be a quarrelsome person, and I have no inclinations to be deliberately disagreeable. I would much rather simply walk away, rather than stand and face a public showdown with an unreasonable, or violent opponent.

However, I have always been forthright, and I believe in speaking my mind. Pushed into a corner and facing disaster, I will stand my ground... not by indulging in threats and brawling, but by using my intelligence and my sense of what is appropriate and fair.

After my strange day out with PP at Kew, I wasted no time in consulting my GP to request a private referral to see a psychiatrist. I explained it would be necessary for a double appointment to be arranged, as both PP and I would need to be seen.

The appointment came through within a week.

I had already made my feelings absolutely clear to PP. I would never consider resuming the marriage unless he agreed to consult a psychiatrist about his violence, and other forms of unreasonable behaviour, and make every effort he could to sort out his weird selection of perverse behaviour problems.

His deranged behaviour throughout the year of our marriage had been extremely mentally and physically damaging to both my daughters and me. And I was not prepared to ever consider continuing with the marriage unless he was willing to get himself sorted out, and make radical changes to his attitude, and his behaviour.

I had agreed that I would submit myself to being examined by the psychiatrist, although I had absolutely no idea what to expect, or even how the appointment would be conducted.

The two-hour appointment, which was arranged with Professor Van Doorn was turned into a deliberate, calculated fiasco by PP. He spent an hour and forty minutes of the appointment verbally lambasting me, in a continuous diatribe about my selfishness... my greed... my insanity, and the endless other ways he claimed he had justifiable reasons to find fault with me. He included, of course, the old chestnut of my 'throwing his little kiddies out on the street'; and rambled on aggressively, without any pause, as the precious minutes sped by. He never paused or allowed the psychiatrist to say a word, even to ask him any questions.

As I listened to him manufacturing one lie after another about me, my hopes of achieving any sort of solution to the problems crashed in flames. I had suspected he would turn the appointment into a fiasco, and he had. I realised nothing at all was likely to be achieved from the consultation, and I was left completely depressed by how ruthlessly it had been hijacked.

PP's determination from the outset, had been to take command of the time, and control everything that went on. I was being charged for the appointment, but he was there simply to justify his behaviour towards me, and even seek approval for it. His depressing diatribe made me increasingly aware that he would never concede there was anything wrong with his behaviour. In fact, he was at pains to airbrush every aspect of his appalling activities aside, and chose to deny, or justify, everything he had ever done to me... blaming me for forcing him to take steps to discipline me for my unreasonable behaviour towards him.

As I listened, everything he said confirmed my belief that I was married to someone who was, at the very least, an irredeemable and extreme example of male chauvinism, and low-life brutality and domination. Even putting aside his violence, his offensive language and vicious behaviour, along with his entrenched opinion that women were naturally of lesser value, and of inferior intelligence to men; he also considered that treating women like infantile morons was a natural consequence of this inferiority. According to his perverse views, women were, by nature, automatically subordinate to men...weak of intelligence, emotionally fickle, and in need of correction and discipline. Brutal attacks, and mental manipulation were necessary to keep them in their place, and under control. Left to their own devices, women would attempt to rule and humiliate the male species... PP was clearly livid with me for forcing his hand over the consultation, and determined to get his revenge... in front of the psychiatrist.

Eventually, Dr Van Doorn asked him to be quiet, and turning to me asked if I would like to make any comments concerning the marriage? I spent ten minutes briefly outlining my experiences with PP during the past eighteen months, and relating the sadistic change in his behaviour as soon as we were married. I finished by referring to the violent and coercive tactics he had engineered to get my daughters and me out of our home, and his subsequent callous abandonment of us on the removal day.

When I finished speaking, the doctor turned back to PP and, in carefully considered language, effectively tore him to shreds for his disgraceful behaviour towards me. The allotted consultation time eventually overran more than half an hour, by the time Dr Van Doorn had completed his summary.

He ended up by saying, 'Mr PP, I consider you have serious and long-standing sociopathic and relationship problems. You seem to have no concept of equality within a marriage. Nor does it seem you have any appreciation, or respect for your wife's intelligence. Your controlling behaviour, together with your violence, are seriously worrying characteristics. I'm sorry to say it, but there is no quick fix for your personality disorders. I believe you require an extensive course of psychological investigation and psychotherapy, most probably over several years, to properly address your serious sociopathic and narcissistic problems.

'Your behaviour, and particularly your attitude towards your wife, is nothing short of deplorable. You quite obviously show her no consideration, respect, or even minimal affection, and merely regard her as existing to be your servant to carry out your commands. I really cannot imagine what brought the two of you together in the first place.

'I also find your pathological lying, your violence, and your callous bullying, deeply significant, and likely to be causing serious damage to your wife's health and well-being. I admit to being completely at a loss to understand why she did not leave you immediately following her honeymoon experiences.

No woman should ever expect to endure what you have put her through for twelve months.

'This is my initial professional opinion. But of course, you are at liberty to seek a second opinion elsewhere should you so wish. I will let you have my report in writing, within two weeks.'

We left the consulting rooms and set off on foot back to the car, in silence. I said nothing, but I felt bitterly aggrieved by the manner in which PP had virtually hijacked the entire consultation. Very sadly, nothing had been achieved, and PP had not been genuinely affected, or even touched by remorse, from anything the psychiatrist had said.

After a couple of minutes, he said mournfully, 'Well, ee didn't fink much o me, did ee? Blamed uz fer iveryfink an' as good as called uz a bloody bastard an a devil outta hell. Ee sed Ah'd treated yer werse tha' dirt an' yer wuz an angel outta 'eaven puttin up wiv uz, and ever considerin' 'avin uz back.' His tone sounded more like self-pity than his conscience speaking.

After we had walked on for another couple of minutes in mutual silence, his mood suddenly underwent a 360-degree turn around, and I found myself being lambasted in the street... accused of secretly arranging to see Dr Van Doorn privately, ahead of the consultation, to prime the psychiatrist with all the things I wanted him to say, and all the criticisms I intended him to make, against PP.

Seconds later, everything the doctor had said, relating to PP's sociopathic problems had been rubbished and dismissed. 'Stoopid ol' git. Wot the fuck duz ee no abaat diddly-squat onyway? Ee's nowt but a fuckin' forener spoutin' a bloody load uv old twaddle. There's nuffink wrong wiv uz. Yer the fuckin' problem in this marriage. An' yer gor at 'im affor the fuckin' meeting, yer crafty bitch, an' yer telt him what yer wonted 'im ter say. Yer got uz ther, yer bugger, jist ter mek a fool aout uv uz. Well it didn' werk, cos Ah've seen frew yer clivver tricks.'

That was the result of my attempts to get him to confront his anger and violence towards me, and to sort out his serious psychological and behavioural problems. All the opinions and advice of the psychiatrist, were summarily discarded. End of story... very clearly, nothing was ever going to change him.

Why had I ever imagined it would?

With regard to my remaining conditions, he reluctantly conceded that he would contribute to the housekeeping, and that Steve would return to his mother's home. He even promised to sort out the financial problem over the Stevenson Street house, with Liz.

But I suspected these were all pie-in-the-sky promises which he had no intention of ever keeping. I felt I couldn't push the issues too hard. And apart from my determination concerning Steve, I knew I was on fragile ground.

So far as Liz and her massive debts to me were concerned, I discovered soon afterwards that she had already completed her property deals, and was about to move into the bungalow she had already bought. It was obvious PP had been lying to me all along, yet again, and deliberately deceiving me as usual. The wretched girl had already spent the money from the house sale, and he knew it. The problem concerning what she owed me had been quite deliberately obfuscated again... and with her father's collusion as usual.

How that particular thorny problem was ever going to be resolved I had no idea, but it was not a subject I had any intention of letting go. Her cheating me had always been at his instigation, and so-far as I was concerned, the pair of them were equally responsible for the mountain of debts I was owed.

Apart from sorting out the thorny issue of where Steve was going to live in future, nothing else had actually been resolved. But PP insisted he had done everything possible to meet my conditions, and announced he now intended to take up residence with me, in the house where I was living.

A solicitor had told him it was his right, as the joint owner, to co-habit, in spite of whatever I might feel... That statement left me with serious unresolved queries as to ...who the unnamed solicitor might be who had been advising him? Did I perhaps know this person?

When I reluctantly told Samantha and Nathalie that PP was intending to return to live with us, I was left facing a new, and even more distressing personal problem. Samantha, in particular, detested him. There were so many complex reasons for her to despise and loathe him. And for those reasons, along with the vile accusations he had made about her to Norman, she would never forgive him. Her immediate reaction was to tell me, that if he was coming back to the house to live, after all he had put us through, she intended to leave home.

Nothing would dissuade her. She had already discussed the possibility with her boyfriend, Max, and made up her mind... If PP forced himself back on us, she intended to leave school at once, and go to live with Max in his rented accommodation in Southampton, where he was currently at university.

I was devastated by her ultimatum. For me, there was no contest between my emotions. I loved my daughter dearly; she was of infinitely more importance to me than PP would ever be, and her leaving home was the very last thing in the world I wanted. For PP I felt nothing other than contempt...I wanted him out of our lives more than anything; and facing the prospect of Samantha leaving home was heart-breaking. But the reality was I had no legal way of preventing him from returning to the house, nor any feasible way of keeping her there against her wishes. It was an impossible dilemma to resolve.

It ended with my precious girl abandoning her academic studies and leaving home before she was seventeen, to live in Southampton. I was left heart-broken and devastated. I felt totally responsible for ruining her life; as well as being forced to endure what felt to me like another family bereavement. When she left home for the last time, I was distraught.

Within a couple of weeks of PP's return, everything had descended back into the black abyss he had already established in my life. There was still no money being contributed to the housekeeping, and all I had actually gained from his promises, was the return of his son to live at his own mother's home.

However, I resolutely went ahead with having plans drawn up to extend the small house. I intended to do whatever I could to keep him to some of his promises. Obtaining planning permission was not a quick-fire project, and it dragged on for a couple of months. Then once the plans had been drawn, I went ahead and applied for planning approval. Eventually the planning application was granted, and permission to build the extension was approved.

Once these legalities had been settled, I noticed that PP had fallen suspiciously silent on the subject of when he intended to start constructing the promised extension. The excuse I was being given was the weather wasn't suitable.

By now it was March, and the winter had been particularly wet and frosty. Consequently, there wasn't a lot I could say or do... except to remind him from time to time of the promises he had made about constructing the extension.

From the time he re-established himself in the house, he had quickly reverted to his familiar controlling behaviour pattern, although his violent outbursts did temporarily quieten down somewhat.

But every weekend during those winter months, he continued to insist upon us resuming our visits to Salisbury, irrespective of the bitterly cold weather. As the result, our monotonous, exhausting weekends away continued... until one Friday evening something occurred that unexpectedly brought matters to a head.

Usually upon our arrival at the cottage, I took my little dogs into the garden for a night-time run. While I was busy with them, PP went ahead to open the front door, and put the lights and the heating on. However, that Friday night it was so wet and cold I decided I would open the house up myself, and I rushed straight from the car to the front door with the three little ones, without waiting for him to lead the way.

I had a torch with me and my keys already in my hand. Surprise, surprise, I couldn't get the key into the keyhole. No matter how I tried, it just would not fit. I couldn't work out what was wrong, although I knew for sure I was using the right key.

PP quickly came up behind me, blustering about my getting the door keys mixed up. He quickly used his own key, and we all hurried inside.

Intuitively, I knew something was wrong. I was sure I hadn't mixed up my keys. Later, while he was eating, I went back to the door and examined the keys and the lock again. I was shocked to discover that at some point during the months when he had been missing, he had surreptitiously changed the lock to keep me out. No mention had ever been made of this, and neither had I been given any replacement key.

Since his return to the marriage, we had been going to the cottage every weekend, for months, as if everything was back to how it had been. I had been back to trying to cope with all the expectations placed on me... the shopping, cooking gardening, etc., and everything else that I was held responsible for. But during that entire time, I had never had a door key that would open the door. He had quite deliberately continued to keep access barred to me, unless I was with him.

There had never been any goodwill, or the slightest sign of genuine remorse on his part, for any of his dreadful behaviour towards me. My accidental discovery of this ongoing devious trick conclusively confirmed what a scumbag he had always been. There had been no change whatsoever in either his attitude or his behaviour. My fury was instant, and my decision absolute.

The house had been entirely furnished by me, to the last teaspoon. Yet for months he had been treating me as someone incidental... nothing more than a casual visitor there, or a servant. I had been callously disrespected throughout. My presence had been taken for granted, and I had been expected to return to all the usual duties for his sole benefit...I was conveyed there to carry out the menial domestic tasks he refused to undertake. He of course had resumed lying in bed, taking things easy, and having his lazy weekend breaks, while I had been expected to wait on him hand and foot. It had all been a return to the former self-interest and controlling behaviour... just a continuation of the same old attitude, with him ruling the roost, and me doing all the fetching and carrying.

Legally, I was the joint owner, and his behaviour over my rights of access were not only illegal, they were despicable. This was another of his totally cynical and heartless ways of treating his wife. A sign written on the wall could not have made the situation any clearer.

I was furious when I realised how callously and intentionally, he had continued to disrespect me. In his eyes everything was his property, and he controlled it. So far as PP was concerned, I had never had any personal ownership rights, or freedom of access... He was in charge, and I was there merely to be his servant.

My ultimatum, upon making this discovery, was swift and adamant. I was finished with going to the so-called cottage, and I refused to condone his despicable treatment of me any longer. I was not his servant, and I rapidly gave him a very direct piece of my mind, which ended with my telling him that I had made my last visit and I would never again return there.

He had deliberately chosen to lock me out, and had never mentioned to me what he had secretly done with the locks. Nor had he made any subsequent attempt to put matters right. To my mind, such behaviour was unforgivable, and a clear demonstration of how despicably and negatively he regarded me. I left him in no uncertainty of my anger, or my intentions.

Since the disastrous marriage had taken place I had lived in hell. His entire attitude towards me had been appalling, and he had better be aware that nothing he had ever done to me during that time, was either forgiven or forgotten. His behaviour over the changed locks proved that his selfish controlling behaviour was still as diabolical as ever. Nothing would ever change him into a man I could ever grow to love, or ever willingly want to live with.

Prompted by this latest secretive, blatant demonstration of complete selfishness, I felt entirely justified in returning to the subject of the money I was owed. In putting my outrage on the line, I held nothing back... and demanded he put an end to all the devious procrastination and prevarication. There would be no more delays over the return of my money by his daughter, and no more excuses, from him, or I would carry out my threats, and go to the police to lay charges against the pair of them for fraud.

I gave him three months to sort out the issues surrounding Liz's property extravaganza, and return every penny of what I was owed.

In the meanwhile, what he did with the cottage was up to him. But I made very clear the fact that I intended to remove all my furniture and personal property as soon as I could. The house would be emptied, even if it meant breaking the door down to get inside it, because he had seen fit to deprive me of a key.

Very clearly, there had been no significant changes in his attitude, nor in his behaviour towards me. And quite simply, it was obvious he had never intended to keep any of the promises he had made, or alter his ways by so much as one iota. I had merely been given the answers I had wanted to hear, and then treated with typical contempt, and strung along by the pair of them. They were thieves and pathological liars, and I had finally reached the end-of-the-line over their criminal behaviour.

I held nothing back. If he thought there was any way of breaking my resolve, or ever getting me to change my mind about his son, or the huge debt he and his dreadful daughter owed me, he was seriously mistaken. I was adamant... I would never again return to the cottage. So far as I was concerned, it could stand empty until it fell down. And he had better take note that I would be immediately cancelling my bank's standing order for the council tax payments still being drawn on it.

In future I would enjoy my weekends at home with my daughter Nathalie, doing whatever I wanted to do. But my three little Yorkies and I, would not be visiting Wiltshire again for any reason. My last visit there had been made.

I think, for once, my plain speaking took him unaware, because he seemed too dumbstruck to answer me, or work himself up into launch an attack on me.

Chapter 28

More Lies and Broken Promises

From the beginning of my disastrous marriage to PP, I had found myself in the unhappy situation of having to struggle hard to sustain my mental and physical health. Added to this, I had never known a single moment of peace, happiness, or security with the man. He was constantly scheming against me... forever bullying and manipulating me, and attempting to overwhelm me with demands I could not meet. I was never free from intimidation and mental torment of one kind or another.

Condoning the resumption our relationship had never been a voluntary choice for me. There was legally no way I could prevent his return to the Rathole, once he had made up his mind to resume living there. But there were malicious untruthful and intimidating threats he was holding over me, to prevent my suing him for divorce. Apart from his never-ending intimidating physical threats of violence, he was also effectively blackmailing me into remaining married to him.

The only trump card I held against him in this contentious marriage game was my resolve to sue both himself and his daughter for fraud… unless the two of them repaid every penny of the money they had cheated from me.

These two opposing conflicts had created a sort of Mexican standoff between us. To my mind, the legal circumstances felt more like a political dispute between warring states, than a marriage. But the prevailing conditions illustrated what a meaningless and diabolical kind of relationship we shared.

However, once he had resumed his residence in the Rathole, following his summer-long absence, he wasted no time in reverting to his earlier behaviour of domination and control. He also resumed his malicious intentions of forcing me into an unwanted pregnancy. He had recognised that, while I continued to work, I retained my independence from him. And in those circumstances, he would never be able to fully and completely control and dominate me.

He had enough nous to realise I was capable of making challenging decisions, and I might even, if I became frustrated enough, throw caution and his perpetual intimidation to the wind, and press ahead with a divorce action. At that point, I would be sure to bring into the acrimonious dispute his appalling behaviour, and his criminal financial manipulation of me, and demand restitution of my assets as a major factor in the divorce.

The very last thing he wanted was to lose was his power over me, and find himself facing my accusations in court. Losing control of me meant losing control of my imaginary millions; and that was the last thing he wanted.

Now in his perverse, sadistic mind, he had decided the best way to gain permanent control and domination was to force a child upon me. A pregnancy would seriously weaken my position, and ultimately provide him with the means of coercing me into giving up my career. I would thereby be left with no independent income, and he would hold the financial whip hand over me. I would finally be at his total mercy. That solution would, he believed, put him irrefutably in the permanent position of complete control over my fictional assets.

He had already taken into account that, with my past medical record, a forced pregnancy might even kill me. But no man had ever been accused of murder, or manslaughter, because a woman dies giving birth to a child forced upon her by her violent husband. Either way, if I ended up dead or alive, forcing me into an unwanted pregnancy was a sure-fire way to put him in the pole position. It was the only way he could be sure of coming out of the situation as the winner... and with possession of everything he had his greedy mind set on.

It was an insane concept. But he had no intention of ever allowing me to escape alive, by way of a divorce.

For me, the idea of being forced into a pregnancy with an unwanted child, fathered by him of all people, both terrified and repelled me.

I consider rape to be a disgusting abomination in any situation. But rape within a marriage demonstrates neither love, nor even respect for the abused partner. However, for PP, raping me became a powerful weapon for exerting control and domination, and it became his current weapon of choice, towards achieving his sick intentions.

I well recalled his own accounts of how he had used this same means of controlling his first wife, Beryl. I had already been made very familiar with the gruesome details of their failed marriage, and I had taken note of all the terrible stories he had told me concerning the events leading to its termination.

After eight years, when she was reduced to despair over his promiscuous affairs and his brutality, she had made a determined effort to leave him. For six weeks, she had absconded back to her family in Scotland, taking their two daughters with her. But very quickly she had found herself denied access to their joint bank account.

To my mind, that sounded like the plot of another, much more personal story I was already familiar with... punishment by deprivation of money. It had been exactly how he had intended to control me... having already used the strategy to successful effect with my predecessor, Beryl... He had deprived her of access to their bank account, and left her destitute, in order to drive her back to him.

Once Beryl has been left penniless, her Catholic family had sent her back to Essex with the advice that, as a good Catholic wife, she must try to patch up her marriage, and seek reconciliation with her husband.

PP was remorseless. He had resumed their marriage, on HIS terms; and the price Beryl had been forced to pay, was submission to him, and the acceptance of further pregnancies.

The boy she gave birth to nine months later was Steve. The child had not been conceived out of love, or even from desire, but as a condition for the resumption of their marriage, and as a sign of her subjugation. Mutual love had never come into it. PP was driven only by sick, egotistical revenge, and the relentless motivation to control.

Several months after Steve's birth, Beryl had again become

pregnant, but this time, her pregnancy had ended in a miscarriage...A termination which PP was convinced she had deliberately induced.

I recalled how he had taken venomous delight in describing the gory details to me. The miscarriage had been the final factor which had brought their marriage to an end. He claimed she had deliberately murdered his child to prevent it from being born. And that was something he would never forgive. Thereafter, he took every opportunity to denigrate her, and brand her as insane and promiscuous. His perverse revenge against Beryl was the permanent punishment of never-ending slander...

His twisted, psychopathic mentality, with regard to the endless production of children, was not something to which I would ever be willing to submit myself. I had worked hard for many years to establish my career, and I already had all the children I ever wanted.

However, for a number of terrifying weeks following his return to the Rathole, I became subjected to violent rape, on a regular basis. There was no affection in any of these encounters... just ugly brutality, and emotionless violation, and I had needed to work hard to numb my mind against the sadism of what he was forcing me to endure.

Increasingly as the weeks passed, he became angry and frustrated that I was not falling pregnant. He frequently took to ransacking the bathroom cabinet, and my possessions, to find evidence for this failure, accusing me time and again of surreptitiously using contraception, to deliberately thwart his intentions.

Eventually he decided I had to go into hospital, and be medically investigated for my failure to conceive. Naturally, I refused to cooperate. I believed it would involve a general anaesthetic and invasive surgery, for no other reason than to satisfy his sick obsession. I had no intention of being manipulated against my will, by a man for whom I had no feelings except loathing and hatred.

I considered no child deserved to be born under such a terrible mandate... like an animal in a farmyard, and as the result of a violent act of aggression.

However, having set his mind upon achieving his objective, he moved heaven and earth... bullying me night and day into submission, until eventually an appointment was made for my admission to hospital. My reluctant consent was only given, once I had been assured there was no invasive surgery involved. It was explained to me that I would simply be internally examined under anaesthetic, by means of fibre optics.

On the day of my planned admission I suddenly panicked. I dug in my heels and refused to attend the hospital. Under no circumstances would I ever again willingly risk becoming pregnant. It had lately occurred to me that the result of submitting to whatever the procedure was, might well prove to be an increased likelihood of a pregnancy.

The birth of my younger daughter Samantha had seen me dead on the operating table during an emergency caesarean section. I had only been revived by the will of God and a skilful surgeon, who had managed to sew my severed abdominal aorta together, and begin transfusing me with six pints of blood.

Amazingly, the surgeon had also managed to restart my heart and bring me back from the dead after six minutes without any vital signs. But as a result of the massive haemorrhage, and the trauma which caused a myocardial infarction, my heart had failed. I was lucky to be alive, but left with permanent damage to my heart; and I had been warned never to attempt any further pregnancies, as another might very well kill me.

That afternoon, when I was two hours overdue for my admission, the hospital phoned to see where I was. At that point, PP physically overpowered me and bundled me into the car and drove me there, while I screamed and shouted my objections all the way.

The procedure I underwent found nothing of any significance, and that apart from my heart, my organs were all normal. Any difficulties relating to infertility, were now irrefutably only ascribable to problems existing with PP's sexuality. Something was amiss with the functional masculinity of this vile and loathsome brute, and he was now incapable of fathering a child.

It seemed like a gift from God, for which I was overjoyed.

Of course, being the extreme, macho-pig he was, he refused to concede there could possibly be anything remotely wrong with him in that department, and refused to undergo any medical investigations to see where his own infertility problems might lie.

Happily, one thorny problem had disappeared from my life, and I breathed a silent prayer of thanks for my deliverance.

All the other problems, however, continued being dragged out. The year was passing, and no progress was being made with any of the issues connected with enlarging the small house, or the promised return of my finances. And he was still resolutely refusing to contribute anything to the housekeeping.

Then one morning in July, he suddenly announced he intended to make a start on building a new double garage. As there already were two garages attached to the house, both currently still crammed with my furniture, I queried why we needed two more.

His excuse was he had decided to convert the existing garages into a large kitchen / dining room, before making a start on the planned two-storey extension. In his opinion, making more room downstairs as living space, was much more important than any planned two-storey, extension. The proposed double garage would replace the existing ones, and would be followed by a rapid conversion of the original two, into a large kitchen/diner.

I was surprised but said nothing. There was no point, as he always did exactly what he wanted. There wasn't a lot I could say about his plan; not until I was told I would be working on the project as his labourer.

He was adamant that any work I expected him to carry out at the house, would involve my working as his navvy. He had no intention of doing the work unaided, and he wasn't going to pay anyone to help him. I was being designated to carry the bricks, and hand-mix all the concrete and mortar needed for the project.

He brought in a couple of workmen from his company to dig out the footings before he started the actual construction.

It was a hot July, but he insisted I must be there from dawn to dusk labouring for him. Between times, I would be allowed to take a break to go indoors and cook his meals, and fetch snacks and drinks for him as required. Such selfless generosity!

I had never been afraid of hard work, and I had gardened and helped Alan in all the projects he had undertaken around our home. But physically, I was never built for working as a manual labourer... moving and stacking bricks, and mixing concrete by hand, was a monumental task for a seven-stone woman with a weak heart. On the second day, the strenuous effort of mixing sand, cement, and gravel, using a heavy-duty shovel, caused me to collapse from heatstroke, and a slipped disc.

The GP ordered me to bed until I had recovered, and gave me a stern warning not to attempt any further ridiculous activities, which I was clearly not physically capable of, especially with my dodgy heart. I think he imagined I had set myself the job of mixing concrete and carrying bricks, as some perverse form of keep-fit exercise.

As soon as I was incapacitated, PP wasted no time in bringing an electric cement mixer from his company's premises, along with two labourers, to help him complete the job. No one except for myself, it seemed, would ever be required, to hand-mix his concrete, unaided by a machine.

Once the double garage was finished, all the other plans simply evaporated. There never was any kitchen conversion. Nor was any start made on the plans he had inveigled me into having drawn up. That had all just been another set of glib promises... pie-in-the-sky exaggerations to build up my hopes, before sending them crashing down again.

At the end of August, I was casually informed he had discovered, from conversations with Steve, that Liz had now sold the bungalow she had bought. Naturally, I had been told nothing beforehand about these plans, until she had already cunningly pocketed all the proceeds and decamped to Cyprus, with assets now totalling £100,000. Meanwhile, I was still left still paying the debt I had taken out on her account, and which had currently been transferred from a bank-loan, into a mortgage on the small house where we were living.

Steve considered his sister to be extremely clever, and sarcastically expressed the hope that she would invite him out for a visit. At that point, it came to light she had not merely gone on a two-week holiday; she intended to stay in Cyprus for at least six months.

I was furious when I learned about her latest scam, and I made it very clear to her father that, as soon as she returned to the United Kingdom, I still had every intention of having her charged with fraud. I let him know that nothing was either forgiven or forgotten. I still wanted all my misappropriated money returned plus every penny of profit she had made out of me. And I intended to see I got it, by going to the law if necessary, and suing her.

If he felt the slightest aggravation over her latest outrageous behaviour, he said nothing about it to me.

Then, suddenly and out of the blue, he announced that, as I was refusing to have anything more to do with the Salisbury house, he had decided to place it in the hands of an estate agent. He would sell it, and shut me up once and for all about Liz. He would settle all the debts I was owed, from the proceeds of the house-sale. He claimed he would deal with Liz when she returned from Cyprus; meanwhile, he would see my money was returned, along with all the interest I was owed, so I could forget about my threats to take her to court.

When he first outlined his intentions, they sounded surprisingly conciliatory, and like a serious attempt to resolve my grievances. In truth, they were nothing of the sort, this was just his latest invention designed to shut me up, while he implemented a new way to scam me. Once again, I was being covertly manipulated by one of his devious financial schemes.

However, this time, over the succeeding weeks, and after I'd had a quiet opportunity to think his proposals through carefully, I recognised the truth of the plan for what it was. At face value, the new proposal sounded plausible and a very reasonable solution to a thorny problem. But as usual, it was just his latest cunning plan to manipulate my finances. And as always, it had been inevitably designed for his own advantage and that of his daughter.

Now, instead of carrying out any of the promised alterations and developments to the Rathole, he announced we would cut our losses and move. It was down to me to find a new house; somewhere larger, and more to my liking. He would buy it out of the funds that would be released from selling both our present houses. There would be no further need for me to be involved in paying a mortgage, and we would consolidate everything, by putting both properties on the market right away. Then we could get on with finding a bigger, and more comfortable place to live.

Initially I was sucked into believing this latest scheme, because I was so eager to escape from the cramped space of the Rathole. But foolishly I failed to look more deeply into his proposal, and unravel the devious motives behind it.

With PP, nothing was ever as it seemed. And eventually It dawned upon me that once again I was being hoodwinked, and cleverly blinded to the fact that I would not in actuality be getting any of my funds returned...he was not talking about any cash-return. He was a shameless, and unrepentant villain, who continually worked to deceive me over money. All that I was owed by Liz would still remain in her hands. While her devious father had now devised a plan to trick me into believing he was paying off all her debts to me, along with his own, by selling the Salisbury cottage.

In fact, all he was arranging to do was roll over the complete value of the Rathole, which I had paid for, plus some top-up money skimmed from the sale of the Salisbury cottage to make up the difference in the purchase price of whatever new property we bought. Much of the money he had previously scammed from me had already been invested in the cottage, and the bottom line was...he was never actually going to return any part of the money he had, borrowed from me. Whatever the price of the new property was, it would continue to be held equally in our joint names and continue to be funded, in its entirety, from the collective finances he had conned from me.

On the other hand, his daughter Liz, would remain, happily sunning herself in Cyprus, while still hanging on like a leech, to the proceeds accrued from the various property deals which my assets had financed.

This entire business was nothing more than another con-trick, with neither of them ever intending to repay any part of what they had fraudulently obtained from me.

To add insult to injury, PP made no bones about his intention to bank whatever funds remained from the sale of the cottage, in his own name.

The new scam saved him from the expense of undertaking any of the work he had promised to carry out. It also continued to tie my loaned assets into a house he would continue to occupy as a joint owner; and gave me back nothing from the substantial amount of money I was currently owed by both his daughter and himself.

We were now two years into the marriage, and I was still trying to get my head around the remorseless, manipulative, and criminal mentality of the man I had married.

Unfortunately for me, I was still not fully aware of the vicious depths of depravity and hatred, to which this man and his family-from -hell, were prepared to go to destroy my physical and mental health.

Hatred is a dark, and dangerous bedfellow.

Chapter 29

Researching a Dilemma

Two unbelievably destructive and terrifying years of marriage to PP lay behind me. Twenty-four-hour-long, anguished days, and twenty-four interminable months, where my days and nights had been filled with every kind of abuse imaginable.

My life, my health, and my happiness were of zero consequence to him.

Currently, he was still unflinchingly convinced I was persisting in keeping secret bank accounts stuffed with my vast secret wealth hidden from him; and he was determined to go to any lengths to break me to his will. No one was ever allowed to defy PP... What PP wants... PP gets. That was his life-long mantra.

Living with a deranged man whose greed and violence were focussed upon destroying my physical and mental well-being, meant I never knew what any moment of each day would bring, or how to prepare myself for his next attack. His ability to instantly switch between his two personas of Jekyll and Hyde, was incredible.

And his determined efforts to keep me in a state of nervous tension meant that at any hour of the day or night, he was liable to commence upon an episode of screaming abuse, lashing out with his fists, or grabbing me by my neck with the intention of strangling me. These calculated, but unpredictable and violent episodes continued to seriously damage my mental and physical health. They made him impossible to live with, and kept me in a permanent state of distress, scared out of my wits, and constantly living on my nerves.

My daughters had frequently pleaded with me to leave him... imploring me just to abandon everything, and escape alive before he murdered me. But I knew that running away from him would play right into his thieving hands; and that was something which I would never allow myself to do.

I was well aware that my situation was perilous. I never knew what was coming next, or what devious schemes he was secretly hatching to cause me further harm. There were no rules except the ones he constantly made and changed, and life for me was like existing on the edge of a permanently volatile volcano.

The longer I lived with him, the more convinced I became that something fundamental to his innate psychology was seriously abnormal and unhinged. His everyday behaviour, and his mental processes were unnaturally convoluted and cruel... even at times psychotic and insane.

Insanity... was the favourite accusation he frequently enjoyed throwing at me...but it was a mental condition which seemed much more appropriately ascribable to himself. In the time I had known him I had become increasingly convinced he was controlled by an exceedingly, and serious, abnormal mental psychology.

To resolve my perplexing dilemmas, and as a means of attempting to get to the bottom of what was really wrong with him, I decided I needed to begin researching available works on psychology and psychiatry.

Years previously, when I had been at university, part of my degree work had included the study of criminal psychology. During those academic years, I had visited juvenile Borstal establishments all over the country, and attended lectures on criminal psychology and behaviour, together with time spent observing the evidence of various criminal male psychologies. I had also attended further postgraduate training, and lectures on the subject, given by a notable psychiatrist. Professor I.Z. who was an expert on the deviant narcissistic and psychopathic criminal mind... particularly relating to juvenile males.

I was not a qualified psychiatrist, but I began to consider collating my current personal, real-life experiences, along with my previous academic and postgrad training. Perhaps in that way it might be possible to assemble enough informative diagnostic background material, to make a rational identification of the abnormal mentality lying at the root of PP's deviant psychology, and his criminal...insane... behaviour.

Eventually I decided it would add significantly to my understanding of this man, if I could find some way of delving into his family background. I felt very strongly that the key to his abnormal psychology must originate in his genetic history. I felt it was essential for my personal welfare, and my survival, for me to discover if the dark undercurrents of his warped personality might have been inherited. Had this man actually been born with the warped mind of a psychopath? These, and numerous other related questions, were urging me to find answers.

The only person I could think of who might be able to enlighten me on the history of his strangely twisted, sadistic personality, was his mother. But realistically I could see no possibility of turning up at her home to begin asking her questions about their family history.

PP was her only son, and she had always spoken of him very affectionately. So obviously, she was unlikely to tell me anything detrimental about him. And it was self-evident, that if I attempted to question her, there would certainly be serious repercussions for me, as she would be sure to repeat whatever questions I might ask, to PP the next time she saw him.

The possibilities of my ever being able to resolve my dilemma through this approach seemed mere wishful thinking, and my investigations looked like they were at a dead-end, with no way of obtaining any confirmation of my suspicions, or ever being able to discover what I needed to know regarding PP's early history. If I was to gain clearer insight, all I could do was try to research the subject as thoroughly as possible from available professional literature.

Some months earlier, during our joint consultation with Professor Van Doorn, he had identified PP's abnormal personality as being somewhere on the sociopathy scale. But he had clearly indicated his opinion required much deeper consideration; and that years of investigative therapy would be necessary before a full, and accurate, diagnosis could be made.

I decided that the psychiatrist's informed opinion would make a practical and valid starting point for my intended research.

I believed, that if I could accurately piece together some

scientifically established facts, for comparison, and arrive at the truth behind PP's wildly sadistic, deviant behaviour, it might be possible to deduce what was actually wrong with him.

Eventually, after going through seemingly endless works on psychiatry, which did not help much at all, I eventually came upon the work of Dr Robert Hare, and read his book Without Conscience: The Disturbing World of the Psychopath among Us. This is recognised as the standard tool for diagnosing psychopathy. I moved on to read H Cleckley's The Mask of Sanity, and then another work by Dr Robert Hare and Dr Paul Babiak, Snakes in Suits. And finally, I read In the Blood, by Steve Jones, and Prone To Violence, by Erin Pizzey and Jeff Shapiro.

I studied these books thoroughly and made copious notes. After careful cross-referencing, and comparing my personal evidence, I found the results extremely informative and enlightening. I followed up by reading everything else, on the subject of psychopathy, available on the internet, and researched the patterns of behaviour of male psychopaths, in both America and the UK, with particular reference to domestic violence, and criminal activities motivated by psychopathic behaviour.

The records were most alarming… particularly those recording the number of women who die every year at the hands of men such as PP. My research proved to be a revelation, and I was convinced, beyond doubt, that I was married to a full-blown, and seriously dangerous psychopath. His condition went way beyond the parameters described as sociopathy. In fact, PP was a man whose extreme symptoms were to be found at the top of the psychopathy scale, not the bottom of it… with the shared traits of numerous convicted, vicious murderers at both sides of the Atlantic.

I already knew that PP was playing sadistic games with my emotions and my life. There was no capacity in this man for remorse or genuine feelings of affection. He was entirely driven by some form of insane jealousy, relating to everything I was, and everything I represented. Destroying my life would be the eventual proof he wanted of his own power and superiority.

I had identified most of the classic psychopathic symptoms, and now I came to realise his entire life had been built on the clever mimicry of other people's feelings and emotions. By nature, he was incapable of any genuine feelings of his own. But he was a skilful observer, and a cunning mimic of other, normal people's psychologies. He was entirely egocentric, controlling, and aggressive; and a lifelong pathological liar, who lived his life devoid of conscience or remorse.

PP had no potential to be anything other than a hollow cruel mockery of a man. His was a clever and complex personality, but he was someone who irredeemably belonging within the dark triad of narcissism, psychopathy, and Machiavellianism. As the consequence, he was possessed of a fundamentally deep and implacable malevolence.

I felt vindicated when I eventually comprehended what PP really was... an emotionless monster in human form; a cold and scheming predator, who took particular sick pleasure from manipulating anyone who came within his remit. His behaviour was entirely unpredictable, irascible, and exceedingly violent; and I was finally convinced he would eventually reach a point where he would make a serious attempt to kill me.

Something inside him was constantly driving him to crush the life out of me. It drove him on, relentlessly undermining my physical and emotional well-being. And I had many times witnessed the sadistic pleasure he derived from seeing me emotionally, and physically prostrate, during his calculated, murderous attacks on me.

Observing my total distress was the feedback which reinforced his feelings of power and omnipotence, and there was never the least flicker of remorse or compassion.

The analogy eventually came to me that he was akin to an emotionless, grotesque reptile...a pythonid creature with the destructive, crushing instincts of a monstrous python driving him. Just as a python wraps its coils around every part of its victim before crushing the life out it, so his huge hands were always gripped around my neck, tantalising him with an aching urge to press on, block off my air supply, crush my windpipe, and fatally strangle me. I had sensed many times that every one of his sadistic instincts was urging him towards crushing me to death... every time he grabbed me by my neck it provided him with a sick form of anticipated pleasure; and I knew that the final destructive act of killing was something with which he had frequently toyed.

Something inside his brain motivated an increasing hunger in him for the ultimate feeling of triumphant power he would achieve, from crushing the last vestige of physical life out of another human being.

I finally recognised I was confronting something irredeemably evil and emotionally destructive. There was...a killer... lurking inside of him.

The illusion that PP was anything approaching a normal, if volatile man, completely vanished, and I was left with the recognition that all his charades, and games were nothing other than clever cunning devices to hide the awful reality of the feral, emotionless creature he really was.

In finally stripping away the mask, from his particular brand of insanity, the reality I was left with was terrifying. I had been selected as the eventual victim of something innately inhuman… a man, with the metamorphosed brain of a killing machine…a psychopython.

It was not my imagination. PP was not playing some erratic, or perverse sexual fantasy game with me. The emotionless energies controlling the brain of this man, were working to crush, and eventually annihilate me. His twisted instincts lay beyond my comprehension; but I was well able to recognise that he derived pleasure from inflicting pain, and perverse satisfaction from the vicious activities he carried out upon me. He couldn't stop…there always had to be something even more cruel and diabolical with which he could persecute me.

My academic research had taken me as far as I could go. Now I needed some practical confirmation to support my conclusions. I had identified my enemy as 'the psychopython', and recognised the abnormal and dangerous perversion of humanity with which I was contending.

I would never be able to anticipate the ultimate, or read his grotesque thoughts, or pre-empt his murderous schemes; and I would never dare relax or trust him. A day would inevitably come when, completely unexpectedly, he would no longer walk away from the temptation to terminate my life.

He had already come close to that situation many times already… and I clearly recalled how often had he suddenly walked away from further, more extreme temptation, mid-way through an aggressive attack.

Now I felt very really pressing reasons to seek more insight into the invidious situation I was constantly exposed to… and, hopefully find some way of defending myself, or escaping from him.

Divorcing him would never guarantee my safety... such was his irrational, vindictive drive to avenge himself, I doubted if I would ever be safe even years later. I already knew his capacity for holding a grudge, and for exacting remorseless revenge, even after many years.

It seemed there was no feasible way to address my concerns. I was still no nearer accessing any family information to confirm whether his condition was a lifelong behavioural pattern with a genetic pre-disposition. I felt as though I was left facing a blank wall, with nothing further I would ever be able to do to confirm or deny the validity of my suspicions.

And this was how things seemed destined to remain, until several weeks later, when a strange chain of events, unexpectedly provided the opportunity I had been hoping for, to speak with his mother. I had always believed she held the key to her strange son's dark and convoluted personal history. She had known him all his life in the ways only a mother ever knows her child. She had brought him into the world, and she had watched his character develop from infancy.

We hadn't seen his parents for quite some time, when out of the blue, PP had a phone call from his sister, Mavis. She had recently been over from Hamburg to spend some time with her daughters, and the three of them had dropped by to visit the old couple. Mavis informed her brother, in no uncertain terms, that their mother was seriously ill, and he ought to go over and see what he could do to help. The doctor was visiting regularly because she had dangerously high blood pressure, and there was the distinct possibility of her suffering a stroke and dying.

The following Sunday, we drove over to his parents' home. His mother was confined to bed, but she seemed very pleased to see us, and eagerly propped herself up to talk. It was impossible to make conversation with his father, as he was stone deaf, and simply kept on repeating that the doctor had visited and said Gladys's blood pressure was dangerously high, and she might have a stroke at any time.

PP never felt any genuine sympathy with other people's illnesses, and he quickly found being in his mother's sickroom confining and completely boring. That afternoon, after a few minutes of pacing about telling her, she needed to get more fresh air, and look after herself better, he disappeared downstairs to spend time with his father, watching the horse racing on TV, which was continually turned up loud enough to raise the dead.

I remained upstairs with Gladys, keeping her company in her bedroom, and listening to her reminiscences of times gone by. She was genuinely delighted to see me, and clung to me like a child.

'Oh, my dear,' she cried, 'you're just how I've always imagined my little Joanie would've been, if only she'd lived. I'm so pleased you've come.'

I gave her a hug and sat down on the edge of the bed, holding her hand in mine.

'I've been lying here for days,' she said, 'just thinking about things. Charlie's very deaf, and he doesn't have much to say. And having to shout makes me exhausted, so I can't talk to him. And when Mavis came over from Germany, she couldn't stay long. She had to leave early, because her daughters were taking her out for a meal before she went to catch the eleven o'clock ferry. But now you're here, you will stay a while, won't you?'

'I'll stay until you feel too tired to talk,' I said, patting her hand. 'I can see you've got things on your mind. But I don't want you to tire yourself or get yourself upset. You're supposed to be resting and taking things easy, aren't you? That's what the doctor ordered, and I don't want to be responsible for you wearing yourself out by talking to me.'

I watched as she reached for a handkerchief and wiped her eyes. It was obvious she was becoming agitated. And from her tears, and the way she kept shaking her head, I could see something was distressing her.

'What's on your mind?' I said. 'Is something troubling you?'

She tucked her handkerchief away, and silently pointed towards the bedroom door. 'Just see it's shut, dear, will you?' she said. 'I would rather speak in private. I don't want my son suddenly walking in. He does that, you know. He always has, ever since he was a teenager. He has a funny way with him, where he creeps around the house and listens outside of doors, and then suddenly bursts in and starts shouting all kinds of awful accusations. I'm afraid he easily gets suspicions in his head, and he can be very aggressive, you know.'

I closed the door quietly, feeling slightly apprehensive as I returned to my place on her bed.

Speaking in a low voice, she said, 'I'd rather say what I need to say in private. There's been such a jumble of sad things preying on my mind for a long time... family things I've been wanting to get out into the open. But nobody wants to listen. My daughter didn't want to hear anything I had to say when she was here. She just pooh-poohed me, and said what I remember about the past doesn't matter anymore, and it's of no interest to anyone.

'But I want to say things, all sorts of things I've had to keep to myself all my life… sad things that have caused me endless grief. I've got a strange feeling, if I don't say what's on my mind now, I may never get the chance again.'

I held her hand and said, 'I'm here, Gladys, and I'm listening. You can talk about whatever is bothering you if it will make you feel better. I have all the time in the world to listen.'

That reassurance seemed to satisfy her, and she lay back on her mound of pillows and relaxed. I watched as she closed her eyes, with a deep contented sigh.

Chapter 30

The Sins of the Fathers

The closed bedroom door suppressed some of the blaring noise coming from the TV in the living room downstairs. For a while, I thought Gladys had fallen asleep; she seemed so still and so quiet.

Then unexpectedly she began speaking. Her voice was almost inaudible, and it seemed as if she was thinking aloud... just mumbling to herself, and quietly repeating a story she had been rehearsing inside her head for a very long time. I needed to sit very close to hear what she was saying.

The story that poured from her came in a flat dreamy voice, not much above a whisper. And every now and then, she needed to take a drink of water before picking up her thread again.

'We used to live in Catford when I was young,' she began, with the flicker of a smile crossing her pale lips. 'My father was a fishmonger in the high street, and the two of us lived in a flat above the shop. He had a really good business, you know, and he was well thought of in the Catford business community. He was quite well off. In fact, he owned a motor car, which was very unusual in those days. It was a black thing... a big black Ford, quite a classy American automobile. I used to joke it was like the one Al Capone used to drive. He was prouder of his gangster car than anything else he owned. But it did make him much envied by the other tradesmen in the high street.

'The problem that always troubled me, when I was young, was I couldn't remember my mother, you see, or my young brother, Robert. All Father would tell me was that they'd both died; but he would never tell me where they were buried, or even how they'd died. Asking questions about them just made him angry with me.

'He was always a man with a very violent temper, and I had to watch what I said, or he would beat me. He had a really mean heartless streak. But I was always desperate to know about my mother and my brother, and I would persist in talking about them. It was like a kind of hunger in me that was never satisfied. Well it's natural, isn't it? We all want to know about our close relatives, especially about a parent, if they've died and we can't remember them.

'From the time I was a little child, I had longed, more than anything, to have something to remember my mother by. But Father had kept nothing. There were no photos... not even a piece of her clothing, or anything to do with Robert either. There was no trace of them anywhere in the flat. Everything had been burned, and all signs wiped away. It was as though they had never existed, and I'd never really had a mother or a brother.

'My father's sister, Hester, lived near us. She was my only other relative. She was widowed, but most of her days were spent at the flat looking after me and Father. I sort of looked on her as a substitute mother. But she was a very stiff sort of woman, very bossy and controlling, just like Father... not at all the way I imagined my mother would've been.

'I couldn't remember anything at all about my mother, but I used to dream about her. In my mind, she was a beautiful slender lady, with blonde hair done up in a chignon, like the fashion of the Edwardians. I liked to imagine how soft and loving she would've been, and how much she would've loved cuddling me and Robert, and telling us she loved us. Father never did anything affectionate like that. He never touched me, unless it was to hit me.

'But aunt Hester wouldn't tell me anything. And she got very angry if I tried to talk about them. It was as if I had no right to know anything at all about my mother and my brother. She even refused to tell me if I had any grandparents or other relatives still living. It was all down to my father, you see. He had forbidden her from telling me anything at all about our family, and Hester never went against his orders.

'Aunt Hester wasn't at all maternal. In fact, she was as hard as nails. I've often wondered if she and my father had cruel parents of their own... a family that had made them into the callous hard-hearted people they were. But I never knew anything about my relatives. I never even knew where they had lived. I sometimes even wondered if I'd had any real relatives at all, or if I was just found somewhere, like in an orphanage. That's how lonely I felt as a child.

'Hester had no children of her own, and I was her only niece. So apart from my father, she was the only other person who knew anything about my mother or my brother, or anybody else I might've been related to. But she would never tell me.

'I was just a young girl, and desperate for someone to help me fill the unbearable gaps in my memory. I wanted to know about my family... what they looked like, and the things they'd enjoyed doing. I often used to wonder if I looked anything like my mother, and I would try to persuade Hester to tell me. My head was full of natural curiosity... normal questions any bereaved child is desperate to ask. I especially wanted to know the sort of things we all want to know about our mothers.'

Gladys suddenly started to weep profusely. I helped her with a glass of water and her tablets, and gradually she calmed down again. It crossed my mind that she might be getting exhausted and sending her blood pressure up, so I made no attempt to press her or ask questions. I simply sat quietly beside her, stroking her hand.

However, as soon as she had settled back among her pillows, her quiet recital recommenced. She drifted away seamlessly into her semi dream state, and went wandering off, reliving far away events from another time. I have no idea why my presence had prompted her to talk about her past in this way. But perhaps she felt she had finally found a willing listener, and was content to unload her store of sad memories onto me. Or maybe my being there had given her one final opportunity to get things off her chest, so to speak.

Many of her reminiscences related to her father. But they were mixed up with all sorts of other stuff... sad things left unspoken for a long while, and quietly festering in her mind for years.

For me, the afternoon was an unexpected revelation. But the most enlightening parts were those relating to her son, PP, the twisted character I had married, and who was the monstrous blight upon my own life. For two hours that afternoon, Gladys talked and rested and talked some more, quietly rambling from one thing onto another, as she revealed her strange family history. It was a recital full of significant and tragic experiences… some of which she had been brooding about for most of her life. She seemed to be full of sorrow about so many things, and all of them still made her weep.

But there was no trace of bitterness in anything she said. She spoke in a way that implied she now accepted that her strange story almost belonged in some kind of alternative dimension, where what she had experienced was merely the inevitable and mysterious workings of fate. And so her reminiscences continued, sotto voce, while I listened silently, and enthralled.

'My father was a hard man to like, and harder still to love. He had a cruel unfeeling nature, and he was constantly driven to control everyone who came close to him. He was remorseless when roused, and I always suspected there was something strange about his emotions… something not quite right, something very dark and secret. He was like no one else I had ever met.

'He had to be right about everything, you see, and he would never accept any opposition, even over little things. He was so secretive and unpredictable I could never guess what he was thinking, or what he would do next. And I never knew how to please him. He was like a volcano. You never knew when he would choose to explode, or who he would injure when he suddenly started lashing out.

'I grew up realising I could never believe or trust anything he ever said. He had terrible moods that changed like the wind. And as far as it went, the truth was always variable. He'd just say whatever came into his head, and for some reason, he constantly seemed driven to lying about everything and manipulating the truth, all to suit himself. I really think there must have been some dark hidden secrets he wanted no one ever to find out about him. One day, he would say something, and swear it was the truth. And the next day, he would angrily deny he'd ever said it, and call me a liar.

'He shouted and swore at everyone, and drove loads of his customers away with his terrible abusive language. But he never apologised for anything, and never showed he was sorry, no matter what he'd said or done. According to his beliefs, to back down in any way showed weakness, and he was never weak and never wrong. In his eyes, anyone who apologised just proved they were as weak as dishwater.

'He was a man without a conscience, you see, and he didn't care about anyone else's feelings except his own. We could never keep a servant because of his terrible temper and his physical violence. If he didn't like something, he would lash out with his fists and his tongue, screaming and bellowing at whoever he was blaming, before he went storming off in a terrible temper. He never waited to hear what anyone else might have to say. His opinion was always the last word on any subject.

'That's why Hester was the only person who ever tolerated him, and even she was kept under control and scared of him. If he paid her for all she did around the flat, like the cleaning and cooking, I would be surprised. He was the most tight-fisted man you could ever meet. But she was too frightened of him to complain. Yes, he certainly had Hester well under control.

'I'm certain she knew what had happened to my mother and my brother, but she would never tell. They just suddenly vanished from my childhood, and all I was ever told was that they'd both died. Over the years, I often wondered if that story was just another of his lies. Maybe his terrible violence and temper had driven my mother away. I did sometimes wonder if, perhaps, she might not be dead at all.

'But if she was alive, and living somewhere else, I could never understand why she hadn't taken me with her, along with Robert, or why she had never tried to contact me, just to say … hello, or enquire how I was getting on. And if she really was dead, I did sometimes secretly wonder if father had killed her in one of his violent rages. Nothing would have surprised me about my father. But I would never have dared to accuse him. I just lived in a state of never knowing what to believe.

'Sometimes, when I was younger, I imagined my mother had run away to escape from him. I used to daydream that she and my brother were living happily somewhere, both safe and sound, and out of Father's reach. I even made myself believe that, one day, she would come back and take me away with her... away from all the anger and violence, and the endless unhappiness of my life with Father.

'He was always a vain man, you see. He liked fancy clothes and enjoyed dressing up and playing at being a dandy. Every Saturday night, he got himself fixed up in his best suit and went out on the town drinking and socialising, as he called it. I used to suspect he was messing about with different women, but I could never be sure. Then all day on Sunday, he was like a bear with a sore head, and no one dared go near him. Hester used to leave a tray of food outside his bedroom door and tap gently, to let him know it was there. But it was more than her life was worth to go inside or wake him when he was snoring fit to wake the dead.

'He got real enjoyment out of intimidating people. I remember how he bullied delivery boys. I once saw him pick one young man up bodily and throw him, and his bicycle, across the road, just because he claimed a parcel the lad had delivered was slightly torn. I never understood why it gave him so much pleasure always finding fault with people, just to make them miserable. I think it must have been to do with the feeling of power it gave him, but I could never understand why.

'I never wanted to invite any friends home from school because of his bad temper and his nasty ways. You see, he enjoyed saying wicked things, just to humiliate me. No one at school had a father like mine. He could pretend to be all jokey and funny and silly one minute, and then go off like a bomb the next, and terrify everyone. He was so unpredictable you never knew where you were with him.

'There was one young chap, a painter and decorator, who'd done some painting work sprucing up the shopfront. Father had agreed a price before the work began. Then when it was finished, he refused to pay him, and threw both him and his ladder into the street. He kicked him savagely, and beat him up because he said the work had taken too long to finish. I remembering him saying, "You're not getting a penny out of me, my lad. All I am giving you is a valuable tip, and that is work faster in future."

'When I was twelve years old, I had to start working in the shop after school and at weekends. He said, if I wanted to eat, I had to start earning my keep. Then when I was fourteen and left school, I wasn't allowed to get the job I wanted in a ladies' dress shop, because I had to start working full-time in Duckworth's Fish Emporium. That was on the sign above Father's shop. It was all painted in fancy gold letters and very swish.

'I was gutting fish and scraping fish scales, and scouring stinking trays from seven in the morning until eight at night. He even left me running the place on my own, when he went up to Billingsgate to buy fresh supplies every morning. I had to do the job on my own because he wouldn't pay a lad's wages to work for him. Like he told me, he didn't keep a dog to bark himself.

'For two years, he gave me a half-crown on Fridays and called it my wages.

'Some while later, a year or so after I'd left school, he brought a young Irish woman home to be a servant, and help Hester around the flat. She was called Elspeth, and I really liked her. She was just eighteen and full of life. Elspeth was great fun, and we became good friends. She had lovely curly auburn hair and freckles on her nose.

'When father wasn't around, she taught me to do the Charleston and the Black Bottom, and lots of other popular dances. I'm talking about the twenties. you know. Oh, what fun we had, Elspeth and me; we did used to laugh. Of course, Hester always tried shutting us up, and lecturing us with her sour-puss face. She said Father wouldn't approve. But that didn't stop Elspeth and me enjoying ourselves whenever he wasn't around to pour cold water on our fun.

'Then Elspeth fell pregnant. Well it's my belief Father took advantage of her. Months later, when it was obvious to the world, she was going to have a baby, he finally married her. So officially she became my stepmother, and in a while, she had a baby girl she called Wendy.

'I loved my little half-sister Wendy. She was the loveliest little baby in the world, with bright red curls, and the sweetest smile. She was a beautiful little thing, and I loved Elspeth too.

'But once Father had married her, everything changed. The dancing and all the fun stopped, and Elspeth wasn't allowed to go out unless father knew exactly where she was going, and how long she would be. She wasn't allowed to see any of her old friends, and he wouldn't even let anybody visit the baby. She could only take little Wendy into the back yard. He even refused to buy her a pram. He said pushing a pram around the streets encouraged a woman to be idle, and go wandering about talking to strange men, and flirting with them and getting up to no good, instead of being at home working and attending to her duties as a wife. With no pram or baby buggy, Elspeth had to carry Wendy with her everywhere she went...it was quite shameful.

'Then he began complaining the baby cried too much, and that Elspeth was making demands on him for money to waste on baby clothes and toys. He accused her of not doing her share of the housework, and leaving too much for Hester to do. More and more, he was shouting at her and hitting her, or finding fault with her. He became increasingly bitter, even about little Wendy for some reason or another.

'Once the baby came, he really seemed to take a dislike to Elspeth. It seemed to me he'd set about destroying her personality with his violence and his control of her. I never actually saw him hit her; I think he was too clever for that. But I did see her change very quickly into someone who was always silent and covered in bruises. From being full of fun and bright and bubbly, Elspeth changed into a sad girl, who spent most of her days in tears. Father was really nasty. He never spoke to her kindly, and just ordered her about and criticised her. And he hardly took any notice at all of poor little Wendy. You would never think she was actually his child.

'I once overheard him yelling at Elspeth that she'd let him down, and was a useless bitch who couldn't get anything right.

She couldn't even produce a son for him. He seemed to hate Wendy because she wasn't a boy. Father's excuses for Elspeth's constant bruised arms, and her poor damaged face and black eyes, was she was a clumsy Irish bitch, and having the baby had made her depressed, so she fell over a lot and bruised easily.

'Then, when Wendy was two years old, she and Elspeth suddenly disappeared. It was all very strange. I'd overheard a terrible row going on during the night, with father shouting and screaming, and banging things about in their bedroom, while Wendy was crying her little heart out. Suddenly, they both went quiet, so I thought they must have gone to sleep. But a while later, I heard a lot of thumping and banging on the stairs, like big boxes being moved about. After that, I heard Father drive off in the Ford, and he didn't come back until dawn.

'That morning, when Elspeth didn't come down for breakfast, I went looking for her. But she and Wendy were gone. All their things were still in the cupboards and drawers, but there was no sign of either of them.

'Father said Elspeth had run away to Ireland with a gypsy bloke, and had taken Wendy with her. He said the noises I'd heard must have been Elspeth running away. But when I told him all her clothes were still upstairs in the bedroom, and she hadn't taken anything with her, not even things for Wendy, he got angry and cuffed me around my head. Then he threatened to knock my teeth out, or break my nose for sticking it into business that had nothing to do with me. Later that morning, I watched as he took all Elspeth's stuff into the back yard and burned it.

'What really happened to Elspeth and Wendy I never knew, but Father never mentioned either of them ever again. He was always very hard-hearted, you see, and could easily shut things out that he didn't want to remember. If Elspeth did run off, she never got in touch. I never heard from her again. And I did so miss her and little Wendy.

'Father was an astute businessman, but he was also deceitful and secretive. And he was very clever at making up cunning lies and excuses to cover up things he didn't want anyone to know about. Sometimes I wondered if he'd done something terrible to Elspeth and my little sister. I just couldn't understand why they never came back. But sometimes I used to imagine they were happy and living safely in Ireland. I never did know for certain. Father just blanked them out of our lives, and forbade me from mentioning them.

'I recall hearing unpleasant whispers going around the neighbourhood for months, that father had done away with them. Someone said they had seen him beating the poor girl with a walking stick, and others said he'd only married her because he'd got her into trouble. Some said he didn't want to have to pay her for the baby, or give her anymore wages, so he'd done away with both mother and child.

'Well, people will talk, won't they? And there was already the strange disappearance of my mother and brother to gossip about. People remember things. And in a close neighbourhood, they like gossiping about strange events. Elspeth's disappearance meant two women had gone missing from our address, and two little children. It was hard to understand, and harder still to explain. And it did give rise to a lot of unpleasant gossip. But Father just ignored it all and carried on his life as usual for the next two years.

'Then things got so bad for me at home I couldn't stand anymore of his violence. He was turning me into a slave, and lashing out whenever it suited him. I decided I had to find some way to leave home, and get away from him. I was eighteen by then, and my friend Judy and me used to go ballroom dancing every Saturday evening at the local palais.

'After a few weeks, I met a young soldier there called Albert, and we started going out. He was a very handsome young man, very tall and smart. And eventually we got engaged. He bought me a lovely gold ring with real little rubies in it, and we started planning to get married once we'd saved up.

'Things at home were just as bad as ever, with father's controlling ways and his violent outbursts, and me always having to work like a slave, and do exactly what I was told. I'd been asking him for months to increase the wages he was paying me, because I wanted to save up to get married, you see. But his answer was always the same. He claimed he fed and kept me and bought my clothes, and that what I was getting from him as wages was enough to waste on the stupid things I bought. He considered he overpaid me anyway for what I did in the shop.

'I felt I'd been working hard for him since before I left school, and I deserved more money. In four years, he had only ever increased my wages to ten shillings a week. I knew it was nowhere near what I could earn in a proper job. And if I went into domestic service, I would be able to live in and get my evenings and Sundays off, plus a decent wage.

'Well...when Albert heard he was being transferred to Richmond in Yorkshire, I decided to give Father an ultimatum. Either he started to pay me a proper wage, and give me more time off from the shop, or I was going to leave home and get a job in service up north in Richmond, near Albert's barracks.

'At first, he simply ridiculed me, and said ten-bob was all I was worth. Then he turned nasty and said, if I dared to leave him, he would cut me out of his will, and I'd get not a farthing when he died. He worked himself up into such a fury I really thought he was going to kill me.

'Well that was the last straw so far as I was concerned. Eventually, the only way I could get away from the shop and Father permanently, was to do a moonlight flit. I packed my case and caught a train to the north one Saturday night while he was out. I found myself some cheap lodgings. And then, within a couple of days, I'd found myself a really good job as a lady's maid in a very nice house...no cooking, no cleaning, no stinky fish to clean, and a pound a week in my pocket, with all the usual benefits of room and board, and a smart uniform, including laundry.

'A few weeks later, Father drove up to Yorkshire to find me. He tried hard to persuade me to go home with him, and swore everything would change. He even promised he would treat me differently and pay me more than I was now getting as wages.

'But I knew nothing would ever be any different. He was an out-and-out liar, who never kept his promises. He would say anything just to get what he wanted, and then change his mind once he'd got it. I refused to go back to Catford with him, and I stayed in Richmond. It was really nice there.

'But life's very strange, isn't it? A few months after being in my new job, I met Charlie. With him and me, it was love at first sight. And it was Charlie I eventually married, not Albert. That was when we moved south to live in Essex, near where his family lived.

'Charlie couldn't afford an engagement ring, so he tied a piece of cord around my finger till he could afford something better. Even a silver one from Woolworth's would've been nice. But it never happened that we had any spare money for such a trinket. Anyway, not having a fancy ring didn't change how we felt about each other. So, I never did get another engagement ring. But I had my gold wedding band, and nothing could mean more to me than that.

'I've sometimes wondered if maybe I broke Albert's heart, jilting him like I did. I can't be sure. But somehow, I doubt it. A smart military uniform is always a magnet for us girls, and I'm sure he soon got over me and married someone else.

'I don't regret anything. I've been happy in Essex, and Charlie's always been the love of my life. But I still remember the last words my father said when he left me that day in Richmond. He said, "Marry that fool, and he'll always keep you dirt-poor. He's just a farm labourer, and you'll never be sure where your next meal's coming from. But you can be sure as hell, you'll never get a penny from me."

'Well, I suppose in a way he was right. Charlie and me have never had any money, and we've always been poor. But we've been devoted to one another through all the good times, and the bad ones. Charlie always worked hard up in the woods. And he's never stopped doing his best to provide for me, tending his vegetable garden, and bringing me bunches of the flowers he's grown. Our life together has been mostly happy.

'I'm not saying he's perfect. He's always liked his cigarettes, and a good drink of a weekend. And we've had many a battle over his wages, and how much he wanted to keep for his spends, 'specially when the kids were little.

'But Charlie's never been a cruel man, and he's as straight and true as any man could ever be. He's never been a liar, or messed about with other women, and he's never raised a hand to me, or ever tried to control me. Charlie respects me. He's nothing like my father ever was. Charlie would give me the shirt off his back if I said I needed it, and never ask why.

'We've had some happy times, and I don't regret a minute of our life together. The first year we were married, we had Mavis. Then two years later, along came our son, young Charlie. Then five years more, and we had dear little Joanie.'

Suddenly Gladys' face was wet again with tears, and she began sobbing. I bent over her, and she dabbed her eyes while I gave her another sip of water. She took a drink and then quickly pushed the glass away, eager to struggle on with her story, while fighting back the obvious burden of emotional pain she was carrying.

'Oh, my little baby girl was beautiful,' she whispered, biting her lip to stop the tears, 'like a little angel out of heaven, she was. She put me in mind of that little sister, Wendy, I'd once had, only her hair was golden and not red. My darling little Joanie, how she loved her big brother. She followed him everywhere, like a puppy. But being the rough-sort of boy he was, he didn't want her with him, and he used to try running away and leaving her up in the woods.

'I think he was jealous of her. Well he'd been the baby of the family for five years, you see, and he had always got his own way in everything, until Joanie came along. I suppose he resented having his nose pushed out of joint by a new baby, especially her being a girl. He's never had any respect for girls. Sons were always what he wanted, just like my own father.

'Anyway, when little Joanie was just about reaching her third birthday, that was when the terrible accident happened. Our boy was seven, and one afternoon he came home without her. I knew she had been with him when he went up to the woods, but I noticed him come creeping back on his own and go sneaking into the outhouse. He closed the door quietly, but I knew he was hiding so as not to be found. Anyway, I went out and brought him indoors and asked him to tell me where Joanie was. He stared at me defiantly with those pale empty eyes of his, but just kept shrugging his shoulders and wouldn't say anything. We tried every which way to make him tell us what he'd done, but he just stood there, stubborn as a mule, shrugging his shoulders and refusing to speak.

'Well, Charlie and me went searching for her. We knew he'd taken her up to the woods. The neighbours had seen them go. And that's where we found her, hidden under a tree. There were leaves and branches piled over her, poor little mite. But there was nothing Charlie or me or anybody else could do. She was dead, with two rifle bullets in her chest.'

At that point Gladys burst into floods of tears, and sobbed fit to break her heart. I put my arm around her and hugged her until she calmed down.

Then, after drying her eyes, she insisted on continuing her story. 'Yes, some of the neighbours said they'd seen my little lamb walking hand in hand up the hill towards the woods with her brother. We knew it was his favourite place to play. You see, he liked messing about with the rifle cartridges and live ammunition he found. It was wartime then, and the soldiers were often up there on their training manoeuvres... using live ammunition. The boy used to be fascinated with guns and such. He liked scavenging around among the trees, collecting all the used brass cartridges the soldiers left behind. And there were often live ones left lying about as well... Charlie once told me he knew the boy had worked out a way to make them explode.

He said he'd seen the lad fix them between stones and bang on the detonator end with a sharp flint, so they went off... exploded just like being fired from a rifle.

'But the boy would never tell us anything about what had happened that day, or how Joanie got two bullets buried in her little chest. We never did get the truth out of him. He was always a big strapping lad... a big baby from when he was born, a real man-child, I called him. But he always was a proper little devil.

'As soon as he was able to crawl, he was into every sort of trouble imaginable... wilful in every way. Well, his dad always suspected ... It was such a shock about Joanie ... Well, I know what Charlie suspected. But I can't say exactly for sure ... It was too cruel to imagine. And the boy was only seven, you see. But he's always been secretive ... and he had a very cruel streak in him we could never break.' Gladys wiped the tears from her eyes and took a sip of water before continuing her sorrowful story.

'I still remember how he would hide behind the sofa and sneak out to pick up Charlie's cigarette butts from the hearth, where he'd thrown his half-smoked Woodbines. Then he'd sit and puff away on them out of sight, and him only three years old at the time.

'We lived in an old, tied farm-cottage in those days... an old wreck of a place that went with Charlie's job in the woods. It's long gone now... pulled down before it fell down. But the old place was rotten with damp, and there was no electricity or any proper sanitation, just an outside earth closet; and oil lamps and a cold-water handpump in the kitchen sink. The plaster was falling off the walls with the dampness, so they'd been lined with hessian sacking, stretched on a wooden frame. It soaked up the moisture, you see. But there were rats living behind the sacking. When it was quiet of an evening, we could watch them moving about. And by the time the boy was six, his favourite game was hunting them and killing them with a thick stick.

'Sometimes he would disappear up into the woods with a catapult to shoot squirrels. He's always enjoyed killing things, you see. He had a game knocking their nests out of the trees and stamping on the young 'uns to kill them. He never did care much for animals.

'My God, the things I could tell you about what he got up to would make your hair stand on end. He was always a young imp. In fact, he caused a lot of rows between me and Charlie over money. Well, we never had much, you see, and I used to work in the fields and orchards at different times of the year for ten bob a week, to help out with the housekeeping. But if the lad could get his sneaky hands on my purse, he would help himself to whatever he wanted and then lay the blame on his dad. He'd pinch maybe sixpence or a shilling and go off and buy cigarettes. Then he'd hide in the earth closet at the bottom of the garden and smoke them.

'Then one day I found myself embarrassed and short when I went for my groceries at the shop. I knew I'd had enough in my purse to pay for what I wanted, but that day a half-crown was missing, and I was short. The shopkeeper said young Charlie had been in to get his dad his cigarettes as usual, and he'd paid with a half-crown. Then he mentioned the boy often went in to buy cigarettes. He always said his dad had given him the money, and the fags were for him. No one thought anything of it, or even to mention anything to me about what he was doing.

'Well I went home and let rip at Charlie about taking my housekeeping, and leaving me short. There was a real humdinger of a row, I can tell you. When things calmed down, and we talked things over reasonable like, it turned out he'd never sent the boy to the shop to buy his cigarettes, or ever thought of taking money from my purse.

'It was the young 'un. He'd been helping himself whenever he wanted, taking sixpence here and there, so I'd never really noticed, until the time he took the half-crown, and that brought everything out into the open.

'He was always a sly little monkey over money. Could never get his hands on enough of it. And he enjoyed causing trouble between his dad and me. He would sit at the table, listening to rows he'd caused with a grin on his face like a Cheshire cat.

'I remember the time when I'd saved up for weeks in a clothing club, and gone without all sorts myself to buy him a smart blue velvet suit. As soon as he saw it, he flew into a tantrum and screamed that he hated it and wouldn't wear it. So, when I insisted on dressing him in it to take him up to his grandparents' for tea, he ran outside and climbed into the water butt while I was getting myself ready. He ruined the suit, but he didn't care how upset he'd made me, or what I'd gone without to buy it for him. I forget now what it had cost, but the suit was no more use when he finished tearing it to shreds.

'I was so cross with him I smacked him across the legs with the stick I used for the wash boiler. But quick as a flash, the little imp turned on me and wrestled the stick from my hands and set about hitting me with it, until his father came and got the stick off him. He was a little monster... left me black and blue, and the new velvet suit in rags after he tore it to pieces in his fury.

'He's always had a terrible temper and been dead set on getting revenge if anyone crosses him... just like my father always was. He neither knows nor cares what damage he does, and he's never known his own strength.

'And as for telling tall stories and downright lies, well, from first being able to talk, Charlie and me could never believe a word he said. And the bigger he grew, the more he put me in mind of my own father. He was a demon, storming and raging, and throwing his temper tantrums, smashing furniture into pieces, and wrecking things whenever someone crossed him or if he couldn't get his own way.

'Nobody's ever managed to control my son, and I doubt they ever will. When he's in one of his rages, he doesn't know his own strength. And he'll attack anybody, man or woman, until he's beaten them to pulp. It's like there's a devil inside him, fighting to get out. Nothing, and nobody, has ever been able to control him.

'From the time he was five. he regularly got sent home from school for fighting and swearing, and stealing and lying. Eventually when he got to the secondary school, they expelled him after two years. They said he was uncontrollable, antisocial, and an aggressive bully. They branded him a juvenile delinquent, and said they could do nothing more with him. He was accused of habitual truanting, constantly lying, cheating other kids out of their dinner money, fighting and beating the smaller kids up, and of insolence to the teachers. He even threatened to beat them up as well, when they found fault with him.

'Nobody ever knew what to do with him, or how to get him to change his ways. You see, he's always fought against any sort of authority or punishment, and turned on anyone who tried to control him, even when he'd done something really bad.

'The last straw came when he was sent to the headmaster to be punished for lying and stealing money from the office. He snatched the cane from the master's hands and lashed him across the face with it...cut him really badly across his cheek and left him scarred. Well, that finished his schooldays. But he didn't care. The boy never ever said he was sorry for anything he ever did. You see, he never actually ever feels sorry for anything, and he never sees any need to apologise for anything because he always believes he's right.

'Even before his expulsion, he hadn't been at school much. He'd been skiving off most of the time anyway, and his attendance record was dreadful. He just didn't like anyone telling him what he had to do. So, he ran away each morning, and then sneaked back home at teatime, pretending he'd been at school.

'We never suspected anything, and were completely taken in by him. You see, he's very convincing in what he says, and very secretive. And he only ever tells anyone what he really wants them to believe.

'When the school finally sent for me to talk about his terrible record, and how he hadn't been attending school for almost a year, I couldn't believe it. I told them I couldn't understand what had been happening, because I'd been putting him on the eight o'clock train every morning myself. But they explained he just got off at the next station, and spent his days hiding in the woods, like something half-wild... catching animals and killing them, often mutilating them and cutting off their tails and their paws, or nailing them to trees. If he wasn't up in the woods killing things, he was roaming the town stealing from the shops. It horrified me when I found out what he had really been up to when I thought he was at school. Eventually the police came around because he'd been caught shoplifting, stealing things to sell for cigarettes and beer.

'After he was thirteen, he never went to school. They refused to have him back, so it meant he never did get a proper education, you see. He wouldn't listen to reason, or do anything we asked, and just ran wild up in the woods. Charlie couldn't handle him or even talk to him because, at thirteen, he was bigger than his dad, and could knock him down with one hand tied behind his back.

'We kept hoping when he eventually had to go into the army to do his National Service, they would discipline him and straighten him out... you know, make him toe the line, teach him some discipline, and calm him down.

'When he was fifteen, I managed to get him an apprenticeship with a local builder. He was never stupid, quite bright really, and certainly very cunning. But he had a strange way with him that I never understood. It's like a sort of strange gift; it's amazing the way he can convince anyone of almost anything. Nobody could ever tell a more convincing story than he could. But he always used his intelligence for the wrong reasons. He enjoyed making fools of people, you see... manipulating them to get what he wanted.

'Getting the apprenticeship was the best thing for him. For once, he seemed to be a round peg in a round hole. Anyway, he took to it and enjoyed learning to be a builder. It was something practical he could do with his hands, and he didn't have to stay glued to a seat, or even stay in the same place all the time. He has to be moving around, you see, and can't put his mind on just one thing. He can't abide to be bored. There's always some scheme or another going on inside his head. Sometimes, he just deliberately goes off and finds some sort of trouble to occupy himself with.

'Then there was the problem we had with him over girls. Once he got to fifteen, he couldn't control his sexual urges, you see, or his violence if any of them rejected him. He caused a lot of trouble with some of the local families, I can tell you. Things got really bad, and he worried me a lot. He was always getting up to some tricks with the girls, and forever in trouble over what he'd been doing to them. We had some terrible things to put up with from some of our neighbours over what their girls had been saying about him.

'There was one girl in particular. I think he used to call her Topsie. Well, she came crying to our door saying he'd got her pregnant, and she needed money to get rid of the baby. Well, you can imagine what my son had to say about that. He had no money, and neither did we. It was a really bad scene she made in the street outside our house. In any case, he denied it was anything to do with him... called her a liar, and knocked her down he did, and called her a trollop to her face.

'He got married to Beryl when he was nineteen, just before the army called him up, which was just as well. And by the time he went off to do his two years, she was already pregnant with Mandy. He'd met her when he was working at the cottage hospital. She was a nurse there and a few years older than him.

'But him getting her pregnant just before the army sent him to Malaya meant she had to give up her job as a nurse, and her flat, and come to live with Charlie and me. She had no money and no place to live, because a national serviceman's married allowance wasn't much for her to live on and pay rent, especially with a baby on the way.

'But, like the boy said, it was a good thing she was at home with us. That way, he always knew exactly where she was, and she couldn't be getting up to any funny business with other blokes while he was away, or me and his dad would be sure to tell him.

'He's my son, and I love him. But he's been a worry to me all his life. He can't control his temper, you see, and he never says anything you can believe. It grieves me to admit it... but he's the spitting image of my own father, both in his looks and in his ways... There's no softness in him... and no conscience either... I don't believe he has it in him to be genuinely kind or loving to anyone.

'Oh dear, he's always been aggressive and determined to get his own way, by saying and doing whatever suits him. He's hurt a lot of people, I know. He just has to control everything. And he can never admit anything he ever does is wrong. It's always made me unhappy that he's got my father's unfeeling selfish streak... He doesn't care who he hurts or what harm he does... as long as he's getting what he wants. I don't think he'll ever understand how to be ...'

She gave a deep sigh, and her quiet voice, which had been slowly fading to a subdued mumble, suddenly fell silent.

When I looked closer, I saw she had fallen asleep mid-sentence.

It had been a melancholy afternoon. I'd spent it listening to her tragic story, and she had unburdened herself in a way I hoped had given her some comfort. She had certainly left me with a clearer picture of the twisted family legacy handed down from her father to her son... and, so it would seem, even to her grandchildren.

Without ever being aware of it, Gladys' revelations about her strange parent, and her unhappy family background, had told me everything I had been anxious to know. Her recital had certainly helped to clarify my understanding of her son's malevolent personality disorder.

Sadly, that afternoon I spent with Gladys was the last time I ever saw her. At some point during the night she attempted to get out of bed. But being very deaf, Charlie hadn't heard her.

The poor lady had somehow missed her footing in the darkness, and had fallen, badly breaking her hip. She had lain on the floor, struggling in agony for hours, unable to make Charlie hear her distressed cries, until eventually she'd suffered a serious stroke.

The next morning, she was found unconscious and suffering from mild hypothermia. An ambulance took her into hospital, where she was nursed for two weeks in intensive care.

Unfortunately, while she was there, she had several more mini-strokes and developed pneumonia, which all seriously worsened her condition.

Eventually she had a second massive stroke, from which she never recovered. Her life ended peacefully a month later, without her ever regaining consciousness.

Gladys was a lovely lady. She'd had a hard life, and had very little to leave behind after seventy-four years of struggle. That last time I saw her she had willingly opened up to me about her son's troubled background, and had related all the unhappy things she had kept to herself for years. Everything locked in her memory had been poured out without my asking one solitary question. Gladys had awakened the long dormant recesses of her memory... relating stories from PP's early childhood, to his deranged adult behaviour. And quite inadvertently, she had answered all the questions I had wanted to ask her but had felt unable to. She had left me with a deeply significant parting gift, and had confirmed in every way, that my darkest suspicions about the mentally unbalanced man I had married, were correct.

I have no doubt that she had loved him all his troubled life, with the unconditional love only a mother can give a seriously disturbed child. But she had always realised there was something dark and twisted about his character, and had recognised in him the same cruel and heartless traits her father had exhibited.

It was a dangerous, and destructive family legacy that PP had inherited, and it seemed to have already been passed on to the next generation. It left me wondering how many more children would be born to carry that terrible tainted inheritance of cruelty and evil into the future.

In some part of her failing consciousness, Glady's seemed fully aware of her terrible son's evil personality. She recognised the truth behind the wicked things he had done in his life. Yet on her death-bed I believe she longed to separate the reality of the depraved, cold-hearted monster from the child she had brought into the world. She had always loved him…he was her precious son… and she desperately wanted to go on believing that, deep down, he had always loved her.

I believe that as her life was drawing to its end, she wanted to disassociate the child she loved from the sadistic, emotionless monster within him. Perhaps in some way she wanted to redeem him.? I don't really think she had ever wanted to accept the truth of how truly, and unrepentantly, malevolent he actually was.

But there was no way I could ever completely understand what she really felt about him…deep down that remained an enigma which she took to her grave.

What I had gained from our afternoon together left me with a deep and genuine sense of gratitude for her honest revelations, and for the graphic word-pictures she had drawn of my sadistic adversary. Everything she had said, had confirmed my suspicions about PP's psychopathic inheritance. And everything I had learned at her bed-side had added significant insight to my understanding of the dark energies which clearly drove him.

Unfortunately, what I now knew had also reinforced the hopelessness of my personal situation. I had no remaining doubts that the man I was married to really was capable of any depths of depravity... including murder. But the knowledge I had gained had brought me nowhere nearer any solution to my sickening dilemma... I was still his prisoner.

For many weeks following my afternoon with Gladys, I could think of little else. My mind continued to revolve at desperation point, with no idea how much longer I could survive PP's evil manipulations. His constant behaviour was a cruel, destructive game, maliciously played to torment the life out of me with one sick episode after another. And each scheme he invented made my continued existence ever more unbearable, and drove me deeper into despair.

He had coldly and cynically demonstrated many times, in sickening detail, exactly what he would do to me if I ever attempted to divorce or leave him. And every one of his sadistic plans invariably ended with my death.

I saw myself trapped in a situation from which I could not escape. I tried to remain calm; but the reality was, I was fundamentally terrified of him, and intimidated into inactivity by his threats and his relentless cruelty.

The prospects for my future seemed bleak. Years of fear and violence stretching ahead... each one crammed full of heaven only knew what diabolical schemes I would be forced to endure.

I had never felt so abandoned, or so unloved and isolated. My life seemed to have descended into a hopeless day to day struggle for survival. I was fighting against an implacable enemy; a tormentor who had no intention of releasing me so long as either of us had breath in our bodies. The more deeply I thought about my situation, the more I realised I needed to find strength and courage to resolve my dilemma. Either I must resign myself to go on enduring in misery, or I had to take the terrible decision to put an end to my own life, and escape. Whatever I did I felt PP would eventually triumph. My future seemed an unresolvable inevitability.

I began to consider... was death my only possible route to freedom? Insanity or death... they had always been the only exits from the marriage PP had offered me. He believed himself to be invincible, and that in the end he would be triumphant, and live forever.

Viewed through the eyes of my bleak despair there seemed to be no tolerable or liveable future left for me. All I could do was come to a decision on how, when, and where I would finally put an end to my desperate unhappiness.

Several weeks dragged by mired in this misery, while I contemplated my wretched state. The depths of my grief and confusion persisted, until quite unexpectedly one morning, something changed.

When I was floundering at my lowest emotional point, out of nowhere something came to raise me up. It was a gift of truly heaven-sent insight, and came as a wonderful vivid lightning flash inside my mind. It illuminated my clouded thoughts, and brought me an unexpected and uplifting revelation. Suddenly I became aware that my future was not the inevitable one I had believed it to be.

In a few brief and incredibly insightful moments, many hidden things which had been weighing me down were suddenly clarified. I became aware that for each human soul there is a spiritual book of life, which begins as a natal document of empty pages. Each human life can only be written line by line, and page by page, as that life is lived. I was reminded that it was my responsibility to survive, and complete the empty pages still left in my own book.

What I saw clearly, in my mind's eye, was the promise of a future, and the reassurance that my life really was still worth living, however hard it might seem. I was made aware that God was the real power in my life... not PP... My responsibility was to continue to meet the difficult challenges ahead, and strive to endure in spite of them...I must never surrender to hopelessness or despair.

I had already made one huge, and ill-advised mistake when I had married this man. But taking my own life because of him, would be an unforgiveable act of defeat... something that would bring terrible harm to my children.

Unexpectedly, in the clarity of those brief moments, I realised that I must look beyond my emotional despair, and focus upon my personal survival. I must gather what remained of my determination and courage and hold on, even in the face of all the pain and sorrow currently working to destroy me. Life always has a purpose... If you search hard enough, you can find it.

My daughters were young, and I was the only person left in the world who cared about them. It was my responsibility to them and to Alan, to navigate a course through the sick games PP was playing with my mind and my life...I must be strong...I had to endure... My beloved Alan was never far away, and I must keep faith with him.

This inspirational insight provided the spiritual strength I needed. It had brought me a glimpse behind the smoke and mirrors of PP's deplorable schemes, and shown me what I was experiencing was a series of cunning psychopathic constructs...

cruel, devilish plans devised by his warped mind to take control of my life and destroy it.

Something intrinsically human was missing from his brain; and his malicious emotionless activities were all manifestations of the malevolent... psychopython which had replaced his withered soul... his missing conscience...Something essentially spiritual and human was absent from his brain...and something dark and distorted had taken its place, and totally controlled him...Now I realised...the evil within him would never leave...it was an intrinsic part of what he was.

My despair faded beneath this inspiring revelation; and I was left with the clear understanding that all situations eventually come to an end.

I must stay resilient, and hold fast to my life; keeping faith and trusting in God's loving mercy. Even a psychopython cannot live forever.

At some point, PP's vicious games were destined to end; and perhaps one day, Nemesis, the ancient instrument of Divine Justice, would fall upon my enemy...

Or perhaps God's promise would finally prevail in answer to my desperate prayers... 'Vengeance is mine; I will Repay, saith The Lord' (Romans 12:19–20).

END OF PART 1

Delias's story continues as...

Psychopython Part 2: NEMESIS, and

Psychopython Part 3: THE MILLS OF GOD.

www.ingramcontent.com/pod-product-compliance
Lightning Source LLC
Chambersburg PA
CBHW061049210726
48294CB00001B/70